Praise for Nisha Minhas's first novel,
Chapatti or Chips?

'Wonderfully vibrant characters . . . beautifully (and
sometimes painfully) observed' Chris Manby

'That old dilemma of sex and passion versus prudence
and a healthy bank balance is given an entertaining
Eastern spin' *Marie Claire*

'An entertaining read with characters you can easily
warm to' *Asian Woman*

'A funny look at the East-West culture clash' *Heat*

'A sparky debut novel . . . superbly written and
wonderfully observed' *Glasgow Evening Times*

'Tradition and family loyalty collides with desire,
resulting in a story that is interesting, funny and
insightful . . . The characters are outrageous but also
so real' Faith Bleasdale

Also by Nisha Minhas
Chapatti or Chips?

In her early thirties, Nisha Minhas lives in Milton
Keynes with her partner and two cats. *Sari & Sins* is
her second novel.

SARI & SINS

NISHA MINHAS

POCKET
BOOKS

LONDON • SYDNEY • NEW YORK • TOKYO • SINGAPORE • TORONTO

First published in Great Britain by Simon & Schuster, 2003
This edition first published by Pocket Books, 2003
An imprint of Simon & Schuster UK
A Viacom company

1 3 5 7 9 10 8 6 4 2

Simon & Schuster UK Ltd
Africa House
64-78 Kingsway
London WC2B 6AH

www.simonsays.co.uk

Simon & Schuster Australia
Sydney

A CIP catalogue record for this book is available from the British Library

ISBN 0-7434-3046-8

Typeset by SX Composing DTP, Rayleigh, Essex
Printed and bound in Great Britain by Cox & Wyman Ltd, Reading, Berks

For the love of my life, Dave.
∞0X9!

And in loving memory of his dad,
Brian Carney. You're not forgotten.
Rest In Peace.

Acknowledgements

My editor, Kate Lyall Grant – What can I say except thanks once again for your brilliant and thoughtful editing. For putting botox in the book's wrinkles. And for being an absolute pleasure to work with.

My agent, Lorella Belli – Thanks for your continuous encouragement and enthusiasm. For all your expert knowledge and professionalism. And a special thanks for all your friendly advice and chats – not to mention your fabulous cooking.

To everyone at Simon & Schuster who have helped bring this book to the shelves. Many thanks.

And especially to Dave, my partner – Thank you for all the help and support you've given me from start until finish. Thanks for the jokes and title. I couldn't have done it without you. I couldn't be without you.

My dear parents and family – for the heartache – I'm sorry.

If I was born under an Indian sun
then maybe I could see.
As I was born under an English sun
I want my life to be free.

by Dave Bell Carney

Chapter One

Even though in the sexual prime of his life, and blessed with desperately good looks, Jordan made a stiff promise with himself not to have sex for two years. Twenty-four months without feeling a woman was not going to be easy. Seven-hundred and thirty days of fighting nature would need discipline. Seventeen thousand five hundred and twenty hours without an erection was going to be impossible – he normally had two an hour – but he would have to try. Even if he had to ask God for help he would, but there was no way he was going to have sex in prison. No way.

Three years later, after serving an extra year for bad behaviour without bending over for anyone's soap, Jordan was free to go.

'Sign here, here, here, here and here,' the boxy guard said, standing behind the grill, handing Jordan back his meagre belongings in a cellophane bag. 'I envy you, Jordan.'

Jordan raised one eyebrow as he scribbled his signature. 'And why's that, Screw?'

'Well . . . I used to read your mail, didn't I? She's got a right dirty mind, ain't she? Your girlfriend. Sordid.' The guard rattled the grill with his chubby fingers. 'Getting angry are we, Jordan? Not sure whether to lash out or not, eh? Getting a little agitated are we?' He shook the meshed metal like an excitable gibbon. 'She loved being frisked, we could all smell her getting turned on.' He smirked.

The musty chamber collected prisoners' belongings like dust. It was freedom's waiting room for an assortment of lighters, keys and wallets. In here, your get-out-of-jail-free card was validated and you were just one step away from being released. It was customary not to attack the release guard.

Jordan smiled up at the camera, then back at the screw. 'Nice try, Pork Pie. Be a sweetheart and let the ex-con out, would you?'

One minute later the door banged shut behind him and he stood staring skywards at the army of marching grey clouds letting loose with their battalions of belting rain. It may have been war overhead, but it was peaceful in Jordan's heart. His blood now warming after a cold freeze of three long years. And if absence makes the heart grow fonder, then prison makes the dick go harder. That's why they're called hardened criminals.

He walked the lonely path that surrounded the prison premises, already taking for granted that he could tread more than twenty yards without turning.

The friendly cons inside had warned him, 'Don't watch *Crimewatch*. It'll give you nightmares.' He headed towards the last post with its red and white barrier. Even though Jordan was not in a car, the guard still lifted it up, waving him through.

He glanced back to his recent digs, the military-style complex was cold and foreboding. Jordan knew he would return.

But just to visit.

A car horn, followed by a wolf whistle seized his attention. The holly green of his eyes seemed to dull. Ryan, his best mate, had promised to fetch him from the slammer in style. A rusty white Luton Box van dirtied the road. Ryan stood next to it dressed as Ronald McDonald, two helium balloons hanging from his ears, while 'Freedom' by George Michael blasted from the van's speakers. This was style!

It wasn't cool for men to hug, but Jordan and Ryan hugged uncoolly. They'd been mates since they were sperm, Reliable Ryan and Junket Jordan, split from the very same corrupted atoms. And both had one thing in common: dead mothers.

Ryan couldn't wait to tell his joke that had taken a month to think up. 'Margaret Thatcher has had a sex change . . .' Chuckling, he rubbed his flashing pink nose. 'She's now called . . . wait for it . . . Lady Thatcher.' With his floppy red boots, he struggled to the rear of the van, throwing back the doors. 'Surprise, surprise.'

Jordan climbed in. Two beanbags on a grubby rug, one small coffee table and a bottle of champers. This was a surprise.

'Nice.' Jordan removed his soaked Valentino suit

3

jacket, lobbed it across the greasy floor and slumped into a Snoopy beanbag. 'Very nice. Where's Cloey? I thought she'd be here by now.' Queen's 'I Want To Break Free' rocked harshly.

'What is this, forty questions? Drink up. Can't you spend a little time with your buddy first?' From under his curly orange wig Ryan removed two perfectly rolled monster spliffs. Handing Jordan one, he lit the other. 'Anyway, there's only two beanbags. Be patient, she might have got the wrong day. I saw this film once where the woman turned up five years too late.'

Jordan lit up, frowning, eyeing the two metallic-pink balloons now stuck to the van roof. 'Did you now?' He stood up, balancing the spliff on the tinfoil ashtray. 'And in this film, did Ronald McDonald get his arse kicked in the back of a van? Where is she, Ryan?'

'Who?'

'Ryan.' Jordan began to make breathing difficult for his mate as he strangled him. 'Now, where is she?'

'I'll tell you,' he puffed, as Jordan dropped back onto the beanbag. 'Remember, don't shoot the messenger. I'm going to be frank. It's going to hurt. You may want to be left alone to cry.'

The rain sounded like boulders hitting the roof. Jordan peered upwards, already weary with impatience. 'She's okay, isn't she? I couldn't . . . she is all right, isn't she?'

Ryan breathed in sharply. 'She's fine.' He looked out of the back of the van at the rain as dense as fog. 'You know that day you went into prison? A few years back? About three years ago today? Well, two

4

days after you were incarcerated, she opened her legs for another man.' He wished he hadn't painted that huge lipstick smile on his face now. 'She got a taste for it, it became her new hobby really. Don't ask me how many men she's slept with, Jordan, because I lost count after six.'

'Did you sleep with her?'

'Don't be so fucking stupid, I'm your best mate.' He swigged the champagne, feeling the cold liquid mixing with his breakfast beans. 'And that's why I didn't tell you, your life was shit enough as it was on the inside.'

Immediately feeling as though he were encased in a straitjacket, Jordan climbed down onto the road. He leaned forward against the side of the van using his hands for support, the fierce rain pummelling against his drenched courtroom shirt. He would have died for Cloey and now it felt like he had. No one touched his heart like she did.

He'd been such a fool. How could he have taken the path that had led him to prison and thrown Cloey into the arms of other men? She obviously needed some company. It wasn't her fault she'd been left to fend for herself. He shouted up to the skies, 'It wasn't her fault she needed a fuck after only two pissing days, was it?' He wished he had the champagne bottle so he could have smashed it, sending the celebratory fizz down the drain. Then he might just hop in after it.

He returned to the van. 'Drive me to Cloey's!'

Forty-five minutes later they were in the village where Jordan grew up, Bruckley, in the heart of Buckinghamshire, with its free-range biddies and tweed-jacket stuffy-nosed men. Even the duck pond had a sign: *No Stale Bread Please*. It was the perfect place to bring up a spoilt brat. Frightfully frightfully frightfully will get you a long way in Bruckley, but juicy gossip will get you further. Talk round the village at the moment, as Ryan explained, centred on the arrival of some unsavoury gypsies in the neighbouring town of Milton Keynes and whether, if necessary, the villagers could put up a blockade, a didicoi dam, to prevent the virus spreading the twelve miles from MK to Bruckley.

But Jordan was back in town now, and he was disease of a different kind. He banged his hand down on Ryan's shoulder. 'Cheers for the lift, mate. Back to what I said earlier: I appreciate you being honest about Cloey. If I was you and found out your wife was doing the rounds, I may have done the same.'

Ryan turned off his flashing clown nose. 'There's only one mug doing the rounds with my wife. Me.' He looked to his feet. 'Anyway, if it makes you feel any better, I heard the blokes she shagged were all wankers.' He handed Jordan a stodgy envelope. 'I was going to say save it for a rainy day. There's enough dosh in there to keep you sweet for a while.'

The two mates parted, Ryan with a hoot of the horn, Jordan with a glint in his eye. He had asked to be dropped off some way away from Cloey's. Maybe she was shagging one of those wankers right now. Maybe Jordan would be going back to prison sooner than he'd thought. It was a perfect day to have blood on his hands, the rain would just wash it off. He jumped over the gate to Lemonly Cottage, ignoring how fucking cosy it looked, and rapped on the front door with his knuckles.

'Cloey,' he shouted through the letterbox, 'answer the fucking door – *darling*!'

A top window opened and shut quickly, ten seconds later Cloey was standing at the door wearing a crime of a red satin dress which would appear to have only one motive: to turn men on. Giving Jordan the briefest of looks, she stepped forward and slid her hands under his wet shirt, hugging him close, feeling his hardness. His poor cock had been in solitary confinement for three years. He must be gagging for her, she thought, gyrating her hips, fingering his spine.

He gently pushed her off. 'Have you been sleeping with other men?'

Ignoring him, she pinched the clinging damp fabric away from her stomach and in the snootiest voice said, 'You've made me all wet and not in the right place either. Next time, change your clothes when you hug me. The rain has probably ruined this designer number. It's a one off, you can't buy this in any old—'

'Answer the *fucking* question. Have you been sleeping around?'

Cloey smiled, lengthening the moment as if counting in her head. 'Ten.' She held up her fingers and thumbs. 'Ten whole men. *Yummy.*'

Jordan tried to control his imagination, but it was already out of the pen, galloping away, hurdling over one hunk after the other. The race was on for him to control his anger. Ever since, as a young lad, he had smashed up his Speak 'n' Spell for spelling 'colour' as 'color', ever since taking his dead goldfish back to the fair and threatening to burn the big wheel down if they didn't give him one that swam, ever since coming home from school and being told his mother had died, Jordan had struggled to keep a lid on the pressure cooker inside him. Finding out his childhood sweetheart had shared herself with ten men while fooling him into believing she was waiting for him on the outside, was beyond pressure. It was plain and simply – like the Speak 'n' Spell Yankee man said when Jordan typed in the word 'colour' – WRONG. But so is leaving the love of your life for three long years.

Jordan shook his dripping conker-brown hair made almost black from the rain. 'Well, in some ways that's a compliment, Cloey. It takes ten men to fill my boots.' He paused. 'If I just shrug at what you've told me, it's not because I don't care, it's because I do care. I love you, and the fact that you had a little bit of company when I was inside hurts, but it ain't gonna kill me.' He brushed the back of his hand against her cheek. 'People like us don't split up. We made a blood tie.' He raised his eyebrows. 'I won't ever mention this again. And I promise I won't go looking for them with a knife in the middle of the night.'

Cloey laughed, holding on to his hand. 'You've got gorgeous looks, Jordan, God spoilt you. And our sex is mind-blowing.' She tilted her head, wiping a dewdrop of rain from his nose with her little finger. 'You really are a dream man and I know how much you love me, but it makes me so sad to see you like this – grovelling. Shall we face facts? You're an ex-convict, Jordan. You've been to prison. Who's going to employ you now? Your CV will go straight in the dustbin.' She stepped back. 'This is going to hurt, but I've met another man. He owns his own security business and . . . we're in love. His name's Sammy.' Her grin was mocking.

There's nothing special about hearing another bloke's name – unless he's the man who has taken your woman. Then you'll remember that name for the rest of your life.

Jordan's view extended past Cloey's shoulder, into the cottage, and he looked for signs of this Sammy. 'Your letters and visits were the only thing that made prison bearable. But now you're telling me you've been feeding me a load of horse shit.' He shook his head. 'You even wrote an apology in one of them for an unreadable paragraph, saying that your tears had spilt out of control and splodged the ink. And all the time you'd been screwing around with other men.'

Cloey smirked provocatively. 'Well, excuse me for giving you something to live for.'

'Well, fuck you.' He turned to leave.

'Oh, by the by, I didn't bother putting flowers on your mother's grave this month, I thought I'd leave that up to you now that you're a free man. Ciao!' She slammed the door.

Cloey's words to him before he went to court three years ago kept repeating in his mind: 'I love you, Jordan. Even death won't separate us.'

Jordan reluctantly dragged himself away from Lemonly Cottage towards the Holy Cross Church, where his mum lay buried among the wild flowers.

Kneeling down by her grave, he picked up the small bunch of pink roses that must have been put there by his dad, Bernie, who came once a week, keeping the grave tidy, replacing the old flowers with new. The headstone had a simple message, it was all Bernie could afford at the time: *We Shared Everything. Except This.* Jordan crossed himself, the only figure mad enough to say a prayer in the hellish rain, and dipped his head. He had dreamed of a good life with

Cloey, and a dream was all it had turned out to be.

From the age of thirteen, they had pledged themselves to each other. To separate their lives would have been to obliterate their lives. And Jordan now felt obliterated. Something told him not to; an age-old voice explained that it was uncool for a twenty-six-year-old man to cry. And so, very uncoolly, he cried.

If the last three years of his life had been black then the next year of his life was white. Like the white inside a coconut, or the white of an American's smile, but especially the white of snow. Jordan found his new love, not in a woman, but in a snowboard, twisting down the mountain peaks of Les Trois Vallées.

His older brother, Antone (he removed the y when he first arrived in France) was a chef at the resort, peeling onions during the day and women's underwear in the evening. He offered Jordan the largest bed in his log cabin: the floor.

Before long, Jordan became a bit of a local hero, winning snowboarding trophy after trophy. His brother shook his head at the compliments to Jordan, how people said he was such a natural on the piste. Both Jordan and Antone knew the secret of Jordan's success: their dad's bad back. When Jordan was five he used to have to stand on his dad's wobbling back, keeping his balance, massaging it with his tiny feet. He wasn't a natural, just good at balancing on a fat man.

Jordan embraced the life of the slopes: skiing and snowboarding in the snowy season; sunbathing and sightseeing in the sunny season. But his home was in

England. He returned to Milton Keynes after a year having picked up a lot of French. He even managed to learn some of their language as well.

Then . . . Zara hit him like a sledgehammer. Barely had his feet hit soggy England, when her beauty knocked him off his soggy feet. She swept him away from the very first shag, replacing the hole that Cloey had left. Within four years they were devoted to each other by which time Zara had long since become used to the dawn police raids and Jordan had become used to Zara's designer friends.

At thirty-one, in the middle of a crispy hot August, Jordan fitted the description, not of a police wanted picture, but of a happy man.

Chapter Two

Kareena was going to lose her virginity before midnight to a virtual stranger. She pressed her face against the hotel mirror that stood opposite the huge four-poster bed. Maybe she'd been watching too many episodes of *Big Brother*, but she was sure she could see a shape moving behind it. She hadn't waited twenty-seven years of her life to have her first bonk broadcast over the Internet, so she draped a burgundy bath towel over the peeping Tom, still overwhelmed by the luxury that surrounded her.

Samir, her new thirty-one-year-old husband, could be heard brushing his teeth from the en-suite bathroom. He'd been swishing and swoshing, gurgling, spluttering and spitting, for over half an hour now. Either that or he had the nervous runs. They'd spent only about five hours alone with one another before today and now they would spend the night together. In Rome you must do as the Romans do, but in

England, Indians do as the Indians do. And Indians have arranged marriages, and that means no hanky panky before wedlock. And that even includes blowing kisses.

The honeymoon suite in the five-star Grand Pavilion Palace Hotel in Poole, Dorset was testament to a thousand passionate nights. A leather-bound maroon book sat insignificantly on a corner table. It was up to you whether you wanted to make a written entry in the Pavilion Book of Passion. Kareena flicked it open, then immediately slammed it shut again, the five stars of the hotel now reduced to one, the condom stuck between the pages still leaking from last night's guest.

Repulsed, Kareena returned to the bed, its red and green crushed velvet clashing with her pink and gold bridal sari, her mind clashing with reality. Tonight was really going to happen, and God she was nervous. What if he was disappointed in her body? What if she was a total flop in bed? What if . . .

Samir walked in, shrouded in worry, furrows creasing his forehead. Kareena smiled weakly, but he just stared, as if having trouble recognizing her. 'Uhm, it's a bit embarrassing . . . uhm . . . oh shit . . . uhm.' His coffee-coloured eyes locked on the champagne bottle chilling in a bucket. 'I forgot to pack . . . Look, I'll be back in a few minutes,' he said, grabbing his suit jacket from the back of a chair.

Kareena looked puzzled. 'What did you forget to pack?'

At the door he turned. 'The rubber johnnies.' He twisted the big brass knob, his red carnation falling to the plush carpet. 'Back in a tick.'

The hotel was huge, like in *The Shining*, except with less blood. An architectural masterpiece of endless corridors, enormous banqueting rooms and high, elaborately decorated ceilings. Samir pressed the illuminated 'down' arrow for the lift. At this moment 'down' seemed to be exactly where his life was heading.

The bell tinkled and he got in. His reflection in the lift mirror revealed a pensive, worried expression. There was no way he could have sex with Kareena today. Or any day for that matter.

The lift stopped, he passed quickly through the spacious Reception with its automated receptionist, out through the swivel doors and into the night. In the August sky overhead, the stars were in Zodiac mood, showing off Aries the ram and Gemini the twins. Custodians of fate. The dice cups of destiny. Samir switched on his mobile, staring skywards, praying for a little help from above.

He punched in a number and spoke, 'Sorry it's a bit late, but I was missing you. I hate these business meetings, they really eat into our time. You okay?'

A pause, then a well-spoken voice, 'I can't concentrate when you're not here, Sammy, I feel feverish.' Cloey twirled the phone cord round her finger. 'You know I'm at my most excitable at this time of the month. I wish you'd picked another week for this important meeting or whatever you say it is. You haven't let any women chat you up, have you?'

Samir felt the urge to jump into his Mercedes, drive to Bruckley and snuggle up with the woman he loved and not stay here in this palace with the woman his parents wanted him to love. He sighed. 'And how am

I supposed to fit in anything of that sort with the horrendous list of meetings I have to get through?' And a wedding. 'I'm one of those men who when they fall, they fall all the way, Cloey. You should know that by now.' He paused. 'Anyway, why would I look at another woman, when right now, even as I stand here, I am gazing at your Polaroid. Hang on.' He made a kissing noise in his hand. 'I *love* you, Cloey.'

She giggled. 'Kiss me again, harder.' She waited for the smacking noise. 'Sammy, let's have phone sex.'

'Uhm.'

'Come on, it'll be fun.'

Samir looked around quickly. 'I'm not wearing any protection.' He chuckled. 'Anyway, wouldn't it be better if we waited until I came home? Think about it, imagine how hot we'll be.'

Cloey giggled again. 'Just hurry back.'

A few minutes of flirting later, he switched off his mobile and pulled the condoms out of his jacket pocket. The question was: could he be unfaithful to Cloey? They'd been together for six fantastic years, he couldn't waste what they had for just one night of passion with his wife, could he?

Back in the hotel, still staring at the box of Durex, he waited for the lift to arrive. Cloey had been the world's best kept secret since Bletchley Park. An Asian Enigma. If his parents had ever found out about her, blood vessels would have burst. Mum and Dad would have rushed to the temple, their noses hitting the *gurdwara* floor so quick you'd think they were sniffing for truffles. If they ever found out Samir had been with a white woman and given her a taste of India, it would mean only one thing: disownment –

the symbolic burning of his birth certificate. In their eyes, from that moment on, it would be as though their son had never been born.

Samir paused at the door. Room 217 – the Honeymoon Suite. Kareena was probably the prettiest Indian woman he'd ever seen, and he knew underneath her sari she wasn't going to be a disappointment; making love to her should be easy. But keeping her a secret from Cloey was going to be hard.

He unlocked the door, walked in and threw the condoms on the bed. The rubbers bounced.

Kareena switched off the TV, checked the wall clock, and stood staring, unsure, an innocence adhering to her like a faint perfume. This was *the* moment. Kareena had heard it hurt like hell and she was itching to dial room service to order an epidural. If they can have them for giving birth to babies then why not for making them? This was probably the only time in a woman's life she hoped her husband had a small willy.

She watched Samir remove his red silk tie and throw it to her. She caught it deftly.

Samir smiled. 'Do you want to help me get undressed?' He dithered and backtracked. 'Of course, I can do it myself. I do know how. I just thought you might . . . You know? . . . To get us in the mood?' He paused, her heavily hennaed hands, slightly shaking, were already working on his shirt buttons. 'I know we don't know each other,' he went on, connecting with her reddish-brown eyes, 'and it feels like we've been thrown in at the deep end, but . . . hold on a sec.' Reaching behind him, he pulled from his trouser pocket his pre-written speech. He glanced it over, then passed it to her. 'You may as well read it. Be warned, I had a few pints before I wrote it.'

Wedding Night Speech

I know we don't know each other, and it feels like we've been thrown in at the deep end, which we have (pause to stare deeply in her eyes), but I'm not a murderer and I'm not a pervert (squeeze her hand).
I don't want sex with you,
if you don't want sex with me.
I'm not one of these blokes who expects their women to give me one (fake laugh) out of duty.
Now get your knickers off!

Kareena just shook her head, laughing. Here was a man who was charming the sari off her. The first time she had seen him, nearly a year ago, she felt something connect, something beyond his fantastic looks that is. Samir was the third guy her parents had presented her with, and he was the only one she had taken to bed in her dreams. The five hours they had spent together before today had been filled with laughter. She would have been a fool to turn him down. If an Indian girl is introduced to an Indian boy she fancies, she doesn't drop the ball.

In the dim hotel-room light, Kareena helped Samir become naked. His skin was like painted gold dust, a golden brown that spoke of the Mediterranean rather than of India. Kareena stood there in her sari, relishing each touch of her hands on his fantastically toned body. Her pink and white wedding bangles softly tickled his skin. She let her hands be guided down his tight flat stomach, his breathing becoming deeper, her excitement becoming purer. She couldn't believe that she was finally touching a man. And what a man! And he was all hers.

He let her hands go, still looking into each other's eyes, and she knew where he wanted her fingers to crawl to. She hadn't even glanced down there yet but, somehow, she could feel it staring up at her through its one unwinking eye. Kareena sneaked a quick look below and stalled. Forget how big it was, how much did it weigh? Her eyes became wide as her breathing quickened. She told herself to calm down. Of course it was going to fit inside.

Samir spoke, 'If you want to, we can turn out the lights.'

Kareena still stared down. 'No, I'm okay.'

'Are you sure? I see you've put a towel over the mirror. You shouldn't be ashamed of your body, Kareena. Honestly, those grandparents we put up with, always trying to get us to cover ourselves up.'

She smiled. God, he was almost perfect. Those doubts she'd had about tonight were dissolving like soap suds. She should have known just to look at him that he wouldn't have ruined this night. He was so edible, with eyes so alive and his square jaw perfect for a Bic razor advert. He had the kind of gorgeous looks that would scratch a record and stop a party.

Samir began to unwrap her silk sari, its heavy embroidery becoming lighter and lighter as the material gradually exposed more and more of her slim figure. Oh God, she thought, *Oh God*. She would soon be as naked as he was. During their first meeting together, he had quietly confessed to his previous experience of sleeping with two Indian women (not at the same time), and she had welcomed his honesty. Most Indian men would have taken details like that to their grave. Now she worried that he might be comparing her body to theirs. She prayed those two Indian women had been weighty warthogs.

Samir offered to remove her clay wedding bangles. It was bad luck to take them off, you should really let them break off naturally, but it would be worse luck to make love and then wake up in the morning with pottery shrapnel lodged in your backside.

So she let him remove them, watching his eyes as they travelled up and down her body. It felt like taking an exam, waiting for the smile, hoping for his approval. If he laughed at her, then the next forty years of her life would be shit. This was the best her body was ever going to be. She'd spent hours in the gym for the past year toning her muscles for this one day. Samir still stared.

'You're totally gorgeous, Kareena. Beautiful,' he said. 'Wow!'

There was a silence in the room, but in Samir's head a board meeting was taking place. The message from the managing director was clear: don't sleep with Kareena, if you want to keep Cloey. You can't have both.

Samir kissed her mouth, knowing that there is always a simple way to keep two women if you try hard enough: you lie through your arse. And as Samir enjoyed the warmth of Kareena's kiss, he gave an inner chuckle. There was no finer liar on this planet than he.

He gently pushed her back on the bed, and showed her how to roll on the condom. 'It's as simple as that,' he said, removing it. 'Now *you* try.'

19

She smiled, her lust coated with nerves. 'You will be gentle with me when you . . . you know?'

He wiped his greasy fingers on the sheet. 'You're in safe hands, I've done this a million times before.' He paused. 'But, given the choice, I would swap all those shags for this moment. Sometimes I wish I'd held on to my cherry.'

She held the condom with both hands, trying to slip it on to Samir's willy, but it refused to stay still, bobbing this way, then that. It was like trying to refuel in mid-air.

'Look, Kareena, you're going to have to touch it. If you don't put its coat on, it'll get cold.'

They both laughed as Samir helped her out with the condom. He could tell she was uneasy. And why wouldn't she be? She barely knew him from Adamjeet, and now she was being asked to roll latex onto his cock.

He kissed her gently on the lips, trying to relax her, hoping her tenseness would ease, hoping his guilt would cease. It felt like they were aboard a raft adrift at sea. Two strangers thrown together and told to survive come what may. She trusted him with her life, her parents had entrusted him with their daughter, and yet, he knew he was a fake. A bogus boyfriend to Cloey and a hoax of a husband to Kareena. There was no confusion in his mind as to what he had now become – *haram da*. Or in English – a bastard.

But Kareena saw only the catch of the century lying on top of her. She could feel his hardness brushing against her thigh, rubbing closer upwards, then teasingly pulling away. They could have been any-where at this moment, the Ritz, a camper van, Dr

Who's Tardis, and it wouldn't have mattered, she knew what was required of her: it was her Indian duty to lie back and be screwed.

Samir asked permission with his eyes, a polite knock on the door before he got out his battering ram. She opened her legs wider, giving him consent to continue, but her mind was in turmoil, a party of emotions ready to commit anarchy. On the one hand he was a stranger and on the other he was her husband, and, right down the middle, he was gob-smackingly gorgeous. Like many women, Kareena had dreamt of a stranger performing sordid, shame-less, sex upon her submissive body – and now her dream was real. Her planned words, 'Take me roughly, unknown person' disappeared down her throat as his cock entered her sharply and began to thrust slowly, then faster. Finally his body lurched into spasm, and she opened her eyes to watch his face. The first few words that came out of his mouth were barely audible, but the next four nearly made her giggle. 'Oh, God, I'm cummmming.' The frenzy was over.

'It was wonderful,' she said, smiling.

He brushed away some wisps of her long hair. 'Don't lie. It was shit and you know it.' She laughed, and he kissed her. 'I'll be recharged in five minutes, then I'll try and make it wonderful,' he said, rolling off her and grabbing the champagne bottle from its silver bucket of partially melted heart-shaped ice – noting perturbingly how befitting the ice hearts were. Surely only a man with a heart made of ice could do what he was doing? He had never felt so guilty in all his life.

21

'Don't you want to check the sheet?' She spoke to his bare back.

He took off the foil cap, undid the wire and popped the cork. 'For what?'

'Blood? To check that I was really a—'

He butted in, chuckling. 'A vampire?' He turned round to face her, smoke rising from the opened bottle. 'You mean to see if you were pure?' His voice was edged with sarcasm. 'Blokes don't care about that sort of thing.'

She watched him pour out two glasses of fizz. 'But Indian men do.'

'Well, I'm not your typical Indian man,' he said crawling across the bed to hand her the drink.

Kareena mused on the moment. Whoever was writing the screenplay for her life must have been reading her mind, delving into her young-girl dreams and pulling out a prince. But every prince needed a princess.

She only hoped she matched up.

Chapter Three

Jordan had done many shameful things in his life, and he was ashamed of some of them. If he was not quite knocking on the devil's door, he was certainly peeping through the letterbox. He knew that one day there'd be a day of reckoning, he reckoned so anyway and, this week, he'd set himself the task of trying to make up for some of the bad he'd done. In his mind, there was no better place to start paying for your sins than a church. And there was no better church than the one where his mother lay buried – the Holy Cross Church in Bruckley.

Cranking up the handbrake, he stared up the steep lane that led to the church. A pretty wall of Japanese cherry trees blocked the spire-topped building from view, their fallen pink petals lay scattered on the ground. It was such an enchanting entrance, no one would believe that evil lurked behind those holy walls. But evil did, disguised in the cloth, in the name of the church, in the name of the father, in the name of Father Luke. Jordan hated that man. And that man hated Jordan.

The sound of horses' hooves roused him from his thoughts, and Jordan watched two women riders clippitty-clop by, each looking down into his Lexus' window, their smiles as bright as the weather, the smell of horse dung as sweet as their smiles.

As they disappeared round the corner, he switched on the CD player smashing out James's 'Sit Down'. It was time for a fag and a think. His girlfriend wanted a baby, and the timing was perfect: their finances were good, their love for each other intense and Next were bringing out a new baby catalogue for the winter collection. Zara had already scanned Jordan's and her photo into the computer and sent it off to some company to see what their baby would look like. In tears she'd shown the result to Jordan who hadn't been too impressed. 'Our baby is going to look like a freak. The world is too small for two Mick Hucknalls.' But he did want a baby, he'd been fostering the idea himself for a while. They'd even turned the spare room into a nursery. It was just that there was the same old shit hanging around that wrecks relationships: secrets. There were things Zara should know about him. He'd left them simmering too long in his head and if he didn't tell her soon, they'd boil over.

Getting out of the car, he flicked his fag on the ground, opened up the boot and heaved out a can of Dulux undercoat. This was his fifth day on the trot painting. He'd given himself two weeks to undercoat the church fence and two weeks to topcoat. It felt good to do something so noble and worthwhile and the council felt good that it was being done for free. Only Father Luke questioned the arrangement. Jordan never did anything for free – what was the catch? He would be keeping a close watch on Jordan, for it was improbable that Jordan had seen the light: criminals were normally born with blinkers on. Highly improbable.

Today, at 93°F, it was an improbably hot day too. Jordan slammed the car boot shut, his dark-green John Lennon shades over his eyes, his snowboarding O'Neill shorts and Billabong T-shirt covering his tanned, muscly body. He might be a crap painter, but he sure looked cool.

'It's a lovely day, isn't it, Jordan?' said a woman's voice behind him.

He spun round, catching the scent of her strong perfume as he did so. Jordan was now viewing a subtlety-free woman. Her clothes were impossibly skimpy but also looked impossibly expensive. His memory failed to recollect the stunning, leggy, blonde beauty now standing with one foot out in front of her like the helm of a sexy ship, but he could already guess what she would look like naked underneath him. He cursed himself quietly for, one, thinking such filth right in front of a church; two, for the fact that he should be saving those thoughts for Zara; and three, his second erection of the hour was coming early.

He set the paint tin down by his Nikes and spoke, 'You know me and I don't know you, that means one of us round here drinks too much.'

'No, you don't know me. My name's Cherry and don't flatter yourself, I'm not here for your cheap one-liners,' she said, perching her bum on his car, its flashy indigo-coloured shell polished like a gem. 'Who d'you dream about at night, Jordan?'

'None of your business. Now get your arse off my car – it's not insured for buffaloes.'

'Touchy. Did I hit a nerve, Jordan? A raw nerve? You still dream about her, don't you? And we both know who I'm talking about.' Cherry jumped off the boot. 'You can't ignore her, pretending she was *nothing* in your life when we all know she was *everything* in your life . . . everything.'

A woman and child whizzed by on bicycles, free-wheeling down the lane. Jordan waited until they were in the distance. 'You don't know shit about me. I take it you're talking about that fucking bitch, Cloey? Oh yeah, I go to bed dreaming about her all right, but not the kind of dreams you're talking about. Now get out of my face.' He picked the tin off the ground, and began to walk away.

There was the sound of high heels following, stumbling behind him. 'I've got a message from Cloey.' He stopped dead and turned. Cherry continued, her smile already victorious, 'If you ignore her again, she'll slap you. You don't freeze out someone like Cloey. Twice she's been up here this week and both times you had the audacity to snub her.' She went up on tip-toes, looking into his shades. 'She made eye contact with you and *you* had the nerve to look away. It won't happen again, will it, Convict?'

Jordan remained calm, his mind dodging thoughts of pouring the sludgy paint over her pretty little face. Who the hell did she and Cloey think they were? Spotting a firm wedge of warm horse manure steaming on the road, he told himself, 'No, Jordan. No.'

'Tell Cloey, I used to love her, but it's dead and buried now.' He paused to wipe his brow. 'Now, would you be so kind and fuck off.'

From 93°F to freezing, hot to cold, sun to snow. Hearing the word Cloey was like taking the wrong pill in the *Matrix* – it wrecked your reality. Right now, Jordan felt like getting hold of a virtual-reality bomb and sticking it right under her cottage in Bruckley. He had always wanted to know how high a bitch could jump. He flung open his locker in the indoor ski-slope changing rooms – the sign on the outside read, *Ski Instructor's Locker*. He knew he'd hate himself later for doing this, but he did it all the same.

Underneath a neatly laundered pile of snow-boarding clothes, he'd hidden a small box inside a sock. And in that small box was hidden a forgotten dream – Cloey's engagement ring. It should have been put on her finger a long time ago, the day he came out of prison to be exact. Now he pulled it out of the hazardous-looking sock, where unknown bacteria seemed to have taken hold of the toe area, and popped open the lid.

The sapphires and diamonds sparkled happily – oblivious to the fact that they'd been cut from aeons-old rock only to be placed next to a team of verrucae – and Jordan couldn't help but think, if only.

It was a bad thought at the best of times. He closed the box and threw it angrily back into the locker, wondering why he'd kept it all this time. It was like keeping a bloody bandage from an old wound, simply to remind yourself of the pain you'd suffered. You can't step into a rosy future if you keep tripping up on the thorns of your past. But sometimes it can't be avoided.

Last week in the churchyard, as he painted his way slowly round the fence, Cloey had sprung up like a miserable leak. Her eloquent voice, drifting over the headstones like fog across the moors, had caused him to look up. And there she was, with a friend, watching him from across the cemetery. Only then did he realize it had been five long years since he'd last laid eyes on her, as he stared across at the woman who had once held his heart. And he'd torn his eyes away from the woman who had broken it.

The next day as he painted the same old plank of wood – *déjà vu* – it happened all over again. Their eyes had locked, their shared history mutely discussed, and his pain unbearable. He thought to himself right there and then, Why have you crucified me, Cloey? and he had turned away once more. He made love to Zara like a guilty man that night, angry at himself for reminiscing, unwilling to accept that he had any feelings still remaining for Cloey.

But today, when the blonde Cherry had mentioned Cloey's name, Jordan knew for sure that while his feelings may have lain low, they had never entirely gone away, and like a sleeping volcano they had now erupted. Sometimes you just can't hold nature back.

But sometimes you can change nature. As he stood at the top of the crystallized ice and looked down the monster slope, Jordan took in the view he never tired of: snow. A mountain indoors, made by man and surfed by madmen. His thoughts of Cloey began to freeze over. People paid him good money to teach them how to ski and snowboard, their healthy cheques funding most of Zara's wardrobe. But money was nothing compared to that buzz of throwing yourself to the mercy of slippery gravity. And Jordan was ready to rock 'n' roll.

Goggles down, fixed-on grin, Isaac Newton do your thing.

Jordan cut the first quarter of the steep slope like a shark fin through water, building up speed for the first jump. Balance was the key here. Did he want to live or did he want to die? He flew up the ramp of snow dangerously fast, aware of the multitude of eyes trained on him. Tucking a high twist, he spun his body twice round, pulling in his arms for a tight landing. Except, just before touchdown, his concentration slipped. Instead of the dazzling clean snow in his view, he saw a vision of Cloey, naked, smiling up at him. He crashed 'n' burned to the loud applause of his audience and closed his eyes. Slipping just wasn't his bag.

He lay there groaning quietly like a wounded animal. This ski-slope, 'Xscape', was where he came to escape from his problems. It was the skiing equivalent of a bottle of vodka. Even if his life was in turmoil outside – in here it was normally at peace. So why was Cloey shivering in his mind?

A man's voice said, 'Are you Jordan Lewis?'

Jordan raised his head from the snow. 'Yes.'

'I heard that you could ski.' The large man held out his hand to help Jordan to his feet. 'I'm Barry, your four o'clock appointment. Advanced slalom? We spoke on the phone – you said that you could turn me into a champion skier.'

Jordan took a quick look at Barry's enormous midriff and thought: I could turn you into a champion ski-slope, Barry.

'And what else did I mention on the phone, Barry?' He paused for him to answer. 'The importance of wearing the correct protective clothing? Why are you wearing a motorbike crash helmet?'

Barry lifted up his visor. 'Don't know.'

Jordan felt guilty taking money off people like Barry whose minds were fed by Sky Sports with visions of Olympic stardom. No one had the right to take away their dreams. If Barry wanted to be a champion slalom skier, then Jordan would help him.

'Tell you what I'm going to do, Barry,' he said, popping his feet back on the freestyle board. 'I'm going to lend you my goggles for today. And I'm also going to give you this lesson for free – to see if you like my style of tuition. Sound all right?' It was hardly going to break the bank, but it felt good to be kind . . . sometimes.

Barry grinned.

'Settled then.'

After Barry's lesson, Jordan sat on the top of the slope watching the skiers, wanting to join them, but wanting more to get Cloey out of his brain. She'd already completely screwed it up once before and he wasn't going to let it happen again.

As he snowboarded down to the bottom, he spotted Zara waiting in the coffee shop behind the safety glass. He gave her a wave. Tonight when he made love to her, he'd make sure Cloey wasn't in the bedroom with them.

Slipping wasn't his bag and threesomes weren't his bag either.

He smiled at Zara. God forbid, shopping was *her* bag and look at them! Designer bags everywhere.

And later that evening, the next day to be precise, at 3.00 a.m., while Samir lay beside Kareena thinking of Cloey, and Jordan lay beside Zara thinking of Cloey, Mickey got out of *his* bag: his sleeping bag. Mickey was Samir's mistake. He was the most dishonest man Samir's company, NightOwl Group Security employed. But he had a face like an angel. And he hated working on the Johnny-no-friends shift, looking after a poxy office that would never be burgled, so he slept through it, for £8.00 per hour.

Mickey rolled his sleeping bag into a tight ball and then finished packing the items he had stolen from Communiqué Communications in a cardboard box. It was a fine office, kitted out for very important office people. Mickey dumped the box outside the MD's door and wandered in. A quick look at the boss's picture of his wife – very ugly – then he walked up to the phone, picked it up and farted in the mouthpiece. His shift was now over.

The dual carriageway was empty at this time in the morning and the tarmac was his. In no time at all, he arrived at NightOwl Group Security in Stacey Bushes. It was quiet down this end of Milton Keynes, a few garages, a KFC and plenty of office space for lease. The brand new NightOwl units overlooked a huge, wild, open field ready for the developments of the future.

Inside, in the central nervous system of NightOwl,

a lone duty-control operator sat at an enormous desk. Three embroidered gold stars shone from each shoulder, an earpiece was tucked snugly in his ear. Mickey sat down opposite him and rested his feet on the table.

'All right, Alf, keeping busy?'

'Alfred to you and get your boots off my desk.' He tapped away at the computer.

'Between you and me, Alfred, you're a twat. The sooner Samir comes back from his Gales honey honeymoon, the sooner your bad attitude will . . . erm . . . erm . . .'

'Disappear?'

'Yeah, Twat, disappear.' Mickey stood. 'I'm in there, filling out my holiday sheet.' He grabbed a pink form and entered Samir's office, locking the door behind him.

The place was immaculate, a sturdy half-moon desk by the window with a brown leather swivel chair, filing cabinets, bookshelf, cold water dispenser and . . . it made Mickey sick, why couldn't he have an office like this? He sat in the chair and spun, thinking. He'd slogged his guts out for this company. It was about time he was . . . erm . . . erm . . . appreciated.

Mickey jumped up and karate chopped his way to the wooden filing cabinets, hitting out at imaginary intruders in his path. He wanted to know what was written on his personnel file and he was damn well going to find out, he thought, as he expertly eased open the lock with his trusty penknife. Samir's secrets were now his secrets. He knew Indians loved keeping secrets. After all, they'd managed to keep curry a secret for two thousand years. It wouldn't be too long, he was sure, before MI5 cracked what was hidden under their turbans.

He riffled through the blue concertina files in the top drawer, checking over each computer label. Mohammed A., Mohammed G., Singh D., Patel A., Mohammed L., Kapany N., Sethi P., Mohammed W., Sagoo K., Smith J., Mohammed V. . . . Bundles and bundles of foreigners, thought Mickey, no wonder his promotion was not forthcoming. Samir was employing his brothers – sheer nepotism! The evidence was damning. Mickey threw back the drawer, disgusted.

The second drawer was boring: holiday sheets, uniform sheets, shift sheets.

'What a load of sheet,' he said, slamming the drawer shut with his hip. Opening the third, he was still muttering to himself. His nostrils suddenly flared. Either his boss was a poof or else he got turned on by women's perfume. It was a couple of private queer jokes later before Mickey spotted the source of the smell: a folder marked clearly CLOEY. And a couple of seconds later it was open.

Mickey dribbled with excitement. Scented love letters, poems, birthday, Valentine and Christmas cards. Even thank you cards.

No, *Thank You*, Samir, thought Mickey, as he flipped through a handful of photographs picturing Samir and Cloey happily flirting with the camera. Cloey was a stunner, no two ways about it. Samir was a lucky man. Mickey would have paid a month's wages for one naked hour with Cloey. Currently he wouldn't pay the cost of a hot dog for a naked hour with his own girlfriend.

Mickey lifted up the venetian blinds with a finger

and viewed the road. Sometimes in the still of the early morning he glimpsed a red fox down this end. Sneaky, sly, intelligent foxes. They reminded him of himself. He sat back down, quite bored by reading Cloey's lengthy love letters. They were so Mills and Boon. He hated women who used the word *penis*, why couldn't they use its real name *cock*? About to give up, he noticed another letter. Not *to* Samir but *from* Samir.

My darling Cloey
They say the pen is mightier than the sword, but I don't feel mighty writing this, I should be saying it to your face. By the time you read this I will be married to an Indian woman I don't know and don't care about. You have got to understand that I did this for my parents. I love you and that will never change. My wife will only be my wife, she will never be my lover, my friend, my reason to get up in the morning.
Your parents are Catholic and mine are Sikh. It was a shame that our love had to be kept a secret from them. Maybe we might understand better when our kids ask us if they might marry someone from Mars.
I feel like a shit writing this letter . . .

Mickey turned the page, feeling conned that the letter was unfinished, but if Samir needed to stop writing to take a shit, then good on him. As his mind returned to the subject of promotion and Samir's favouritism, Mickey folded the paper up and tucked it in his trouser pocket. The unfinished billet-doux could be used to hold Samir to ransom. If he didn't promote Mickey in the next month, he would show him the letter and explain that it might be okay for him to take our white women, but it was not okay for him not to promote the white man. It's called racism. And it hurts.

Chapter Four

Samir watched Kareena's eyes widen as she took in the full view of his huge five-bedroom house from the driveway. He was only slightly disappointed that her eyes were wider now than when she had first seen his willy. She hooked her arm through his and gave him a beaming smile. 'I can't believe this is all ours, it's a dream house.'

It reminded Samir of the same look Cloey had given him when he had finally forked out for the deposit two years ago. Cloey had insisted that if they were to get married, she would only accept one of the posher areas of Milton Keynes for her home. And areas didn't get any posher than Applecroft. Its isolation, the estate agent had said, brought the cream of Milton Keynes to the top.

Kareena and Cloey had the same taste in houses and in men. It would be interesting, thought Samir, to see whether they would both have the same taste in furnishings.

'Samir, it's fantastic,' said Kareena, running though the dining room. 'So homely.'

Samir scarcely spoke as he watched the momentum of his wife's excitement build. He wondered if she would spot some of the little touches that Cloey had spent months perfecting. The little things that men had no eye for, but which they would miss if they were gone. The little magic that makes a house a home. The little swipes on his credit card had nearly sent him into cardiac arrest when the *little* Visa bills dropped through the letterbox of the grand house that Cloey should have been moving into, had he been man enough to swim upstream in a family with two thousand years of tradition flowing downstream.

'What's this?' Kareena asked, standing in the monster conservatory.

'A conservatory.'

'No, *this*. I don't want to touch it.' She pointed to the jar.

Samir thought back to Africa, to the safari holiday he and Cloey had enjoyed there together. He remembered what the tribesman had told him was in the glass container. Kareena was right not to want to touch it.

'It's sperm. Tribal sperm. It was given to me by a shaman, it's a fertility gift. I think the chief's name was Abui Berdongi.'

Kareena giggled. There was not much she could say to that. She just felt blessed for being here at all.

Her Indian friends, when discussing arranged marriages, spoke of them as prisons. Home was a prison where you were cooped up like a songbird waiting for freedom, but that freedom never came. What happened was that mum and dad married you off to Mr Right, who most likely would be Mr Wrong. You moved out of your home prison to an upgraded version with an upgraded prison warden – the mother-in-law.

And that's why Kareena was so happy. Her mother-in-law was a million miles away, in Hayes.

The last two nights had been like a dream, a perfect dream. In the late hours of yesterday they had discussed his past Indian lovers, family, ambitions and fantasies. She had asked him what he respected, demanded, expected in a relationship and he had one answer to all three: HONESTY, in big capital letters. He had been raised on it like Ready Brek and it gave him a warm glow inside.

Samir led her up the thickly carpeted stairs onto the well-lit landing. 'I'm a sucker for dried flowers,' he said, wishing he'd thought to remove some of Cloey's bouquets beforehand.

Kareena agreed with a nod; one dropped match and the house would go wooosh, she thought. She followed him into a study fit for Dickens. Wooden panels, floor-to-ceiling empty oak bookcases thirsty for books and a computer on the desk. The place was odourless and clean. Where did he keep his clutter? All men had clutter, that was one thing Kareena knew for a fact.

The next room popped the cloud Kareena's head was floating in. Shrivelled nerves in her stomach opened like cooked mussel shells, and she didn't know why.

Samir looked on edge as he tried to explain. 'Not

my idea. It was here when I bought the house. It gives me nightmares to be honest.' He cringed. 'Unfortunately, it still stinks of paint.'

Cloey had locked the door to this room for three days and nights, forbidding him to see it until the effect was finished. She had told Samir that all good artists had a dark side, but only the best artists could bring it to a canvas, could convey the pain of their lives through the brush. Sometimes Cloey's mind scared Samir.

'What is *that*?' Kareena pointed to the painted basket of amputated toes, part of a wall-hogging mural. The title was *Frostbite*.

'That? Erm, no idea. I hate this room, let's go.'

Kareena took a few more seconds to get to grips with the full horror of the room's decor. Painted across half the ceiling was a black snowboard with two silver handcuffs attached to, what seemed like, two large arteries belching blood, entitled, *We're Handcuffed by Blood*, and on the wall next to the window, a colourful staring picture of two huge eyes. In the left pupil were scrawled the words, *I'm Not Watching You*. In the right, *I'm Waiting For You*.

She found Samir standing outside.

'It's like I'm selling you the house; it feels weird,' he said.

'Well, if I saw that room, my offer would be nil.' She saw his face drop and regretted the real Kareena coming out temporarily. Although officially lovers, it would be a while before she could read his signals. Until then, just like strangers do, she would have to rely on her instincts. And instincts told her to leave any questions about the house for another day. She tried to fill the sudden silence. 'Even though, erh, odd, I wish I could paint like that. Artistic talent isn't something I was born with, I'm afraid.'

He kissed her. 'You were a teacher, that's talent. Now.' He laughed. 'Let me show you where I show off *my* talent.' He pulled her into the master bedroom.

A gargantuan bed, like the one in *Bedknobs and Broomsticks*, seemed to grow out of the dark polished oak floor. French doors with flowing white flimsy muslin curtains led to the outside balcony which overlooked a secluded garden, the size of three tennis courts. A wooden birdtable, a separate barbecue area and a small summerhouse nestled among red and yellow rose bushes. Beyond were fields – what a fantastic view!

Kareena reflected on her situation for a moment. Here she stood a few days after her wedding, with a man who seemed perfectly chosen for her by her parents: he was kind, reassuring, funny and gorgeous. And this house was all a happy couple could want. She had hit the jackpot.

In front of her, a bed dressed to the nines in purest virgin white. Pillows plumped sky high and a matching white duvet spread so evenly and blemish free, without so much as a feathered crease. It was time to look sexy.

She lifted up her long hair and fell back on the soft, white folds. *Crunch*!

Samir ran to her rescue. 'Are you okay? I should have warned you, the bed's like rocks.'

Kareena went as red as her skin would allow. 'I'm fine.' She struggled up with the help of his hand. 'You actually sleep on this?'

'Don't mock it until you try it. Our ancestors slept on nails.'

She kicked her sandals off. 'You're full of crap.' Quickly she covered her mouth. 'Whoops, sorry, I shouldn't say that. Sorry.' Kareena lowered her head in shame. This was no way to talk to her husband. Her mother had warned her to think rude things in Punjabi but to say only nice things in English. Never, ever, degrade your husband. She frowned. 'I'm really sorry.'

He dived onto the rock bed. 'Don't be.' Then tilted up her chin with his finger. 'Be yourself.'

Kareena wrapped her arms around his neck and kissed him. When she was a teenager, the girls at her school would boast of the hunks they would end up marrying. Rockstars, filmstars, soapstars. They had asked Kareena who she wanted to marry.

'Whoever my parents think is right for me and who treats me well,' she had replied to a suddenly hushed classroom. The silence was broken by their laughter. The worst kind of laughter. Bitchy girls laughing. 'Mummy and Daddy will choose Mr Right for me,' they mocked her as they laughed. Until the day they returned from the town toilet with a pregnancy test – positive – and a dunce of a boyfriend with zits on every part of his body except his teeth and a confused expression, wondering why he was being hurried towards Mothercare and not the needle exchange like she had promised.

There was a knock at the door.

Samir jumped up, hoping some of the blood in his nether regions would return back to his brain promptly. The last time he'd answered the door with a stiffy, the Bible bashers had nearly had a fit. They had fled even more quickly than when he'd chased them with a picture of Guru Nanak the time before.

He opened the door.

'It took me ages to find this place. Right in the sticks. Nice gaff though. Aren't you going to ask me in?' She pushed open the door, and had a look round the entrance. 'Right posh little place you've got here. What's the mortgage on this then? Seven hundred? Eight hundred a month?' She put her hand up. 'No don't tell me, a grand?'

Samir shoved the door closed and watched her disappear down the hall in her highest slingbacks and tightest black dress leaving the oxygen in the room gagging for breath, her perfume so strong it stung his eyes. His nose was saying tart. His eyes were saying tart. But she was Kareena's twenty-five-year-old sister, he couldn't think of her as a tart.

Abruptly the stereo in the sitting room came on full blast. Louder and louder. The music was Eric Clapton, but at 200 watts it sounded like thrash metal. Louder and louder. Samir tried to adjust his thinking. He tried not to think with the brutality of a murderer but tried instead to think about Avani with the gentle glow of a new brother-in-law. Louder and louder.

Then, as suddenly as it had started, it stopped. Avani's head appeared at the living-room door with a smile. He stared at her.

'You passed my test, Samir,' she said.

'What test?'

Avani squinted. 'I wanted to see if you were the sort

42

of man who would hit a woman. I wanted to find out right now. I wouldn't want to have found out from my sister in years to come that you'd been belting her around.'

'Simply put, Avani, I'm glad your sister was born before you.'

Suddenly, what sounded like a screech of car tyres filled the air. A car crash? In his own house? No, it was Kareena and Avani meeting in a sisterly embrace. As both sisters turned to face him, it dawned on him like nothing had ever dawned on him before: he hadn't just married Kareena, he'd married her sister as well.

Avani spoke, 'I've been so worried about you, Kareena, marrying a man you don't even know. God, my mind's been going haywire thinking of all the nasty things he might have done to you. I mean, they look perfect on the outside but who knows what evil swims within.' Avani's heavily mascaraed eyes cruised up and down Samir's body. 'Look at him. On paper his credentials look fine, top notch: the house, the Merc, the business, the looks.' She stared back at Kareena. 'But he's a man after all, and we all know what lies they're capable of.'

'But . . .' Samir began.

'Go on then, hit me,' Avani provoked. 'Go on, get it over with. It's not too late for an annulment.'

Kareena walked over to Samir. 'Leave him alone, he's lovely.'

A huge wretching noise spewed from Avani. 'Yuck or what?'

Half an hour of Avani tests later, Samir was beginning to feel he was finally making headway up her

Christmas-card list. He listened to the two sisters talk, gossip, chat, slag, bitch, slander, with the frenzy of mutes who had grown tongues overnight. Never had he seen two people go at it with so much passion. They were like two dogs wrestling over a bloody steak. Twisting the conversation this way and that. He obviously wasn't needed here, so he rose up to go.

'Kareena, I'm going to go and check out the office and make sure everything is all—'

'Do you want me to come with you?' She felt an elbow in her ribs. 'Do you want *us* to come with you?'

Samir pondered, as if this was a very difficult decision. 'No, no, you two have obviously got a lot of catching up to do. If things get too hairy at the office, or one of the sites, then I'll call in some hours from Mohammed. I know I shouldn't go, it's a bit rude, but a lot can happen in one day let alone—'

'I understand.'

He leant in to kiss her, then decided against it. Avani was watching, she might consider it rape.

On the way out, he turned back. 'You've got my mobile number if you need me.'

Samir left the two with their mouths on fast forward. Leaping into his Mercedes, he put the air-conditioning on full blast and headed out of Milton Keynes towards the village of Bruckley. He wasn't looking forward to the stink of cow pooh, but he was looking forward to seeing Cloey.

But how could he look Cloey in the eyes knowing he had been unfaithful to her? The gnawing guilt of his betrayal gnashed its teeth.

Chapter Five

It's so simple to swap from twenty-first century-man to primitive, thought Samir, as he looked down at his hand-stitched shoes, coated now in silky brown cow dung. The romantic novelty of turning up at Cloey's cottage stinking of bovine motions had long since worn off, but this was the only route that avoided the nosy villagers. It was also the only route that avoided self-respect.

Tractor tracks lay in front of him and he followed the ploughed grooves hopping over any puddles in his way, listening out for the sound of barking dogs whereupon he would dive into the bushes, wishing he'd worn a crash turban. He'd remained unseen by the villagers for six years; the only clue they had that something eerie was going on back yonder in the farmer's field was the odd Patak's Pappadums packet they found from time to time. Samir's rations.

Cloey's cottage rooftop came into view and Samir

trudged onwards, the evening sun bowing low in the pale-blue sky. How had it come to this? he wondered. He had deceived his parents, he had deceived Kareena, and now he was deceiving Cloey. From being born with just the one face, he was at present a man with three. But, right now, as he jumped over the small stile, as he sweated like an onion, all three faces were smiling. And they should be. Samir had a plan.

Last night after having sex with Kareena for the second time, he'd lain awake as she snored gently, working out ways to wiggle free from a future of loveless boredom. He struggled with the complexity of the problem. Indian parents are creatures of habit, a two-thousand-year old habit; their children's wedding is their crack-cocaine fix and hypocritically they hate rocky marriages.

By morning, Samir had found the solution to ending the marriage: he would approach his father in two weeks' time and explain that even though on paper he and Kareena were a perfect match, in reality, they were as unmatched as curry and ice cream: both undeniably lovely on their own, but when mixed together – sickening. Samir would also tell his father that he was having a hard job ignoring the fact that Kareena used to be a teacher. Every time he had a question for her, he had to put his hand up and say 'Miss'. The plan was brilliant, and in the meantime he would keep Kareena a secret from Cloey.

He knocked on the back door to Lemonly Cottage, discarding his muddy shoes on a metal grill, whistling contentedly, waiting for Cloey to undo the five NightOwl security bolts and open the bulky door.

'Sammy,' Cloey cried, cuddling him tightly. 'I can

always tell when you're coming, there's a silence, like nature is holding its breath.' She kissed his lips, towing him behind her into the kitchen.

Samir stared. He was always knocked back by her overflowing beauty. He'd catch himself ogling her sometimes, amazed at how she could be so perfect and yet so kind. Her long straight brown hair always shone and her mischievous hazel eyes always danced. And her body would scare most women straight to the gym.

He pressed her up against the table, softly kissing her perfumed neck. 'That's it, never again. I've just wasted the last week with a bunch of jerks. Next time I go on a business trip I'll book a double room and you can come with me. Either that or I won't go at all.'

'Good!' She pulled away from him, her face becoming anxious and serious. 'I cried over you last night. Claudette was so mean, I hate living with her sometimes, I swear she's trying to destroy my love for you. She knew that I was missing you and she did her best to . . . to . . . oh, Sammy.' And she began to bawl. Through the spluttering, she managed to gasp out, 'She said I was only after you for your money. She said I don't really love you.'

Samir gave her a 'there there' hug. 'And she's the expert on love, is she? Her last boyfriend ate her angelfish.'

'We don't know that, Gabriel just went missing. He might turn up yet. Anyway, you're forgetting the important thing, Sammy, I cried over you.' She purposefully marched over to the door and opened it. 'If you think I'm after you for your money, Sammy, then you must go now. Rid yourself of this scrounger,

47

turn your head away from this bludger.' Her tears were like melted wax and her eyes like fiery candles. 'I love you, Sammy, and always will. I would even love you if you were reduced to poverty like your destitute relatives in India. Because love is priceless, Sammy.' She crossed herself and accepted Samir's hug.

The large kitchen looked like a cake laboratory. A warm cove for calorie-rich creations. Apart from the Ferrari-red Aga set into the outside wall, the room was a pleasant mix of delicate creams and oak-wood beams, with a weighty wooden table in the middle of the stone floor. It was the one room in the cottage which Claudette's parents had forbidden them to alter; and built into their rental agreement was a clause to that effect: 'Keep Cloey's art box on a leash in the kitchen (no wild colours please)'. But the clause said nothing about wild sex.

Cloey was in Samir's boxers already, her suspicious mind urging her to rip his clothes off and do what she normally did, check thoroughly for love bites. There were plenty of kitchen utensils ready if she found one. In which case, Sammy's errant member would end up resembling the bag of diced carrots currently sitting in the freezer.

'I feel like I want to explode, Cloey, I've been gagging for sex since I left you. Just gagging.' He admired how seductively she slipped onto the table, he'd never seen anything like that in *Ready Steady Cook*. He might have watched it more often if he had. At that moment a vision of Fern Britton bulldozed into his mind wearing nothing but a red tomato and a green pepper. 'You know what I'm like, seven days without sex is virtually castration for me, it's like—'

'Sammy! You're wrecking my mood, now bring me that rolling pin.' She pointed to his willy.

Hovering at the adulterer's border, he spared a quick thought for his wife, before he crossed over like the dishonest smuggler he was, leaving his guilt at border control. Cloey was his woman, lying *to* her was going to be hard, but it wouldn't stop him lying *on* her.

The two made love as only long-established lovers can, sharing each other, enjoying each moment. How trivial his wedding night seemed in comparison. Having sex with Kareena was enjoyable, but bare of feeling. It was a horrible thing to think about your own wife, but to Samir, Kareena could have been anyone and it wouldn't have felt any different. It was unsexy sex.

Samir gazed into Cloey's dark eyes as he brushed away a few long strands of sweaty hair stuck to her nose. It was amazing what the two of them had been through: the secrets and lies to their families; the fear of being found out; the shame of falling in love with someone you shouldn't.

Cloey watched Samir get dressed. She loved his body; her artistic eye could appreciate its perfect symmetry. The way his shoulders tapered down to his fat-free waist and the wonderfully balanced arms, not too big and not skinny. She watched him slip his muscular thighs into his jeans, enjoying his fumbles with the leather belt, almost giggling at how just missing the right hole in a belt could make someone so angry.

Still naked, she hopped off the table to give her man

a hand with his belt. But, as she did so, the dazzle of something metallic caught her eye, shining from his left hand, and she grabbed it like a magpie.

Her face was rigid. 'Please, no. Tell me, Sammy, this isn't what I think it is.'

Samir saw his brilliant plan flattened. How the hell could he expect to keep his wedding a secret when he had forgotten to take off his wedding ring?

He managed just one word, 'Erm . . .' before Cloey broke down in tears.

Avani slouched back on the rose-white leather sofa. 'So, did he like his ring?'

'Loved it,' replied Kareena, sipping her wine. 'Perfect fit.'

Without pause for punctuation, the two sisters had been at it since Samir left. At one point Avani was gabbling so fast, Kareena thought she was talking in Punjabi. It was only when she heard the words 'homegirl' and 'Haveyousmelthisnumbertwoyet?' that she realized it was English, Avani's Watford accent crossed with London English (with a touch of Ali G).

Avani had asked a million questions about the love-making and Kareena had done her best to answer them without compromizing the privacy of Samir's and her relationship. Older Indian sisters are obligated by an unsaid law to explain to their younger sisters what's hidden under an Indian man's *kacchas* – underpants – and what will befall her on her wedding night. Indian mothers will only go so far with the grisly details. And younger Indian sisters always want the gristle.

Avani stood up and walked over to the fireplace. 'Shall I tell you what I'm noticing?'

Kareena looked up. 'What?'

'This new husband of yours, how selfish he is. All these photos of him and his family but I can't seem to find even one of you.'

'Well, give him a chance. The wedding photos haven't come through yet.'

Avani shook her head. 'What about that roll we sent him of your engagement photos?' She sat back down. 'We're going to have to let him know that this might have been his house once – now it's yours. Lay down the rules, otherwise he's going to treat you just like a typical Indian woman, stuck cooking *dhal* in the kitchen while you're carrying his son and listening to his mother spouting off down the phone. And I know you, Kareena, cooking *dhal* all day would demoralize you beyond repair.'

Avani had a point, she always did. Samir might be all sweetness and light now, but his sweetness could dissolve like sugar in Darjeeling tea if Kareena risked arguing against his mother.

Kareena would have to try and fray that interfering Indian motherly bond somehow. To live away from the mother-in-law was a privilege that few Indian girls enjoyed, but it didn't stop them phoning every day. Even over a phone line an Indian mother-in-law could weave her ghastly hold. Sons had been known to ring their mothers during intercourse to keep them updated on the progress of their future grandsons. Before long it would be webcam intercourse with the mother-in-law directing, Kareena ruefully reflected. Bollybonking on the net.

Kareena admired the strength in her sister and was glad she spoke her mind, even if she was brutal at times. For an Indian woman to hold her head high in an Indian man's world takes courage. And Avani, luckily, had bags of it.

Kareena poured out more wine. 'I don't mind cooking for him. But I'll tell you now, when it's time for children in this house it will be when Samir and I decide, not some busybody old bat.'

Avani glowered. 'And me. Don't I get a say in the matter? Come on, we've always done everything together. Our periods even come on at the same time.'

Kareena ignored her, deciding it was time to play a joke. 'I've got a feeling that Samir wants to start a family soon. He's already made a start on the nursery. You should see the cute pictures.'

Thirty seconds later a blood-curdling scream echoed through the house. Avani had just witnessed a portion of Cloey's mural: a painting of a man's chest. His left pectoral was scarred, the flaps of the skin exposing maggots crawling out of the wound wearing ski masks. The title: *Your Pain Is My Gain*.

Cloey looked both frightened and hurt. Samir had never seen her this way before. As far as he could remember, this was the first time in his life he had hated a precious metal, that he has despised the warm glow of gold. Cloey stared at the ring on Samir's wedding finger, the circle of betrayal that said he was a married man.

'Take it off,' Cloey demanded, fiddling with her own fake wedding ring (worn to keep dribbling men at bay).

Samir had hurt people in his life before. And it hurt to hurt. His mum and dad hadn't spoken to him for a month when he had first explained his intentions to move to Milton Keynes and start his own security business, when they had wanted him to say in Hayes and start his own hospital. But hurting parents was one thing, hurting the woman you loved was another.

'I'm sorry, Cloey, but . . .'

Through the blur of tear-filled eyes she frantically began to put her clothes back on. 'But you did it for your parents.' She pulled her skimpy T-shirt over her head. 'Have you slept with her yet? Your wife.'

'No.'

'Liar! You liar!' Her words were stark and filled with envy. No doubt his new wife was beautiful, young, intelligent. And Indian.

'You haven't got to worry about a thing, Cloey.' Samir walked towards her, holding out his arms placatingly. 'Mum picked an ugly one, she's like a gargoyle.'

'And you just had to marry her, didn't you? You couldn't let your family down could you? Samir always pleasing everyone. Pleasing your security guards, pleasing your neighbours, even pleasing that stupid idiot who works in McDonald's who never gets your order right.' Cloey lifted his hands away from her waist and stood by the back door sniffing. 'But you couldn't please me, could you?'

For the first three years or so, Cloey had resigned herself to the fact that Samir would eventually have an arranged marriage and do the Indian thing, settling down with a woman chosen for him more or less by a random computer number cruncher. But as their relationship grew stronger and more settled, the feeling that Samir would give her up for another woman began to disappear. She genuinely thought he would stay hers for ever, she genuinely thought she had won him over. Genuine thoughts, however, are sometimes built on fragile foundations of wishful thinking. And now, Cloey's wishful thinking was crumbling before the mighty sword of truth: he'd been unfaithful to her.

'Cloey, I love you, you know that. She means nothing to me.' Samir strode over to her, cuddling her rigid body from behind. 'I was going to tell you. I had it all worked out. I was going to sit you down and explain how much you mean to me. I even wrote you a letter, but I thought only wimps write letters . . .' He trailed off, thinking: only wimps get married to mum's choice of bride.

Cloey silenced him with a cold glare. 'So, this was your business trip?'

He shrugged.

'If you love me, Sammy . . .' Cloey paused, deliberating. 'I want you to get rid of her and I want you to marry *me*. You don't just pop off on some pretend business trip and come back married. Not with me you don't. Now, you go back and you explain to that naive little wife of yours that it's over. You tell her that.' She pushed him gently out of the way. 'Just fucking sort it out!'

'Cloey,' he said feebly.

She turned round. 'Don't you "Cloey" me. Six years I've been with you, six years of lying to my family about you, and all for what? All for you to turn up with cow poop on your shoes and a kilo of gold hanging off your finger.'

Samir looked down at the ring. She was right, Kareena had gone a bit wild with the gold. It felt like he was carrying a twenty-four-carat gear knob in his hand. And talk about knobs! What a knob he was for leaving the ring on in the first place.

Even as he had walked up Cloey's back garden path earlier, he'd been telling himself to be clever about this situation. Not to get caught. Not to say or do anything stupid or suspicious. He'd even congratulated himself for finding a loose wisp of Kareena's hair on his T-shirt and smiled as the wind had taken it from his fingers.

He followed Cloey through the hall until, as though she'd been shot with a tranquilliser dart, she crumpled at the bottom of the stairs and began to wail, her breathing becoming more and more erratic as she gulped in air in stops and starts. Samir tried to soothe her, rubbing her back gently, but she glared up at him, her face creased with biting anger.

'You've hurt me so badly,' she shouted. 'Just like that, you have destroyed my life. I can never be happy again now, can I?'

'Look, I don't love her, I love you. I promise you on my life that I haven't even touched her. I couldn't. I just had to go through the ceremony to keep my family sweet. I know it's hard to understand, but I honestly thought it would be better if you didn't know about it until after I had separated from her.'

She sniffed. 'Which will be when?'

He grinned. 'Only two weeks time. And I can guarantee you that I won't kiss her, or touch her or even speak to her in all that time. I'll lock her in one of the spare rooms, then that way there's no chance in hell that I can shag her. I mean, even *I* can't knock down those NightOwl security doors. Nothing gets through. And—'

Cloey interrupted him, a picture forming in her mind's eye. 'You mean to tell me she's in our house?' She leapt to her feet. 'You mean to say that your wife is shacked up in the house that I worked my knuckles white trying to get in a liveable state?' She slapped him as hard as she could. 'I'm warning you right now, Samir,' she screamed right into his face, 'you get that woman out of our house and you make sure she doesn't touch *anything*. Now get out of my sight.'

'Cloey, you—'

'LEAVE!'

Samir found himself nervously running out of the house in his socks and up the forbidden front path. He'd never left this way before, but he'd never seen Cloey this way before either. He'd once had a dream where he was being spit-roasted over a fire by Madhur Jaffrey. It had been his worst nightmare until just now.

Cloey stood at the door, suddenly smiling, her arms folded contemptuously. She yelled after him, 'You make sure you do the right thing, Samir, I can have you replaced within a week. It's easy for me to pick up one of *you*, but think how difficult it is for you to pick up one of *me*. Now hurry along.'

He looked back. 'Say that again.'

She sneered and clicked her fingers together. 'Just like that. There's one billion of you lot, Samir, all dying for a slice of what I can offer. Think about it. Now go! This village is suffering with every second you stand by my lawn. Go. Go. GO!'

He froze in shock for a second before pulling open

the gate, then he turned and shouted, 'All you think about is this village. You could drop an atom bomb on this weird neighbourhood and no one would give a toss. Rejects, the lot of them.' And he kicked the gate shut with his foot, nearly knocking over Claudette, who was on her way in.

'What have you done now to upset Cloey?' she hissed.

Cloey ran up the path in her bare feet, yelling, 'Remember, Sammy, I'll have you replaced in a week.'

From across the once quiet road, Morris the shopkeeper and Glenys, his shop shelf filler and wife, watched the unfolding drama with curious eyes. Curtains twitched. Wide eyes stared.

Stared at the brown man.

Stared at the brown man leaving Lemonly Cottage.

Ignoring Claudette, Samir made towards his Mercedes which was parked a mile up the road. He blipped the car and his phone blipped back. It was a text:

> *Samir. Big pizza. On journey home*
> *you pick up, or else. Avani.*
> *Loving sister-in-law.*

He jumped in the car, revved up the engine and shot off. 'I hate women. I really hate them,' he said out loud as he steamed out of Bruckley.

His eyes caught the dashboard clock, 21.00, as the church bell tolled in the distance. Amazing, he thought, for a place so backward in time its church clock was dead on.

Chapter Six

Jordan felt the irritating vibration of the church bell right down to his nuts. Obviously making up for a lack of steeple size, it compensated with its extra large ring, hammering away at the hours, twenty-four hours a day. Between gongs you could ask yourself: how am I filling my life? How can I snap the bell rope without involving the police? What did I achieve in the last hour?

And in the last hour, as the lid of night came down, and the street lamps lit up, Jordan had achieved nothing. Just leant against his car, smoking a relay of fags, suspiciously watching a certain Father Luke unloading the contents of a shining new hearse. Jordan wondered what Father Luke could be keeping in the stack of wooden boxes now forming before the iron gate of the Holy Cross Church. Pygmy choir boys? He would wait until the last box was unloaded, then head on over to help.

He stubbed out his fag with his trainer, eyeballing Father Luke's dress sense. Maybe he would say a prayer for him tonight, asking God to help him get to grips with fashion. Purple corduroys and a checked yellow shirt as old as the Turin shroud, teamed with red wellingtons. He jogged the short distance to where the beacon of Father's Luke's partially bald head was reflecting the lamp light.

'Lukie Baby, wozzzz upp?'

Father Luke had been aware of the lone spectator watching him from afar and knew it was only a matter of time before he came over. People like Jordan, scum that they were, couldn't ever keep their noses out of other people's business. He was like the village flea jumping from one crime to the next. Since he was just a nipper, things in Bruckley had gone astray. And unlike most common thieves he didn't start small and work his way up, oh no, poor farmer Ridels never did get over his tractor going missing back in 1982. Very puzzling.

But the villagers had given Jordan the benefit of the doubt, feeling the pain that he and his family must have been going through when Jordan's mother died so tragically young. It would have been wrong to hold a witch hunt when the family was still in mourning. That was their mistake. They should have hounded that family right out of Bucks while they had a chance.

Father Luke closed the back of the hearse, leaving his hand on the handle. 'What is it you want, Jordan?'

'I want you to recommend me a good book. Any suggestions? I want something really way out, with loads of characters, with magic and punishment and traitors. I want heroes and—'

Father Luke turned, his fat red cheeks threaded with veins. 'I get the picture, Jordan. You refer to the Bible?'

'Uhm, I was thinking more *Lord of the Rings* actually.' He chuckled, his eyes steady and sure. 'I know why you've always hated me, Lukie Baby. It's because people like me stretch your faith, isn't it?' He noticed Father Luke's jaw tense. 'Every time you see someone like me, your belief in God is tested, and it scares you witless doesn't it? All those dreams of getting in that spaceship and heading off to the shining light are ruined, because of people like me.' He lifted the flap on one of the boxes, disappointed to find only flowers inside. 'Well, you're God's mouthpiece, let's hear what he has to say.'

Father Luke swung his domed head left, then right, as if he were about to whisper, but he spoke loudly. 'The foundation of my faith is hardly going to crumble because of a hooligan like you.' He smiled. 'And if you must know, it's not a spaceship we go up in, we enter heaven through a spinning wormhole with angels following behind with our belongings. Now if you please, I have flowers that need tending. Goodnight.'

Jordan laughed, then lifted the rusty gate latch for Father Luke, letting it swing open with a groan. 'Have he who is free from sin throw the first stone, Lukie Baby.' And he turned to leave.

'It's "*let* he who is free from sin" not "*have* he who is free from sin". And by the way, could you get a move on painting the fence? It should be a quick job. Just yesterday Mrs Portman was finding it very hard to mourn her late husband with you slurping Pot

Noodle only feet away from his grave. And your lack of clothes in the churchyard is causing quite a stir with the local young women. Cloey and Claudette are thinking of making a complaint to the council.'

Jordan lit up a fag. 'My my, Cloey and Claudette, the two bitches. Now that's a farce from the past,' he remarked sarcastically, edging closer to Lukie Baby. 'Let me see if I remember this right. It all makes for a cosy little story, doesn't it? You, me and Cloey. I bet it all looked quite magical from your end didn't it? The blue neon lights flashing across the headstones, the sound of the helicopters chopping in the air and the barking of the police dogs ready to rip my flesh. I bet you just howled with laughter when they cuffed me, you fucking grass. And poor little Cloey cried then, didn't she? All tucked up under your arm, panicking about what her mother would say.' Jordan's eyes glinted. 'I loved that girl and I did time for her. And you know the truth; you saw just as well as God did what happened that night.' He dragged deep on his fag. 'So, don't you dare mention Cloey in front of me again. I don't need reminding of her.'

As he sped out of sight in the darkness towards the lights of his hometown, Milton Keynes, Jordan asked himself why the dust from his past could never be totally wiped away. Zara and he had a good life together. Why couldn't he just forget about Cloey?

Claudette comforted her tearful friend. Samir had been gone two hours. 'Sometimes I think this place needs a good dose of bubonic plague,' she said, trying to raise a smile. 'They still live in the dark ages when it comes to right and wrong. Samir's right. I think this nosy village needs a nuclear holocaust or a plague of locusts, anything to take their mind away from other people's business.' She paused. 'Oh, God, I forgot to tell you . . . Mrs Birkins didn't pay her TV licence. They caught her red-handed and you'll never guess . . .'

Cloey sniffed into a soggy tissue and blinked at Claudette, whose T-shirt read, 'Woman in a Bad Mood'. 'Forget the bloody village, I've lost him.'

'But you'll shag and make up.' Claudette sat Cloey down on the sofa in the living room. 'He loves you. God knows why, but he does. Some men just like drab, I suppose.'

Among the teasing flickers of candle light and the gentle chimes of Mike Oldfield's *Tubular Bells*, Cloey viewed her best friend's silhouette. Claudette had the sort of face which deserved a good kicking: sneering and scoffing at every woman in eyeshot, forever scrutinizing and slating. Yet, with her shabby dyed-blonde hair and her twelve-togs-of-make-up face, she regarded herself as Miss World. It was a crying shame.

'I'm hurting, Claudette, I don't think you realize the gravity of the situation. He could be making love to her right now, so lay off!' She pinched Claudette's bare arm. 'Now listen to me. He's married. He had an *arranged* marriage. Wimp gave in to his parents and wasn't man enough to hold onto what he loved.' She dabbed the corner of her eyes. 'I can't believe he couldn't stand up to them for me.'

Claudette sneered. 'Wimp!'

'He doesn't even love the tramp.'

'Well, get him back then, arrange the split.'

Cloey looked up and smiled. The same smile that once haunted the teachers at Hartwell School.

Claudette remembered many a time when it had been the two of them against the teachers, with Jordan in the middle of the naughty sandwich.

The headmistress, Mrs Wilders, was also their RE teacher, a grey, forbidding woman who discouraged any fun and games in the classrooms. Until the day that Cloey decided to teach Mrs Wilders a thing or two. Or more like a sin or two.

'Wild Animal,' she began. 'Oh Lord and mercy on the soul etcetera, but, if the Virgin Mary had Jesus without even having sex, would she have had twins if she took the pill?'

Mrs Wilders crossed herself. 'There was a time, Cloey, when I thought that these innocent questions of yours were simply born of ignorance. But now, I know that they are intended to shock and insult. I will be speaking to your mother, again. You should know better with the devout example she sets.'

Jordan had stood up, his mouth full of gum. 'When you speak to Cloey's mother, Wild Animal, ask her where she keeps that pirate copy of the *Exorcist*. I've looked everywhere.'

'Out, the pair of you.'

And *out* was exactly where Cloey and Jordan had wanted to be, away from the dreary lessons. Out kissing, while everyone else studied. Jordan said he got his biggest erection knowing Wild Animal was just behind the door.

Cloey and Claudette, Jordan and Ryan were the outcasts of Hartwell School. Hailed as one of the strictest schools in Buckinghamshire, it didn't seem the right place for possibly the four most abusive children that the staff had ever seen. Although they were all naturally bright, their teachers predicted a rather dull future for all of them:

Cloey –	McDonald's
Claudette –	McDonald's
Ryan –	suicide
Jordan –	McDonald's (supervisor)

Three years after leaving school they all returned to boast to Wild Animal of what they had achieved with their lives. Their lies were phenomenal. Wild Animal nearly had kittens.

Cloey –	owner of three art galleries
Claudette –	owner of three beauty salons.
Ryan –	owner of three Formula One cars
Jordan –	owner of three criminal records. (With another one on the way for murdering headmistresses, he shouted, as he chased Wild Animal into the staff room.)

In those days, Jordan and Cloey were glued at the hip. Bound by love's twine. No one would have been able to predict what the future really held in store. Not even God.

Claudette crunched up the Diamond White cider can and snapped open another. She liked the feeling of being the commander for a change, having to come up with answers that could win the war. And it was always a war. The war against men.

She spoke, 'Every second you waste, Sammy spends another second in his wife's knickers. Think about it,

Cloey. Every minute he spends with her is a minute spent not thinking about you. In the end, he'll get used to not having you in his thoughts.' She gulped her cider. 'You've got to look at it like this.' She belched. 'It's easier for him to stay with her than it is to leave. Simple as that. You've got to ask yourself, are you going to miss his wallet that much? Look, I'll chip in with the bills if that's the real problem . . .'

Cloey stood up and walked over to the window, peeping through the gap in the centre of the curtains. The road outside was empty and silent. Bruckley was like a millpond, flat, boring, the only excitement was the odd bubble from the odd fart that floated to the top. But stagnant was how the Brucklians liked it.

She returned to her seat. 'The money was handy, but it was the house I really wanted. Of course I love him, who wouldn't? The house has got three bathrooms for God's sake.'

'But he's not Jordan, is he?'

Cloey closed her eyes, enjoying the fizzy taste of cider on her tongue. 'No, he's not Jordan. There's only one of him.' She thought to when Dimbo Bimbo Blonde Cherry had come back from the churchyard with Jordan's message the other day. 'I used to love her, but it's dead and buried now. She was crap in bed anyway.' She had slapped Cherry for the news and explained that she and Claudette would no longer be requiring Cherry's friendship any more. But the news had hurt. And judging by Cherry's mascara-clogged tears, so had the slap.

Cloey suddenly sat up. 'Jordan's a loser, and Samir is not. This is a simple thing we're talking about here, Claudette. It's called looking to your future. Samir has one, Jordan hasn't. Simple.'

Claudette loved to hear fighting talk. She rummaged around in her snake-skin handbag searching for the perfect girl's ammunition. A mirror. 'See, look at you. You're so pretty.' She held the mirror up to Cloey's puffed-up eyes, let her have the briefest of glances and then stared into it herself. 'And so am I. All the men in Buckinghamshire should watch out with us two jaw-droppers walking about.'

Grabbing the mirror, Cloey gazed at her own reflection. 'I will never be the love widow, I'm going to get him back. He loves me not her. The house is mine, I've invested in that house.' She adjusted her pose, smiled at the result and repeated, 'I, Cloey, will never be the love widow.' And she cackled, misting her reflection with condensation.

So, without a witches' cauldron and without eye of toad and tail of newt, the two devious women prepared a plan so cunning, so utterly perfect, it could almost be compared to a spell. The spell of the Bruckley coven. Samir and Kareena would be in the divorce courts before the werewolves could howl at the next full moon, leaving Cloey and Samir where they had left off – in paradise.

Cloey allowed one evil thought to creep into her pure mind. She would also make Jordan suffer for not loving her any more. How dare he? How fucking dare he? He should be pining for her eternally. Promises were not meant to be broken: he had promised he would love her until the day he died and he was going to keep that promise whether he liked it or not.

She smiled a drunk smile at the crucifix over the fireplace. 'I dare you to stop me.'

Chapter Seven

Bernie, Jordan's father and also Bruckley's milkman, nodded his head woefully at Cloey's and Claudette's place, debating whether or not he wanted business from a residence which harboured foreigners. Bruckley village had survived the plague. It had laughed in the face of World War One and World War Two. Bernie picked up a bottle of semi-skimmed. Surely it wasn't going to fall to pieces because a dark man was staying with the girls in that cottage? Surely the villagers last night in the pub were overreacting when they said the invasion had started? How it only takes a speck of black to turn a tin of white paint grey. House prices would fall and the bridle paths would be turned into flea markets for spices and fruit. Crop rotation would suffer with the overuse of the fallow fields for coriander. Harvesting would become a thing of the past and farmers would all wear turbans or *keffiyehs*. The population of Bruckley would increase twofold, threefold, a hundred thousand foreigners in a thousand houses. Drugs! The church would be burnt to the ground, the shops turned into shrines. Buddhism, Hinduism, Sikhism, Unemployedism. The spirit of Bruckley would become lost to the peoples of other lands. Overreacting?

Just then he spotted Cloey's mother.

She banged hard on her daughter's cottage door. Bernie watched still holding the pint, dithering. He was quite partial to watching other people argue, especially relatives. It was like a cold flannel applied to the headache produced by his own criminal son, Jordan. It was comforting to know that other families had, to quote his own father, 'Fucked up' with their kids as well. He sat back in the milk float, lit a cigar, and eyed the goings-on from afar. This could become very interesting, worth a few pints down the King George later; it was his noble duty to keep the villagers informed.

Claudette removed her satin eyeshades, presuming she must have had the bed to herself last night. She would never let a man see her in eyeshades. The clock showed 6.30 a.m. and the sun was up, along with the rude person knocking discourteously on the front door. Claudette had once had a fantasy about an early morning police raid. They burst into her bedroom with an assortment of whips, chains and shackles, and, of course, she was naked. The policemen happened all to be six foot tall, blue-eyed, half dressed, with big, big, big muscles and even bigger truncheons – obviously she was being arrested for being too damn pretty.

The knocking persisted and she glanced at the reflection of the pre-make-up Claudette in the mirror.

Suddenly she knew why men never called her again. Chewed up and spat out blonde hair, sleep the size and colour of Brussels sprouts in her eyes, and a false eyelash stuck to her top lip. She breathed into her hand and sniffed. Sure enough, she not only looked like a dog, but she smelt like one too. Maybe she'd supply the men with her eyeshades in future so they didn't have to look at her the next morning.

Claudette peered out of the bedroom window, to see who was banging, careful not to show her face, then skidded over to Cloey's room.

'Darth Vader's here.'

Cloey's eyelids must have been attached to mouse-trap springs, they snapped open so quickly. Her mother was here. It was no laughing matter, which was why no one was laughing. Cloey and Claudette, with a speed normally reserved for last orders, had a few minutes to complete a mission: to turn the cottage religious. It was like their home was on death row, with the girls playing priest, trying to convert it before the Grim Reaper appeared.

The cupboard under the stairs held all the secrets, a box of religious goodies that would help keep Aileen happy. The knocking continued, lively and energetic now, it sounded like someone was livid. Cloey stared nervously at Claudette as she hung up crucifix number six. They both had an inkling as to why Aileen was here, and it didn't look good.

Claudette picked out the last item from the sacred box: a framed picture of the Virgin Mary, and polished it with the end of her baggy T-shirt. Holding it up to the light, she nodded with approval, placing it above the fireplace.

'Good luck, I'll pray for you upstairs.'

Cloey waited for Claudette to reach the top step before opening the front door.

'Is it Dad? Has something happened? Is it his heart?' She creased her forehead. 'Is it worse than that? Is he d-d-d-d dead?'

Aileen's eyes gave little away, but her Laura Ashley dress said it all. She was a stickler for the prim and proper, taking great pains with her appearance. Cleanliness was next to godliness, which meant the Daz challenge was a religious calling. She looked ten years younger than her fifty-eight years, on a diet of manicures, pedicures, rollers, chin wax, facials and liquified carrots. She was the beta carotene queen, it gave her a healthy orange glow and perfect night vision. How she found time for God, God only knew. But she did.

'Of course he's not dead, I'm not finished with him yet.' Aileen's eyes settled disapprovingly on her daughter's bare legs, then slipped past looking over Cloey's shoulders and up the stairs. 'Where is he? Everybody's talking about him.' She stared at her daughter. 'I thought you and I were getting somewhere, but obviously you don't take the church seriously.' Her nostrils expanded, sniffing the air. 'Alcohol. Cigarettes. What is this? A whore house?' She shoved Cloey to one side and climbed the stairs two at a time.

Outside Claudette's room, Aileen paused before she knocked. 'What on earth are you doing in there?' she asked.

Claudette spoke, 'I'm—'

'You are a disgusting young woman,' Aileen spat,

referring to the humming noise within.

'I'm shaving my legs, Aileen.' Claudette clenched her teeth and whispered under her breath, 'You stigmatic dragon.'

There was a pause. 'Good.' Aileen crossed herself for having the wrong vision. 'Good, Claudette.'

Cloey stood watching her mum from behind. 'You won't find him here. It's not what you think it is—'

The words were ignored as Aileen pushed open Cloey's bedroom door, her probing eyes collecting evidence from all corners. She stared at the wall over Cloey's unmade bed, expecting to see Jesus hanging there; instead, a black and white print of a topless black man holding a white baby met her horrified gaze. Cloey had forgotten to remove this in her panic.

Cloey said, 'How about a cuppa?'

Aileen continued scrutinizing the picture, fixated, almost in denial. The villagers were right. Her own daughter, her own flesh and blood, had a . . . a . . . *thing* for dark men. She crossed herself again, then turned to face Cloey. 'I want you round at my house in twenty minutes.'

'But—'

But there were no buts with Aileen.

But there was with Bernie. He had a massive butt and Cloey felt like giving it a good running kick as he bent in front of his milk float whistling cheerfully fifty yards up the road. How a bum that big could be related to Jordan's, she would never know. How a bum that big *got* that big she would never know. But she strolled past, wondering how she could avoid having to speak to Bernie while also trying hard to

71

think up an excuse as to why Samir had been seen by half the village arguing with her on her front lawn yesterday. Any reason to stop her mother going into ethnic overload.

Bernie continued whistling, or was it wheezing? Cloey looked round, he seemed to be struggling to breathe and she felt that awful fear that paramedics must have when faced with the prospect of giving mouth-to-mouth to a lardarse. Then she felt guilty and walked over, touching him lightly on the shoulder.

'Are you okay?' she asked. 'Bernie?'

Bernie's gasps were not encouraging, but he managed to struggle out a few broken syllables. 'Wer . . . tch.' He rummaged round in his pocket, producing a blue asthma puffer. Giving it a shake and inhaling – puff . . . puff . . . puff – he tried again. 'You little witch!' He stood breathing in, flooding his oversized lungs with Salbutamol, freeing up his tightened lifeline, paying back the oxygen deficit. 'Jordan did time because of you. Too nice to snitch you up, wasn't he? I always knew this village had one bad egg and everyone says it's my lad. But we knows the truth now, doesn't we? Maybe this village has had about enough of you. Maybe you'll finally get what's coming to you.'

Cloey ignored him as she normally did and walked on by, wondering why he always had to be quite so nasty. For eight years he had greeted her the same way, going over old ground, never willing to forgive and forget. It was amazing that he hadn't told the village the truth by now, although somehow Cloey knew he never would. Bernie and Jordan might not have arses in common, but they did have principles, and snitching and squealing didn't feature on their agenda. Strolling onwards, she could feel Bernie still watching her and she turned, making her way quickly back to him.

She spoke hesitantly, embarrassed to be showing such an interest. 'So, is Jordan married? Has he got kids?'

Bernie slammed the orange bread crate on the metal floor of the float. 'Ask him yourself, I'm sure he's got all the time in the world for a back-stabber like you.' He plucked out a wholemeal loaf, and his pupils curled tight like two woodlice. 'I hates to be bitchy, that's your job, but my son is getting on with his life good and proper. He's forgotten all about you. His woman makes you look like a . . . dog's dinner. Lovely she is, plain and simply lovely. Given up three years of his life already, he has for you. It should have been you in prison, it should have been you, it . . .'

Cloey charged ahead, feeling a jealous green tinge colouring her blood. She'd got quite used to the idea that Jordan probably lived alone in some derelict squat dreaming of what could have been. Even when she was making love to Samir, just before she fell asleep, a smile crossed her lips, knowing that Jordan was most likely crying over her somewhere. It felt secure to know that at any second she could blow a whistle and, like a dog, he would come running. Unfortunately, two graveyard visits, two snubs and a visit from Dimbo Bimbo Blonde Cherry later, the truth was slowly eroding her belief. Jordan, it seemed, had the nerve to live quite happily without her. Maybe he needed reminding of what he was missing. A Cloey top-up. She surged up the road smiling at the thought.

Her parents' house was the last in the village. It was like a bookend to a shelf of pulp novels. Each one told a different story, and some were scarier than others.

Cloey unlatched the metal gate and approached the four-bedroomed mint-coloured house with a shudder, as memories of her most weird of upbringings returned to haunt her. It was a tangled ball of religious string, knotted up with Christ Almighty, Mum's love and Dad's indifference. Jesus Christ was the light, Mum was blinded by the light and Dad, he was just blind to everything.

Her father, Maxwell, occasionally visited the house, preferring to spend as much time as possible away from his wife on his many golfing holidays and business trips. Cloey suspected he had another woman, and hoped for Dad's sake she wasn't like Mum. Cloey didn't know if she loved her father, she hardly knew him, but she guessed she did.

The door opened and Aileen snatched Cloey's hand, leading her to the study. The scent of freshly polished wood hung in the air, shoulder to shoulder with the musty odour of ancient religious books. It was in this very room, Cloey had decided that God most likely didn't exist. It was in this room her virginity had fallen in the heat of battle. Jordan was excellent, the best warrior, the best secret. Mum didn't even have an inkling that Jordan had played a significant part in Cloey's life, she certainly didn't know that he had put his rather enormous part in her. And it was in this room her mother would make Cloey tell the truth.

'Take the book!' Aileen ordered.

Cloey held the Bible and closed her eyes. The

leather-bound volume had been Cloey's alibi on many occasions. As far as Cloey's mother was concerned, no one in their right mind would lie while holding the Bible – especially her own daughter.

'Say it, Cloey!'

Cloey gave a long sigh and in a bored, toneless voice began to speak, 'I swear to you on the Bible, Mum, that I am still a virgin.' She opened her eyes and faced her mum. 'Satisfied now?'

Apparently she was. Aileen's smile was thin, revealing tiny teeth. 'They are all talking about him. Who was he? You know the—'

'The Indian?' Cloey interrupted.

The thin smile disappeared. 'The asylum seeker.'

Cloey began in a matter of fact tone. 'Look, I design greeting cards for him. He told me that I lacked talent, so I ordered him to leave the house. Then your little gossip mongers just blew it out of all proportion. Like you are right now.' She paused running her fingers through her long shiny hair. 'Mum, asylum seekers? Where do you come up with your ideas?'

Cloey sat on the edge of the desk. The old-fashioned inkwell was full and she tried not to mess up Dad's writing area. 'Look, I promised you I wouldn't have sex outside marriage,' she said, straightening up a few loose A4 sheets. 'You have to believe me when I tell you that I can't wait to settle down with a good wholesome man. It's just so unfair that I can't find one. But I know God will bring him to me, and Mum.' Cloey stared at her mother who nodded. 'I am a patient woman. Not like all those, excuse my language . . . slags in Milton Keynes who have kids before they can ride a bike.'

Aileen kissed her daughter's cheek and lifted her face to see the innocence in her eyes. It felt awkward to cuddle Cloey, to show physically the warmth she felt for her daughter. But she cuddled her now, grabbing hold of her only child in a firm embrace of love, aware that her powers of protection over Cloey were dwindling away fast.

'What about the Negro on your wall?'

'Erm.' Cloey thought back to when she'd bought the photo after being inspired at Notting Hill Carnival, where she was doing her shake-my-tussy-and-rattle-my-pussy dance in time with the throbbing 2000 watt Afro beat. 'I was sure I saw Mother Teresa with just the same photo in *OK* magazine a few years back. I think the Negro in question who you're referring to is in actual fact a young Nelson Mandela. I think the baby in his arms is William Hague.' She paused. 'Look, Mum, I would never lie to you while holding the Bible.' She jumped off the desk. 'Would I?'

Aileen hugged her daughter closer. 'I was so worried. I thought we had lost you to a jungle bunny.'

Cloey returned the embrace thinking to herself: Mother, I think I've lost *you* to the Lord.

76

Chapter Eight

Kareena had never seen her parents touch. Not even the subtlest of brushes. An invisible barrier held their bodies apart like opposing magnets. And yet, they couldn't have been opposites, even when her grandparents had arranged their marriage back in the dark ages, great effort would have been made to discover if they were compatible. So they must have had things in common.

She had imagined when they went to sleep at night a great barrier of pillows lay down the centre of the bed in case they accidentally touched each other. Only when sex was due would the makeshift barrier come down.

But you don't need barriers when you're sleeping on the floor. Kareena looked up at Samir's sleeping feet protruding over the side of the bed while she lay awake on the Oriental rug which covered much of the wooden floor. Most of the night she had fidgeted in the near blackness wondering why everything seems exaggerated in the dark, why seconds seem like hours, why creaks in the house were burglars, why a slight headache was a brain tumour. And what was that faint smell wafting through the room as the gentle breeze lifted the curtains, she pondered, the scent of a woman's perfume?

Morning broke at last with the sun surfing through the open balcony doors. It was great to watch the world wake up. Even better, Kareena thought, if her new husband would.

Finally, Samir awoke with a greedy yawn, and for one second he was still a bachelor. Free to do what he wanted, the full day his playground. Then, like a serpent rising from the sea, Kareena's head rose above the ripples of the duvet. The bachelor party was over, it was the beginning of his fourth day of marriage, it was time to be the lying bastard husband once more and the grovelling boyfriend to Cloey.

Samir eyed Kareena's unique morning look; unique in the fact she still looked beautiful. He'd seen what women were capable of looking like first thing in the morning, and it wasn't a pretty sight. His very own mother showed Yeti tendencies before *paratha* breakfast, plucking out chin hairs ten to the dozen.

He spoke through another yawn, wondering why she had slept on the floor. 'You were talking in your sleep last night.'

Kareena shuffled in beside him in the bed. 'What did I say?'

'It was really weird, you said, "This crappy bed, this crappy, crappy, crappy bed".'

She grimaced. 'I wasn't talking in my sleep. I didn't

get to sleep. How you can sleep on this, I don't know. Maybe we could use a mattress from the spare room?'

Samir reflected that if he was going to get rid of his wife in two weeks, then the least he could do in the meantime was to see to her needs. And if her needs included a new mattress, then a new mattress she would get.

He kissed her on the lips. 'I won't take no for an answer, Kareena, no wife of mine is sleeping on the spare-room mattress. We shall order a brand-new one today. No expense will be spared.'

Eddie, the owner of Edward's Specialist Bed Warehouse, had known doting couples to become quite self-absorbed in their hunt for *the* perfect bed. Sometimes he witnessed movements beneath the shop duvet that made his mind boggle, and the amount of times he'd heard parents scolding their kids when asking for a bonk-bed and not a bunk-bed, he'd lost count. His wife Doris thought him a prude because he wouldn't grant her request to make love after hours on the bed of the month:

'Doris, I don't take my work home with me and I don't take my home into work. We have a perfectly good pocket-sprung bed at home. As you well know.'

Today Eddie and Doris were in the middle of an argument of epic proportions.

'Listen, muggins,' Eddie began, clipboard in one hand, invoice in the other, 'if I put a picture of you up, I'll scare away the customers.' The door chimed and Eddie's eyes greeted the entrants. 'Doris,' he hissed, 'two Bangladeshis. Big smiles now, big smiles, I smell money, leave all the talking to me.' He walked off to greet them, his wife staring scornfully at Eddie's bedside manner. He reserved all his romantic gestures for his customers rather than for her – the bald git.

Samir shook Eddie's sweaty hand. 'My wife and I are interested in purchasing a king-size mattress.' His eyes travelled the length and breadth of the shop. It took all of one second. 'Have you any in stock?'

'Depends which one you choose, sir. Normally we're looking at six to eight weeks for delivery.' Eddie turned to the six beds in the warehouse. 'I mean, take the Mayfair mattress, tweaked to perfection. Each spring is part of a team.' He smiled at them both. 'A team to make your nights as comfortable as Cupid's love cradle. The night will float . . .' He rabbited on and on and on.

Samir tried all the tricks known to man to rid themselves of the salesman and was down to the last one. 'I find that with such a pressurized job working for the Inland Revenue and all the trappings that go with being a tax inspector, I really need a good night's sleep to keep me on my toes to catch all the fiddlers . . .' Eddie was gone.

Kareena giggled, plopping herself on a bed, bouncing up and down on the plastic covering. 'Seems really comfy.' She stood, lifting up the price tag. 'God! It should be at this price.' She held the tag under Samir's eyes.

'Fuck!' His gaze located Eddie. 'Two and a half grand, for a mattress? I hope we get a free pillow with it. That's mad money.'

And staring from the wall was the mad man who had priced it. Samir stepped over to inspect the framed photograph further; Edward with a sleazy grin, four strands of hair slicked back from his high forehead trying to look twenty years younger by sucking in his cheeks. Underneath the frame was inscribed: 'Employee of the Month'. What was this place?

He looked at Kareena, now bouncing on the cheapest mattress, her turquoise *shalwar kameez* flowing gently about her. She was so pretty with that gorgeous smile. He felt really guilty at what he was planning to do to her. Then he remembered Cloey, and reminded himself that he couldn't afford to feel sympathy for his new bride. Besides, Cloey was more than happy with the bed at home. She was the one who'd chosen it after all.

After bouncing their way round the shop, they stood by Eddie's desk debating from the vast selection of six.

Samir spoke, 'Choose whichever one you want; it doesn't matter about the dosh. You only get one back in life and you have to take care of it.' He stooped, crooking his spine. 'Or else we'll end up walking like this.' A few minutes later he was writing out a cheque.

The door bell chimed, and Eddie flew past them like a cruise missile, homing in on his new target: a middle-aged couple. After exchanging a few words with his latest victims, the cruise missile did a U-turn and returned to Doris, rubbing his hands. 'Marriage break up. Separate rooms. Doris, what does that mean? I'll tell you what it means: separate beds.' And the cruise missile returned to the sad-looking couple handing them both a single-bed brochure.

Samir watched with interest. What a come down. One minute they're both gazing into each other's eyes signing the wedding register; next, they're staring at a single-bed brochure. One minute they're planning luxury holidays together, next they're fighting over who owns the hamster. He remembered Cloey saying to him that, if they ever decided to split up, she wanted only one thing from him and one thing only. For him to look her in the eyes and tell her he didn't love her.

When Samir had returned from Cloey's yesterday evening, carrying three large boxes of pizza, he had spent nearly an hour explaining to both Kareena and Avani why he was not wearing shoes. They couldn't believe what a nice person he was. Only someone as nice as Samir would have lent his own three-hundred-pound hand-stitched shoes to a security guard who had forgotten to bring his boots into work. It had dawned on him then, as it was dawning on him now, that his life was becoming too complicated. Too complicated because of two women, because he wasn't man enough to be a man; wasn't man enough to face his traditionally minded parents, sit them down, and watch the disappointment on their faces as he told them he loved an English woman and wished to marry her; wasn't man enough to explain to them that just because he loved someone of a different culture didn't mean they had brought him up badly, didn't mean he didn't love them and it didn't mean he was letting go of his Indian heritage.

But the disappointment on their faces would still remain. Faces that had seen both the Indian sun and the English sun. His dear parents, who had come to England against the odds, with no guarantees, just hope for the future, and as many of their Indian belongings as could be stuffed in two suitcases, but with the whole of India's spirit inside each of their hearts.

Samir had seen his parents struggle. Even as a kid he'd seen the bruises Britain sometimes inflicted on them. He never wanted to hurt them by selling out. He recalled his dad sitting him on his knee once as they watched England get trounced by India at cricket on TV. Each time India scored a six, his dad would bounce young Samir up and down on his knee. Each time England scored a boundary, Samir clapped. Until his father became ruffled by his son's behaviour.

'You're an Indian. Look at yourself in the mirror. Now clap for India.'

'But we live in London,' Samir had protested.

'Shut up and clap for India. And boo for England.' Case closed.

An identity crisis. Forever trying to be both Indian and English. He became sick of his parents preaching to him about how brilliant the motherland was. He became sick of his English mates trying to lead him astray. And he was sick of every Tom, Dick and Harrieta asking him the correct way to cook *jashasha hunza baltit* with Uncle Ben's rice. Sick of it all, until he met Cloey.

Ironically, it was Cloey more than anyone else who had taught him to be proud of his Indian roots, who had taught him to take the best of both worlds and think himself lucky his parents had risked coming to England in the 1960s. They had opened the gates to a better way of living, she explained, rather than being penned into a life inside a backward rural village. A village with a well for its water, a dusty trail for its road, a barn for its school and where your death certificate is written in the strength of your bones. A much harder life.

To put it bluntly, she said, he owed them.

To put it bluntly, he did.

Kareena smiled to herself as they drove away from the warehouse. She had just made her first marital decision, and she couldn't wait to sleep on it. In six weeks time when the new mattress arrived, she was sure she would know Samir a whole lot better.

By the grace of the gurus, she might also be in love with him by then, too.

She crossed her fingers and psyched herself up for six weeks of sleeping on a lumpy mattress.

It takes great discipline to walk past Greedy's without walking in, and even greater discipline to walk out of Greedy's without a well-stuffed belly. Jordan sat inside the swanky coffee and cake shop, in MK, reading the *Sun*, enjoying the comfort of the spongy armchair, ignoring Vivaldi's racket from the speakers, oblivious to the ringing of the busy tills. The place was nearly always bustling and had already made its first million from the gold crowns that fell out of people's teeth when their jaw hit the table at the prices they charged.

A brass engraved plaque stood on the counter, 'We Measure by your Pleasure' next to another sign: 'Gratuities', with a credit-card machine attached to it by a chain.

Jordan folded his paper, and stared through the

tinted windows to the picnic green opposite, its short grass was scattered with bodies burning in the stinging sun. His eye was keenly focused on a substantial red-raw body on the verge of self-combusting. He imagined she could explode with quite a force and checked the strength of the glass. He smiled. Safe as houses.

Then his smile deepened. A woman who fit the description of a Blonde Babe had stolen his attention and, judging by the raising of heads on the green as she walked past, she'd stolen everyone else's as well. Wearing clothes that would be considered too risqué in a nudist camp, she wiggled her size 8 hips, working the walk, driving her heels down the central path.

Some women, Jordan had noticed in passing, couldn't balance properly on high heels, wobbling out of control, walking like Tina Turner. But this babe, in her glittering pink six-inch stiletto mules, had style.

The Blonde Babe entered Greedy's, slipped her designer shades on top of her head and stared at a view she saw often: men with their mouths open, like a scene from *The Body Snatchers*. She walked across the wooden floor, easing herself between the tables, her heels tapping in time to the sway of her long hair. Finally, she arrived at Jordan's table, shaking her head disapprovingly, and from her pink Gucci bag, she pulled out a small box and tossed it at his chest.

Jordan picked the condoms from his lap and placed them on the table next to his fags. 'Not here, Zara.'

She sat opposite him, dodging his kiss. 'Condoms are what we will be using from now on, Jordy. You don't seem to touch me otherwise.' She uncrossed one tanned leg and crossed it over the other. 'I tested you this morning and you failed. I asked you for a quickie and you gave me one – the quickest escape I've ever seen.' Her huff lingered.

'I didn't know you wanted sex, I thought you said bacon and eggs.'

'And I didn't get those either. I want a baby, Jordy, and you're not providing. Every time I come off the pill you hardly touch me.' She fanned herself with the menu. 'I've spoken to a few people and we've concluded that you have a mental problem. And mental people, Jordy, need coaxing.'

Jordan came in close, like a rugby scrum team talk. 'We had sex the other day. There! Two days in a row. I've got a mate who only gives his wife one on their anniversary and spends the rest of the year dreading the next one.'

'Yes, Jordy, we did have sex – only just, though – all of five minutes worth.' Zara watched him scowl.

She checked the menu and ordered their food from the waitress. Not only did Zara want a baby, but she was getting sick of people telling her how she was slim only because she hadn't had one yet. 'Oh, you wait until you've had a few brats, you'll be a right fat cow afterwards. You'll see,' said a woman whose stretch marks could be seen from the moon, and with an arse the same size as the moon, too. Zara had been stocking up on vitamin E cream ever since.

Jordan had been good in some ways though, decorating the nursery, trying to give up smoking, he'd even made a cute baby mobile out of two police truncheons and a set of dangling handcuffs. But with all that, her question remained, did he really want to have a baby with her?

The salmon, lemon and cream cheese bagel arrived. Still warm, always mouth-watering. She daintily divided the bagel in four, then continued with her lecture.

'I'll tell you what I propose to do, Jordy, and don't interrupt.' She picked up the condoms. 'See these? You're fine with them. No problem, we have sex every day when you wear one.' She paused. 'And I need a baby. So, what I'm going to do, and remember I've got the full backing of my friends on this, I'm going to puncture one of them, and not tell you when. Okay? That should sort out your mental problem.' Then she whispered, 'Partially at least.'

Jordan had a thought, while he tucked into his tomato (or as Greedy's called it, the Quafier Salad) and watched the woman he knew he could make happy. He realized his time to tell the truth was nearly spent. It was now or never.

He decided it would be now. 'Zara, how would you feel if I told you that since we'd been together I've been telling you a big whopping lie? The biggest fucking lie you've ever known?' He saw her face change. 'Only joking. How's your bagel?' At least he'd tried, he thought.

'The bagel's fine, and if your *whopping lie*, the same lie you throw at me every time, is that the snow reduces your sperm count, then I never believed it anyway. Thank you.' She bit into her bagel, cream cheese spilling out. 'If that was the case I would have banned you from snowboarding years ago, Jordy.'

On the green, two jovial young lads were floating a frisbee over the head of a sunbather, each subsequent throw dropping closer and closer to the sleeping man's nose. Jordan watched enthusiastically as the lads upped the ante on the game by unleashing their dog. He barely noticed Zara leaving for the Ladies', so preoccupied was he in mulling over his guilty conscience.

Why was it so difficult to come clean sometimes? Cloey was the dark stain that showed up on the X-ray. An incurable disease that hacked away at his insides. How could he fully commit to Zara when a big part of him still loved Cloey? Zara didn't even know Cloey existed, and she certainly didn't know that he had once loved a woman so much, he had gone to prison for her. She thought he'd done time for his own crimes, like normal people did.

Ignoring the fact that he was supposed to be giving up smoking, he lit a fag and drew on it deeply. Zara was right, he was mental, only a mental person would live in the crumbling past when the future was neatly laid out in front of him. Zara was intelligent, funny, immensely beautiful, kind hearted, and he loved her. It was time to cut the apron strings of his first love.

Zara returned and smiled. 'Don't worry about the bill, you've already paid it.' She handed him back his credit card.

He took it, and sure enough it felt lighter. The receipt duly arrived on a silver plate, the waiter bowed, 'Sir,' then scuttled away. Jordan shook his head in disgust at the price.

'I hate this fucking place,' he said standing. 'Sixty-five fucking quid!'

'Well, I had to give him a big tip. Apparently a few of the customers complained when they heard the word . . .' She whispered in his ear, 'Sperm.'

Jordan smiled, eyeing the snotty-nosed gits. 'Really?' He grabbed her hand and walked towards the door desperate to hurl back abuse. But, this was where Zara and her friends came for lunches after having their nails done. He didn't want to get her a bad name in her regular hangout.

Outside, he laced his hands behind her waist. 'Look into my shades, Zara.' She lifted them off his face. 'Tonight, we shag.' He kissed her, noticing the unimpressed look in her eyes. 'Er . . . without condoms? Look, what I'm trying to say is that, when you were in the Ladies' doing a poo—'

'I was *not* doing a—'

'Whatever. Anyway, I want this baby. Light the candles, wear something sexy, do what you want, I'll be there at seven.' He kissed her on her lipsticked lips. 'I do love you, Zara.'

She giggled and gave him a hug.

They went their separate ways to their separate cars. From his parked Lexus, he watched her drive past honking the horn, the soft roof on her red BMW down, her hair trailing behind like a comet's tail. It was time to bury his secret for ever. But he knew it was going be hard burying something that wasn't yet quite dead.

As Samir's blue Merc zoomed into the drive he was saddened to note his house had been burgled. A NightOwl security van parked on the lawn, three flashing lights on the roof and a vicious mixture of shrills, wailing and barking from the NightOwl burglar alarm, meant the one thing that Samir had boasted could never happen, would never happen, had in fact happened: he'd been broken into. The owner of the top security company in the area had been *done over*. He could see the local headlines now: 'Samir's Shit Security Sucks'.

There's never a good time to imagine your living-room walls covered in kakka, thought Samir, but if he was going to imagine it, then now was the time. He ran inside the house to check the walls, with Kareena not far behind.

They were met in the hallway by Alf, all suited up for his labour of love – security. He coughed before he spoke, 'At fourteen hundred hours I received a call.' He flipped through his leather notebook, checking for details. 'Let me see, ahh, yes, a few of us bundled into the van and drove here at top speed, sir. We arrived at . . .' he read from the page, 'fourteen-hundred hours and however long it took to get here, sir.'

Samir punched in a security code, disabling the alarm racket. 'So, was anything stolen?'

'With respect, sir, I wouldn't know, I don't live here. But, the conservatory window was smashed.' He replaced the notebook in his back pocket, and coughed again. 'I'm of the opinion that . . . Could we talk in private, sir?' He raised his eyebrows in apology to Kareena. 'Security red tape.'

Samir asked Alf to wait downstairs while Kareena and he checked over the house. He would have that *little* chat afterwards. And if it was about that *little* bonus Alf was after, he'd get a big NO – with a big red tape round it.

Room to room, heartbeat to heartbeat, Kareena and Samir checked the entire upstairs. Each time Samir sighed in relief, Kareena followed suit. The whole drama brought to mind a time when she and Avani had been watching an episode of *Crime Stoppers* where a woman had been crying after her house had been burgled.

'Why did they pick on me?' the woman had said. 'I haven't harmed anyone.'

Kareena remembered thinking shamefully, 'That's what they all say', as she and Avani had laughed wickedly at the silhouette of the poor woman's massive hairdo on the TV.

'She's hardly going to keep her identity a secret with a four-storey-high perm, is she?' Avani had said as they both continued to laugh hysterically.

Their mum had then butted in, 'Careful when you laugh at others less fortunate than yourself. You never know, it could be you next.' And then Mum too saw the silhouette of the monstrous hairdo and she laughed along with them.

Upstairs was untouched, now for the downstairs. Samir and Kareena descended cautiously through the games room with its snooker table, into the dining room with its huge dining table, and into the kitchen with its . . . Samir stopped just outside the kitchen, his hand held up to quieten Kareena.

'Shhh.' He pressed his ear to the wooden door, trying to decipher the sounds from within. Sticking up two fingers, Samir turned to Kareena, mouthing, 'I think there's two people in there.' His ear was back to the door like a toilet plunger sucking out the voices within.

'I've never seen chunks this big before, check this out!' said a voice.

'Nice, nice.' A deeper voice.

'From India.'

'Very nice. Hopefully very tasty.'

A pause and then a metallic tapping sound. 'Ahhh, lime pickle. I see this man likes variety.' Then a loud chuckle. 'Just like his women.'

Samir angrily pushed open the door to see his employee Mickey sitting on his marbled kitchen table with his legs dangling, talking to himself among the open jars of pickles. Bombay mix was scattered everywhere. On the stove, a saucepan of rice boiled quietly.

Mickey glanced up, quickly sliding off the table. 'All right, Chief, how's tricks?' He crunched on a dried green pea.

Samir held himself back from unleashing a string of abuse. 'I know you're thick, Mickey, and you can't help it. But surely you can't be that thick – you passed your driving test, after all. We've got people coming round tomorrow, Mickey, and I was just wondering what the fuck you're doing in my kitchen eating their food?' Samir's eyes spotted an enormous can of ghee with a screwdriver rammed through the lid.

'Well, in case it slipped your mind, Chief, your house alarm activated. Emergency procedure stipulates that upon said call, security officers on duty must attend said scene of break in. So here I am. I don't see any Mohammeds here, do you?' He crunched another pea. 'Lucky I came instead of one of those Indian Mohammeds that you're so keen on. A right mess here it was, all that broken glass. I bet Mohammed wouldn't have cleaned up the glass like I did. They don't show any inish . . . inisy . . . inishot—'

'Initiative, Mickey. Well done.'

Samir thanked him politely for acting so responsibly. He also explained that the pictures on the walls of Guru Nanak were not of Father Christmas on a holiday in India. Not everyone with a white flowing beard is Santa.

To find out that the house hadn't been burgled was a great relief, but the relief turned to anger when Kareena and Samir learned the reason why the NightOwl alarm had been activated.

'Bricks?' Samir repeated, following Alf through to the conservatory as Kareena helped Mickey drain his rice. 'Why would someone want to throw bricks?'

Alf had laid out the projectiles in order of missile size on the bamboo furniture. Starting from a quarter brick, to half a brick, to a full brick.

Alf made a quick survey of the door, and then with a sleight of hand worthy of Cardini himself, he passed Samir a piece of paper. 'This was attached to one of the bricks. I didn't think you'd want your misses to see it. Mickey was in the toilet when I found it, so don't worry, and the other guys had long gone by then.'

Samir didn't know which was more scary. The thought of Mickey using his toilet or what was written on the scented note paper Alf had handed him. Having the sense to leave Samir alone to read it, Alf had headed out to join Kareena in the kitchen to see what was cooking in the frying pan.

And Samir was out of the frying pan and into the fire. The note might as well have been written in blood. Samir's blood. He was cooked.

You can't run away, unless you've got your shoes, Sammy.

Because that's what you are doing, running from yourself.

The longer you leave it, the harder it'll get, and the angrier I'll get.

GET RID OF HER.

C.

PS Darling, I chose and designed that conservatory. I'll do what I want with it. Think how many other things I chose. LOEY.

Chapter Nine

Fifty-three photographs lay neatly in a spiral on Cloey's patchwork quilt. At the end of the spiral was the latest photo of Samir and Cloey together at Claudette's thirty-first birthday party seven weeks ago. In the centre of the photo swirl lay the oldest picture. This was the most precious of all. A photo of the two of them when they had first met at a mutual friend's house six years ago. When their galaxy began. The big bang. Cloey feared after yesterday's brick-throwing episode that her universe with Samir might now be heading for the big crunch. The end of their era. Her dreams of luxuriating in the splendours of wealth with a man who was very nearly trained to her exacting standard were rushing away at the speed of light.

Cloey stood at the window. The view from her bedroom always eased her mood. But looking out on the fields coated in a summer flourish of rape and bundles of hay could do nothing for her today. She had a wife to get rid of.

She felt her blood thicken and clots of jealousy ride her veins, imagining Samir facing his Indian bride as they made love on their wedding night. His whole mind, body and spirit devoted to the naked Indian woman wriggling beneath him as he gave himself to her. As he made blind love. His real love forsaken as he fornicated with the woman his parents had chosen for him. Indian weddings – humbug!

Samir had explained the Indian marriage customs to her once, and she had sat there pretending to be interested, 'Oh really, Sammy, you must tell me more.' Just like she pretended to be interested in everything else he said. Until his wallet came out.

Cloey looked round the room. Disregarding the bed, antique toy box and a few pairs of knickers, Samir's cash had bought nearly everything in here. From the top of the range drawing board, artist's materials, Apple Mac computer, scanner, printer, even down to the artist's rubber she had sent him out in the snow to fetch over four years ago.

Her ability to earn income from greeting cards and paintings was reliant on Samir's credit cards. Artist's supplies cost an Indian arm and leg these days. And, according to Cloey, artist's supplies included a full-blown designer wardrobe. It was so much easier to apply herself and be inspired in the morning, knowing a snappy pair of thigh-length crocodile boots were waiting to be picked up from Oxford in the afternoon.

She returned to the photos. Her cup of lemon tea, like her envious heart, was now cold. She'd spent her whole relationship with Samir pretending to be someone she wasn't, and now, as the image of his wedding ring firmly sealed itself in her mind, she wondered if he too had been pretending. Had he known all along that their paths would eventually separate? Was she just Samir's spare? The stunt double for his wife? Cloey fumed. If anyone was going to be doing any stunts round here, then it would be Samir's wife as she was kicked from the top of a multistorey car park. She'd invested too much in Samir to let some trollop trot in and take him away, just like that.

Cloey looked in desperation through every photo to see if a clue of Samir's coming betrayal could be discerned in his image. But apart from the odd red-eye effect, there was nothing. Just his kind, gorgeous face and crushing smile. For one second she forgot his money as she stared at the picture in her hand. God, they made a good couple.

She put the 'big bang' photo down. He hadn't even phoned to see if she had dislocated her shoulder throwing the bricks from the rockery in his garden; *their* garden. The garden she had spent most of last summer spending his money on. The garden which was sown by one woman but which would be reaped by another.

Apart from her cherished photos of Sammy, there was one more photo which Cloey could not bear to part with. Between the pages of a book, *The Encyclopaedia of Cruel and Unusual Punishment* by Brian Lane, a solitary picture of Jordan lay hidden, but not forgotten.

On a sudden impulse, Cloey picked up the book, shook out the photograph and watched it glide to the carpet in three sweeping movements, landing face down. Typical, she thought, the one day she could bear to look at him, and he couldn't bear to look back at her. Bending down, she flipped the photo over and smiled in spite of herself. Twenty-three-years of mischief was wrapped up in his cheeky grin and it weakened her heart. She kissed him gently, and suddenly the tears began to fall. To hold them back any longer would have been impossible. They'd been waiting to fall for years. She collapsed face down on the bed, sobbing into her pillow.

Over five years ago, from her living-room window, she had watched Jordan hop back over the gate, and walk down Conker Avenue in the hammering rain. His first day out of prison and turned away at his first door. She remembered the feeling of satisfaction as his face had dropped upon hearing she was in love with Sammy. A twinge of euphoria had jumped up her spine like voltage. But she knew, in her heart of hearts, he would return. He loved her and he would beg to be taken back.

But he never came back.

He never *ever* came back.

Cloey stared at the photo of Jordan again. If he thought that his love for her had died, then he could bloody well think again. No man got to ditch his love for her without her say-so. No man got to ignore her as Jordan had done down at the Holy Cross Church the other day. It would be interesting, she thought, if he could ignore her in *this*. She picked out the smallest, tartiest dress in the wardrobe. The label inside, not much bigger than the dress itself, said, Only To Be Worn In Fantasies.

By the time she'd finished with Jordan today he'd be in a little fantasy of his own. And she was getting wet just thinking about it.

An Indian kitchen is a noisy kitchen. If the noise is missing, then, so too normally, is the flavour. Kareena had learnt her culinary skills via her mum. Starting with basic *chapatti*-making she'd worked her way through *dhal* and *bhajee* school until by the time she'd received the relatives' nod of approval – the Indiploma – she was capable of cooking for a temple brimful of hungry Sikhs.

Being accomplished in the kitchen, her dad would say, through a mouthful of *aloo chat*, spraying the table with bits of food, was more important than speaking good English or showing good manners. The sudden burp which usually followed this pronouncement often led her brother Arun, Avani and Kareena to wonder if their dad knew the real meaning of manners or etiquette at all. The fact that he always tried his hardest to break wind during the queen's speech should have given the game away years ago.

Kareena loved her new kitchen. She had made it very clear to Samir, 'I just love this kitchen,' she'd said. Casually asking him whether or not he liked to cook, she had been relieved to find out that he didn't. Casually asking him whether or not he liked to wash up, he had pointed in answer at the dishwasher. She hadn't tested out Avani's theory yet, but, apparently, in just your socks, you could slide down from one end of the kitchen to the other on the black marble floor. Avani had tried it out, playing drums on the hanging brass-bottomed saucepans as she did so. 'Even Delia

Smith could cook something exciting in a kitchen like this. I bet her husband is sick to death of white eggs.'

Kareena switched on Horizon Radio. Today she was preparing a meal for Samir's family while he was at work. Everything had to be spot on. She glanced round, getting her bearings. Frosted-glass-fronted cupboards covered most of the wall space and all the extras that Samir had had built in would keep *Gadget* magazine busy for weeks. There was no way she could complain that she didn't have enough utensils – and, equally there was no way she could simply melt a wad of cheese, chuck a few bread sticks on the table and tell them to stop their moaning and eat the fondue, either. They expected Indian. Indians always expected Indian, and it was crucial they got Indian.

The noise of chopping soon took on its own dull beat, as Kareena reflected how much her life had changed in such a short space of time. It was not that long ago she had been a primary school teacher in Watford, pointing the kids in the right direction, trying to give them the best start in life. Explaining to young Timmy why putting fridge magnets on his lunch box wouldn't necessarily mean that his sandwiches would keep cold. Telling Mary to stop eating her ear wax. Reprimanding Tobias for telling Mary that her ears were full of honey. That life felt so far away.

Kareena stood poised with a silver spoon over the bubbling mixture in the *karahi*. A heap of chillies, red with rage, stood ready to enter the magma. The question was: how much chilli to put in? If she guessed wrong the guests would sing a song, and the toilet would pong from that day on. So it was always best not to guess.

Kareena picked up the kitchen phone and dialled her mother, the oracle of Indian cuisine. After polite hellos, how are yous, I miss you already, Kareena got to the seeds of her problem: chillies.

She spoke in Punjabi, 'I'm cooking for seven, I expect you're going to tell me that a dessert spoonful each is too much?'

'You are making me very nervous, Kareena. You'll be divorced within the week. Even your own father would have to use the downstairs toilet after that amount of chilli, and you know how much he despises the downstairs toilet . . .'

Kareena listened intently. Not only was today a very important occasion for Kareena, it was an important occasion for her mum. Tonight, Samir's mother would find out how well Kareena had been trained in the kitchen. It was imperative she didn't screw up. Mud sticks in an Indian family and nothing is stickier than a badly cooked meal.

Her mother continued, 'So, if it all goes horribly wrong, you must make it very clear that this was the one dish I never taught you. Clear?'

'Yes, Mum.'

'And repeat back to me what I explained about your manners. Your mouth, Kareena, it worries both your father and I. You must always think before you open it. Now repeat.'

This was getting repetitive. For the month leading up to the wedding, her mother had drilled the rules into her. Kareena sighed, 'I must keep my head covered when his parents are present. I must never ask questions. I must answer all questions politely. Never smile unless smiled upon.' She paused, trying to think of the most important *must*. 'Er . . . oh yeah, I must always oblige.' Kareena felt her face flush. 'I must always satisfy Samir in the . . . bedroom.'

'And have you?'

'I haven't said no.'

'Good. I haven't said no to your father for thirty years. And I know it will be hard sometimes, but you must always say yes.'

So with the food and sex out of the way, there was nothing more to discuss.

Kareena returned to her chopping, grabbing an apron from a door peg. The fun design made her snigger: a cartoon of a monkey talking to a polar bear in the desert, the caption was, 'I don't understand how you can be lost, you're a pole-a-bear.' It was now time for turmeric sprinkling and capsicum crushing.

Kareena had always been told by her father never to judge herself by someone else's standards. She thought of his words now as she stared out at the magnificent garden that summed up August perfectly with its rash of red roses and a flush of pink sweet peas decorating little nooks and crannies like elf plots. And here, inside this dream house, she was cooking for her perfect husband.

Some Indian women would say she had landed on her feet. Some Indian women would have every right to say so. And that was the point of an arranged marriage. It could appear that you had landed on your feet from the outside, but inside you could be swaying to and fro, not sure whether you even liked the person your parents had chosen for you, not sure if the cars, house, bank account would really be able to make up for the feeling that somehow, somewhere, you might have missed out on something – that something often referred to as love.

Kareena asked herself, would she ever love Samir? Could it be possible that her parents had found her 'The One'?

She sliced through a handful of tacky ladies' fingers, smiling. Her father had told her not to judge herself by others, but she couldn't help it. Compared to her Indian friends and cousins, compared to relatives abroad, she had definitely landed on her feet. Exfoliated, buffed, pedicured, painted and massaged. Oh boy, had she landed on her feet! And it was looking very promising that love might well creep into their relationship at some stage.

And she couldn't wait to love Samir.

Chapter Ten

Cloey loved graveyards. She loved to look at couples who had been buried side by side. All those petty arguments meant nothing now. They were maggot food. She bobbed in and out of the gravestones like a will-o'-the-wisp in her tiny, fuschia-coloured dress, her eyes scanning the grounds for Jordan. Eventually she spotted him sprawled out on a blanket of moss on top of a tombstone worshipping the sun.

Enjoying the view of his semi-naked body, she stood camouflaged in the bushes debating her opening line. Debating how, with some sexual flaunting, she could make him hers again.

In her six-inch Rodolphe Menudier stilettos, Cloey crept closer, drawn by the wonderful smell of his aftershave. She used to wonder what type of woman Jordan would have ended up with had he not been so fortunate to meet her. And now that wonder had twisted and gnarled into a compulsion to know. Cloey had always been intensely jealous as far as Jordan was concerned. She remembered walking into a party with him once and noting to her horror that there were two women prettier than her in the room. It was the quickest migraine she had ever had. As Jordan mused afterwards, it was probably the only time in the world a woman had said, 'I've got a headache, I need to make love.' He had called it 'Nurofen Nookie'. But he was never allowed down that end of Milton Keynes again.

Cloey checked her shiny pink handbag to make sure she had got rid of anything sharp, just in case he mentioned kids, marriage or engagement. Even she couldn't kill a man with a tampon. Within a few metres of his body, her smile broke. She had spotted what she hoped she would see: his wedding finger without a wedding ring, Jordan was still on the scrap heap. She glanced back to the grey of the church – thank you, Lord.

As Cloey edged nearer, she found herself drooling over the man who used to be hers, the man who used to fix all her problems, who used to wipe away her tears. She admired the tanned, chiselled body, the muscles in his legs and shoulders, his tight six-pack, the strong muscular arms, his gorgeous face. God, how she wanted to kiss him! To touch him again and feel what he used to do to her.

Her French-manicured fingers hesitated before nudging him awake. She stood over him with the pepper spray aimed at his eyes; it more or less guaranteed some civility between them.

It was rare to wake up to a nightmare, and Jordan left

the word 'bitch' at the back of his throat while he made a sly snatch for his John Lennon shades lying beside his shorts. What the . . . was going on? He covered his eyes and pushed Cloey out of the way so he could stand up.

Cloey spoke, 'I love watching you sleep, Jordan.'

'Well, why the fuck did you wake me up then?' He switched the radio off.

'Because we—'

The church bell tolled, interrupting her.

Jordan combed his fingers through his dark hair. 'If you're here to paint a fence to atone for your sins, I hear Woburn Abbey's perimeter fence needs painting, I think it's about thirty miles long. That should take care of a couple of your minor wrongdoings.' He brushed off the moss from his shorts, watching the green dust fall into the can of white paint.

'This is all a bit low key for you isn't it? You used to graffiti walls and now you're painting them. You've become so boring, Jordan.'

'Yeah, yeah, I'm a boring bastard.' He found his cigarettes under his O'Neill snowboarding T-shirt and lit up, eyeing her suspiciously. He chucked the fag down. 'What's the score with the tarty dress? Trying to give the stiffs a stiffy?'

'You're so vulgar.'

He smiled, then his face became serious. 'Look, I don't care why you're here. I'll tell you what you want. Yes, you are still very beautiful, yes, your body is fantastic. Turn around.' She twirled. 'Yes, your bum is number one in my book, and yes, we had a beautiful relationship once. But,' he came in real close. 'Now listen very carefully. You are one sick woman. Now fuck off!'

Cloey's smugness held firm, secured by her self-esteem. 'You can't just wipe me from your mind, Jordan. You know my favourite colour is purple, so every time you see something purple, you think about me. Each time you see a beautiful painting, you wonder what I'm doing. When my birthday comes round, Christmas, Valentine's . . . You can't get away from your first love, Jordan. It's the same for me, every time I see a police car I think about you.' She grabbed his hand, expecting him to pull away, but he didn't. 'And when I sleep with a man, I always think it would be better with you.' She planted a long kiss on his lips. 'So much better.'

Through his shades, Jordan stared upwards at the emerald-green sky. The theory of the philosopher Descartes sprang to mind: I think therefore I am. In prison, a copy of Descartes had been passed from cell to cell and it had had a profound effect on Jordan's prison life. Hidden between the hollowed-out pages of the book had been fine-quality ganga. You needed the ganga to understand the freaking thing. One aspect did make sense though: use reason to guide your passion and you will be happier. In other words: don't follow your knob.

Jordan found his sense of reason and pushed Cloey away. 'I won't lie to you, Cloey, you nearly fucked my life up. You came this close.' His thumb and forefinger measured an inch. 'If someone were to have told me that one day I would stop loving you and end up hating you instead, I would have thought them mental. I would have explained . . . Oh fuck it, I don't know why I'm bothering.' Bending down, he picked up the dried-out paint brush. 'Got to get on. It was a blinding reunion.'

And the words 'get on' stuck in Cloey's mind. It was just like Bernie had said, Jordan was getting on – without her. It was disgruntling to see how well he was looking, she had hoped to see him thinned to the bone with love sickness. Instead, he was all muscled up with confidence, all geared up to get on with his life without her, while her life with Samir was falling to bits, her dream house was crumbling to dust, and no one seemed to love her any more.

She followed him over to the part-painted fence. The chest-high church boundary was made of half wood and half worm and, in keeping with the rest of Bruckley's fences, was held together more by luck than by anything else. Jordan slapped on the green and white paint angrily, while he tried to clear his head.

Cloey spoke to his bronzed back. 'Are you happy with her? Do you love her like you used to love me?'

'Go away, Cloey.'

'I'll go if you show me your bum.'

Jordan turned round and yanked down his shorts, his bits dangling freely; Cloey's eyes greedily toured his nakedness. Then she bent down, unable to believe what she was seeing.

Father Luke watched the scene from a distance with interest, unable to believe what he was seeing either. The last time he'd seen these two together was just seconds before Jordan had been handcuffed and led away in a police van. He remembered the wondrous feeling he'd had when making that anonymous phone call to Milton Keynes police station and dropping Jordan in it – he believed the term the policeman used was 'snitching'. He believed the term they might use for giving false information was lying. But it was so easy for a priest to lie and be believed. Sometimes being a priest was more like being God. And right now, he was sure God would not like what he was seeing – Jesus!

Cloey still studied Jordan's bottom. 'I can't believe you got rid of it, Jordan.' She seemed genuinely hurt. 'You said it was for life. It's so tacky for a person to cover their tattoos. Even tackier when they cover a classy name like Cloey with a shoddy seahorse.' She slapped his buttocks hard.

'I don't think your name deserves to be on my arse now, do you?' The breeze was quite cooling and reluctantly Jordan pulled up his shorts.

Cloey stepped forward, her eyes centred on his pecs. 'You may have got rid of my name, but you can't get rid of this.' Her fingernail traced its way across a four-inch scar on his chest. 'I prefer the knife to the needle any day.' She paused, wondering if now was time for the fatal blow. It was. 'I still love you, Jordan, I never stopped.'

Jordan watched a grey squirrel scoot across the grass and up a tree. He sighed. 'I love someone else. It's too late.'

This was not what Cloey had expected. If anyone was going to say it was 'too late', or 'I love someone else' it should be her. She hated people who broke her rules.

She flung her arms round his neck, sobbing. 'It's not too late, it's never too late. I love you, I know you love me, you may think you don't but I know you do. That day you came out of prison, when I told you I loved someone else . . . you don't understand.' A tear trickled down her cheek onto his bare shoulder. 'He hits me, Jordan, he frightens me. As soon as I shut the door on you he . . . he . . . punished me.' She pulled her head back to peek at him. 'It was bad . . . it was really . . .'

Jordan stroked her hair soothingly. 'Slow down. Who? Who are you talking about?'

Cloey had practised the next bit and now had it down pat. 'Saaaaaaaaammy.'

Hugging her tight, he rocked her from side to side, trying to calm her, trying to make things better. Why was the world so shitty to people sometimes? he thought, staring up at the cross on the church. Why did fuckers like this Sammy exist at all? What purpose had God put scum like that on this earth for? Over Cloey's shoulder he spotted Lukie Baby pruning the shrubs and staring at them with contempt. Jordan gave him his middle finger. Prune that!

Gently he pulled away, his chest now peppered with tears. 'This may be a daft question, but are you still with him?'

Cloey looked scornful. 'You don't understand, I can't leave him, he scares me. I've been with him all this time.' Her eyes pleaded with him. 'Six years of being battered. And the worst thing is, I couldn't tell anyone about it. No one knows but you, Jordan, not even Claudette.'

Jordan refused the urge to spit at the mention of Claudette's name. 'Why the fuck didn't you say something before? I was at the door, you know what I'm like, I would have fucking killed him.'

Cloey squinted and, letting the tears form once more, she brushed the back of her hand against his cheek. 'That's why. I know what you're like. You would have gone straight back to prison. I couldn't do it to you again. It was better this way.'

Jordan fumbled for his fags.

She sat on a gravestone. 'I shouldn't have told you, but I couldn't have you hate me like you do. I should go.' She wiped her sore eyes with her hand. 'He's coming round later. Just forget I told you.'

Jordan's mind was made up before his mouth opened. 'It stops today, Cloey. What time is he coming over?' He threw her his T-shirt. 'Use that.'

She dried her eyes on his top, smelling the scent of a woman, the obvious smell of a woman looking after him and washing his clothes in Comfort. 'I wish I hadn't told you. Look, he won't hit me if I behave myself. I think he's going to leave me anyway, he brags he's found someone else. Don't come over, or he'll cause trouble. He bears grudges, I know he does. He'll pay me back if he ever found out. It's best he just goes of his own accord. Promise on your life you won't come over. Promise.'

'Cloey, this is all so . . .'

'Just promise.'

Jordan picked up his mobile, and from the casing he handed her a business card. 'Ring me if he touches you again. I mean it, Cloey, I'll make his life a fucking misery.'

Ten minutes later, Cloey was smiling to herself. Jordan was such a sucker. Easy peasy let's get squeezy. The plan was simple. She would make him sleep with her, which would ultimately wreck his pathetic relationship with his girlfriend. In the meantime, Sammy would be blackmailed some more if he didn't leave his wife. She didn't let men walk over *her*, she walked over *them*.

In her stilettos, Cloey marched away from the Holy Cross Church, Jordan's business card clamped in her fingers. She peeked at the embossed card, before opening her Megane door.

Jordan Lewis
Peak Sensation Snow Coach.
Snowboarding, Skiing & Thrills
45 Foxes Dean, Waterfalls, Milton Keynes
0314 1592653

'My my,' she said, grinning like a pool's winner. 'Jordan *has* moved up market. Waterfalls.'

Chapter Eleven

On the roof of NightOwl Group Security's one-storey building a two-metre-high owl perched. Steel girders kept the wooden owl from flying away. The eyes were two 200-watt, green, fairground bulbs and its fixed gaze stared owl-like. Mushaf, Samir's cousin, had done a grand job. He called himself the Indian Michelangelo with the brilliance of Stan Lee. Many clients had commented on the realism of the Uzis and the Gatling guns hanging from the owl's holster. The slogan underneath the bird read, Don't mess with the best. He's sitting in a nest. It used to read: Twit-too-woo, I'm coming for yoou. Samir still thought there was room for improvement.

Samir and Gilbert stared at the owl. One eye was winking erratically. The smell of Kentucky Fried Chicken wafted from across the road. Samir had a choice: should he fix a bird or should he eat one? The policeman had said that it was fairly important that the sign was fixed soon, before there was another near collision on the nearby dual carriageway. All attempts so far to get a Mohammed up a ladder had been to no avail. Apparently, Allah – may peace be upon you – forbade it.

Gilbert rubbed his unshaven chin. 'Sometimes I wish I wasn't your fucking mate, Sam my man, because if you wasn't my mate, I would be charging one hundred and fifty smackeroonies for that job. The roof's a death trap.'

To Gilbert's shock, Samir produced his wallet and counted out the money. Married life had already changed his mate, he guessed, his mind boggling at what might have happened if Samir had been a Mormon instead of a Sikh. Gilbert grabbed the cash and stashed it in his leather tool belt already weighed down with a hammer and various screwdrivers.

From egg to owl, Gilbert had seen Samir's company grow. Working as his alarm fitter, locksmith and glazier, he'd witnessed at first hand the correlation between hard work and success. To watch Samir graft in the early days was to watch Samir sweat. He had asked Samir once what drove him so passionately and his answer was simple: my dad. And through seven years of moans and groans, Gilbert had come to admire Samir and his ethics and had felt privileged to sometimes give him guidance.

But today, Samir was after guidance of a different kind. Marriage guidance. The winking owl could wait for now.

Across the road in the window seat of KFC, as the bleach smell from the floor mingled with the colonial colonel's eleven herbs and spices, Gilbert listened with an open mind while Samir explained his moral dilemma: how to get rid of Kareena without feeling like a bastard.

Pouring his beans into his coleslaw, Gilbert stirred them with a plastic fork. 'I already gave you my advice months ago, and you didn't listen. And now poor Cloey is suffering because of you.' He paused with the beans in front of his mouth. 'What did she call you again when she found out?'

Samir bit his bottom lip, and rolled up his shirt sleeves. 'Er . . . a sick Sikh.'

'Well, you are a sick Sikh.' Gilbert forked in the beans and munched, 'Edward the Eighth abdicated his throne for that lass Wallis Simpson because he loved her and you won't even explain to your family that you love a white woman. That's why you're in this mess, because you're a wimp.' Gilbert sucked up his milkshake. 'Besides, I still find it hard to grasp why you let your parents decide your wife for you. It's so backward it's almost Jurassic. It's not like you're an ugly fuck, is it? Or you needed help? You were doing fine and dandy on your own. Cloey is gorgeous, intelligent, funny. You're like two peas in a pod, you are, or should I say one haricot bean and one black-eyed bean?' He chuckled.

The Kentucky fried its chicken, letting in the hungry, letting out the full. Bob Marley sang in the background, trying very carefully to keep his dreadlocks out of the deep-fat fryer. Samir looked again, oh no it wasn't Bob Marley, just someone who thought he could sing like him with a corn cob in his hand. Samir smiled and returned to Gilbert's analysis of arranged marriages, while picking at a hot wing.

Gilbert did have a point. How could it be reasonable to expect his parents to choose the correct woman for him to settle down with? And yet he'd seen the trouble they had gone to to make the right choice. His mother had been adamant that his wife should be good with children and know how to instil discipline. His father had been of the strong opinion that his wife should not be from Liverpool as the accent grated on him.

In an effort to appear modern about choosing a wife, Samir's parents had even tried the Internet. Samir had watched as pictures of Indian women appeared on the screen. Pretty Asian women all waiting to be picked by parents. It was amazing, he'd thought, either all the ugly Asian women were in hiding, or there was a censor only letting the pretty ones through.

He saw his father checking their qualifications, calculating the earning potential of various brides in the few years they might have before they started producing babies. He saw his mother jump with joy when she saw an Indian woman with relatives from the same village she came from. She had tried desperately to get Samir at least to agree to see her so she could catch up on village gossip. And he saw both of them frown in disgust when a woman came on the screen who appeared to be white. God forbid if Samir should choose a white woman.

The Internet idea lost its appeal with his parents when they opened an attachment one day which showed a naked Asian woman with some attachments of her own. The name should have given it away: Allido Issuck. After that, Samir's parents resorted to the old-fashioned word of mouth method. And the word was that Kareena, the primary school teacher, would be the one. The perfect wife and potentially the perfect mother. The karma was good.

Samir and Gilbert listened to 'No Woman No Cry' two more times before heading off to the winking owl to remove its cataract and restore its vision. Nothing is worse than seeing things through a cloudy lens, thought Samir, knowing how short-sighted he'd been himself lately.

Gilbert rested the aluminium ladder against the roof guttering, staring up at the ledge as if it were a cliff face, a worried expression on his face at the daunting ascent. 'I've got two kids, you know. I couldn't bear them to be orphaned.'

Samir shook his head. 'It's one-storey high.'

With one foot on the second rung, Gilbert turned. 'In case I don't come back, you know what you've got to do?' He took another step, not waiting for an answer. 'Cloey's so beautiful she could pick up any man tomorrow.' Another step. 'If you let her go you'll regret it.' Another step. 'Forget your parents, forget your wife, think about your future happiness.' Another step. 'Stop being a wishy washy wimpy wankey wimp . . . Fuck, Samir, I'm serious. Stop wobbling the ladder.'

As Gilbert made it safely to the top, all eight steps up, Samir sat on the bottom rung waiting. Gilbert was not always wise, but he sometimes showed good sense. He could pick out the live wire among a tangle of earths. And right now, Samir hoped that he hadn't cut the wrong wire with Cloey and short-circuited their relationship. It was one trip he could do without.

*

Chariot's Bar, in downtown MK, was the opposite to *Cheers*. In Chariot's, nobody knew your name which was just the way Jordan liked it. Apart from the lit-up bar the place was dressed in gloom. Voices only became faces when lighting a fag, and the sole question asked was, 'Are you using that ashtray?'

Jordan sunk a pint, counting the problems in his life. Disregarding Cloey, he had none. Today, at the church, when she had arrived dressed as sin itself, his life had altered course yet again. His reliable moral compass was now messed up by his meddlesome past. He watched the bartender pull a pint, the furry liquid climbing the glass. It was the only pulling that ever went on in here.

'You smoke your fags real funny,' the middle-aged bartender remarked, sliding over another pint. 'And yet you drink like a pro.'

Jordan looked at his half-burnt fag, the smoke streaming up in an unbroken flow. 'I'm a passive smoker. A hands-on passive smoker.' He eyed the skinny man, an earring would have doubled his weight. 'I've got a question which only a barman can answer.'

The bartender leaned against the bar, with the knowing nod of a spiritual leader. 'Ahhh, women, health or money?' He grabbed Jordan's wrist. 'The Rolex is real, so money's out. And, you're a good-looking chap so it can't be women. And,' he came in closer, 'no liver spots, so it ain't health. I give up . . . unless, of course, it's toiletry scenarios, in which case I'd rather not know.'

Jordan smiled. 'I was going to ask you if your barrel

needs changing, this lager is rank. But you were close. It is women. Two actually.'

'Get away.'

And he did, with the bartender winking in the background.

Jordan found the seclusion of a corner table, which was appropriate, as right now he felt cornered. In no man's land. His mind was playing war games battling his past against his present. As always in war there are casualties. In this one, he feared the casualty would be Zara.

Honesty would win him no medals, but it might clear the minefield. He loved Zara with all his broken heart. But here was the point: he could never love her like he loved the person who had broken it. Cloey was as much a part of him now as she had ever been.

Jordan stared through the pall of smoke, wondering how feelings he had thought long-dead could have risen again: the resurrection of his love for Cloey. In his mind, he'd erected a wall built from bricks of betrayal, where he'd locked any thoughts of her away, entombing her in his hatred. But today he'd learnt the truth. Sammy was dominating Cloey's life and forcing her to obey him with his fist. The bricks were crumbling to dust, his wall was becoming a ruin. Cloey still loved him and the only thing preventing them from being together was Zara. But it didn't make sense for a man of sound mind to contemplate life without Zara once he'd experienced life with her.

Zara could walk into anyone's life and splash it with colour. She was the woman young blokes dream about when they needed a nurse to check them over: 'Yes, Nurse Zara, I do think if you suck it, the pain will go away.' She was the blonde who gave blondes a bad name – she was intelligent. She was January to December's centre spread. Busty, lusty, gutsy, she really should have been living in Beverly Hills. Plain and simply, Zara was a man magnet. And yet it was she who had done all the chasing with Jordan.

Four years back, wearing more nerves than clothes, she'd planted her long legs astride one of his as he'd sat smoking on a metal bench under the palm trees inside the shopping centre.

'You and me, babe, how 'bout it?' Zara had asked, cringing back at her two giggling friends hiding behind a craft barrow. The chat-up line had been concocted by all three girls as they had stalked Jordan through the centre in their painful high-heels, picking up clues of his interests en route. He had stopped at WH Smith and checked out the surfing mags, he'd popped to the ski-slope for ten minutes and watched the skiers, he'd eaten two ice creams, and had an animated discussion with a patrolling Bobby. 'You and me, babe, how 'bout it?' had seemed like a winner.

'How 'bout fucking what?' Jordan replied.

'Er . . .' More cringing back at her friends. 'This is the first time I've ever chatted up a man, if you could at least help me along. I'm Zara by the way . . . and that's with a Z.'

'Could you spell that?' he said, enjoying what little she wore.

She took a deep breath. 'That's Z A R and then at the end there's an A. Zara.'

'So you *can* spell, then?'

She gave him a sexy, sultry smile. 'Oh, ring a ding

dong, it's Mr Preconceived, Mr Instinctive, Mr Judgmental, Mr I Woke Up One Morning And Decided I'm An Expert On Human Behaviourism, Mr Sheep, Mr Ice.' Running her fingers seductively through his hair, she spoke with a patronizing air, 'And Mr Gorgeous who won't be getting inside Zara's lacy G-strings, and that's G for goodbye. *Goodbye* Mr Ice Machine.' Zara would never again ask a man out.

And she didn't need to, Jordan was already hooked on her. He grabbed her hand and pulled her back. 'Here's my opening chat-up line: my name is Jordan, I've served time, my solicitor is on my friends and family list, you're beautiful and I've concluded you're not wearing a G-string. So, yeah, how 'bout it?'

'Can I call you Jordy?'

'If you want.'

'Yum yum.'

And their life together had been yummy ever since. Until now.

Too drunk to drive, Jordan wondered if he was too drunk to ski. He gulped the last of his pint and headed out into the blinking sunshine, then, slightly embarrassed quickly returned the pub its ashtray. Leaving his car parked, he made his way towards the silver-domed Xscape like a homing pigeon. The ski-slope would cool him off on the outside, he hoped it would do the same on the inside. The thought of Sammy laying into Cloey had roused him to boiling point. There was no way that that crime was going unpunished. No way!

Samir was raised believing it was rude to turn up at someone's house unannounced. His father had also explained that if notice wasn't given the larder might be empty. Bearing that in mind, he picked up his mobile and phoned Cloey from her back door. Five boot-licking text messages later, she opened it.

Samir's pupils grew from raisin size to olive size, his eyes out on stalks. In all their years together, he'd never seen Cloey so dolled up and daring. And the irony was, he was here to win her back, not the other way round. He followed her into the kitchen, gawking at her long slender legs, drooling at the way the pink dress clung like static. She was like a wet dream.

'I'm gob-smacked, Cloey, I can't believe you transformed yourself like that in between my texts.' He pulled out a chair, lifted some magazines off the seat and sat down. 'You don't need to dress so minimally to show me what I'm missing.' He gave her a caring look. 'Believe me, *I know* what I'll be missing if we split. It would be like my soul had committed hara-kiri.'

She filled the copper kettle with water, set it on the hob, then turned. 'I put myself back on the market today. It's not an easy adjustment to make when you're hurting. Who knows which man's arms I'll end up in when I'm on the rebound?' She grinned sweetly. 'I just hope he's less careless than the hunk I bumped into today. Now would you just take a look at this paint.' Cloey picked at the white specks from Jordan's paint brush. 'Let's say these white stains could so easily have been something else, Sammy. Let's just say next time they might be . . . Biscuits? I've got your favourites.'

His face remained fixed. It was no surprise to Samir that she would try to make him jealous, and each dig was easily ignored. More important was to find out how much he had hurt her and whether their relationship was fixable. If she had done the same to him, he would have given her one-way directions to radioactive Chernobyl – it would have been safer than staying with a man glowing green with jealousy.

Cloey slumped on his lap. 'I've made a decision. It involves someone getting hurt. Any guesses who the person I'm referring to is?'

Samir shrugged. 'Me?'

She kissed him on his cheek and ruffled his hair. 'That's what I love about you, Sammy, you're always thinking about yourself. The person is your wife, silly.' She giggled and moved to the Aga.

'I know she's going to get hurt. I just wish you wouldn't look so pleased about it.'

Cloey lifted the whistling kettle off the hob and made two mugs of coffee. She placed them on a wooden tray with a plate of neatly arranged homemade coconut and cherry cookies. If her mother had known she had been baking biscuits for an asylum seeker and not her daughter she would have put less cherries in.

He followed Cloey into the living room and sat on the cream-coloured sofa. The room was either yin or yang. Today it was yang, the principle of light, Jesus was here. Nailed to the vertical wooden beams were five crucifixes of various sizes. On the antique sideboard stood china figurines from the Bible, and on the coffee table, the Bible itself, leather bound, resting on a red cloth, a gift from the man of the cloth, Father Luke. It was a sure sign that Cloey had been visited by a demon.

'I take it your mother's been round?' said Samir, stuffing a biscuit in his gob.

Cloey snuggled down beside him. 'Yesterday morning. I couldn't be bothered to remove all the stuff. I had other things on my mind far more important.' She passed him his coffee. 'I'm sorry for smashing your conservatory; it was very out of character. Aggression rarely solves anything.' She paused, her voice went an octave lower. 'Instead, we have to sort this out rationally. Your wife, she is a problem, and she needs solving, Sammy. I don't know her and I don't ever want to know her. You made the mistake of marrying her and I will help you divorce her.' She snapped a biscuit in half and fed it to him. 'We mustn't humiliate her any more than necessary. I couldn't bear the thought of her suffering because of your stupidity.' A thought occured to her. 'Will she be shunned by her own family when she goes back red faced and crying?'

He nodded.

'Oh, that is a frightful shame. Frightful,' she said in her immaculate well-spoken voice. 'You must do it when you get home today, before her feelings for you become too strong. Then we can go back to having fun.' She kissed him as if that settled it.

But it wasn't settled, not by a long shot. Samir felt as if there were a crowd of Cloeys in the room, a press gang, a threatening rabble. He stood up to walk over to the window, then remembered he wasn't allowed near the window. Clenching his fists, he was about to swear, then remembered he wasn't allowed to swear in front of Jesus. There must be something he was allowed to do in this room, he thought, then he remembered there was: he was allowed to sit there like a lemon.

Sitting back down, he felt a new sense of purpose. Cloey must be more deeply in love with him than he'd thought. To forgive him so easily for his treachery showed a caring and an understanding that went beyond mere love. It was as though she'd walked out of a mangled car crash without so much as a scratch. It showed she really understood his predicament, his family pressures and traditions. She was a remarkable woman and he was a lucky man.

He took her hand in his. 'I'll tell her tomorrow, I can't do it today. My parents are coming round. It will be easier tomorrow.'

She removed her hand. 'You are *so* selfish. This is not just about me, this is about her as well. You're leading her on. Each minute she spends with you is galvanizing your lie, Sammy. You must obey the laws of kindness here. Besides, it's perfect if your parents are there, they can take the poor wretch home afterwards and stave off her tears.' She took his hand again. 'My love is non-negotiable, Sammy, I won't take no for an answer in this. I can't have her sleeping in my house another night.'

'Cloey, I can't. Not today. We're having a special meal to celebrate our marriage. It would be sick to do it tonight.'

'If you don't do it today, then I'll know you prefer her over me, and I would therefore never want to see you again. I want her out of the house by midnight. I'll wait for your phone call.'

A few hugs and kisses later, she waved him off as he took to the back fields. The kitchen clock showed

5.15 p.m. as she slammed and bolted the door, a sly smile on her face. Victory was less than seven hours away.

Cloey topped up her coffee, still smiling. She hoped his wife cried until it hurt. How dare she try and muscle in on her dream house. How fucking dare she.

Chapter Twelve

Kareena lay the silk sari on the bed. Six metres of peacock blue embroidered in gold. When she was little, she used to gaze at pictures of beautiful Indian brides gracefully decorated in fiery red and long for her wedding day so she could wear one too. Kareena ran her painted fingernail over the fine thread work, her thoughts on the significance of this piece of material. From peasant to queen the sari reigns supreme, from Bollywood to royalty the sari says India. But a requirement written by history dictates when an Indian can wear one. Until you are married, the sari remains a romantic dream. But once you are married, Kareena lifted up the sari and held it to her in view of the full-length mirror, once you are married you could even wear one to clean the blinking floor.

Her thoughts turned to Samir sitting downstairs exhausted from his day's work. How lucky she was. With him around, she wouldn't be cleaning any floors. His words on their wedding day had been music to her ears: 'You are not my skivy; I don't expect you to do anything.' It was a world apart from her Aunty Banjinder who even had to clean the fluff from her husband's navel. The times were changing. Women had nearly as many rights as men.

And talking of the rights of men, she could hear Samir shouting at someone on the phone from here. His family were due within the hour. Kareena smiled. She was worried but also hopeful that tonight would run smoothly. Why shouldn't it? She had prepared a good meal, she had a gorgeous bloke downstairs, and she was about to dress up in a £400 sari.

Checking herself out in the mirror, she thought of the one ingredient that could wreck the evening: Samir's bloodline – his parents, two sisters and brother. A mixed bag of snobbery and superiority gelled with a warped sense of humour. They had applied to appear on *Family Fortunes* four times and had been turned down four times over an entry on their application form that gave the producers cause for worry. The question, 'What type of family are you?' had been answered with, 'We are a non-violent organization. We wish you no harm. We just want to have a good time. And we are MAAAAAAD.'

Kareena wrapped the sari round and round her slim hips, bandaging herself in. Her mother had shown her how to do it plenty of times, but this was the first time she had put on a sari alone. And your first time, as with most things, is never your best: Kareena was making a hash of it; too loose and it falls off; too tight and you fall to the floor. Kareena fell to the floor. She wondered if the house insurance covered sari slipping. If not, why not?

What is it with Indians and wrapping? she thought. Turbans, you wrap. Saris, you wrap. Samosas, you wrap. But when it comes to presents, it's, 'Here you go', and a Netto carrier bag is lobbed across the room, with an out of date Easter Egg spilling out in transit. She thought back to Avani's advice to wear a tight black skimpy lycra dress.

'But I won't look Indian,' Kareena had said.

'Well slap a *bindi* on your forehead. *Voilà!*'

Finally it was done. She wished she'd marinated the sari in Sure deodorant now, the amount of sweat she'd lost putting it on. She toddled over to the balcony to let the cool air of the evening fan her.

Her life had changed so much in five days. Uprooted from her own family and adopted by a new one. Leaving the bedroom she used to share with Avani, to share a bed with Samir. Her whole world back in Watford was carrying on just as before. Carrying on without her. Kareena breathed in the fresh scent of flowers and watched as a black and white cat sharpened its claws on a tree by the summer house, its bum wiggling like a Hawaiian grass-skirt dancer. A plane overhead grabbed its attention – a delivery of catnip from the Far East perhaps? Its head stretched upwards and the bum-wiggling ceased.

Kareena headed downstairs to join her husband in the living room where Samir explained that no matter what she saw in the next few hours he was not a psychopath. He did not have two personalities, just two modes: parent mode and non-parent mode. The prime characteristic of parent mode was agreement; agreement with anything the parents said.

Samir continued with his tutoring. 'Right. Now,

when I do this,' he raised his eyebrows twice. 'What do you do?'

'Agree and back you up,' she said, pouring out Bombay mix into tiny glass bowls.

'Good.' He slid his hand sexily through his hair. 'What does that mean?'

She smiled. 'I must roar with laughter. Whether I think you're funny or not.'

Samir slapped his hands together in celebration. 'Excellent. You're a quick learner.' He jumped up and picked his way through a selection of DVDs stored underneath the Goliath TV. '*Platoon*, no. *An Audience with Freddie Star*, no. *Memento*, no. *The Craft*, no. It's going to have to be *Tera Jaadu Chaal Gaya*. If my memory serves me correctly the woman is kidnapped by bandits and found on top of a mountain singing. Her face was scarred by hot *ghee*. Who would marry her after that? Except our hero.' He slotted it into the DVD player. 'It's a gritty love story with barbaric undertones,' he said turning round. But Kareena was gone.

With the night fast approaching, Samir found himself thinking of Cloey's deadline: 'Get rid of your wife by midnight!' And with his parents due any minute, even a month of midnights didn't seem enough time to explain to them: 'Thanks for trying, but Kareena ain't the one. Oh yeah, forgot to mention, found myself a lovely Catholic woman. You'll love her. She's all white.' No, tonight was not the time to tell his parents. Midnight would have to wait. And so would Cloey.

Popping in a mouthful of Bombay mix, he was just starting to wonder where Kareena had disappeared to, when the doorbell set off the NightOwl dog alarm.

The top of the range K9 alarm barked each time the doorbell was rung, warning would-be burglars that a ferocious Rottweiler or Russian wolfhound guarded the premises. The chihuahua setting was rarely used.

In the hall, he found Kareena spraying enough lavender Glade in the air to keep a zoo fresh. He'd already complimented her on how fantastic she looked in her sari, and now, as he watched her kill off the last remaining pockets of oxygen, he underscored that thought in his mind. God, she was beautiful, and before he had time to think about what he was doing, he was across the hall and kissing her, and then apologizing for not swallowing his Bombay mix first.

The door opened, and Samir's family, all spruced up for an entertaining evening, stared at Samir's clothes with disdain. A family sneer at his choice of Oxfam clothes: a Metallica T-shirt half in half out of his scruffy jeans and a pair of brown slippers squashed at the back by his heels. The only clue that Samir had made any effort at all was that his flys were zipped up.

As Samir stepped aside, a gasp came from his mum. She'd seen some dazzling brides in her time, herself included, but Kareena really surpassed them all. She smiled at her new daughter-in-law so warmly that Kareena nearly forgot her manners. But she remembered herself just in time to cover her head with the tail of the sari, a mark of respect which preceded another: foot touching. She bent low and touched the shoes of her father-in-law and waited for him to wave her to her feet. 'Hurry up,' thought Kareena, desperately holding her breath, for whatever lay hidden underneath his socks did not smell pleasant.

Hanging up the shawls and coats, Kareena took the

drink orders and headed off for waitress duty in the kitchen. Manisha, Samir's twenty-five-year-old sister, followed her. For some reason Kareena sensed trouble already. Perhaps Manisha was still feeling aggrieved with her for wearing pink at her wedding and not the traditional red? Or was she about to issue a warning to keep Samir happy possibly? Or even . . .

Manisha spoke quickly and quietly. 'I know you don't know me and please don't think of me as a weirdo, but I need some alcohol sharpish.' She grabbed Kareena's wrist. 'I'm not an alky or anything like that. It's just that my parents drive me to it.'

Kareena watched her knock back a Stella in two gulps, then produce a packet of cigarettes from her tiny beaded handbag. It was hard not to stare at Manisha. Her beauty was totally bewitching. From her cropped hair streaked with red to the metallic silver *lengha* suit, she could have just slipped through a time warp and travelled back from a distant dimension. A dimension where men were slaves and were subjected to daily humiliation.

Manisha switched on the extractor fan over the cooker. 'I always sneak a fag in here.' She lit up and drew in. 'That's when Samir's not too busy to invite us round . . . which is hardly ever. Always busy he is, so he says. It's a miracle he ever got married.'

Kareena poured out the drinks. Fresh orange juice for the women and lagers for the men. She said, 'What do you mean, "a miracle"?'

'Well, Indian families are famous for applying pressure – and God, did Samir get pressure.' She puffed. 'If mum's tear ducts were connected to the Ganges she would have drained it to a mud bank, she cried that much over Samir. None of us got a moment's peace until he was married off. Finally, finally, finally he agreed.' She stubbed out her fag and stared at Kareena unblinking. 'It's me next, you know. They've already started looking, telling prospective buyers that I'm an angel. And look.' She stood with her back to the door, lifted up her top and pulled down one cup of her silver bra.

Kareena edged in to take a closer look at the tattoo. 'Erm . . . is it a flying pineapple?'

'No! It's a bumble bee, and fuck did it sting. If they thought Samir was hard to get shot of, they haven't seen what tactics I've got planned.' She giggled, then put her hand to her mouth. 'God, do I talk too much?'

Inside the living room it was talk of a different kind as Kareena filed in behind Manisha with the drinks to join in the discussion. The topic of discussion being her face. Her and Samir's wedding photos were being passed from lap to lap.

Her mother-in-law spoke in Punjabi, 'Cameras are horrible things, don't you think, Kareena? The way they distort and make your face look bigger.'

Samir jumped in, he was getting sick of this. It was his mother's tenth comment on the width of Kareena's features. 'I love fat faces.' He smiled across at his wife, who shrugged.

His mother, wise to Samir's reverse psychology, continued, 'Oh, I don't know.' She turned the photo upside down. 'It's such a shame when the bride's face is so inflated. Look, Kareena, don't you agree? If you would have listened to me and worn red, your face would look comparatively normal.' Her smug sigh nearly sucked the teeth from her gums. 'Of course, I wore red at my own wedding.'

Samir stared at his family. Surely someone was going to stand up to his mother? He looked at Ajay, his brother, his brain still in hiding since his last batch of weed. Then to his two sisters, both impulsive, but batty, both looking bored. And then to his father, engrossed in the Bollywood DVD. It was obvious who wore the *kacchas* in this house.

'Look,' Samir said, startled at his own anger. 'Does it *really* matter that she wanted to wear pink?'

His mother sipped her orange juice defiantly. 'Pink's a cheap colour. I can't believe that you're already taking her side over your own mother.' She sniffed. 'You wouldn't even be with her if it wasn't for my forcefulness. You said yourself that you were too yo—'

Her husband interrupted her with a burst of laughter, pointing at the TV. 'He just fell over. Did you all see that? He just fell over.'

The family gave a pitiful shake of the head towards him. But the timing was perfect, thought Samir, ushering everyone to the dining room, praying that the chapatties were doughy enough to shut his mother up.

Sex by silhouette, Cloey had seen that before, two ramblers in a tent. Murder by silhouette, she'd seen that too – *Psycho* was a favourite film of hers. But a wife and husband splitting up by silhouette, this was a first and she wanted to enjoy it fully.

She sat, looking from a distance at the curtains of Samir's dining room. Her car was cool, keeping the heat of excitement at bay. Air conditioning was a must when you were about to win your man back. It wouldn't do for Samir to dispose of his wife tonight to find that his woman in waiting had turned into a sweat pot, with her make-up all melted and congealed to the prime whale fat it was.

The shadows were murky, floating across the curtain. Cloey craned her head forward and twisted the focus on the tiny binoculars. She could make out Samir's strong features easily. Her heart thumped to think that his wife was in that room with him. The unseen enemy. She gave a thin smile. No, Cloey, it is you who is the unseen enemy.

Hidden out here in the darkness amongst the thick bushes, Cloey had the best seat in the house. She was impatient for the show to begin, waiting with baited breath for his wife to come running out in a flood of tears, Samir standing on the porch yelling, 'Good riddance. You were a joke in bed.' And he would then dial Cloey's number immediately. Ideal.

Minutes passed. Cloey waited, her eyes flicking nervously from the clock then back to the shadows. 10.30, then 10.31, then 10.32. Time trickled. Every now and again, an enormous shadow worked its way across the curtains like an eclipse. It took a few minutes for her to realize that turbans don't cause eclipses. Itchy scalps maybe, but not eclipses. 10.36. What was taking him so long?

She unzipped her overnight tapestry bag and pulled out a lace and satin passion sweetener: a wine-coloured chemise, chosen today, thought about all afternoon, to be worn and ripped off tonight. She re-applied her make-up and re-affirmed the list in her mind of what she would and what she wouldn't let Samir do to her body later on.

Her smile thickened. She would let him undress her;

he'd suffered enough looking at the awful body his wife undoubtedly had. Cloey rubbed her hands down her smooth calves. Legs this smooth should be illegal. Samir would be allowed to run his hands up and down these legs, she thought. He'd suffered enough having to put up with the baboon-like legs of his wife. Cloey smiled again. Samir had fantastic hands. Hands that responded to her subtle signs and teased the hell out of every inch of her. She would allow Samir to touch her all over, after he had cleansed himself from his wife, after he had . . . Cloey threw the binoculars down in disgust. Jesus Christ, Samir, it can't be that hard to explain to a woman you hardly know that you have another life planned with the woman you love. She felt her arteries thicken with hot-blooded temper.

Feeling claustrophobic, Cloey stepped out of the car and strolled a few metres down the lane. Right now her head was filled with only one thought. That house. To lose it now would be a disaster. And this world was already filled with too many of those, she thought, smiling to herself as she returned to her yellow Megane and reached down into the boot.

She lovingly touched the wooden box, caressing the label she'd printed.

Sammy and His Parents' Choice of a Wife.
Separation Fireworks.

The clock showed that it was nearly 11.00 p.m. and it would soon be time to watch the display. Her laughter scuttled through the hedges. For fuck's sake, Sammy, will you ditch the bitch!

Chapter Thirteen

It was past midnight and Cloey drove along an empty road with her head filled with bitter thoughts. Her last hope that Samir and his wife slept in separate rooms had been dashed. The vision of Samir gently unwrapping his wife's sari was now branded in her mind. Through her binoculars, she couldn't fail to see the terrific teasing effect that the sari cast on her man. For each metre of material unwrapped, Samir's cock rose an inch more.

She had wanted to ram her fist on the car hooter and wreck their moment. But she refrained, driving away at full pelt, keeping a tight lid on her bitter rage and envy. She'd get her own back, she told herself. She'd wreck their loveless, fake marriage if it was the last thing she did.

Each imagined kiss Samir planted on his wife's lips, each passionate word he whispered to her was like pilfering bricks from Cloey's house, signing the deeds over in a sweaty embrace. Her earlier vision of Samir's wife as a morose woman in a sari at a women's refuge was fading fast, being replaced by a vision of a happy woman in a sari hanging washing out to dry on *her* washing line, outside *her* house, in *her* garden. If Shakespeare were alive today he'd alter a line of *Julius Caesar*. Et tu, Samir, tu bastard.

She continued driving down a long road with fields of untamed grass on either side. The moors of Milton Keynes. The perfect place to break down and get murdered. Cloey pushed her foot down and headed towards the glowing beacon of Tesco's Extra. She snorted at the humour of the supermarket planners. Place a twenty-four-hour Tesco on the edge of town, miles from any houses, where they make *Born Free* films, and wait. Build it and they will come. Build it and the greedy, grabby, gannets of Milton Keynes will always find a way to get there, you'll see.

Cloey parked up in a disabled spot. The rules of night shopping were different to those of the day; no one made eye contact, in case you happened to be the night-time nutcase. And it wasn't trendy to look trendy here, food was your priority not your Moschino pants.

Music blared through ceiling speakers, and shelf stockers on roller blades zoomed in and out of the aisles. Cloey filled her basket with edibles – anything containing sugar or chocolate would do – and placed the one non-edible item among them, a street *A to Z* of Milton Keynes.

She stood directly under a security camera and ate her Snicker bar, smiling up at it with an 'I dare you!' look. And if dares were the order of tonight, then what she was about to do in the next half hour was a double dare. She was going to use the sins of her past to reap the rewards of the future. Cloey had always known that falling in love with a criminal would come in handy one day. And no one came in handier than Jordan when it came to crime.

Besides, it would be a crime to waste legs as smooth as this on Tesco. She hadn't shaved her legs that close just to be eyed up by the four-year-old spotty cashier who was grinning with his tongue out as she placed the items on the conveyer belt.

'Oi. Need some 'elp wiv yer packin', luv?' he asked politely.

Cloey shook her head. 'No. No thank you.'

She imagined the numbers on his till would be covered with bogeys. She imagined sex with him would last approximately two seconds. She imagined him not to wear pants and have skid marks on the inside of his trousers. She felt sick.

Cloey tried not to look at him as his tongue dribbled saliva. 'Can I have forty pounds cash back please?' She passed a credit card to a sovereign-ringed hand.

The lad's tongue slipped back inside his mouth, retracting like a snail's tentacle. He tried to make skin contact with Cloey, chasing her hand round the counter. Finally, he gave up and put the money on the plastic top. The tongue was back. 'I'm surprised yer hubby lets a gorgeous babe like you out on yer own this late.' His gaze was fixed on her wedding band.

She grabbed the money and looked him squarely in the eye. 'My husband died today. Goodnight!'

Cloey parked the car fifty yards from Jordan's residence in Foxes Dean. She walked quickly towards it down the ghostly pavement like a gunslinger, her pepper spray in one hand and her personal attack alarm in the other.

On the short journey here, she'd prepared her mind for a few things: Jordan's initial anger at her imposition; her initial anger at his girlfriend's pretty looks; the sight of both their faces dropping as she dropped her bombshell. But she had not prepared herself for the sumptuous-looking house he lived in.

From across the road, Cloey squirmed as she took in the modern glass-fronted building. It was so obviously designed to make people jealous, she thought jealously. A tantalizing glimpse of a wooden spiral staircase could be seen leading up to a large landing, which no doubt led to even larger bedrooms. Only one top light was on, sending a candle-like glow down the stairs.

The thought of Jordan living in squalor was one thing, but she couldn't handle the idea of him living in splendour. With a pretty woman? With a future to look forward to? When her own life was down the pan. No bloody way. She roughed up her flimsy black chiffon dress, ripped off two top buttons and yanked down one shoulder strap. Then she grabbed a small handful of mud, rubbed it in her face and crunched angrily up his front drive in her stilettos.

Cloey rang the doorbell while simultaneously hammering with the knocker.

The door opened to reveal Jordan standing there with a baseball bat, slapping it in his hand. 'Fuck, Cloey, this isn't a good time. Go away!' His green eyes softened from annoyance to concern. 'Jesus, what happened?'

She didn't know what was more violent, his *Mr Bump* boxer shorts or his wielding of the bat. With her eyes wide in shock, she spoke deliberately and quietly. 'I don't want to cause any trouble with you and your girlfriend. But I had no one else to turn to. Sammy tried to strangle me.'

'What?'

Cloey knew she looked ugly when she cried, but it was worth it in the circumstances, and her dishonest dirty tears flowed down her muddy cheeks, as she let her shoulders slump and her arms fall by her sides. *Pitiful* was the look she was after.

Jordan's instincts urged him to drop the bat and cuddle this damsel in distress. To think someone had dared to harm her filled his mind with nefarious thoughts. She looked so pitiful, he thought, so vulnerable and lost. He reached out a hand and then . . .

'Jordy!' Zara yelled. 'Who is it?'

He turned his head back. 'I don't fucking know, I haven't asked her yet.'

'Her?' Thud thud thud down the stairs. Patter patter patter across the wooden floor. Zara appeared at the door next to Jordan, her half-drunk eyes half focused on Cloey. 'Oh my God, what happened to you?'

Cloey's fake tears were replaced by real ones – Zara was picture-perfect pretty. She answered through jerky sobs, 'I was jumped on from the bushes by a man. He pushed me to the ground and told me he was going to . . . to . . .'

Zara moved outside, put her arm round Cloey's shoulder and walked her through the door. 'You'd better come in.'

She was led into the open-plan downstairs. A chrome kitchen, a vast dining room and living area. White sofas and chairs were spread shouting-distance apart and a tiny model of the house had been placed centrally on a low glass table. No pictures, no ornaments, just a Technics stereo, a flat cinema-size TV screen pretending to be a wall and a cabinet filled with silver snowboarding trophies. Sparse was an overstatement.

Within fifteen minutes, Cloey was wearing Zara's clothes, drinking Zara's brandy and sobbing into Zara's arms. Jordan watched anxiously from the kitchen stool as an apparent bond began to form between the two women he loved. Zara made friends easily. Just as easily as Cloey made enemies.

Cloey sniffed. 'You're so kind, such a lovely nature about you. I'm Catherine by the way.'

Jordan coughed.

'I'm Zara. And that's Zara with a Z. Z for zebra or,' she giggled, 'Z for Zara. And that's Jordan.'

Cloey spoke to the shadow in the kitchen. 'Nice to meet you, Jordan.'

'Likewise, Catherine.'

Zara pulled a strand of matted hair away from Cloey's eyes. 'Do you think you're up to talking to the police now? They're very sweet, aren't they, Jordy?' She giggled again. 'He knows them all, don't you, Jordy?' She whispered, 'Just the sound of a siren gives him the cold shakes.' Then she shouted, 'Doesn't it, Jordy?'

Cloey glanced at Jordan as he sunk into a sofa-chair. She'd never seen him this nervous before. Apart from, perhaps, that time they were being chased at 90 mph by MK City's police cars. The thought of that night had given her nightmares ever since. Just inches away from death while she had struggled to maintain control of Jordan's motor as a swarm of squad cars gave chase through the back lanes of Bruckley:

'They won't look for us in a boneyard,' Jordan had claimed as the car skidded on to the Holy Cross Church lawn. And they wouldn't have looked for them in the boneyard – had it not been for Father Luke and his one to one chat with CID. Cloey wondered if Father Luke had gone to confession after the police left.

Jordan had saved her bacon that cold November evening. And, some might say, saved her from the bacon.

Cloey felt the warm tug of brandy in her stomach. This evening wasn't about reminiscing, it was about lost property. Jordan's love belonged to her and this bimbo here wasn't allowed to lay claim to it, just because she'd found it lying around some place.

'You've both been so sweet, but I don't want to waste police time,' Cloey began, standing up. 'They've got enough on their plate with the criminals in this town,' she went on, directing her gaze at Jordan. 'I feel so much better. I'm sure the rapist is long gone now. I'll just walk home very quickly.'

'Nonsense.' Zara rose. 'Jordan will give you a lift, won't you, Jordy? I can vouch for him, he's the gentlest man you could imagine. But he's vicious when we women need protecting from groping men, isn't that right?' Zara gulped down the rest of Cloey's glass of brandy. 'I love him so much.'

Zara folded up Cloey's dress, and placed it in a carrier bag along with her pepper spray, personal alarm and a complimentary Zara gift – a box of Diary Milk. 'Don't let this beat you, Catherine.' She smiled warmly, giving Cloey her mobile number. 'Take this. Any time you need to call, then, by all means, call. And you can keep my clothes, they suit you better than me anyway.' She kissed them both goodbye at the door and mouthed to Jordan, 'Ahhh, she's lovely.'

Underneath the spotlight of the drive, Cloey waited as Jordan reversed his Lexus from the double garage, noting with frustration that the second car, belonging to that stupid bimbo indoors, was a bloody BMW. Samir had only bought her a pathetic Megane while Jordan was providing his woman with a spanking new BMW. He was also providing his woman with too many clothes, she thought, feeling the quality of the designer lycra dress she wore and feeling the too-comfy fit of a dress one size too small. She only wished Claudette was here with her one size bigger hips to make her feel normal again.

Cloey spoke as soon as the car was moving, 'You make a lovely couple, Jordan. I can see you both love each other dearly and I regret to have laid this on you but you're the only one I can trust.'

Jordan concentrated on the road. 'Why did you call yourself Catherine? Out of all the names, why pick my mum's?'

She placed her hand on his knee. 'I didn't think. I'm sorry. It's the first name that came to me.'

'And why didn't you ring before you came over? Fucking hell, I can't be doing with all this lying and stuff. You realize I've got to lie to Zara now, don't you? And that makes me feel like shit. I love her, Cloey, and you've put me in an awkward position.

And it's sad that your boyfriend strangles you, but, I'll fucking strangle you myself if you do anything like this again.' He pulled into a BP garage and turned to face her. 'Right, where does this Sammy live?'

Even though it was late, the forecourt was busy, its bright lights attracting traffic like moths. Cloey fiddled with the tassels on Zara's bubblegum-coloured cashmere pashmina wondering how to play this hand she'd been dealt. Should she go for the grand slam? Or should she just play the dummy?

She picked up a CD from the floor – Talking Heads. 'It's not as simple as that, Jordy.'

'Jordan to you.'

'Jordan. You can't fix this with fists, they'll lock you up *again*. Think about Zara for a minute. Do you want her to go through what I went through? It was a living hell. Do you know how many showers I had to take to get rid of the prison stink after my visits? I don't think people realize that we prison maidens suffer more than you do: our lives on hold; living for the day the convicts are released. It's no joke I can tell you, it's—'

'It's bollocks. In fact, it was ten sets of bollocks if I remember rightly. Ten men you slept with when I was inside, wasn't it? While you were suffering with your life on hold.' He lit up a fag, remembered his promise to Zara, stared at the fag as though it were poisoned, then chucked it out of the window.

Within seconds a do-gooder had legged it over and stamped on it, mouthing angrily, 'Petrol! Petrol! Petrol! *Wanker*.' When he saw the size Jordan was as he got out of the car, he added, 'It's cheap petrol here! I can't wait to see the next *tanker*, buddy!'

Ignoring his buddy, Jordan filled his Lexus with the *cheap* petrol, battling with a whole list of emotions. Just Cloey's smell, a certain perfume she always used, was driving him nuts. The whereabouts of his sanity was unknown, because even though she was making him furious, all he could think about was fucking her. Fucking her furiously. It was probably the wrong time to be sticking a nozzle in a petrol tank.

Inside the car, Cloey eyed him through the vanity mirror. There was great pleasure to be had watching Jordan become annoyed, she thought, grinning. Knowing the connection was still wired up and all the old buttons still worked after so many years was a thrill. It was as though her past had been given a facelift by the scalpel of her lying mouth. Jordan was now unsure what might have happened between them if he'd stuck around instead of vanishing all those years ago. And when a man is unsure, you take advantage.

She stared across the forecourt at the cashier in the kiosk as he scratched his head, wondering how he was going to pass the pizza Pringles through the night slide to a customer. It would come as no surprise if he began to pass them through individually. Jordan joined the quickly forming queue that was popping with agitation. Finally a compromise was reached and four packets of salt and vinegar Discos were passed underneath by the delinquent cashier. Jordan laughed at a comment made by an attractive woman standing behind him. He made a comment back and she touched his arm then cracked up laughing herself.

Cloey fumed. 'Why don't you two just take your clothes off and be done with it?' she said to herself, glaring at the pretty brunette. 'Don't mind me, the woman who has just been—' and she frantically wound down her window and shouted out, 'STRANGLED, Jordan!' She didn't bother to wait for the response, quickly finding the Talking Heads CD, and snapping it in half. 'Decapitated Heads!' Her pulse rate remained steady.

Ignoring anything that might lead to the topic of strangulation, Jordan made small talk as he drove Cloey back to her car still parked outside his house. The sooner he returned her the better, her flirtatious traffic light was all green, go Go GO. But his instincts were red, no No NO. The car hummed down Watling Street and Jordan switched on his police scanner. There was no point in doing a ton twenty in Milton Keynes if you were going to get caught. There was no point in risking a ton forty unless you had someone to share it with. Cloey's screams of delight as he floored the accelerator gave Jordan a warm feeling inside. Just like old times. And his mind began to race, just like old times.

He pulled up behind her Megane. From where they sat on the road, every light in every house was out. He wondered if any of the sleeping husbands and wives within were dreaming about someone else tonight. Like he had done for a zillion nights. And now, the person he'd dreamed about was here. Right here next to him.

Cloey said in a whisper, 'I'd better go now, Jordan. I've tried to lower your guard, but you obviously love Zara too much to wreck things. You are someone I will always compare other men to, you know that?' She kissed him on the cheek and lingered with her lips.

'I know you loved me once. And I know I ruined it all. Will you thank Zara for me?' The car light flicked on as she opened the door.

Jordan's mind was having a jamming session, the strumming bass of loyalty setting the rhythm as the big bongo drums of his hormones came crashing in. The huge brass band of his past joined in too. By the end, the strumming loyalty was but a faint tapping on the side of his head.

'Pagoda?' he said urgently, reaching out to grab her arm.

'Pagoda.' She nodded, swinging her legs back in the car, wrestling with her facial muscles to keep them ladylike as she turned to face him with a dignified smile. But there was nothing dignified or ladylike in the way her hand went for his crotch. It was time to switch on that police scanner again. The Town Clowns never slept in this town, even at 3.00 a.m. Nor did the criminals.

The car lurched on to the gravel car park, tossing up the stones, clouding up the cool morning air with dust. A few seconds later they were running up the wooden steps just like they used to, each worn step bringing them nearer and nearer to their goal. Many people climb the countless steps to the Peace Pagoda on the crest of MK's highest hill for a spiritual make-over, to enjoy the calming silence of the huge Buddhist temple. But Cloey and Jordan were after spirituality of a different kind.

Jordan put his arm round Cloey's waist, and for a few heartbeats they gazed down the huge hill to the twinkling lights of Milton Keynes. Words would have wrecked this moment. A poet was worthless up here.

On the cold stone of the white marbled floor, Jordan began to remove Cloey's (Zara's) dress under the moonlight shadow of the gold canopy roof. Two flame-breathing dragons circled above, caught in repose among the peak of the canopy, their sculptured wooden bodies painted the colour of bloody fire. And tonight, Jordan's heart was on fire, ablaze with awe at the sight before his eyes. Cloey was sensual pandemonium. Her exposed skin doused his guilt and fanned his excitement. To touch her body once again was like waking up from the best dream and finding out it's real. There had been lonely nights in prison when he'd thought that if the screws would let him out to spend just one night with her, he would happily have let them add another year to his sentence. Then he would wake up to the greasy-bile farts of Bubber Smith, his cell mate, and think: 'Fuck that, I'll have a wank instead.'

Cloey unzipped his jeans, while her other hand slid under his T-shirt and roamed. With a body like his it was obvious that Zara's hands would have been everywhere, making sure he had a good time, and it was therefore of grave importance that she impressed him tonight. She removed his *Mr Bump* boxers and dropped them, standing on the blue-bandaged man to keep her tootsies warm.

She kissed him as sensually as she could, then pulled back. 'I probably look like an elephant compared to Zara.'

Jordan smiled. 'African or Indian?'

'I'm being serious here, you're hurting my feelings. I mean it, Zara is a size eight.'

'I'll be diplomatic. You both look better with your

clothes off.' He paused. 'Come on, Cloey, you know you're beautiful; you don't need my compliments.'

She giggled, then lay back on Zara's pashmina pulling him down with her.

Jordan knew where her weaknesses lay and touched her like he used to, his pupils deep and wide like pools of pure sin. He pushed his cock slowly inside, watching her eyes, listening to her moan, with the wind a silent curse on his back, Jordan made love to her, relishing each thrust inside her, enjoying every groan. Before, when they had made love as teenagers, they had always been in a hurry, 'Quick, Cloey, pull your knickers down, I've got a math's exam in eleven minutes.' It had been innocent and free. But today, on the peak of Milton Keynes, older, wiser and more experienced, he became what he despised: an adulterer.

Like a picture developing, the sun slowly brought the view from the Pagoda to life. A lake with a small grassy island at the bottom of the hill, a faded chalk maze on the far side and in the distance the roofs and bell tower of the village of Bruckley.

Cloey slipped back into the dress. The cold and damp that had earlier been a blanket of comfort from the heat of their passion was now an interfering nuisance that gave goose bumps to her legs and shivers to her bones. Jordan stared out over the city as though he were searching for an SOS flare. He certainly needed rescuing now.

He lit a fag, then threw it down. 'Cliché time. I made a fucking mistake.' His words stumbled out, 'It was a once-only type of mistake . . . a one-off . . . a never again.' He pulled her towards him. 'I didn't mean that. Oh, shit. My big mouth.'

She smirked, and wrapped her arms round him. 'Feeling guilty, Jordan? Me too. We should have done this a long time ago.'

They walked back down to the car, holding hands, waking the birds up for a change with their chatter. There was still so much to talk about, and back inside the car they continued their discussion about Sammy. Cloey explained, between tears, that Sammy was an animal who had beaten her so savagely, with such hate, that she now knew what death felt like. Her chemist gave her a discount because of the amount of painkillers she regularly consumed. Cloey explained to Jordan that just once, when things were really bad, she had wanted to consume all the painkillers together.

'I really can't see how I can help you, Cloey. You won't go to the police and you forbid me to lay a finger on him.' He checked his watch, 4.45 a.m., and prayed that Zara was asleep.

'You *can* help me.' She paused and inhaled deeply. 'I took photos of some of the bruises and cuts he gave me. I don't know why I did it, morbid really, but I did.' She wiped her finger across the squeaky window condensation. 'I hid them in his house. He goes through my things, but he wouldn't think to look in his own house.'

'And?'

'Well, he told me last night he had got married, I knew it was on the cards, and now he's got a wife he doesn't want to see me again. He tried to strangle me as a threat to keep his beatings a secret.' She rubbed her neck. 'Still hurts. Lucky I didn't bruise'

'And?'

151

'I want the photos back, in case he ever comes back for me. It's my safeguard.'

An ancient park ranger drew up in his Range Rover, suspiciously eyed Jordan's Lexus, then jumped down from his seat holding a pooper-scooper. His job application had insisted on 20/20 vision – he'd assumed for seeking out wild animals, not to hunt for a weasel's stools. He nodded in Jordan's direction, 'Youngsters, I don't know,' and trotted off into a thicket of bushes, his green uniform melting into the leaves.

Cloey continued, 'It's a lot to ask, I know, but I need you to help me break into the house. I feel awful even asking you.'

He shook his head slowly. 'I'd much rather beat him up.'

She took his hand and looked him sadly in the eyes. 'I've lost you, Jordan, I accept that. I've lost the only man on this earth who I truly care about. I've just about learnt to live without you but I can't live in fear of being beaten. I can't make you do it, but, I—'

'I'll do it. Come here.' He cradled her head in his lap, and stroked her long silky brown hair while she cried.

Cloey elaborated on her foolproof plan. She knew the security code and password and only needed Jordan's help to gain entry. Once inside, she would disable the alarm, collect her photos, and leave. Sunday was Sammy's temple day, he rarely missed it, and he would be none the wiser. And if the police did happen to turn up, she would lead them straight to the photographs and see if Sammy still wanted to press charges after that.

Jordan lit a fag and smoked it. 'Give me the address and phone number, I need to scout the place out before Sunday and work out the entry point.' He leant over to the glove compartment and produced a pen and a business card. 'Jot it down, and try to smile, everything will turn out fine.'

She wrote down the address, joyful at how well her plan was panning out. She wondered who would cry the loudest: Sammy's wife or Zara? Both would be losing their men by the time this month was out, and she would have her dream house back.

'You're right, everything will be fine.' She smiled at Jordan. 'So, when can I sleep with you again?'

'Never.'

Her face remained smiling as her thoughts became hateful: That's what you think, Jordy, you criminal. I'm the organ grinder round here, you're just the grease monkey. I decide when we're finished sleeping with each other. And until I've made that decision, you will do as I say, when I say. Got it, crim?

Chapter Fourteen

Kareena lay next to Samir as the morning sun broke through the bedroom curtains. A dancing beam of dust sliced the room in two. She glanced across again, hoping he would join her in the land of the living. It would be nice to have an early morning chat in bed before he had to scurry off to NightOwl.

She was beginning to feel at ease with their marriage. Her mum had told her ease wouldn't come easy. 'He could carve you up with a chainsaw on your wedding night for all we know,' she had said, half joking. But the day before Kareena's wedding, she had sat beside her and tried to soothe away some of her daughter's fears.

'We would only choose the best for you. Samir is bright, charming, confident, he is very good-looking and we are sure that even if you had the tools to build a man yourself, you could not build a better one than

Samir. You should have seen the man your sister Avani was trying to have you married off to. He shot his own legs off to claim invalidity benefit and needed a wife to wheel him around.'

Kareena had laughed nervously, but she had still worried. She had wondered when in India's history women and men had lost their desire for romance. Where had the thousands of years hidden the pleasures of true love? The lost treasure of India.

Kareena peered at Samir's flat stomach, watching it rise and fall like a gentle wave on a sea of liquid bronze. The white sheet covered the part she wanted to caress right now, the part which had caressed her last night. Maybe romance was alive and well, she thought, putting her hand under the sheet and eyeing Samir's face stir pleasantly in his dreams.

Her mum had explained that sex was valueless if a man was not fulfilled. To know when a man wanted sex was just as important as to know how to perform it. Sex was all about the little signs he gave out. Kareena stared at the tent rising on the bed in front of her eyes. Surely this was one of those signs, she thought, feeling quite powerful because of her ability to cause such arousal. She watched Samir blink awake.

'I see you're up.' She giggled.

He glared, a powerful anger ripping through his insides. 'If you think I'm excited right now just because I've got a hard-on, think again. I always wake up with one. Ask anyone.'

Kareena shied away from his body. 'I was only . . .'

'This is all moving too quickly for my liking, Kareena, way, way too quick.'

'But we're married. We can't move too quickly.'

'Of course we can. We've got all our lives to do this. It's not a race. Haven't you heard about the tortoise and the hare? Well, Indians are tortoises.'

He pushed her away and jumped out of bed on to the carpet of clothes. He picked up a sock and slam-dunked it over his erect willy, still fuming. The last thing he remembered about last night was a brief picture of himself collapsing on the floor after sex like a stringless puppet. Now the morning had arrived, so, too, had the regrets. And regrets always lead to more regrets.

'I can't just drop my standards like that. We're not your typical English couple who wake up to some rumpy pumpy. We're Indians, and Indians make money. Now, do you want some breakfast?' he asked. 'Or not.'

She turned her head away from his nakedness now that his bitter tongue had turned his sexy body into a hideous turn-off. 'I'm not going to ask you if I have done anything wrong, because I know I haven't. So why don't you just naff off to work,' she said, throwing on her blue satin nightgown and leaving the room feeling cheated.

And Samir stood on the balcony feeling like the cheat.

He chewed on some facts as the sun painted tree shadows on the lawn. Cloey had become all the missing parts his life had needed. She had grown so deeply into his world that his veins sometimes seemed filled with her blood as well as his own. Samir found a loose piece of stone from the plant pot and tossed it at a hedge below, the noise scared a bird in a birch tree about a hundred yards away. This was as confusing a time in his life as ever there could be.

Last night Cloey had believed he was going to say the words that would bring shame to all who heard them. Last night he had been ready to tell his parents that he wanted out of this marriage; but instead he had made love to his wife, and for the first time had enjoyed it.

He remembered often saying to his brother that making love to a woman you hadn't chosen for yourself could never be *enjoyable*. Ajay had agreed, but his principles thrust deeper, and he had shown more guts than Samir when arguing with their parents. Ajay had always waged a war against his parents: attacking the values they held; explaining that taking away choice from a human being, taking away his freedom to choose his own wife, was like trying to remove a natural instinct. It was wrong and nature would prove it.

'And is it wrong to take away the razor blade from an infant because the infant chose it over the toy car?' his mother had replied. 'Are we wrong, your father and I? Are your uncles and aunts and grandparents all wrong? And the five hundred million other Indians of the present and the billions of other Indians of the past, are they all wrong as well? Hey, Ajay, are we all wrong?'

'Yes.'

'We didn't travel halfway round the globe so you could become white. Now let me watch *EastEnders* in peace. Dad will be back with fish and chips soon.'

Samir didn't like the idea of being gutless. He disliked being *thought* of as gutless even more. And as

157

he was the eldest child his responsibility was therefore the greatest. Any bad habits picked up by his brother and sisters would automatically be blamed on him. He was forever trying to convince his parents that his sisters and brother had minds of their own.

It had been a very testing time for him when his brother had come home from school one day wearing a white frilly blouse. Samir had tried to explain to his parents the theory of New Romantics and how this phase of Ajay's might worsen: how make-up was now as important to a young man as football. But explaining to Indian parents that one day their youngest son might come through the front door dressed like a complete queer was not easy. Especially when Ajay sat eating poppadums dunked in jam, wearing a white silk scarf round his neck listening to Tainted Love on repeat, with glitter on his eyelids. A very testing time indeed. Samir pulled the sock off his cock and headed into the shower.

Maybe a deluge of water would save him from having his mind completely flooded by guilt. As the streaming hot spray jetted against his face, he wondered if there was any possible way he could leave Kareena, live with Cloey and keep his family happy without the liberal use of Prozac.

The fact was that the two women in his life deserved a man – not a gutless wuss. Both were probably better off without him. He'd made a promise to Cloey, and like a wimp he'd broken it. Pictures of Cloey waiting by the phone, counting the minutes, biting her nails, began to fill his head. When he was gasping for air and Kareena was screaming with delight, Cloey must have been checking text on

TV to make sure that Milton Keynes had not been hit by an asteroid. While he was snuggling up to Kareena and promising her that life would only get better, Cloey must have been going out of her mind with worry. Samir grabbed a towel; he needed to hear her voice.

He dialled her number from his mobile while drying his backside with the towel.

Claudette answered in her squeaky phone voice and explained that Cloey was not available at the moment.

Samir spoke quietly, 'It's important, Claudette.'

'So's my birthday, but you never send me a card. Anyway, she's in bed asleep. Poor little mite didn't get in till gone six this morning. I have strict instructions not to disturb her.'

'But . . .'

She squeaked loudly, 'Even by you, Samir.'

His thoughts became rotten. Samir strode out to the balcony and raised his voice, 'Look you little stirrer, just put her on the fucking phone.'

'More, Samir, talk dirty to me more. Say the C word, please.'

He held his anger. 'Catholic! Now please get me Cloey, Claudette.'

'Hang on.' A minute later she returned. 'She's asleep. She's out of it.'

The rotten thoughts had won, Samir feared the worst. 'She hasn't taken an overdose, has she?'

Uncontrollable laughter purged Samir's ears. 'As if she'd take an overdose over *you*. You could die tomorrow, Samir, and she wouldn't miss a wink of sleep. In fact . . . she's over you.' Claudette paused and enjoyed the silence. 'She came in smelling of aftershave this morning. Stayed out all night with a man. She had a shower as soon as she came in . . . and we all know that only means one thing, doesn't it, Samir? So, you just stay with your little Asian wife and let Cloey enjoy her new man.' The line went dead.

Samir angrily threw the towel, it landed in the garden.

Kareena watched the towel land from the kitchen window.

The Germans were here.

Chapter Fifteen

Aileen, Cloey's mother, saw old age as the height of respectability. It was certain proof, in her eyes, that the Lord was keen to keep you hanging around. Scanning the obituaries for pre-1900 birthdays was a favourite hobby of hers, and she dreamed one day of receiving the telegram from the queen herself. Or from the king if the queen was dead. Or from Camilla if the king was dead or . . . It didn't matter. She just wanted the fucking telegram.

But being old was not about being wrinkly, she thought, grabbing a tiny straw basket filled with life-extending vitamins from her kitchen cabinet. Little did they know in the village that she was taking a concoction of minerals and amino acids which kept her skin looking as tight as a drum while that of the rest of the women in the community looked like paint on a battered barge boat. When your hormones begin to pack up, the body becomes a guest house to its new lodgers; arthritis, osteoporosis, toilet troubles and BMS – Bitter Mouth Syndrome. Aileen looked at the label on her last pot, Ornithine Alpha-ketoglutarate, it sounded mightily impressive, so she swallowed a couple of tablets. As she waited for her body to absorb them, she checked out her complexion in the hallway mirror. Mightily impressive. She was looking younger already.

And fitter already, she thought, as she marched briskly towards the church holding a cardboard cake box, with her pulse meter not hitting above 100-bpm all the way. She'd walked this route ten thousand times, and she knew the exact atomic structure of every single house that lined the path. If a front door had been painted or a flower had died, she'd know. She was the ears and the eyes of the village. Nothing could escape her subconscious surveillance – apparently.

Among the smell of wild flowers and berries that cloaked the gardens of the Holy Cross Church, a pungent twist of Dulux outdoor paint scuffed the air. Jordan was whistling along to Kylie Minogue – 'Can't Get You Out of My Head' – as the radio blasted from on top of Mr Reeve's headstone. The white paint on the church fence had gone through puberty this morning, paint-brush hairs sprouted from beneath his sloppy paintwork. But Jordan was beyond caring, he wasn't getting paid, he wasn't getting job satisfaction, but he was getting hot. Removing his Airwalk snowboarding T-shirt, and placing it to dry on Mrs Reeve's headstone, he spotted Darth Vader approaching.

'Oggy oggy oggy, Aileen.' Jordan waved.

Ignoring him, she opened the gate and walked up the small path which circled the church.

Father Luke was down on one knee dead-heading flowers with his secateurs. Aileen crept up behind him and rattled the cake box in his ear, making him jump and nearly slice off a finger. The bald patch on his perfectly round head changed from its usual pink to match the crimson colour of the roses. She'd heard of people beginning to look like their pets before, but to look like your plants – well, it was a new one on her. Then she thought of Julia Roberts and that Venus flytrap mouth of hers. Maybe not so new.

'Lovely morning, don't you think, Father Luke?' she said, cupping a beefy yellow rose and sniffing.

He stood up. 'We're blessed, Aileen, that we are. I'm glad you've found the time for our chat.'

Aileen extended the box at arm's length, as if she was water skiing. 'I baked these biscuits for you this morning. Your favourite, nuts and chocolate.'

He took them eagerly. 'Thank you. Shall we go inside, Aileen, away from the sound of that racket Jordan insists has to be played to motivate him to paint? I've told him he'll wake the dead.'

The heat blistered outside, but in the Holy Cross Church the air was marble cold. The grey stone walls were built thick and high, supporting the ceiling which was the colour of a storm. And the eyes of Jesus stared down from a six-foot crucifix. They stared down at you and into you.

'I have some troubling news for you, Aileen. It is of a delicate matter. I had intended coming over this evening before the information became common knowledge.' He beckoned for her to sit down on the wooden pew. 'It's regarding your Cloey.'

From church fetes to Sunday prayer, Cloey, in one

way or another, had been a scapegoat for the mothers and fathers of Bruckley. If someone had done something bad, there was always Cloey who had done something worse. Aileen was confident that Cloey never made matters easy for herself. Whether it be using jelly moulds in the shape of a penis for the church fete or sending home-made Christmas cards written in Punjabi to the church devotees wishing them a *baisakhi* New Year, Cloey's track record lapped everyone else's. Except, of course, Jordan's when he had lived here. But he didn't count. Poor people never did in Bruckley.

Aileen felt as though she were about to regurgitate one of her Ornithine Alpha-ketoglutarate tablets as she sat down on the pew with a worrying thump. 'If this is about the asylum seeker, then it was a misunderstanding. She was making greeting cards for him. Quite respectable, nothing awry in that, Father.'

Father Luke shook his bowling-ball head. 'It's about Jordan and Cloey and what they were doing in the church grounds yesterday.' He pulled his cassock to one side and slotted in next to her. 'This is a family church; people come here to pay their respect not to see others in compromising positions, Aileen.' He stared ahead. 'A very delicate matter this one, Aileen. A very delicate matter indeed.'

She laughed nervously. 'Jordan? No, no, you must be mistaken, Cloey despises him.'

Father Luke glanced quickly into all the corners of the church, then he turned and lifted his chin. 'Fellatio, Aileen. Fellatio. In my church grounds.'

She swallowed hard. 'No, not my Cloey.'

He opened the box of biscuits and began to nibble

on the end of a nutty hob nob. 'I saw it with my own eyes. Jordan had his shorts to his ankles.' He nibbled some more. 'Your Cloey bent down and . . . fellatio, Aileen, in God's back yard. She even blasphemed harshly before she took to her knees.'

Aileen crossed herself and tried to take stock of the situation, sensing the eyes of the Lord judging her from the blues, reds and yellows of the stained-glass windows. She could see her 'Reserved for Aileen' place card being removed from God's round table. This was hellfire with knobs on.

She calmed her breathing, her pulse meter now close to 150-bpm. She should be dead. She wanted to be dead. Forget the telegram, forget Miss Granny Glutes 2025, forget it all.

Through echoing sobs, she sniffed out a few words. 'You . . . mustn't tell any . . . one. Please!'

Father Luke patted her on the back. 'These things are sent to try us. Be strong, Aileen, I want you to be strong. Do you think you can do that for me?'

'I'll try.' She sniffed again.

Father Luke focused on the crucifix. 'Good, because I have to tell you that Olivia knows. She was placing flowers on her husband's grave.' He closed his eyes. 'Lovely flowers. And then . . .' He looked at Aileen, his bushy eyebrows climbing his forehead like two worn paint rollers.

'No, not Olivia.'

'Yes, I'm afraid she saw the indecent act. The tattoo on Jordan's buttocks will forever haunt her more than the . . . Let me make you a nice cup of hot tea and we can pray together.'

*

Welcome to my zoo, thought Kareena, watching Samir screech out of the drive in the Merc. The housewife zoo. A symbolic cage of loneliness could sometimes be worse than real shackles and bars. And even though this was only her first week of marriage, Kareena could already feel the boredom nibbling at her sanity. Nibbles which could easily lead to bites. Until one day, possibly next week, her sanity would all be eaten and she would be Kareena the-no-brain-foaming-at-the-mouth vegetable. Simply put, she would become a run of the mill housewife.

She sneered at Samir's towel, rumpled and drying in the midday sun. No matter what, she decided, there was no way she was picking that towel up off the grass, especially after his grumpy attitude this morning. It could change from towel to turf, for all she cared, because right now she didn't give a toss what the rules were for a good Indian wife.

Mum had warned her always to clear up after Samir, 'Apart from days when you are in childbirth, you must always attend to his mess without a fuss.' But Kareena knew of the consequences of letting a man become used to things being cleared up after him. Some of her relatives in Leicester would actually wait outside the toilet while their husbands did their business, then they'd run right in with the toilet brush at the ready to clear away his bum soot. Kareena climbed the stairs. A woman should not have to go anywhere near a man's bum soot. It was bad enough she had to go near her own, she thought, admiring the captivating landscape spread out before her through the massive arched window at the top of the landing.

Kareena loved her new house. It was like a new

friend who she knew would become very close. It sat proud in Applecroft, with a view that screamed *paint me* to worthy artists. Each room felt planned, meticulously arranged, so that only an acute eye would spot the details that tied it all together. Kareena wandered round the rooms, subconsciously collecting all the clues and sending them to the suspicious part of her brain: man management. The colours and cushions, the placing of lamps, the odds and sods, the vases, pictures, ornaments, dried flowers, the bed. It all looked so perfect and ready for a newly married couple to move into, clink champagne glasses and toast the future. It all looked perfect except for one thing: she hadn't chosen a single item, not *one* single thing had been her choice. It was as though this house already belonged to a different couple. For all she knew Debbie Magee and Paul Daniels lived in one of the spare rooms. The idea amused her.

Not a lot.

She sat down on the cool leather sofa drinking Colombian coffee, mulling over the facts. Samir's explanation why the house had a feminine feel was simple – he boasted that keeping the reins on his galloping artistic talent was like trying to tame a wild stallion. He was, quite simply, a genius, and kept referring to how amazed she would be when she saw the owl on his NightOwl sign. 'The detail in the Uzi guns will blow you away,' he had said. 'It's a wonder we don't have owls trying to mate up on that roof it looks so realistic.'

Kareena sipped her coffee. Painting guns on owls was one thing, but crocheted tampon-box holders was quite another. There was more to this house than met the eye. And there was one room in this house that shouldn't have met her eye. Why hadn't Samir painted over the freaky murals in the spare room? Who in their right mind would keep a room with a sign over the door that said, 'Watch your step. It could be your last'. God, this house gave rise to a lot of questions. She wished the walls could talk.

She walked to the window and pulled the netting to one side. The black and white rogue cat, now christened Streakers, was jumping and twisting, trying to add a Red Admiral to his butterfly collection. As Kareena pressed her nose to the glass and watched the tumbling cat become frustrated, the smell of Windolene rebounded off the pane and Kareena's mind became suspicious again. This place was so clean. The frame of the window was immaculate, the netting whiter than white. Behind the TV, clean. Under the sofa, clean. Even the top of the door frame was clean.

But men were not supposed to be this clean. Cavemen left bones to be cleared up, Henry VIII chucked chicken on the floor, Sid Vicious spat at his fans. They put ferrets down their trousers, they collected fungi on their feet, they grew maggots, fished with maggots, they are maggots. Dirty grimy filthy men. Don't you just love them? she thought.

As she sipped her coffee, her eyes noticed another interesting thing. Sitting right there in her hands was a Botanic Garden's mug. Samir was more of a plastic-beaker man, she guessed. Only someone with a womb would have chosen a Botanic Garden's mug. It was nearly time to overreact. But first she needed permission from her sister, Avani. The last time Kareena overreacted she had nearly been sacked from her teaching post. The headmaster had asked her to wipe off the red dot on her forehead and she'd replied, 'Pass me the Tipp-Ex, you oaf.'

Sitting at the bottom of the stairs, she dialled Avani's mobile. 'Can you talk?'

Avani was filling samosas with vegetables. Her parents had told her to study at school. 'Study hard, Avani, or you will end up with a rubbish job.' That's what all Indian parents say, she'd thought. I will prove that Indians *can* make it without *Letts Study Guides* or revision. Unfortunately, her exam results had concluded otherwise and she soon became known as, 'The dopey Indian girl who fills samosas down at the samosa factory.' Her parents were disgusted with her. If only she had studied.

Avani put the phone between her neck and shoulder and carried on stuffing the pastry triangles while she talked. 'What's up? Missing your little sister already?'

Kareena paused at the accuracy of the shot. 'Sort of. I miss you all a bit.'

Avani dropped a samosa, kicked it towards Ranjit, who picked it up and added it to her pile. 'How's Samir? Has he hit you yet?'

'Not yet, but . . .'

'But, he threatened to hit you?'

'No. Stop talking about violence.' Kareena paused. 'He was off with me this morning for no reason. I told him to naff off.'

'Oh shit, time to find yourself a good solicitor. I see a divorce looming, Kareena. Take the silver and hide it.'

'This is serious, Avani. I don't want to put a foot wrong. That comment just slipped out, I couldn't stop it; what if next week the F word comes out. I'll be so embarrassed.'

'I haven't got a fucking clue what word you're talking about, Kareena, not a fucking clue,' she said laughing and accidentally spitting into the vegetable mix.

'Oh . . . just . . . forget it. I had something else to tell you as well.'

Avani calmed down instantly. 'Go on, sis, seriously, you know I'm a good listener. Fire away.'

Kareena wondered if she should speak her thoughts aloud then she remembered how Avani was an expert at diffusing worry. 'This may sound silly, but I think Mum and Dad have lied to me about Samir.'

Avani adjusted her hair net. 'Seriously? Like, lied in what way?' She was about to make a joke about Samir and a GBH record, but thought better of it.

'They told me, and Samir himself told me, that I was the only girl he had seen. I was told he hadn't shown any interest in any other girls his parents had in mind for him.'

Avani was impatient. 'Yes, so what's the lie? What's the big conspiracy?'

'Don't laugh, but this house, everything about it, was meant for another woman. I think Samir already had his heart set on another bride. Then, as their wedding approached, he decorated the house to her taste, or they decorated it together, who knows? And then . . .'

Avani was intrigued. 'What?'

Kareena went red with embarrassment. 'She died.' There was a hush down the line until Kareena prompted. 'So?'

Muffled laughter. 'So, you're reserve?'

'Yes, I was second choice and that's why the wedding was such a big rush, and that's why he loves leaving me on my own, and that's . . .' She began to cry. 'He will never love me, Avani. His true bride is now dust and ashes. His heart will always be hers.'

The muffled sobs became hysterical. Avani found it very hard to sympathize with someone whose fears were all in their imagination. But she had a soft spot for Kareena, so she tried to ease her mind. 'He's a bastard.'

Kareena sniffed. 'Do you think I'm going mad?'

Avani ducked from a flying samosa. 'Look, I'm going to have to go.' She nodded her head at her supervisor. 'I don't know what bedtime stories he's reading you, but, can't you accept that he decorated the house for you? You should really be talking to him, not me. Maybe—' The phone went dead.

'Bye, Avani.'

Kareena stood up and walked out to the garden, dragging a stool behind her. She smiled as she saw the bulky body of Streakers laid out on top of the towel. Bless, cats had it so easy, she thought. Streakers proudly turned round with a butterfly wing hanging from his mouth, the makings of a smile hidden beneath his long whiskers. The remains of a Red Admiral hors d'oeuvres lay in his stomach. Not so bless.

She sat on the stool soaking up the UV rays. Avani had shaken away some doubts. Maybe it was time to talk to Samir and ask him once and for all what the deal was with the house. It was also apology time. She felt bad for speaking disrespectfully to him. But there was naff all she could do about that until she saw him tonight.

Or maybe there was. She got off the stool and dragged it back into the house. It was about time she saw NightOwl and the Uzis for herself.

Chapter Sixteen

Jordan wiped his brow and squinted at the sun floating with its orange burn just above the church spire. The church roof sloped unevenly down on one side, as though it had had a stroke. Jordan tutted; they still hadn't fixed it. For years they'd been promising the village they would, squeezing pennies from everyone's pockets to raise funds. Even as a youngster he could remember the rattle of the collection box being thrust in his face. And some people could remember the face of the youngster who ran off with the rattling collection box over twenty years ago. *2000 AD* magazines were far more important to a seven-year-old kid than any crummy God-box.

Two hours had passed since Aileen had entered the church with Father Luke. Him above was missing out on a tremendous opportunity, thought Jordan, it was the perfect time for the roof to collapse. He stamped his trainer down on the paint-tin lid and lit up a fag. Sometimes the strain of trying to skive out of work was harder than the work itself. Most of the morning and some of the afternoon he'd been walking backwards and forwards doing nothing in a cemetery where there was nothing doing. He was beginning to regret having volunteered to paint the fence. The novelty of Jordan's Crusade was wearing as thin as his turpentine and he could hear his ice mountain calling. What he wouldn't give now to be chasing gravity down the snow slope.

He pulled out another Coke from his cool box and gulped a fizzy mouthful. Fizzy Coke, flat Jordan. The Coke tasted the same as yesterday's, and the sun was as hot as yesterday, even the huge painful burp he did sounded the same as yesterday. But today he was a different man. Today he was a cheat. And he couldn't feel any flatter than that.

When he'd crept into the house in the early hours of the morning his attention had been arrested by a rather angry, upset-looking Zara waiting on the sofa, tucked up in a duvet, snivelling into a tissue.

'I thought you'd had an accident, Jordy. Why didn't you take your mobile with you? Why didn't you ring?'

And it was in that statement that his lie was born. He'd explained with as much sincerity as he could, that Clarice, Chastity or Clingfilm – whatever her name was – had begun to feel faint. He'd had no choice but to take her to hospital where they waited in the out-patients for nearly four hours. He hadn't liked to phone Zara in case he woke her. The worst part of it all was that Zara believed the lie so easily. She hadn't even put up a fight, which proved she trusted him wholly. It proved she trusted a lying cheat.

Jordan crunched up the Coke can. It was time to investigate the happenings inside the church. He'd once seen an episode of *Inspector Morse* where the vicar killed people. He'd once seen *Songs of Praise* and wanted to kill himself. He took a quick look at the two planks of wood he had managed to paint today and headed for the church door.

There was something enticing about catching someone out. At school, he and his classmates were sure that Mrs Birkwood, the history teacher, had false teeth. Proof was all they needed, so they started a rota of getting up extra early to get to school in the hope that they would catch her in the process of filling her mouth with dentures. A month passed without any proof. Jordan suggested to a close-knit group of friends that his reputation was at stake here and if proof of her dentures did not come quickly then they would all be a laughing stock. Jordan, as always, had the solution. 'We knock her teeth out.'

Catching Mrs Birkwood out was one thing, but catching Father Luke with holier than thou Aileen in a compromising position would be halfway to paradise. Jordan chucked away his fag and sneaked open the aged oval door, thanking God for the silence of the hinges. Dropping to all fours, he crept like a dog into the main entrance of the church, where the voices of Father Luke and Aileen overlaid the slapping of his palms on the cold stone of the floor. He guessed by the clarity of their conversation that they were only a few feet away. Leaning against a supporting pillar, he decided to listen in to what no doubt would be a boring bunch of codswallop . . .

'Fellatio, Aileen, fellatio.'

'I know. Fellatio.'

'I only pray that Our Lady was blinded by the severity of the sun when the obscene act was in progress.'

Jordan peeped round, his body cramping with the effort of withholding his laughter. Only a halo's toss away from the altar were the two people he hated the most talking about what he loved the most – blow jobs. There was a God after all. He was in paradise. If he held his laugh in any longer, he was liable to send a volley of snot across the church.

Finally, he could control himself no longer and he staggered to his feet. 'I'm amazed, Aileen. I didn't even know you had the guts to put the word in your mouth, let alone a cock.' He paused briefly to see what effect he was having. 'Fellatio, Aileen. Don't let me interrupt you two, you just carry on with your sordid conversation. I'll pray later. Mum's the word.' He winked at Aileen and whispered to her under his breath, 'How much?'

'HOW DARE YOU!' she screamed.

A beeping noise seemed to be coming from Aileen's wrist – her pulse meter was going haywire, warning of impending death. Jordan saw the frenzy in her eyes. He'd seen *that* look in Cloey's eyes before. It meant, in the words of *Robocop*, 'Trouble'. He legged it out of there.

Jordan frantically opened the Dulux can with a screwdriver, sending a slurry of undercoat on to Mrs Reeve's headstone and his drying T-shirt. He heard a tittering of laughter as he began to paint the fence and soon realized that it was himself.

Footsteps approached with such speed that he

expected a sonic boom to follow. His nervous excitement was overcome by curiosity of what her face looked like, and more importantly – he strained his ears – had she brought the biscuits with her?

Jordan had a love–hate relationship with Aileen's cookies. He loved the taste, but he hated who baked them. Even when he was just thirteen, Aileen had made Jordan feel unwelcome. It was the little things she said, 'I was in labour for twenty hours with my Cloey. I did not go through all that pain for you to latch on to her, Jordan.'

Unfortunately, Aileen was an inescapable part of Jordan's life. Without her, Cloey and he would never have been together. And in another context, without her, Cloey and he might well still be together. He was quite aware of a mum's propensity to wrap her daughter in cotton wool. But barbed wire? With a minefield and a forty-foot moat? It was a wonder they had ever managed to get up to what they did – and sometimes right under Aileen's pointy little nose, too, the interfering witch.

But dwelling on the past is as pointless as dreaming of the future; prison had taught him that. Endless letters to Cloey detailing his dreams of their future together. Words he would never write to another woman. All as dead and meaningless as the words inscribed upon these gravestones that no one ever bothered to read.

Jordan could feel Aileen's eyes boring into his bare back, hotter than the sun, more intense than a supernova.

'I want a word with you. Put down that brush,' she demanded.

He turned, grinning, dropped the brush in the tin, and flipped a fag in his mouth. 'Aileen, I suggest you warm up your cranky old knees before kneeling down for a blow job.' He lit the fag.

'They should have thrown away the key. Devil's Island, that's where you should be.'

'Where's your Christian spirit? Forgiving and forgetting.'

She stood closer. 'I have my own interpretation of the Lord's words, Jordan.'

He offered her a puff on his fag. 'And I'm sure the Lord has got his own interpretation of you, you old cow. Now let me get on with my work.' He turned his back on her and picked up the paint brush. 'Cheerio.'

Aileen had spent most of her life trying to avoid men like Jordan. And if by chance men like him crossed her path, then it should be her snubbing him and not him snubbing her. 'Cheerio'. How dare he! She could see, in her peripheral vision, a young couple attending a grave. This was a place of peace, a place of mourning, a place of remembrance. Oblivious, Jordan sang along to 'Mr Bombastic' on his radio, slapping on paint, wiggling his bottom in time to the music.

A place for a clip round the ear. 'Sinner.' She hit him firmly on the head. 'Have you no respect?' She bent down, picked up the neon-blue plastic radio and deftly removed the batteries. The music died.

Jordan spun round. 'I'm not even going to ask you why you want the batteries, Aileen. No doubt you've got your own interpretation of what construes heaven. I'm more of a hands-on man myself, don't like gadgets.' He dug deep for a nasty. 'Penis envy, I think they call it.'

178

Aileen's pulse meter was bleeping again. 'I'm warning you, stay away from my Cloey.'

Her eyes stared fixedly at his tanned bare chest. Oh, what she would do to have young skin like that again. She thought of Maxwell, her husband, with his wide girth. His skin was reptilian now, with bulbous fat cells like cellulite chain-mail covering every inch. And his appendage, his manhood, was withered and dry like autumn's last leaf; it hung with two raisins in a scaly elf's rucksack.

Her gaze dipped down to the top of Jordan's shorts, just above his lunchbox. She felt repulsed that her daughter had been near that. Repulsed, but in some ways, envious.

'No more shenanigans with my Cloey,' she barked, her eyelids sliding slowly over her black pupils. 'Have you no shame? This is where your own mother lies buried, God rest her soul. And it is here that you decide to force my daughter to her knees and demand her to perform all sorts of sexual acts upon you. It will not do, do you hear me? It will not do. Do you understand?' She shook a shiver from her body. 'Father Luke was gravely distressed.'

'Gravely, isn't that what you have on your Sunday roast?' He flinched in case she hit him again. 'Listen here, you antiquated turnip picker. I haven't even begun with your daughter, not even started yet. Her body, her virginity, is mine. I will not be denied my legacy.'

Aileen stepped forward and grabbed Jordan's wrist. 'Over my dead body.' She glared at him. 'Scum, all of your family, scum.'

He yanked his arm away and rubbed his chin as if

thinking. 'Can't decide where I'm going to fuck her first. I want to make it special for her, you know, especially as it's her first time. Really special.' His fingers massaged his chin roughly. 'I'm going to make her go to bed thinking about me.' He grabbed his crotch like Michael Jackson. 'I am going to have so much fun with your virgin Cloey. And there will be nothing you can do, do *you* understand, Turnip Picker?'

She eyed him down her nose. 'I will pray for your painful death tonight.' And she walked away .

Jordan waved goodbye enthusiastically with his paint brush.

Cloey's throat felt as dry as the toast she was buttering. She sat down in her silk robe, the colour of lemons, and slowly chewed the bread like someone with a bad tooth. The kitchen clock showed 3.00 p.m. and she blew a baby's raspberry at it. 'So what? It's a late breakfast.' Her eyes caught sight of the empty wine bottle. She had consumed the wine at 6.00 a.m. She gave it the middle finger. 'So what? It was an early morning celebration piss up.' Jordan was hers again and with his help, Sammy and the house would be hers again too. It was only surprising that she hadn't drunk more.

Being intimate with Jordan had proven one thing. Once you've tried the best you're never satisfied with less. Ever since Jordan had been in prison, her orgasms had never had that certain 'Oh my God I don't care if the world ends right now because I'm on a different planet anyway' feeling. There had been times in their past when all she could think about for the entire day was the sinful feeling he would give her when she next saw him. Those were long days.

Last night on that cold, grassy hill, in the presence of nothing but the stars in the sky, he had showed he still loved her. She could tell Zara would never have received the attention she had received by the Pagoda. There was no way a man could look *that* way at two women. But he was a criminal. And he was unreliable. And he didn't have that beautiful house.

She dragged her feet to the kitchen door. The warm country air, like an invisible wall of cow dung, struck her nose as soon as she opened the door. The birds stopped singing, waiting to see what mood she was in today. She strolled across the garden barefoot and stared back at the cottage, its thatched roof and white walls presenting the cosiest of pictures.

If a woman in a straw hat with a basket of blackberries had emerged from the bushes and gone inside, you wouldn't have been too surprised. Except that a picky historian might query the satellite dish on the roof, and the burglar alarm camouflaged in bright red, and the fact that the bushes had never produced blackberries since Claudette poured her hair peroxide on the roots, and that the house was home to – she thought of Claudette's one-night stands, she thought of having sex with Jordan in the Pagoda a few hours back – the idyllic cottage in respectable Bruckley was home to two slappers. The birds began to sing.

After showering, she let the breeze coming through the open bedroom window chase away the wetness from her skin. Mum had always shunned the naked body. 'Make sure that when you finally allow a man to see you, Cloey, you expose yourself little by little.

Never let a man oggle and goggle. Your body took years to get to maturity, don't rush things just to please a lustful man.'

Cloey stood naked as the kind shine of the sun dried the remainder of her toned figure. She thought back to Samir's little by little view of her body as he oggled and goggled, and decided her mother did not have a striptease in mind when she had said those words.

Sitting on the bed with her portfolio of home-made greeting cards, she yawned. Before her lay the huge volume of samples she showed to craft and card shops. The A–Z of cards with a range of fine messages, from anniversaries to the zodiac. She opened the big black leather-bound book to a section which always sold well, the 'I'm Sorry' section. At a guess, 99 per cent were bought by bastard blokes. She admired one of her finest creations: 'I'm Sorry I Slept Around'. It had a humorous drawing of a woman with a guillotine on a man's penis, her words were, 'How sorry?' Cloey giggled and began working on her new creation, noting that her favourite colour next to purple, was running low: blood red.

Two cups of cappuccino later, she marvelled at the result. It had taken nearly an hour. But what's an hour when her whole life was at stake here. She blew on the ink in a rush to hold the picture to the light. Finally, she excitedly viewed her masterpiece: a picture of an Indian woman holding her suitcases and crying on Samir's drive. The inscription said, 'Find Your Own Fucking Man'.

A thunderous knock at the front door made Cloey drop the card. Her mum's voice bellowed through the letterbox. Cloey's nerves ran rampant. If she had bitten her nails, she would be up to her elbows. If she had bitten her toenails, she would be up to her arse. And that's what she was right now, arse over tit, desperately trying to hang up crucifixes before Armageddon Aileen entered.

She smoothed out her short black skirt, put on a fixed smile and opened the front door. 'Hi, Mum. I was just about to make a cup of tea.' She stepped aside to let her mother in.

Aileen stood firm and grabbed her daughter's biceps. 'You're coming with me.' Cloey was dragged into her front garden.

'Mum, you're hurting me.'

'Not as much as you're hurting *me*, young lady.' They bolted up the path.

Being frog-marched up a village road by your own mother at the age of thirty-one was pants. It was more degrading than bio-detergent.

Cloey tried to warn her. 'Mum, watch the—'

'Don't you "watch the" with me young—' Squelch. Dog shit. Squelch. Both trainers.

Cloey eyed Aileen worriedly as she scraped the muck off her trainers. It was almost a shame she wasn't wearing open-topped sandals. Something in her mother's attitude warned Cloey to tread very carefully. Then she spotted another mess and spoke softly, 'Do you know your clothes are covered in white paint?'

Aileen stopped picking the sticky pooh off her shoes with a stick. She glanced up. 'That peasant boy, Jordan!'

Cloey's jaw slackened somewhat. 'As in, Jordan the criminal?'

Aileen's look said it all – a look torn straight from the pages of Cloey's youth. 'Stay away from him. He was bad news then, he's bad news now.' Aileen spoke, 'And before you think I haven't noticed, young lady, you stink of the bottle. And your skirt speaks of prostitution.' Her strong hand gripped her daughter's wrist tight and mean, like an armwrestler's. 'Sinner!'

The house of dread loomed up ahead. Cloey was coming home again for the second visit this week. And this time she knew it had nothing to do with asylum seekers.

Chapter Seventeen

Every workplace has an idiot. The boss knows who he is. The employees knows who he is. Even the cleaner knows who he is. Only, the idiot doesn't.

Mickey knocked on Samir's office door. 'You called, Chief?' He stared at his boss quizzically. 'Looking a bit peaky, Chief. You coming down with Chinese flu?'

Samir pointed to the seat opposite him and Mickey sat. 'How much did you hear?' he asked, referring to the conversation he had just had with Kareena on the phone. A suspicious noise from the extension in the office next door had been clearly audible as the conversation neared its end, along with the sound of Mickey's laughter.

To lie or not to lie. That was the question. 'I'm ashamed to admit, Chief, I heard it all.' He chuckled. 'I especially liked the bit when she apologized to you about this morning, saying if you didn't want sex with her then that was your prog . . . prod . . .'

'Prerogative.'

'Prerogative. And then you saying that you *did* want sex with her – classic.' Mickey leaned in. 'I hope you don't mind me saying, Chief, tell me if I'm out of line, but are you two having marital problems already?'

Samir shook his head and noticed Mickey's latest home-made badge pinned to his white shirt. It said, Security God. Last week he'd had, Bodyguard to Shania Twain. Looking for signs of intelligence in Mickey's eyes was as ambitious a project as the Mars Lander mission. Possible, but highly unlikely.

Samir spoke, 'As you already heard, my wife is coming in—'

'Yeah, apparently she wants to clear the air with you. It's a bit unprofessional all this though, don't you think? You said never bring your personal problems into work and now, just because you and your missus are infertile, we have to suffer the indignity of a wife on spec. It's not on, Chief.' Mickey enjoyed humorous banter. 'Maybe Mick with the biggest dick could . . .' His eyes were quickly drawn to the green and white piece of paper Samir was scribbling on. Upside down in the corner it read 54d. His mind juggled it round to 54p. It worked harder and harder until it finally calculated it was P45. His worry lines emerged. 'No way, Chief. You can't sack me for having a big dick.'

Samir slid the P45 across. 'I'm not sacking you for having a big dick, you idiot. I will sack you though, for being one. Now, this is a warning. Take a good look at it and maybe if you behave yourself over the next month, I'll rip it up.' Mickey nodded, feeling hurt, and Samir checked his watch. 'My wife will be here any minute. I don't want any of your lip with her, understand?'

Mickey stood and pushed his chair under the desk. 'Roger that, Chief.' Just before he reached the door, he thought about the document he would show the tribally . . . tribumall . . . tribunal for unfair dismissal if he was sacked. Samir's letter proved beyond reasonable doubt that he favoured the white woman in bed, but hated the white man in his office. He turned and said, 'I'll makes sure I let all the *Mohammeds* know not to give your wife, *CLOEY*, cheek.' He pulled an imaginary zipper across his mouth. 'Zip service to their lip service. Anyway, time's a-wasting, Chief, I've got to get back to my solitaire before that screensaver wrecks it again.'

Samir followed Mickey into the main office. Three people can suddenly seem very busy when the boss walks in, thought Samir, watching Cathy the wages clerk instantly become obsessed with her calculator. Madeleine was cranking out a letter on the qwerty for the attention of all security guards in relation to a personal hygiene complaint by one of NightOwl's biggest clients. Selwyn, the ex-army security guard, paced the office with his truncheon, ready for emergency call-outs as opposed to emergency call-ups. He did not take prisoners. And judging by the look Madeleine kept giving Cathy, he did not take baths either. Over in the corner, out of harm's way, was Mickey's desk for the day. A pile of envelopes that he should have sealed up hours ago still stood as a pile of envelopes he should have sealed up hours ago.

Mickey pinched a digestive from Cathy's work top and stood deliberately in Selwyn's path. 'Bomb in the hole,' he said, and the whole biscuit disappeared in his mouth.

Samir ordered him to get to his desk and begin licking. His concerns were building quickly. Kareena was due here any second, and Mickey had just mentioned something he shouldn't have been privy to. Cloey was not a name that was safe in Mickey's hands, along with anything sharp, electrical or fish food (Mickey had actually thought he was saving money by feeding his goldfish only half a tub of food a day). Samir didn't know how Mickey had found out about Cloey, but he didn't want this information to go the same way as the fish: belly side up.

He leaned over Mickey's shoulder and whispered harshly, 'You fucking mention Cloey in front of my wife, and I'll zip you into the body bag myself. Clear enough for you, Mickey?'

Samir waited for him to swallow the digestive mush. He wanted to be sure that Mickey's response showed understanding. The same response you might hope for from a child when he is holding an electric bar heater over your bath.

The main door opened, the taxi skidded off, and Kareena walked in tentatively. Samir squeezed Mickey's shoulderblade as a warning, then introduced Kareena to the staff. Cathy and Madeleine sized up Samir's wife. They had often wondered what type of woman he went for and guessed she would be both pretty and slim. They hadn't guessed she would be wearing a sari. Mickey had told them that he knew for a *fact* that saris were only worn when the women were pregnant. And turbans were only worn during Jewish festivals.

Samir led Kareena to his office, shutting the door firmly behind him.

'I saw your owl on the roof. It looks really owly.' Her eyes roamed the small room.

'Thanks.' He pulled a chair out for her and perched his bottom on the window ledge. 'So, what couldn't wait until I got home?'

Kareena began to pick a sequin off her green and gold sari. 'I want to apologize for the way I spoke to you this morning, it was very rude of me. Barely has my henna faded and already I'm disrespectful to you. I don't want our marriage to get off on the wrong foot because of me.' Hard as it was to look him in the eye, her gaze remained fixed on his to show him her sincerity. 'I'm sorry.'

Samir wheeled over his chair and sat next to her, squeezing her hand. The words 'I'm sorry' made him cringe. He knew of uncles who ruled the roost with discipline, control freaks of the highest magnitude. In some houses, a woman is not a woman, a woman is *only* a woman. And in some cases, she's not even only a woman, she's only a womb. Samir sometimes stood back from the crowds of relatives at family gatherings, weddings, engagements, *akhand paths* (religious book readings), and saw mostly tragedy. Women with that same apologetic look in their eyes. 'I'm sorry'. And it always made him cringe. Sorry for what exactly? Sorry I haven't got a prominent Adam's apple and my period comes once a month?

Samir spoke, 'I don't accept your apology, you've got nothing to apologize for. I, on the other hand, have. I'm sorry for snapping at you this morning. I was whacked out.' Lifting up the phone he buzzed through for some coffee, then continued, 'So, you came all the way here to apologize? Or are you checking up on me?' He regretted it as soon as he said it. 'Not that you ever need to check up on me. I wouldn't ever have an aff—' He angrily picked up the phone again. 'Will you hurry with that coffee, Madeleine, for Pete's sake.'

After apologizing for apologizing, Kareena got to the nitty gritty of her other reason for being here. Worry was like food, you leave it too long and it goes bad.

She stared into his eyes. 'I know there's not even a chance in a million, and I feel dumb asking, but I always used to tell my pupils that if you don't ask you never know. So here goes.' She took a deep breath, while Samir held his. 'I want you to tell me the truth. Was there another woman?' She had meant to hold his gaze, but found his shifty eyes unsettling and looked away. God, this was hard. 'Did you set the house up with her? Was I second best? I need to know.'

Samir's thoughts turned to Cloey. There was no such thing as a second best to Cloey: it was her or no one. Deep in his heart he knew now was the time to tell Kareena the truth: how Cloey and he had thrown away the family rule books each of them had been nurtured on; how being happy was more important than being a Sikh or a Catholic; how religion was all very well, as long as it didn't get in the way.

Samir could see the anxiety in Kareena's eyes. He spoke softly, 'Would you understand me if I said I believe that there is only one man for every one woman in this world?' He blinked slowly, glazing the surface of his deep-brown irises.

'How romantic.' She felt the rush of impatience. 'Probably a load of crap, though. But you didn't answer my question. Was there another woman?'

Samir stood up and walked to the small bookshelf. So many great words here, if only he could find a few himself. 'No, there was no special woman before you.' He sat back down. 'Why all the questions?'

'Oh, I don't know. It's a few things.'

'Like what?'

'They say a gay person can spot another gay a mile off, well, a woman can normally spot another woman's touch in a house. And that house is crawling with femininity.'

Samir faked ignorance. 'Now come on, are you saying the house is a bender? I too have my doubts, I thought I saw the summerhouse winking at it the other day.'

She giggled. 'Seriously, did you get an interior decorator in to do it?'

He shrugged, wishing he was white so he could go red. 'All right, you caught me, I am soooo embarrassed. I haven't got a' – he paused to smile – 'I haven't got a naffing clue about decorating. The only thing I know is to make sure you take the furniture out before you lay the carpet. Or—'

They were interrupted by a sharp knock on the door. Madeleine entered carrying a small tray with coffee and biscuits. Kareena could tell by the way Madeleine walked that she liked the way her breasts bounced. But by the way her breasts bounced, it was amazing she could walk at all. Had she not heard of bras? Madeleine fussed over the coffees, poured out the milk, stirred in the sugar. Kareena wondered if she were to put her nails out on the desk whether Madeleine might oblige her with a manicure. It was obvious she hoped the private chat would continue with her in the room. Unsatisfied, she bounced back out.

Kareena took a sip of her coffee, feeling some of her worries about the house dissipate. A word dithered at her lips. A word she could never use in front of her parents, a word she encouraged her pupils to avoid, and yet she found it about to spew. 'Samir, this is going to sound so inappropriate, but, without making a song and dance about, I'm *bored*. Being left in that house on my own is boring. I was wondering—'

He interrupted her, 'You want to go back to teaching brats?' She nodded. 'This is Milton Keynes, you're going to need to know kung fu and get a gun licence.'

She laughed. This arranged marriage was going to be easier than she had envisaged. Samir's attitude was so relaxed, it was not going to be the *Hammer Tandoori House of Horror* she had thought it might. Her mother had warned her always to be careful about voicing her thoughts out loud, never to be carefree. But her mother wasn't married to Samir.

Kareena spoke freely, 'I really want us to become close. I don't want us to be like those zombie couples who hate spending time together and as soon as one leaves the room, the other sticks their fingers up at the door.' She bit on her Jammie Dodger, the jam as sticky as what she was about to say next. 'And I mean it's sort of pointless for me to go back to teaching if you want us to start a family. I was—'

'Stop!' Samir did some semaphore with his hands. Planes bound for Gatwick would now be landing at Heathrow. 'Stop! It's not *my* decision when we start a family, it's *our* decision. Personally, I think we should wait to get to know each other before we think about brats of our own. So if you want to go back to teaching, then feel free.'

Samir felt his veins shrink-wrapping his blood. Sausages of haemoglobin trapped in a guilty man. He stood up and walked over to the year planner, pretending to yearly plan. He cursed his big mouth, the fucking thing kept getting him deeper and deeper in trouble.

He sat back down and looked at his beautiful, sweet wife: how could he betray her like this? She was planning their future life together, while he was already sweeping her into the dustbin of his past. She had floated into his life on the wind of family traditions, now she could float away again on a gust of reality. It wasn't fair, but maybe that's what love was sometimes. Unfair. There was no way he would let Cloey go. He couldn't drop the precious feelings he had for her and swap them for the pocket-sized feelings he held for his wife. It would be like a kid on *SwapShop* swapping his Scaletrix set for a Pop-a-Point pencil. No deal.

Noises in the office next door sounded as though they came from a zoo, and Samir could see doubt in Kareena's eyes about his choice of employees. He shrugged. 'It's because you're here,' he said. 'Good as gold they are normally. Whenever we get guests they always play up.'

She smiled and rose. 'I'm glad we had this chat. I feel a lot better.'

'Me too.' He walked over and hugged her.

But the hug felt false, out of step with his real emotions. This produced nothing like the tide of feelings he experienced when hugging Cloey; he didn't tingle at Kareena's smell, her touch or her curves. This was more like a dull ebb. It felt wrong. This whole marriage felt wrong. You can't just throw two strangers together and expect fireworks. Religion, tradition and culture do not make good gunpowder. Only love does. You just have to hope it doesn't blow up in your face.

Chapter Eighteen

Violence is noisy like the thunder after lightning. Violence is quiet like the spread of disease. Violence is beautiful like the Arctic ice. And violence is torture like the fear of your parents.

Cloey's fear had grown with her, like a wound that won't heal, like the scar of her mother's religious fanaticism. Each birthday she would promise herself not to let her mother walk over her and not to be intimidated by hell. For as she was told repeatedly, hell was where she was heading – to join Peter Stringfellow and the whole cast of *Baywatch Nights* – if she followed the wrong path.

'Take the Bible, Cloey!' ordered Aileen, for the umpteenth time.

The curtain was drawn in the study keeping the sun from fading the wooden-carved face of the Lord. An *Usborne Book of Insects* lay open on the desk, pictures of beetles staring out of the yellowed pages.

A jam jar stood beside it, its lid tight, imprisoning a crawling chafer beetle, and a can of insect spray waited for the executioner's hood to be donned by Aileen. The beetle bided its time, gasping for that eleventh-hour phone call. Otherwise Aileen would bump it off. Stays of execution only came for those beetles who didn't munch on her purple Iris Profiels, and at the moment, the beetle was having a hard time hiding its purple shit behind a leaf.

Cloey remained seated at the edge of the desk, her face adamant, her thoughts stubborn and rigid. The room groaned with pressure, as neither mother or daughter surrendered.

'No, I'm not going through the charade of holding the Bible again,' Cloey began. 'You talk to me like a mother should to her daughter. Like those mothers who don't drag their daughters halfway up the road. Like those mothers who read nice bedtime stories to their children.' She glared. 'I still can't believe you used to tell me stories about children being cooked in ovens. And this bit makes me sick.' She pointed at Aileen's face. 'The kids in your stories always had to be cooked alive in a fucking Aga, didn't they? Couldn't just be a Creda, could it? No, it had to be an Aga.'

Aileen crossed herself quickly, like the slash of *Zorro*. 'Who taught you to swear like that?' Her thin smile emerged to match her squinting eyes. 'It was that no-good, squalid vessel of filth, penniless, second-rate, wretched man, Jordan. Wasn't it?'

Cloey rolled her eyes. 'Of course it wasn't.'

Aileen lunged forward, grabbing Cloey's hair. Her fingers began to twist, pulling at the roots, while Cloey struggled to free herself from the snake-like grip.

'But he taught you something else, didn't he?' Aileen shouted. 'The whole village is talking about it.' She yanked down hard and Cloey yelped as she bent forward. Aileen's eyes were now full of rage. 'He taught you fellatio. My own daughter, in public, in front of Father Luke. You're a complete embarrassment!' Her grip loosened, followed by a slight rush of wind, bringing Aileen's hand smartly round Cloey's face with a trouncing smack. 'Slut!'

Violence is being slapped hard round the face.

It was painful, but that was only skin deep; the hurt inside felt greater. From a child until now Aileen had served her daughter course after course of misery; a banquet of anguish. Cloey used to think her friends at school were holding back on her, keeping their secret of how to keep mummy happy. Maybe they painted prettier pictures or helped round the house more. She tried it all. Until one day, a certain young lad by the name of Jordan gave her a clue, 'Your mum is a first-class weirdo. A religious, demanding freak. Slip her a few sleeping tablets and pray to God she don't wake up.'

But Cloey had defended her mother, explaining that her mum just loved her more than most mums. She was just being over-protective, that's all.

Even now, as Cloey viewed the clump of hair on the floorboards, she knew that Aileen was being over-protective. Before long the cuddles would come, then the tearful apology, then the promises and then the declaration of Aileen's unlimited love for her daughter. 'You're all I've got. I just don't want a man to take advantage of you . . . my Cloey.'

Cloey rubbed her cheek. 'It's not what you think, he

was just showing me the tattoo on his bottom. I swear.' It sounded crap, but the truth did sometimes.

'Liar. He told me today that he was going to take away your virginity. He should be locked up. I thought prison was supposed to reform the disciples of doom. If this was the Isle of Man he would be birched. And I would be there to watch. String him up, I say.'

There was only one way to bring this conversation to an end.

Cloey took the Bible and held it close to her chest. 'I promise you that I am still a virgin and I will not let Jordan take away my cherished virginity. And I did not give Jordan a . . . blow job.' She turned her head to Aileen, keeping her eyes shut. 'Do you want me to add anything, Mum?'

Aileen delayed answering, watching Cloey's angel face. God had blessed her with a beautiful daughter, and He had given responsibility to Aileen to make sure she remained pure and wholesome. It would be a mistake of the highest order to let that wretch Jordan inch his way back into Cloey's life. Give a man like Jordan an inch and he would take a thousand yards.

'Yes, there is an addition I would like you to make, Cloey. I feel Jesus needs something clarifying. Would you care to promise him how you will never speak to Jordan again? And maybe in return he might find you a good man to rid you of the womanly frustrations you must have from time to time.'

Cloey made the promise and stepped forward to receive the loving hug of her mother.

Aileen smoothed down what was left of Cloey's hair. 'You do know I love you, Cloey. Maxwell loves you dearly too.' She paused. 'And I can understand that you may be curious as to a man's middle region. To his appendage. And I would have to be a pretty silly fool if I didn't suspect that you may have come across the odd drawing or the occasional TV programme displaying one. But believe me, Cloey, when you do get a man, he will not stop thrusting it in your body – and it's not at all pleasant. Revolting creatures.' Aileen stepped back from her daughter. 'Don't embarrass me again. You know what this village is like. Gossipmongers all of them.'

Cloey kissed her mother on the cheek and saw sadness beneath her smile. Aileen's eyes closed tightly, pushing back the threatening tears.

'You do know how much I . . .'

'Of course I know, Mum,' said Cloey, resting the side of her head against Aileen's.

Later, in the garden, Cloey unscrewed the lid of the jam jar and watched the beetle scurry away. No one has the right to play God, she thought, staring up at the blue roof of sky. Do they?

Cloey continued on her way home at a leisurely pace away from the place she used to call home. Just a half mile of road between them. Her acquaintances would say how lucky she was to live such a short distance from her mother. Friends knew otherwise though, and called Cloey a 'poor cow'.

The same friends had cheered when Aileen was featured in the village rag. The headline had been, Local Bruckley Woman Receives BANNED *Exorcist* Video Through Post. It was the best thirty quid Jordan had ever spent. He had even included an invoice for six pounds and sixty-six pence payable to the church. Aileen would never sign for a package so easily again. Especially when the sender was called. Dr. F.O. Urskin.

Cloey bypassed the stares of the neighbours and pushed open her garden gate to find smoke surging from the open front door giving the illusion that the cottage was on fire. She took a deep breath and walked through the hall and into the kitchen as the fumes stung her eyes.

Claudette hovered over a colossal frying pan, singing along to 'Diamond Dogs' by David Bowie. A plastic apron picturing a nude man hung off her hips. She was planning a heavy session of booze tonight and needed to line her stomach with Findus Pancakes. Four frozen ham and mushroom pancakes waited on the side to be incinerated, while the oil spat like a snare drum. Claudette held a lump of Anchor butter over the spluttering oil.

'No, Claudette! Dangerous! Put it down! Dangerous!' screamed Cloey, running across to remove the pan off the heat. 'You can mix your drink and you can mix your men, but never, ever, mix your cooking oils unless I'm here to supervise. You can't be trusted. Nutcase.'

The smoke alarm sounded as soon as Cloey put the removed batteries back in. She gave Claudette a further warning – not to let her freshly washed hair drip into the hot oil unless she wanted to turn up for tonight's lucky date carrying half her face in her precious Vivienne Westwood handbag. Claudette replied that she always carried half her face in her handbag, but she understood what Cloey meant. Men were nasty creatures who would surely laugh if her scorched ears fell off during sex. They laughed enough when her ears stayed on.

Opening the back door, Cloey breathed in the warm fresh air. Her mind began mobilizing her thoughts. Mum, Jordan, Samir and Samir's wife; family, ex-boyfriend, future husband and loser. She felt like driving over to Samir's house right there and then, grabbing his wife by the hair and tossing her out – stay away you little Asian concubine! You can't buy Samir's love with blow jobs in the moonlight or by sending him off to work with a packed lunch. I didn't shag him for six years to make him a good lover for you. I was not pussy practice. Get a life, rip up your marriage certificate and bugger off back to mediocre land, you enfeebled cockroach!

Cloey wiped away her silent tears. She couldn't lose Samir. Losing Samir would mean losing the house. Jordan had told her this morning after they had made love that she'd never know what it felt like to lose someone she really loved until she'd lost someone she really loved. He likened it to the film *Hellraiser*: it will tear your soul apart.

She didn't believe in hell or souls, but she did believe in the obvious pain that Jordan had endured when she had told him she no longer loved him. And she was beginning to know what it felt like to lose some*thing* you love. God, she hoped the house was okay.

High up in the clear sky a silent jet drew a straight white line. Cloey watched. Life was all about going somewhere. As soon as you're going nowhere, you're dead. Life was also about direction. Mum had religion to guide her, and Samir had his family. And Cloey? Who or what did she have?

A voice called from above, and Cloey peered up. Dangling out of her bedroom window was a pair of Donna Karan stilettos. 'Can I wear these?' Claudette asked, as her head popped into view. 'You can't even walk in them properly.'

'Will you be dancing?'

'No, just seducing. I feel sorry for the men who stay in tonight. Because men indoors are—'

'Bores. Yes, you can borrow them,' Cloey said, catching the kiss that Claudette blew her.

Cloey smiled at the battalion of empty wine bottles standing to attention on the patio. Repeated requests to Bruckley Parish Council to have a bottle bank put in the garden had been repeatedly turned down. In return they had had the cheek to make a request of their own: would Claudette and Cloey please think more carefully about the colour of the light bulb they chose for their upstairs landing? Red is a colour often linked to prostitution, and the last prostitute in Bruckley was burnt at the stake in 1674. Legend has it, that just before her head exploded in the flames, she shouted out, 'One day I shall return. By the name of Ann Widdecombe.'

Cloey turned to head back in, when something caught her eyes: a mass of bright-red roses bundled together like firewood lay propped against the wall just to her right. Her heart thumped in time to Claudette's music. She knew instinctively they were from Samir. Maybe life was not just about direction and going somewhere, maybe it was also about signs: life's highway code.

She quickly counted the roses, good luck only came in even numbers. That's why being single was bad luck. Thirty-six in total. A bush's worth. Each one dripping with beauty and a fragrance that won smiles and lost heartbeats. There was nothing more romantic than roses, she thought, clutching them to her chest. Nothing more romantic than – she stared at the envelope which was slipped between the wet stalks – nothing more romantic than the words that came with them.

Placing the flowers down on the kitchen table, she gently opened the peach-coloured envelope. The writing on the matching paper was neat, thoughtful and not rushed. The words were meant to be read slowly.

Dear Cloey,

Once upon a time I fucked up. I once saw a news article about a surgeon who amputated the wrong leg. Well, I fucked up worse than that. A half-sighted man saw half a sign which read, 'Hazard' so he put on his hazard lights and drove off the cliff. I fucked up worse than him. I even saw an Indian man who had it all. A woman he loved infinitely and who loved him in return. A future that burned brighter than the North Star. A woman he called his own but foolishly gave up for someone else. I didn't fuck up worse than him. I am him.

I want us to be as we were. Only trouble is, I am married. I want you to understand that I thought I would be able to give you up. I thought that I would be able to follow the road of

*Indians. Otherwise I wouldn't have married.
And the reason I didn't tell you was that I wanted
to hang on to you until the last possible moment.
I once knew a man who was selfish. I am him.*

*I know I have hurt you beyond repair, Cloey.
I will understand if you don't wait for me. And I
will understand if you hate me. I will understand
if you don't even read this. I'm an understanding
guy – joke. Please let me sort this mess out and
wait for me. Just give me some space. I will make
it up to you, I promise.*

I love you, Cloey.

Sammy X X X

She glared in disbelief at the kisses at the bottom.
He normally did eight; three was unlucky. Surely the
little time away from her had not shrunk Samir's love
from eight kisses to three. She dropped the paper onto
the table and crossed her arms. One foot tapped as her
eyes stared, unblinking, at the low ceiling. For once
she didn't care that Claudette said she looked just like
her mother in that stance. The burning question was
simple; had Samir's love for her been stolen slightly by
his wife? Had Samir forgotten the other five kisses
because his wife was meaning more to him? Was
Samir's wife the owner of five kisses while she owned
just the three?

'Do you want me to bin the roses?' Claudette asked,
traipsing in, stinking of perfume. She picked up the
bunch and sniffed. 'I take it they're from the deserter?'

'In fact they are from a man who loves me so much
he is willing to change his religion, thank you.'

Claudette snorted. 'Forget him, he's dishwater.

204

He's another one of those . . . men. I just can't wait for the day that doctors can sew dicks on wallets. Because that's all men are good for. Cocks and money.'

'He wants me to wait for him. He says he's messed up and will make it up to me.'

Claudette forced out a laugh. 'I'll be honest with you, Cloey. If you were ugly I'd say he left because you're ugly, and if you were fat then I'd say it's because you're fat. As it is, you're neither.' She leaned against the kitchen cupboard. 'Have you looked in the mirror lately? He left because you're not Indian.' Claudette spat on her fingers and rubbed dirt off her heel. 'I'm not an expert or anything, but these people like to stick together. He used you.'

Cloey folded the letter into a dart. 'He didn't use me; he's in love with me. And love makes you colour blind, so there.' She threw the dart and it glided over Claudette's head. 'His family put him under a lot of pressure, you know. It's just like my mother, but ten times as bad. He doesn't want to hurt them. They pressurized him into this marriage; he would never have gone through with it otherwise. But he realizes now that he can't live without me and, if anything, it's made us stronger.'

Claudette applied her eighth coat of frosted-pink lippy and smacked her lips together. 'But you're not even together. He goes to bed with another woman every night, not you. Anyway, I'm running late. Don't do anything stupid.' She made for the door. Then, just before slutting off, she turned back. 'Say what, why don't you just pick up another man with money? That's what you do, isn't it? Tutty bye.'

As Claudette slammed the front door, Cloey

thought fondly of her friend and how positive she always was. She was like one of those Weebles, never falling down. Her life was always full, never hollow; her bag always full with a variety of condoms; her bed always full with a variety of men; and her face, always full with a variety of make-up. Claudette had once said to Cloey that she'd rather have her bikini line waxed with Duck tape than stay in on a Friday night and forego all those potential seed givers. But Cloey could quite easily enjoy a Friday night in. Friday nights out were overrated anyway.

After pouring herself a big glass of white wine, Cloey ran a hot bubble bath while her moussaka cooked in the oven. When she got married she would miss these romantic evenings for one. The honesty of being alone. And when she had children, she'd most likely miss the romantic evenings for two.

She poked her toes through the foam of the bath and looked at the red roses sitting in a crystal vase on the window ledge, their green petals glistening from the steam. If she was straight with herself, she wished Jordan had sent them. If she was totally honest with herself, she also wished he was here in the bath with her. She leaned over the side and picked up her mobile. It was time to make contact with Jordan again.

The Sawn-off Shotgun pub in Milton Keynes or, as it was more commonly known, the Puffing Piccolos, was packed. A pool competition was in progress which meant there would be a fight after hours. You could normally tell the best pool players in this neighbourhood by their missing teeth. There was enough denim in here to keep a stadium of Status Quo fans happy, and the last time a man wore a tie he was chased up the road by fifteen yobbos. It was not the sort of place to bring your mum.

Jordan watched the pool table with casual interest as Ryan fetched another pitcher of beer. If these people knew that Jordan normally managed to reach the £125,000 mark in *Who Wants To Be A Millionaire?*, without using a lifeline, he would be categorized as an intelligent life form, and no intelligent life forms were allowed in the Puffing Piccolos. Which was why Jordan was laughing along with everyone else, trying to sound as thick as everyone else, as Taffy McDuffy regurgitated the pool chalk on to the blue felt playing surface.

Ryan thumped the pitcher angrily on the wonky round table and sat down. As far as Ryan was concerned, his wife came second to Jordan. He'd do anything for his mate, except have sex with him, of course.

'I used to think when Stephanie slept naked it was a real turn-on,' Ryan began, referring to his wife. 'Now, when I wake up and the sunlight lingers on her body, I ask myself, when did she get this big? Wasn't there an in-between stage where I could have stopped it?' He lit up. 'Next time you're round, you take a look at our mattress, the side she sleeps on dips like this.' His hand made a curve. 'Think yourself lucky with Zara. Her mother's slim, isn't she?'

'Pencil slim. You've got to be sensitive though, mate, it's a touchy old subject, weight. If you approach it wrong she'll comfort-eat. Vicious circle. I—'

A text blip stalled the chat and Jordan picked up his mobile and read the message.

Jordan. I'm sitting in the bath thinking about you. I didn't really want to wash away our body fluids. If you were thinking about sending me some flowers then always remember that I hate odd numbers.

See you Sunday. Love Cloey XXX Blood Tied To Death.

Shaking his head, he deleted the message. 'Fucking cheek. Witch!'

Ryan spilt his pint. 'Witch? as in Witch *Cloey*?' Jordan's silent gaze confirmed it was true. 'Jordan, Jordan, Jordan, what are you keeping from Ryan? What shameful deed has wired up your mouth?'

'I accidentally slept with her this morning in front of a Buddha.' His voice was a low grumble. 'I think I'm still in love with her, mate. I've thought of nothing else all day . . .' Jordan went on to explain everything: the hitting, the planned burglary, the sex on the Pagoda hill, the mini-drama worthy of Spanish TV.

If Ryan was shocked by what Jordan told him, he didn't show it, he said it instead, 'You are making the biggest mistake of your life, mate. She's evil. Dogs whimper when she's within five miles. Fucking hell, mate, I've done some stupid things in my time, but this . . . What about Zara? Thought about her for one second, did you, while you were sticking your rod in that sewer? Now get this into your skull: phone that stupid psycho back right now. Tell her you've got a life, she's not in it, and she can eat the fucking grass in the fields along with the other Bruckley cows for all you care. Go on, get on the phone now!'

'You don't like her then?' Jordan gulped beer from the jug. 'She's been through a lot, mate. Didn't you listen to a word I said? She'd been beaten up—'

Ryan butted in, his fingers to his head like a gun. 'Someone shoot me. You stupid twat! You don't believe all that shit, do you? She's playing you. Remember, Jordan, this is the woman who waited only two days before she dropped her drawers while you were serving time for her.' He paused, his own anger making him angrier. 'Remember the mess you were in after you found out about her bed hopping? Remember how low you were? Just be sensible about this; you're a good mate, Zara is a lovely woman, don't fuck up.' He pushed Jordan's mobile across the table. 'Phone her!'

A glass smashed behind the bar and without thinking both Jordan and Ryan cheered along with everyone else, it was the done thing here, but thinking wasn't and Jordan's mind was a seesaw. The question was how low under the moral limbo bar would Cloey go?

'When I was inside, did you ever see her with bruises?' Jordan asked.

'I only saw her a few times, and no, she never had bruises. But she wouldn't, because she's lying. Look, mate, you can't make this real when it isn't. I saw her with a few blokes, all tossers, all wankers, all falling for her little, "Oh look at me I'm so lovely" charade. She never had a cut, a graze, a bruise, a neck harness. She didn't walk funny one day and I never saw her crying. She's lying, mate, she's fooling you. Wise up, Jordan.'

Ryan's attack was good, especially for the spur of the moment without any preparation. It showed a great loyalty to Jordan. But Cloey wasn't here to defend herself, and she had a significant piece of evidence to prove her case. Cloey had the photographs of her wounds and it was up to Jordan to help her retrieve them. There was no way he could walk away from her when she needed him most.

His text bleeped, Cloey again.

Roses Roses Roses Roses.
We are one. Let's have some fun.
Cloey. XXX. One Heart Two Minds.

Jordan deleted the message thinking, 'Yep, she definitely needs me.'

Chapter Nineteen

Waking up beside a woman was a luxury Jordan had never tired of since prison. He'd left a few friends inside who wouldn't be waking up next to a woman for forty years. He sent them pictures of wrinkled pensioners from time to time, to help them get used to the idea of what they might end up with on the outside. They sent him coded death threats from time to time in return.

> *Jordan,*
> *The food in here is ace, the prison officers are*
> *superb, and when I get out, you're eadd mother*
> *uckefr. Send some smokes.*

Today, as the Saturday morning sunshine poured through the open bedroom window, Jordan awoke not with a woman beside him but a feeling inside him, an inkling that the stakes were about to be raised, the dice to be loaded. To a dishonest man only the truth lay ahead, waiting to pounce. Zara had been clear about dishonesty, had made no bones about infidelity, 'If you touch another woman, Jordy, you'll never touch me again.'

Jordan kicked the white duvet off and stretched across, smelling Zara's perfume on the pillowcase. He pushed his hand under her pillow and, like a crab walking, it searched for the coloured card. Pulling it out he rolled over to read it. The red-glittered words were easy to remember, but he looked all the same: *Jordy Jordy Yum Yum*. Zara had told him that by placing it under her pillow, she always had the most rampantly sexual dreams. He slid the card back and closed his eyes.

Zara tip-toed in, her nail-varnished feet sinking easily into the thick cream-coloured carpet and her hot-pink satin slip did all that it was supposed to do – left her bust hanging out. She admired Jordan's tanned muscular physique as he dozed. From the toes up he was sexual dynamite. TN (who needs dildos when you've got that lying on the bed) T. A few scars here and there gave character to his otherwise perfect body, and apart from the neat slash across his chest which he never discussed, the stories as to their occurrence always resulted in 'oohs and ahs' from a thrilled and delighted Zara.

She placed the tray beside him. She loved bringing him breakfast in bed. The whole scene gave her a romantic rush.

'Jordy,' she whispered, nudging him gently. 'Breakfast is ready.'

She had asked her friends whether the desire for

profiteroles and ice cream for breakfast suggested that Jordan was missing a few marbles, it was hardly the breakfast of champions. Their answers always involved sex: who gives a monkeys what a man eats for breakfast, as long as he leaves enough room to eat you afterwards, followed by their girlie laughter. Zara scooped up some cream with her thumb and glazed Jordan's nose with it.

His eyes blinked open, green and bright like a traffic light. 'Hello, gorgeous.' He leant forward and gave her a kiss. 'Not pregnant yet, then?'

'I wish. I had a little nibble on a piece of celery this morning and it made me retch.'

'Can't you do a pregnancy test like everyone else?'

'Ooh, non-believer,' she said, picking up a lump of ice cream and dropping it on his stomach, giggling at Jordan's cries.

And there had been non-believers for generations. On her mother's side of the family tree, all pregnancies were confirmed by the craving for celery. Her great-gran, her gran, her mum, her sister, all fell to the spell of the crunchy stick when preggas. Mum had even written a small leaflet for her daughters, 'Twenty Celery Stick Recipes if You Miss a Period'.

After licking Jordan's stomach clean, Zara's eyes picked up an anomaly on his left oblique muscle. She knew blokes masturbated, she'd watched Jordan countless times, but surely they didn't give themselves love bites.

Her finger paused at the reddish mark. 'I didn't give you that. So it only leaves one question, doesn't it, Jordan?'

'Who did?'

'Yes, who did? Well?'

He sat up wishing he could juggle, then, with Zara's attention on his juggling, he could dive out of the window. But he couldn't juggle, and obviously he couldn't juggle his women either. He should have known Cloey would have left her business card. Yesterday he was hoping the roof would collapse on the church, now his roof was collapsing on him. Be careful what you wish for, the saying goes, it might happen. He stared at Zara, and, oh sweet Mary, was it happening.

'Buffy did it. The Vampire Slayer. Stupid cow. I said, look, Buffy, I'm not inter—' The smack round his face bit into the remark. 'Sorry.'

He quickly studied the reddish bruise to see if it could be mistaken for anything else. Teeth marks round the outside, for example, would be a dead giveaway. Examining it more deeply, while Zara made huffing noises in the background, his face finally broke into a smile. It wasn't even a bloody love bite.

'Silly, Zara, it's a snowboarding bruise. Look.' And he began to suck on his forearm. 'Wait a second.' He thrust his arm under her nose. 'That's what a love bite looks like. Now, compare to my snowboarding bruise. Silly, Zara.'

A kiss and a cuddle later, Jordan could breathe again. Her conclusion was that the ski-slope was trying to make her jealous. If she found any snowballs in the freezer, she would melt them. She wasn't raising another woman's children in her house. Thinking of babies always made her want to make one, and within a few smouldering moments she was as starkers as he was.

Jordan loved the look in Zara's blue eyes as he made love to her. They seemed to become bluer, like the naked flame of a butane burner, and he loved the double-dare of her pupils tempting him to take her to the pleasure dome. That special galaxy where only he and she existed. After sex, it was always the same old story though: Jordan lay half asleep listening to a load of claptrap, while Zara lay wide awake talking it.

With her head resting on his chest, she spoke, 'I was talking to Tiffany and Natasha yesterday about that poor woman who came here the other night.'

'Who? Cloey?'

She lifted her head up and narrowed her eyes. 'No, Catherine!'

'Yeah. I thought Cloey was short for Catherine.'

Zara sat right up. '*Cathy* is short for Catherine, you should know that. Your mother was called Catherine.'

He chuckled. 'I suppose that's why I never called her Cloey then. I called her Mum anyway. Christian names are so confusing.'

'How much did you drink last night, Jordy? Because you're talking rubbish.'

Zara had thrown him a lifeline, drink, and he grabbed it like someone overboard. If seldom used and if used cleverly, the drink excuse could get one out of many an iffy situation.

'How much did I drink? God, have you ever heard the term "a lot"? Well, since you have now quit drinking, because of the baby, and I'm quitting smoking, because of the baby, I couldn't help acting like a baby last night. I drunk loads.' He threw back the duvet, faking concern as he glared at his balls, studying them like the day they had dropped. 'Phew, thank God they're still there. You never know what my mates will get up to when I'm as drunk as I was last night.'

She shook her head despondently. 'Well, as long as they don't interfere with our relationship, Jordy, I don't care.'

Zara had lost friends over Jordan. Apparently most of them could see into the future. In their crystal bollocks they foresaw that Jordan would lead her into the quagmire of jiggery-pokery, where her healthy middle-class morals would be stretched beyond recognition. She would not just be Zara with a Z, but Zara with an H. *Cellblock H.*

Even her own mother had been nervous around Jordan to begin with. Any sudden movements he made had lowered her life expectancy. He had sneezed at the dinner table once and she'd thrown a pork chop across the room at him. Self-defence, she said. Jordan did not have an excuse as to why he had aggressively lobbed it back, apart from 'prison reflex'. Still, a soft spot for Jordan had begun to develop. Especially when she found out his mother had died when he was ten.

'Of what?' she had asked. 'The C word?'

'I don't know,' he'd replied. 'She just went flatline. Just one of those unexplained things, I suppose. I miss her sometimes, though. I can't really picture her in my mind any more without photos. But I'm glad in a way she didn't live to see me in prison, it might have killed her. It was shameful enough that my dad had to visit me. He didn't like to see me in there, and I didn't like to see him in there either.'

'Parents love their children no matter what they've done. Your mother would have been proud of your snowboarding. In some small way, Jordan, I'm proud of you myself.'

But another mother's affection never quite hits the spot like your own mother's. Jordan's parents had both known she was dying, but had never let on. Their battle had been a private one, praying daily, hoping against hope that a blessing would come from the heavens to cure her cancer. A month before her death, his mother had asked for his help putting out the washing in the back garden. Her words hadn't stung then, but they had stung later.

'Jordan, out of all my children, I worry about you the most. You promise mummy that you will make sure you always steer clear of trouble. You promise that for Mummy.' She handed him the tin of pegs.

Jordan smiled cheekily. 'Course', he said, sticking a red peg on his bare stomach.

His mother continued, 'And you'll always make room in your life for poor people.'

'Like us?'

'There's always someone poorer than you, Jordan.'

'You mean the Cambodians?'

'Them too.' She hung up a T-shirt. 'And I know your dad is grouchy sometimes, but he works awfully hard, and make sure, when you can – I know you've got a lot of friends who need your help and advice – but when you can, give your father some help as well.' She gave him a hug, while Jordan stealthily stuck a yellow peg on her woollen hat. 'And make sure you always pray to God. He's grouchy sometimes too, but like your dad, he works awfully hard.'

And then, just as the last item of clothing had been hung out, the heavens had opened, and it had started pouring with rain. A month later she had passed away. And that's when his troubles began. Why should he pray? Why should he help Cambodians? Why should he be nice when God had killed his mum? For many years he had blamed God.

The heat was unbearable and Jordan thanked his lucky stars that he hadn't used Zara's home-made egg-yolk conditioner this morning. The last time he'd used it in a heatwave he turned up to his mate's barbecue with an omelette on his head and a soufflé in his boxers.

It was 1.00 p.m., Zara was shopping in central MK which gave him approximately until tomorrow to do as he pleased.

'Make sure you don't dehydrate, Jordy, have a few beers if you get dizzy,' Zara had said as he kissed her goodbye outside Piri Piri Chicken. Jordan had asked if she planned on buying some clothes as she didn't appear to be wearing any. 'Oh, Jordy, you know I've only got eyes for you. Don't be so jealous, you'll suffocate me.'

And she was gone, along with her long tanned legs, melted-on pink skirt, pierced belly-button and a boob-tube. Around her neck was a donor card. The list of organs had been scrubbed out and written in their place was blonde hair. She would donate her long, knot-free, split-end free, pollution-free hair. It would have only got in the way of her halo anyway.

The thought of Zara grinding down her high heels as she worked her way through countless designer shops, massaging out money from her purse as she went, made him smile. It was a part of her he would never quite understand. Now, as he spied on Sammy's house through the bushes, he was in a part of his world that *she* would never fully understand. Maybe the thrill of shops to her was the same as the thrill of crime to him.

He lit a fag and surveyed the house for a minute. If Loyd Grossman could give you one clue it might be, 'A rich fuck lives here, wot wot.' Apart from the long drive that led out of the gates, the area was surrounded by trees, bushes and flowers. It was almost an entire ecosystem in itself. Inside, Jordan imagined plush carpets, expensive wood, a snooker table, posh taps, a wine cellar, a bar, a massive fridge, beer, more beer, and . . . a safe. Bubber, his old cell mate, was a safe-cracker and used to leave little written notes after his heists. 'I re-christen this metal box UNSAFE and I can't wait to spend your money.' But Bubber was no fool, even though he eventually got caught. He was the Einstein of the prison world working hard on his theories from inside his cage. There were many things he had taught Jordan on the inside: breaking wind and entering, falsifying evidence, the lyrics to Kajagoogoo's hit 'Too Shy'.

Jordan felt the familiar mixture of fear and fun. Breaking into someone's house for his ex-girlfriend was madness. But then again, going to prison for a girlfriend was also madness. Maybe he was just mad.

He gave himself a few more minutes before he ventured any nearer. He needed a good grasp of all the angles of the exterior before he could calculate the entry point for tomorrow's break-in. A rustle nearby broke his concentration and he dropped to a crouching position. He held his breath for two reasons. One, he did not want to be caught. And two, there was a cat crapping about a foot away from his nose.

Shooing the cat away, Jordan continued to move through the bushes, and before long was at the back of the house, looking down the long garden and into the conservatory.

A few statues of – Jordan focused his eyes – elephants of all things, lined a neat slightly pink footpath that pierced the centre of the lawn up to the summerhouse beyond. Jordan rubbed a hand through his hair. This house, from the perspective of a clue-collector was obviously owned by some sort of toff. Someone, Jordan figured, who wouldn't know what to do if you said, 'Fuck off' unless you said 'Forck oorf'. Someone with six sets of knives and forks for six different courses. Someone who probably had a butler to lay out the cutlery for them. But could any butlers be found in Milton Keynes? Maybe not. He moved a little to the left of a pear tree. He plucked one off, gave it the once-over for maggots and bit in.

Voices interrupted his pear-slurping and his eyes homed in on their whereabouts. Coming out of the conservatory were an Indian man and woman. He watched as the man popped back inside and returned with two cushioned sun-loungers. Could have brought three, he thought. For some reason it had never occurred to him that this Sammy bastard was an Indian.

In time, the couple were lost in chat, sizzling under the sun. It was hard to believe that this man, Sammy, who he'd been watching fussing over his wife for the last fifteen minutes was a man who liked to hurt women. But Jordan knew from experience that the gentlest-looking men could have a vicious, violent streak.

In prison, there had been a kindly-looking, fragile old man called Crooner, all skin and calcium deposits. But, as Jordan had found out after a while, he was a known fiend of mammoth proportions. To the ten or so girls he'd mishandled, he was the Devil himself. You just couldn't tell who was who sometimes.

So engrossed in analyzing this Sammy – waiting on standby to run across and pin him to the ground if he so much as raised his voice to his wife – Jordan failed to notice the creeping bundle of fur at his feet. It was like seaweed flowing in and out of his calves.

Then the fur spoke. 'Meeeow!'

He looked down. 'Oh, it's you,' he whispered. 'What d'you want?'

The cat made a little shuffle with its hips, the long whiskers seemed to shrink.

Now Jordan knew one thing about moggies, their whiskers were the same width as their bellies. And if this one's whiskers had just shrunk it could only mean one thing. Its belly was about to shrink too. There was only one way of that happening, thought Jordan, thinking the worst.

'No you do not,' he said, lifting the moggie up and gently lobbing it over the bushes.

The cat glanced back to Jordan as it flew through the air. 'Meeeeeeeeeeeeooooooooooo . . .'

Chapter Twenty

'. . . ooooooooooooowwwwww.' The cat landed, shook its plump body and flopped on the grass.

Samir and Kareena jumped.

'Shit! It was as though it had it stood on a landmine. Did you see it fly?' Samir said, settling back into his lounger.

Kareena was still riding high on the crest of a wave from last night. Samir had done everything right. It proved to her the importance of nipping a problem in the bud, of talking things through. The evening had seemed designed especially for them. A classy Indian restaurant by the name of the Floating Ganges set the mood, with its fountain in the centre of the room, sending tricks of light on the rose-coloured surroundings. The food was sensational, a sensual assault on the tastebuds. The waiters produced course after course with a smile cloaked in confidence: I dare you to try and produce anything this tasty at home. Bring your mama jis, auntie jis, even bring your Jaffrey jis, no one can compete with the Floating Ganges.

As the *sitars* and *tablas* fought a delicate battle with the sizzling of the *shaslicks* and *tikkas*, and the hundred voices of contented customers blended to a babble, Samir and Kareena had become closer through a never-ending stream of chat and an equal measure of wine. Even Streakers the cat had played a part in sparking their feelings. It began with Kareena's description of Streakers attacking the butterfly, which led to talk of *Papillon*, which led to Steve McQueen, which led to *The Royle Family*, which led to Mrs Merton, which led back to alcohol.

'Would you like some more wine?'

'Of course I would.'

And they were off again. Coincidentally, the same taxi driver who had driven them to the restaurant also returned them home. He wanted to know what wine they had been drinking. He also drove with his head out of the window most of the way. His Lisa Simpson air freshener couldn't compete with the aroma of thirty cloves of garlic.

Now, as the sun pressed down, and her sunglasses fended off its rays, Kareena basked in romance. She stared through the dim blue glass lenses at Samir. One man for every woman, he had said. She giggled internally at the way she had thrown herself at him last night. Her head blamed the wine, the slut sauce. And whether it was this gorgeous weather or not, she felt like doing it all again. Maybe the sun was an aphrodisiac. Maybe she had a crush on her husband. Maybe she was falling in love far more quickly than she had thought possible. Samir caught her eye and smiled, maybe he was falling in love with her too.

Her bikini was fluorescent green. You could have seen it from outer space. She would never have worn something like this before. She had been brought up to cover her legs and arms. She assumed Mum and Dad had meant her tits as well. This morning at 10.34, by aisle twenty-three in Tescos, Samir had dropped the radioactive-looking garment into the shopping trolley. Before she had time to protest, he explained the importance of how a couple should also be an individual. How rules were not meant to be followed but were meant to be made up as you went along. Being Indian did not presume Indianness. And unless she wanted to carry the Tescos shopping back to the house on her head, she shouldn't have to live in the past like their parents did. Coming here was different for them, just as being born here is different for us, he'd said. A merging of worlds also meant a merging of ideas. And the bikini, as far as he was concerned, was a brilliant idea.

The next hour passed, with the conversation piece on repeat: it's hot. God it's hot. Shit it's hot. It's so so so hot. Streakers sat in the shade just inside the conservatory, watching. He just could not believe how lazy humans were.

'It's really hot,' moaned Kareena, chucking down her *Marie Claire*. 'You can almost hear the grass dying of thirst.'

Samir could not hold out any longer and collected the canvas canopy from the summerhouse. Kareena watched his every move, giggling at the slapping noises of his flip-flops and enjoying the look of his slightly sweaty torso. His upper-body muscles tensed as he struggled to roll the concrete base over to the canopy. At one point he lost control and Kareena observed her husband struggle to steer it back on course. Finally he managed to set up the sunshade and dragged over his own lounger so they lay side by side. He lay back with a smile, the self-satisfied smile of a man who had just done a good job – or thought he had.

'Shall we go in now?' she asked laughing, as his head touched the pillow.

He hung on for dear life – he wasn't going anywhere. He'd set up camp as far as he was concerned, and it would take a bloody monsoon to move him now.

In time, as the sun swelled in the sky, they snuggled closer together, Samir looking into her eyes and playing with her hair and Kareena enjoying his touch. Sometimes the quality of chat was borderline filth, at other times it was fairly deep. One minute Samir could be asking whether she thought the fall of mankind would be politically motivated by greed and the next they were discussing whether asking a midget to think big was insulting.

Even though the weather was so hot, their conversation never dried up and Samir could feel his thoughts changing direction slightly. Yesterday, they were blowing in Cloey's direction: a force-ten gale of panic when he realized he might be losing her. And when a man panics he knows that only one thing will do: flowers, roses, red ones. Lots and lots of them.

Now, as he lay enjoying his wife's intelligent conversation, Cloey was becoming less and less of an ache in his heart. In fact, if he were to sum up the years he spent with Cloey in one defining word it would be: bossed. She bossed him like no one bossed a man before. Samir, fetch me this; Samir, this room will be decorated in mahogany wood and marzipan-coloured walls. Only the best for us, only the best for me. Hand over your credit card, and stop being a stinge. Oh how women hate stingy men. Samir, Samir Samir!

'Samir, why don't you open a bottle of wine,' suggested Kareena.

Now that was bossing of a different kind. He jumped up quickly, hurdling Streakers. 'Back in a sec.'

Chilled wine filled two shelves of the monster fridge. Fresh salad, pickles and cheese were on another, and on the bottom shelf – he didn't care what was on the bottom shelf, he just wanted the wine. He picked out a California red. It was supposed to taste of raspberry and damson fruit with a toasty oak flavour. It was also supposed to be served warm like all red wines. He poured out two glasses and took a swig from the bottle. To the untrained wino it could have been filtered through Oz Clarke's underpants for all he knew, but it hit the spot.

Some people get depressed on booze, others get silly, some sleepy and a few even get violent. With Samir, he made promises. Big ones.

'And over there,' Samir pointed to the summer-house, 'we will have a riding school. We'll call it . . .' He paused, thinking hard for a good name. 'We'll call it "Kareena's and Samir's Equestrian Centre". Getting planning permission would be a cinch. No problem.'

Some people get flirty on alcohol. Kareena giggled.

'I just love the name. I bet you could get permission for anything.'

He nodded in agreement. 'Mostly.'

'You don't need permission from me though.' She took off her shades, fluttered her eyelashes at him, then put them back on. 'Especially when you wear short shorts that short.'

Some people talk crap when they are drunk.

He leaned over and kissed her, losing himself in the moment, feeling the grip of the booze. His parents complained that drinking cluttered thinking. Samir smiled as he pulled away from Kareena's soft lips. There was nothing cluttered about his thinking right now. Nothing messy or jumbled. It was just plain filth, the top shelf of his mind.

Kareena's long, long fingers found their way inside Samir's short, short shorts, and he smiled, smiled and smiled. God, how he loved booze. Even if it did taste of raspberries, damson fruit and toasty oak; but especially when mixed with the taste of a delicious, up for it woman whose hands were rummaging around in his undies. Some people even get horny when drunk.

He clumsily unhooked her bikini bra and threw it across the lawn.

Eyes only give you two options. To look or not to look.

So Jordan looked. He stared at the topless Indian woman and allowed himself a very quiet wolf-whistle, it almost made up for three hours being held hostage by a bush. From the moment he had seen Sammy position the sun-loungers, his escape route had been thwarted. Foiled by a couple, who as far as he could tell were brown enough, but who wanted to get even browner. Patiently he waited for them to get a life. To go indoors. He wanted to shout out, 'Haven't you two got a curry to cook or something?' This wasn't a stake-out. It was just a mistake-out.

Things were hotting up rather quickly in the garden with each item of their clothing being ripped off as though it burnt. Jordan turned his back on the lovers. It was a private moment and they deserved some privacy: even the cat appeared to have vanished. It may have had something to do with the barking coming from one of them. Time was really pushing on and Jordan found himself willing them both to orgasm. Finally the duo delivered, finally Lassie was quiet, and finally Jordan could go home.

Chapter Twenty-one

Cloey and Claudette had reserved a portion of the evening to discuss men and the benefits of men. Claudette said they would fit the chat in between the sixth ball and the bonus ball of the lottery. After ripping up the tickets they would then take a stroll through the village. Chatting all the way they would pass by Wood. W. Orms Antiques, through the cobbled alley that led to the village bowling green, then on to the centre of the universe: Peter Benchley's Fish Shop.

Ever since they'd moved in together, on the second Saturday of each month, they would make the trip together. Any arguments would be dropped, any sulks would be stopped and any money owed would be paid. Nothing was allowed to get in the way of cod and chips washed down with Vratislav Czech lager. As far as they were concerned it was their call to Mecca.

Claudette had been ensconced in the bathroom for over an hour. She had to look gorgeous for her cod. Trying to explain to her that you don't have to wear half a pound of make-up all the time, was like explaining deep calculus to a three-year-old. She just didn't understand. Just like Cloey didn't understand why some people always had to moan and complain.

She stared down at the letter of complaint. It wasn't the first she had received from potential customers objecting to tasteless remarks on the greeting cards she sent on spec to businesses up and down Bucks. Didn't people comprehend how hard it was to find fitting lines for condolence cards when you were having problems of your own? Wasn't it obvious that when she wrote 'Sorry He Faded Away' her mind was elsewhere? And maybe some people would find comfort in knowing the top fifty personalities who had died in the same month as their loved one? Surely realizing that God didn't just pick non-celebs to die helped some people. And whether they are A list, B list, or even E list, when it comes to the end, they all join the RIP list.

Screwing the letter up in a ball, Cloey lobbed it on her bed and glared out of the window, annoyed at the nerve of some people. In the fields in the distance she watched a man in the long grass repeatedly throwing a stick to a dog she couldn't see. Most likely he came from Milton Keynes, coming out here to seek the peace of the country. Just like Claudette went to Milton Keynes and slept with MK men, giving them her own little piece of the country.

After another twenty minutes, Cloey banged on the bathroom door, and it was finally unlocked. Cloey stood back as she would when opening a dishwasher. She compared it to the pod opening in the film *The Fly*. Masses of steam swirled around a shadow of Claudette, until she appeared through the clouds in her short dress, high heels, bunker-bomb-proof face – reborn. Even her own reflection didn't recognize her. Cloey admitted to herself that, maybe Claudette did need that half pound of make-up after all. She looked stunning.

'Have you got any make-up left I could use?' Cloey asked sarcastically, sitting on the loo doing a pee.

'Maybe if you had worn some before, Sammy might have hung on a little longer,' Claudette replied, admiring her newly dyed blonde hair in the steamed-up mirror. 'Then again, you can't polish shit, can you?' She walked out.

'You managed it,' Cloey shouted, pulling up her jeans, washing her hands, then following Claudette through to her bedroom. 'They kill one whale a week because of you,' she continued, slumping down on to Claudette's unmade bed.

Her eyes were drawn to Claudette's sheets, wondering how she had found the time to try her hand at tie-dying. There were various-sized round patches of colour in random places all over them. Cloey tilted her head to one side to examine a substantial mark near her left leg. Claudette obviously had untapped artistic tendencies. Very impressive.

Claudette pointed to the large stain. 'Sean's. And that one near your hand is Joel's.' She flung the duvet on to the magazines that concealed the floorboards. 'And that one is my latest, Callum. You saw him last night; you probably heard him as well. Animal. I think it's his anyway. We were so drunk last night.'

'Change the sheets you dirty, slovenly cow.' Cloey jumped off the bed.

A knock at the front door prevented a cat fight.

Cloey crept to the window and pulled the netting slowly to one side. At the same time the occupants of the two houses opposite drew back their netting and faces stared out. This meant trouble. Claudette asked who was knocking and Cloey hissed at her to be quiet. Turning back, she spotted a third house with curtains twitching, then a fourth, and up the road a fifth! Who the hell was so important that even Mrs Topps, who struggled round her house with a trolley drip, could risk the journey to the window? Cloey's heart strummed.

The letterbox flapped open. 'Cloey, it's Jordan. Open up, I can see you.'

Cloey faced her friend with a smile of apprehension and excitement. 'Let him in, I've got to get changed. He mustn't see me like this. I've got to look my ultimate best.'

Claudette viewed her stomach from the side and sucked it in. Satisfied that she was still gorgeous she spoke, 'I'll hide me valuables then.' She laughed extra loud.

'He doesn't steal sex toys, Claudette, so don't bother hiding them. Just answer the door.' Cloey was already half undressed and running across the hall into the bathroom. 'And be nice.'

Holding on to the banister, Claudette lowered herself down the narrow stairs in her stilettos, with the top of her dress now exposing more cleavage and the bottom of her dress now showing more thigh. A male visitor of no matter what pedigree, deserved to see what a real woman looked like sometimes.

She smiled as she opened the door. 'Prisoner 4253, if it isn't you. Do come in. Solitary confinement is this way. Follow the female guard.'

Jordan pulled the bottom of his shorts back up. He'd shown his bum to the nosy window watchers enough for one day. Leave 'em wanting.

'Ahhh,' he said opening his arms, 'Princess Vomit Face. God, I've missed you.' He followed her through to the living room.

Claudette pointed to the armchair. 'Don't worry, there's no electricity flowing through it. We don't execute our prisoners any more.' She blew him a kiss, then adjusted her boobs and stared at his ankles. 'My my, no tag, or is it a suppository tag nowadays? Makes more sense, don't you think? I always thought branding was a good idea, lets the innocent know the guilty ones who live among us.' She sat down on the sofa, revealing her knickers, and waited for his response.

Claudette only resented Jordan because he was gorgeous and because she blamed him for turning her into a slag. If only he had kissed her in primary school, she wouldn't have tried to make him jealous by kissing all the other boys. If only he had snogged her in senior school, she might not have sucked so many of the other boys' dicks. And if only he would have shagged her just the once after leaving school, maybe she wouldn't have tried to make him jealous by sleeping with half of Milton Keynes. Jordan was guilty of turning Claudette into a slag and she would hold a grudge against him forever.

Jordan said, 'It's frustrating sitting here with you,

233

Vomit Face. It's hard to insult someone who's been called every name under the sun. I mean, tell me if I'm wrong, but I bet you've been called "a mouldy sackload of cheesy knickers" before, haven't you?'

'Yes, actually, many times,' she replied, chin up, refusing to give him satisfaction.

'Okay.' He lit up, then extinguished the fag, 'What about "a crustated, flaky, scabby, septic tape worm"?' He paused. 'With genital warts.'

She faked a yawn. 'Oh, Jordan, you're definitely losing it. Did prison steal your brain cells?' Their eyes swapped malevolence. 'I love talking about prison, it's so obvious that it hurts you . . . It's a shame that Cloey didn't wait for you. Every time she brought another man back here I would say, "What about poor Jordan stuck in the cells? How could you, Cloey?" But she carried on regardless, one after the other. Orgasm after orgasm.' She watched his face with amusement. 'I'll go and make you some porridge if you like and we could discuss how Cloey burnt all your prison letters. All those feelings you poured out on the page, all those desperate pleas.' Claudette held her necklace and looked out of the window in mock acting mode. 'Oh, Cloey. Oh, Cloey, I miss you so much in here. When I get out we will be together. Oh, Cloey.' Her synthetic sympathetic voice returned. 'But Cloey didn't miss *you*, did she? Poor, poor, desperate, Jordan.'

He stood up and approached her smug face. People had told him that his eyes glinted when he saw red. 'I'm going to walk to your kitchen and come back with a steak knife. If you're still here when I get back, I will slit your throat and kick that ugly head of yours into the nearest dustbin.' He turned to leave, chuckling inside at the sight of her quivering bottom lip. 'I can't wait to go back to prison.'

Claudette's mobile rang – to the tune of Kraftwork's 'Model' – and she warily unclipped it from her suspender. 'Yes?' It was Cloey upstairs asking if she could keep Jordan talking for a few more minutes. 'He said he is going to kill me. He's flipped. I don't think he's joking.'

'Never mind that. Just find out how much he loves Zara. Find out what she means to him. Or if he's got a thing for me.' The line went dead.

Jordan returned with a selection of knives and kitchen tools. He laid them on the coffee table and picked up the meat cleaver, swinging it through the air.

'Get out, this is your last chance, Vomit Face.' He swung the cleaver again.

Claudette threw her stilettos on the floor and ran out at top speed screaming, 'Call the police.'

Sitting back down again, he studied the room. Nothing much had changed since he was last here eight years back. Only the splash of peach-coloured paint on the walls appeared to be different. A fruit bowl containing Jelly Babies stood on the coffee table beside him and he swiped a few, chewing a set of triplets in one go. Another bowl next to it contained scented floating candles in the shape of roses. He took the liberty of lighting two and they promptly sank. He guessed they were bought from the Pound Shop.

Cloey appeared at the door. 'What are you doing here?' She walked over and kissed him on the lips. 'Missing me, were you?'

Jordan knew exactly Cloey's intentions. She left little room for doubt. A lavender chiffon and lace dress clung tightly to her fantastic curves. A dress and a body that could walk into any pub, and out with any man. A dress that really should come supplied with condoms.

'Sorry about sinking the candles,' he said, popping in another set of triplets.

She sat down next to him. 'You don't have to apologize to me, we're lovers.' She neatened up a few of his wobbly hairs that the gel had given up on. 'We never should have lost touch. You and me had something that others never have. Because when I was with Sammy, I always felt something was missing. I did think about you – I cried you know – a few times. He said I'd never stopped loving you, and he was right. That's probably why he hit me.' Playing her fingers through his hair, she continued, 'God, you are so gorgeous. How did I ever lose you?' She rested her head on his shoulder. 'Do you feel like that with Zara? Like something is missing?' Cloey closed her eyes, sniffing his neck.

And Jordan closed his eyes also. Cloey was coming on strong. He wasn't even sure where his own feelings lay concerning Zara but he certainly wasn't going to discuss them with Cloey. If in doubt say nowt. It used to be easy to open his heart to her, but that was before she broke it. And it used to be just as easy to listen to her, but that was before she had perforated his ears with lies. The heavy silence of the room was soon broken by Claudette's jungle music above, kicking them both from their daydreams.

Tip-toeing up his neck with her tongue, Cloey

planted tiny kisses, little seeds of excitement. 'There's twenty-four hours in the day, Jordan, I can't believe you don't think about me in some of them. You must do. I used to try so hard not to think about you, knowing I had failed you. I couldn't even look at your photo for years, let alone say your name out loud.'

'Of course I thought about you. If I hadn't, it would have shown our relationship meant fuck all wouldn't it?' Her hand came to his thigh, sliding up to his crotch and he placed his hand over it to stop her. 'I think we got our just desserts though, don't you? People always get payback. No one really gets away with anything. God must have a lot of fun pulling the carpet from under people.'

'God doesn't exist.' Her voice was like a label gun, pricing up the world in one sentence. 'All we get is this one life on earth, and we should make the most of our time. We don't get a second chance, Jordan.' Her hand caressed his neck, resting on the dull throb of his pulse. 'I'm sure Zara will understand if you explain that you have to leave her.' She felt his pulse quicken. 'You're too good for her.'

'Just like I wasn't good enough for you? How did you put it? "Without money you and me are finished. No one employs ex-cons." I think that's what you said.'

A hush filled the room like the smell of cheap perfume. A small cartoon caricature caught his attention over the fireplace. It was a picture of a bearded man holding a china cup. Underneath, the caption read: The Last Cuppa. Jordan smiled, he was sure Jesus's last drink would have been something stiffer than PG Tips.

The drawing dug up a memory though, of what had attracted him to Cloey in the first place: her sense of humour. Slightly dark and warped, but equally sharp and irreverent. He first knew he had fallen in love with her when she had agreed to light the fuses on the rockets aimed at the empty scout hut. Apparently Jordan's attitude to life did not bode well with the dib dib dib dob dob dob mob. His opening line to Arkala had been, 'I'll join your poofy club, but I'm not wearing a wanky woggle. Got it?' It seemed a lifetime ago.

Cloey stretched over to pick up an orange Jelly Baby, then flopped back. 'If we are going to make a go of this, Jordan, then we're going to have to bury the past. We all say things we don't mean. Are you really going to hold it against me when we could be so good together?' Her fingers manipulated the orange sweet. 'Once you've helped me break into Sammy's house and collect my proof of his beatings, then we can both forget our past partners. You and me, Jordan, can be as one, as is written in our blood.' She plopped the Jelly Baby in his mouth.

Jordan had come to Cloey's cottage with the intention of making arrangements for Sunday to break into Sammy's house, and to explain to Cloey that after that day, they could see each other no more. Now his mind was playing trick or treat, his common sense absent and his future path glazed with fog. He didn't have a clue what he was going to do. Not one.

He walked over to the net curtains and pulled them to. Across the road the faces still watched. 'We're on the TV, Cloey.' Jordan gave the middle finger and was quite amused to see Mrs Topps giving it *large* in return with her eighty-five-year-old middle arthritic finger. Top woman. 'I can't ever leave Zara. I think you know that.' Reluctantly he let the nettings fall back and turned round. 'I love her too much.'

'Ha! That's a joke. You slept with me this week. You would never have slept with anyone else when you were with me. Would you?'

'This isn't about sex. And it's not about love either.' He seemed confused at his own statement.

'Well, what is it about? Breast implants? Bimboness? Blondes?'

'Loyalty. Respect. Being happy. I'd never be happy with you, Cloey.'

Cloey curled into the sofa, her eyes filling with tears. 'I don't believe you would be so selfish as to stay with a brainless airhead. Can't you see these tears are for real, Jordan? Don't you think at a time like this I might need a hug?'

He watched the emotion spill out. Someone like Cloey was dangerous. She was like the naughty niece at the family party showing her knickers to all the guests. When the attention wasn't on her, she fell into a sulk.

Jordan tried to feel some sympathy. But his lasting memory was the way he'd felt when he stood outside the prison on that first day of freedom. There was nothing to beat finding out that the love of your life has deceived and betrayed you. There was nothing to compare with being lied to when you were caged up like an animal. Finding out that his girlfriend's legs had been spread all over Milton Keynes was something he had never got over. If his heart thought of forgiveness, the words in his head were clear: resist, resist, resist.

But as her wails got louder, he *couldn't* resist the deafening demands for a hug, and as he clasped the sobbing Cloey, he found that there was a treacherous part of his brain working out plans of how they could be together without hurting Zara, and without resorting to a cloning experiment.

In time, the plans for breaking into Sammy's house the following day were discussed. It all seemed fairly straightforward: get in, get out. Jordan explained how he'd got the tiniest of glimpses of Sammy and his wife, but he knew better than to confess to Cloey that he'd seen the fantastic body of another woman in the buff.

An hour later, he stood. 'Right, I'll catch you tomorrow then.'

Cloey looked put out. 'Can't bear to be with me another minute? Worried that my bed is only thirteen steps away?' She giggled. 'Can't trust yourself, Jordan? Well, you run along now. You run along to dumbo Zara. Go and have sexual intercourse with her. I'm sure she won't mind; she's only a blow-up doll anyway.' She put her hand to her mouth. 'Whoops, sorry, it's only the drink I'm going to be having later doing the talking.'

'Don't go horrible on me now, I was just beginning to like you again. But that was always your downfall, wasn't it, Cloey? Other women and their pretty looks. And for the record, Zara knocks socks off you in the intelligence stakes. She could talk you under the table about topics you couldn't even pronounce, she could—'

'Shhh,' Cloey said, placing her finger on his lips. 'I was only joking. That's what I love about you, you're so loyal.' Her hand dived into his shorts and she smiled as he became hard. 'She can't be that intelligent though, can she?' Her fingers tightened. 'Because she's going to lose you to me.' She pulled her hand back out.

Watching Jordan's muscular legs as he walked up the garden path gave Cloey a gush of lust. She used to mock the women on TV who fainted in front of their pop idols, but right now, she felt quite faint herself. Wobbling up the path after him, she fell into his arms in an exaggerated slump.

'Kiss me, Jordan.'

Without thinking he put his mouth to hers and enjoyed the untamed passion of his youth, the feeling of being a rebel teenager again. When anything was possible and rules were something that came with a Monopoly set. All he needed now was a joint, a six-pack of lager, some nudity and – he stared at five sets of gawping eyes across the road – some fucking privacy.

Jordan pulled away from Cloey and jumped over the garden gate of Lemonly Cottage. The last time he'd jumped over this gate, his world had been out of orbit, this time, his mind was out of orbit, somewhere in the Kuiper Belt on a collision course to mayhem.

Chapter Twenty-two

The Indian temple holds the spirit of an Indian community in the palms of its hands: the wise in the left palm and the foolish in the right. Each Sunday those hands are clapped together to remind the Sikh worshippers of Guru Nanak's words: everyone is equal, regardless of race, creed, colour or caste. Each Sunday, hordes of brightly dressed Sikhs fill the *gurdwara* floor, as equals, for their weekly prayer, and listen to readings taken from the holy book of scriptures called the *Guru Granth Sahib*.

Samir and Kareena inspected each other's tongues for any tell-tale signs of booze. Turning up for Sunday temple stinking of the bottle, bleary eyed and with tongues you could use for loft insulation, was not on. It amounted to disrespect. No problem if you came in belching out a whole cacophony of *thali* burps. No problem if you hadn't washed under your armpits since the day you were born and you were so smelly your wife stuffs *ghee* up her nostrils when she has to shag you. But come in smelling of wine, Lambett's Ice and Jack Daniel's, then *chunnis* and turbans will turn. A whole brown blanket of faces staring at you with the same mixture of hurt and betrayal. 'Pakistan is testing nuclear weapons and all you can think about is booze.'

Kareena checked out her *shalwar kameez*, its rhubarb colour was thankfully not too bright for eyes that were still curled up asleep at the back of her lids. She could picture the day the fabric had caught her mother's eye on a pre-wedding shopping spree in Soho Road, Birmingham. The whole place, a hub of Asian shops, spicing up the streets with goods shipped in from the East. The whole day, a hub of emotions verging on panic. The carrier bags weighed heavily on her arms by the time the day was through. Each bag was filled with items intended to please a man she barely knew, and that was a weight of a different kind.

Lifting up the tail of the *kameez*, Kareena smiled at a botched stitch she had sewn horribly wrong, remembering the day well. Sitting in total concentration at the dining-room table with a foot on the pedal and an eye on the cotton, she had worked away on the rhubarb-coloured garment. Each stitch sewing up the reality of her approaching wedding to Samir. Each perfect stitch, spaced by a mechanical needle, pierced the silk as though it pierced the unknown future it would be worn in.

Suddenly Avani had shot in, declaring that a sex scene with a *really* sexy man was hotting up on the digital channel. Kareena had leapt up from her seat, snagging the material, and had run through to the sitting room to join in with the drooling. The man was definitely worth missing a stitch or two over. In fact, he was worth missing a period over. He was gorgeous. Later that evening Avani could be found frantically studying the digital guide for repeat showings of the same programme. The next time they would not make the mistake of screaming at the top of their voices when Fabiano Zackeria III slowly turned to the camera and teasingly dropped his towel to the floor looking only *you* in the eyes. Phew! He was hot.

Today, the weather was hot and that was *phew* of a different kind. It was doubtful if anyone at the temple today would be saying, 'Bloody English weather!' More like, 'Bloody English weatherman, I wore my bloody coat, didn't I?'

'Same rules as all temples,' Samir said, as they drove away from the house. 'The women have to remove the shoes of the man they enter with.'

'And if she doesn't?' Kareena asked.

'She has to give me a grope,' he said, signalling left and smiling at her.

'That's not even funny, Samir.' And she put her hand between his legs, giggling.

The car veered to the right.

The drive from house to temple took them along a mainly straight dual carriageway. A mild crush of cars were always held up near the centre of town like lost baggage and so Samir took a coronary bypass down Avebury Boulevard, which ran parallel to it.

His vision of Milton Keynes before he had come to live here had been of a grey, concrete monolith polluted by dull people. But upon his arrival, seven years ago, a sheepish grin had spread over his face. His vision had been wrong. The place was green, fresh and growing. The perfect place to set up a business and maybe the perfect place to set up a family. He had heard people in older towns slagging off the new city. But he was born in a modern age and liked the life of a modern town. If people wanted to live in the bones of the past, let them. But he did agree with one criticism. The Milton Keynes planners had been a bit greedy in the roundabout department.

'Sodding roundabouts!' Samir said angrily. 'I've been trying to get NightOwl advertised on that one.' He pointed to a well-pruned flowery roundabout with its sponsor's name neatly written on an eye-catching sign: DareDevil 24–7 Security. 'Crap company.'

'Why don't you get Mickey to put weedkiller on the flowers?' she said jokingly.

'Bloody good idea,' he said, not joking.

It was becoming harder not to like his wife. He glanced across to Kareena, she was miming along to Eric Clapton's 'Wonderful Tonight'. Samir felt confused. It had only been a heartbeat ago that he had been arguing with Cloey over who was going to be sleeping on the left side of the bed when she finally moved in. Now Kareena slept on the left side. Surely love doesn't change ships that easily? Could a man really divide his love between two such different women?

The car shot down a side road, along a newly laid piece of tarmac and up a small slope to the huge metal gates that guarded the temple. Samir drove through the open gates. You could take a Polaroid of yourself outside the temple and tell people that it had been taken in India. And they would tell you to stop bollocking, that it looked nothing like temples in India. How would you explain the eighty-five yellow Neighbourhood Watch stickers plastered on the windows? Or the huge sign, Milton Keynes Sikh Gurdwara? Or the adjoining brick building called the British Gas Tool Shed, with a subtle addition from the local community, Pakis Keep Out.

Samir had a choice: he could park next to the red Mercedes or the silver Mercedes, or, alternatively, he could mingle with the black Mercedes and the gold Mercedes.

'Can't Indians buy something other than Mercedes?' he said, blipping his blue Mercedes.

He covered his head with a white handkerchief and led Kareena to the entrance steps. She tried to control her nerves. Meeting a new Sikh community was like joining a new school halfway through term: everyone looking at you; wondering who you are; where you came from. Kareena told herself to ride the waves and go with the flow. Who knows, she might even come out with some new friends. She would definitely be coming out with a sore bum.

Jordan leaned against the British Gas shed and threw his fag end over the wall. He wore black shorts and a black Billabong T-shirt. His red John Lennon sunglasses completed the look; whatever look that may have been. The last hour had been an eye-opener. He wouldn't be falling for that old shit of sending money to Bangladeshi charities any more. He hadn't been aware of the wealth that flowed through India's veins. A whole fleet of Mercs, women dripping with gold, and precocious four-year-old kids walking round with their hands-free mobiles shouting down the phone to their butler not to forget to tape *The Money Programme*.

He set his watch to bleep after four hours. Mission Snapshots had begun. He wondered if the other Indian people this Sammy mingled with inside the temple knew how handy he was with his fists? As Sammy knelt and prayed to the god with six arms, or eight arms, or however many arms it had, would the god know how evil Sammy was? Would it have seen him lashing out at Cloey? Would it even care? Jordan walked casually across the car park.

Sammy's car was a beauty. Jordan felt an icy shiver go down his spine as he plunged the six-inch blade through the rear tyre. He dared anyone to catch him as he looked around for any do-gooders who might raise the alarm. The stale air rushed out through the wound, with the smell of dead fish. The car seemed to groan as its back legs began to buckle. With a swift glance round again, Jordan slapped a pre-written note, scribbled in his left hand, on the windscreen.

This car is dangerous to drive, one of the tyres is flat. The kids across the road did it. I tried to look for you, but I don't know what you look like. Sorry.

He returned via the route he'd come and sat in his car about four hundred yards away from the *gurdwara*. He lit up. It would have been a mistake to deflate two tyres. With only one, Sammy would more than likely change it himself, using the spare in the boot. Wrecking two might have led to any number of things happening. He might have decided to send his wife home while he waited for the AA, for example. One tyre wrecked was definitely safer, giving Jordan and Cloey that extra half an hour, if needed.

Puffing on his fag, with the smooth confidence of a plan going to plan, he smiled to himself. Maybe the gods were on his side. An awful thought suddenly occurred to him: what about the Indian gods who had just watched him outside their spiritual temple. What about them? Were they on his side as well?

Or were they on Sammy's side?

Chapter Twenty-three

Over the years since leaving prison Jordan had collected as much DNA as he could from different people. Bundles and bundles of different people's DNA from just a few handfuls of hair off the hairdresser's floor. Perfect to leave at the scene of a crime. Perfect to fool the town clowns. Today, however, he had speciality DNA – prison warder beard hair – only received in the post a few days ago from Bubber's cell. It had cost ten packets of fags, a 180ml bottle of Tabasco Habanero Sauce, and a copy of *Playboy*. If it all went wrong inside Samir's house – the prison warder would cop it.

Jordan tapped his pocket filled with DNA as he walked away from his car holding a black briefcase. Two morning ramblers did a double-take at the sight of a businessman in shorts, T-shirt, trainers and sunglasses. Suspicion is in the eye of the beholder, Jordan thought, and carried on up the long isolated road that led to the entrance of Sammy's house. Already the thrill of crime was turning him on, a mixture of sensations surged through his body. He had tried to explain the buzz to Zara once: 'It's like creeping over ice that could crack at any minute and if you fall . . . you die.' She hadn't understood. He'd tried again. 'It's like creeping over ice that could crack any minute and if you fall . . . you're never allowed to shop again.' She'd understood.

Sammy's house beckoned. Instinctively Jordan remained out of sight, in the thick hedging that bordered the gates. A house this beautiful should not be left unattended, he thought, it would be like leaving your Rolex unattended at the pool side. He checked the time on his Rolex. (Some poor sod had left it at the pool side). It was 9.35 a.m. He made a phone call to Sammy's house in case the place was occupied by a friend or relative. The answerphone switched on and he hung up.

It was time for his disguise. From his case he produced Ryan's trusty old Snoopy mask. The rubber could be smelt from fifty yards away. Snoopy had been worn by Ryan on occasions Jordan didn't really want to think about right now. He was kind of glad Zara wasn't into cartoon sex like Ryan's wife was. Although they had once pretended to be Minnie and Mickey for a night.

Safely disguised, he trotted to the front door and rang the doorbell, setting off the dog alarms. He almost laughed. It sounded like a pack of wolves ripping open a carcass inside. A bit OTT. Checking in the obvious places for a key – under the mat, on top of the door, beneath the plant pots, in the keyhole –

he proceeded to the back of the house, keeping his body close to the wall.

It was never too late to make a mistake. People were so unpredictable. He poked his head round the corner and froze. Then his head snapped back behind the wall and his heart seized up. The sight of a woman, with long jet-black hair crouched over a flower bed, was not what he had expected to see. Jordan decided to take another peek round the wall. This time when he looked, he found he simply couldn't look away again. Why rush when staring back at him was possibly the most beautiful backside in the galaxy. Slow down, slow down, he told his filthy mind, don't be fooled by that perfectly tight pair of round cheeks snugly fitted into an expensive pair of designer jeans. Sometimes the best arses belong to the ugliest faces. And some women have no luck at either end. Bum deal.

Peeking through Snoopy's monster nostrils, where the holes were bigger, he noted the make of the jeans printed down either leg in big bold letters: Versace. Now he knew of only two people who would wear Versace jeans while gardening. And one was at home in bed and the other . . . He coughed.

Cloey turned round and screamed, following it up with a burst of laughter as she realized it was Jordan. His body was a dead give-away, Snoopy mask or no Snoopy mask. Jordan reminded Cloey that this was not Butlins and it was imperative that they kept shtum. Cloey reminded Jordan that this was not carnival day.

'What the fuck is that on your bonce?' he demanded.

'It's a wig. Don't you think I look like the wife?' She twirled round and removed her gardening gloves. 'Well, do I look like her or not?'

'I can't tell, when I saw her she didn't have a fucking grizzly bear on her head.' He walked past her and headed for the conservatory. 'Two questions. One, why are you gardening? And two, why do you want to look like the wife?'

She watched as he knelt before the conservatory door, partly opened the briefcase and took out a pair of black leather gloves. His movements were automated and his eyes fused to the workings of the lock. Watching men do men things never usually excited her. On this occasion, however, she was riveted at the sight of Jordan kneeling before her, risking his own freedom, so he could be part of her life once again. It was almost romantic. There was definitely something about being with a dangerous man, willing to do dangerous things, that sexually aroused her. Her mother had always played safe; Maxwell had been the result. Cloey had played safe herself and Samir was the result of that.

It wasn't as though she wanted to be chained to a motorbike and towed naked through town. Just the occasional step out of line, for God's sake. Instead of Samir unbuttoning her shirts, why not rip off a button or two? Instead of asking for permission for a bonk, why not throw her down and ask permission afterwards? Were we the only animals in the animal kingdom who pretended we weren't animals? Apart from cats that is, for everyone knows they are royalty.

Jordan looked back.

'What?' she said, caressing his neck. 'Is it hard to

concentrate?'

'Why were you gardening?'

She turned her head, the wig was becoming lopsided. 'It took me months to have this garden transformed from a wilderness to a haven. Trollop moves in for five minutes, and already it's been neglected. And before you say, "Why bother?" I've got my pride.' She chewed her bottom lip. 'That's all I have got these days.'

'Whatever you've touched, go and put it back exactly as it was. I explained all this, Cloey. If you want my help, you do as I say. And take that fucking wig off. You look nothing like her.'

'You can be so hurtful. I'll put the weeds back in the garden, but I'm not taking the wig off. It's part of me now. Anyway, you've got your pathetic disguise.' She went back to the half-full wheelbarrow.

Jordan returned to the lock, remembering Bubber's invaluable advice, and from a bunch of skeleton keys he picked the closest match to the lock. It was no good just shoving the skeleton key in and wiggling it, you had to respect the hole, you had to respect what the hole was trying to tell you. Carefully, expertly, Jordan felt his way with the un-moulded key, prodding, poking, teasing even. Soon the resistance to his foreplay began to pay dividends and within half an hour he was carefully sculpturing away at the malleable metal with an assortment of files. The picture in his head was of a three-dimensional lock. And, finally, in his hand he held a three-dimensional key. He placed the key in the keyhole, held his breath and prayed to the locksmith in the sky . . . Cloey was bored and unimpressed by now.

'Bingo,' he said smiling, with his eye on his watch.

'Thank you, Bubber.' He blew away any filings. 'As soon as the door opens, the burglar alarm will blow. Are you sure you know the code? I've got my trainers on, you've got your sodding stilettos on.'

'Meaning, Criminal?'

'Meaning this criminal can run, you can't.'

She knew the code and a second later Cloey was dashing through the downstairs with the alarm screeching, while Jordan kept his eye on the sky. If he saw a cop 'copter, he was out of here.

ALARM ACTIVATED

Marvin searched through the NightOwl manual. He had been told nothing ever happened on Sundays. The computer screen was proving otherwise, flashing its warning.

Page by page he read through the security guide, ignoring Mickey's sarky comments. It seemed to tell you everything but what to do when an alarm activated: instructions as to where Samir kept his emergency mobile top-up cards; a list of take-away numbers; a map of Luton; opening hours for MK shops over Christmas three years ago; the call-out numbers for Klix coffee machines. He bypassed a chapter on the various types of fires and how to control them. A chapter devoted to bomb evacuations. Even how to set up a temporary government if your town was hit by a thermonuclear blast. There was nothing on alarms.

The screen flashed angrily, bleeping progressively louder.

Marvin looked at the monitor. 'Will you fuck off!'

To his surprise it stopped, and in its place a phone

number appeared, with a slightly worrying message above it:

> BOSS'S HOUSE
> I PAY YOUR WAGES
> GET OFF YOUR ARSE AND SEE TO IT!
> MK 5897932
> Code word: Tandoori.

Marvin's sweaty hands shook like two wet fish. He was of an extremely nervous disposition. He'd seen people become a tad flustered when faced with death. He on the other hand only had to see Nick Cotton say 'Maa' to Dot and his face became blotchy. Trying to control those shaky hands with difficulty, he picked up the phone and dialled Samir's number.

Jordan closed the conservatory door just as the phone rang. He looked at a grinning Cloey. 'Go on then, answer it, do your bit.'

She skipped to the hall and picked up the phone, kissing the receiver. 'Hello . . . Sorry about the alarm . . . Clumsy me . . . Samir's not here, I'm his wife . . . Say again . . . You want to eat some cheese? . . . Brie? . . . Oh, breeeeeeach. You mean breach of security. Have you got a stutter?' Jordan was waving for her to stop. 'It's a *horrible* stutter. I'm finding it very hard to understand a word you say . . . I forgot the front door key, silly me, so I came through the back. Be a sweety . . . do-do-do-do-do don't let sum-sum-sum Samir know will ye- ye- ye- you? . . . Ta-ta-ta tandoori . . . Goodbye.'

Marvin placed the receiver down. 'Fer-fer-fer fucking

bitch!'

*

Jordan faced her. 'You heartless, cow. You've probably wrecked his day.' He was annoyed. 'Come on, get your photos and let's go.'

'I'm not finding you very sexy at the moment, Jordan, all bossy and dominating. You did your bit and you were very clever. Did I rush you with the lock? No I didn't. Now, remember, I've got a lot of memories in this house, good and bad. So if you don't mind, I shall be taking my time.' She took his gloved hand. 'And talking of memories, Jordan, I've got something to show you upstairs.'

She knew the house blindfold, its corridors and rooms were engraved on her mind like a map etched on glass. Her personality flowed through these walls like the blood of the house itself. Each colour, fabric, ornament and picture had been chosen carefully by her with affection and tenderness. This house was taken from her dreams and if she couldn't have it, then no one could. If she had to raze it to the ground herself, she would.

Standing outside the weirdly painted room, she faced him. 'I never ever stopped loving you. Ever!' And she pushed open the door, leading him inside. 'I dare you not to be stupefied by this room's beauty.' Her head tilted to the side. 'Never in a million years did I think you'd ever get to see it for yourself. Enjoy. I'll be back in a little while.'

As quick as a smash she was gone, the door slamming shut behind her. Even through the rubber mask, the scent of paint was thick, and Jordan felt his eyes overloading with details. There was definitely an obvious theme in here: him. Four walls, ceiling and a wooden floor all drenched with artwork connected to himself. Wow! Ignoring the entrails and blood, the mural was a visual 'This is Your Life, Jordan'. From boy to man, school to prison, England to France. It was an odd sensation. One segment nearly tore his eyes from their sockets, winding his insides like a blow from Tyson. A painting of himself behind bars staring out at Cloey being burnt on a bonfire. Joan of Arc was lighting the flames. The title? *He Sits Behind Bars. I Sit on a Barbecue. An Angel Lights my Fire.*

Glancing out of the window, his mind felt askew. There was probably more blood in here than when Van Gogh chopped his ear off, but he could tell it had been intended with love. Sammy had obviously brutalized her palette, turning each brush stroke into a knife stroke.

He returned to the mural, his eyes drawn to a picture of an empty crucifix in the snow. A caption on the painting said, 'Gone for Winter'. And below it a small poem titled: 'Gone'.

> *I let you go*
> *and now you're gone*
> *it's all gone badly wrong.*
> ***Blood-tied to death.***
> *I wait for you until I die*
> *then come join me*
> *in the sky.*

Cloey was the love of his life and his world was only half full without her. As the words said, they were blood-tied till dead. He walked out of the room, feeling like the captain of a sinking ship. All those years he'd thought Cloey had shed her love for him like dried skin, when really she had loved him all the time.

Stalking down the corridor he became aware of a burglar's nightmare: noise, and lots of it. Quickly he located the racket, and warily opened the door to the master bedroom. He'd been hit in the face with many things before, shoes, fists, birdcage, snowboard, but he'd never been hit by fifty decibels of palpitating Hindi music until now.

'What the fuck are you doing wearing a sari, Cloey? What is this, Network West?' He located the stereo and flicked it off.

Cloey stopped dancing and pointed to her clothes neatly piled on the bed. 'I'm naked under this.'

Jordan pointed to her breasts spilling out of the badly fitted glittery pink sari. 'I know.'

She giggled wildly. 'What did you think of the room then? My artwork?'

'The artwork?' He didn't really know what he thought of the bizarre collage of memories. The room devoted to his life, and sometimes death, showed warped affection, as if his life was a jugular vein seen through the eyes of a vampire bat: Cloey's intense way of painting her love for him. 'I loved it.' He hovered on his words. 'So, you knew all about my snowboarding then? And France? And . . . what about Zara?'

She hissed, '*Apart* from her. Yes, Jordan, I was obsessed with you. And I still am. I hung on to snippets of information about you when they came my way. You could say that that room was where I hoarded them.' With a huge smile, she gave a twirl. 'Anyway, don't you think I look like the wife now? I think this is her wedding sari from what I can make out of the wedding album.' She smiled. 'But I can't be sure.' Wiggling her hips she walked towards him and let the sari fall to her feet. She was now totally starkers – except for the wig. 'I want you to make love to me, Jordan. I want to make love on that bed, in the house I love, with the man I love. And I want you to do it rough.'

He was male. His blood was red. His blood was hot. What was he to do? The only words he could find were. 'Houston, we've got a problem here.' Then he kissed her on the lips.

'Without the mask, Jordan, kiss me without the mask.'

And Cloey removed Snoopy . . .

Chapter Twenty-four

Aileen pulled her trolley case down Bruckley's main road, her expression grim. No one saw the slim frame as it shuttled away from her house with a bitter twist to its mouth and a certain anger in its feet. No one saw her, and even if they had, they wouldn't have recognized her. Aileen never missed Sunday Mass, so it must be someone else who looked like her.

But it was her, and she was angry, and she was heading straight for Cloey's.

She kicked the bottom of the door with her foot. 'Cloey, it's your mother. Get out of bed.' Aileen checked her watch. 11.40 a.m. Her lips curled. She should have been singing her favourite hymn by now. 'Let me in this instant!' She banged with her foot again and joined in with her fist.

The door opened slowly. Claudette yawned. 'She's not here. Bye.' She closed the door as far as Aileen's foot would allow, and impatiently repeated, 'Look, she's not here.'

Aileen had a fair amount of strength coiled up in her tendons and she let loose with it all, ramming open the door and nearly knocking Claudette over.

'Out of my way, worthless woman!'

She stomped up the stairs, banging the case into the wall, chipping the paint work as she went. Abruptly she entered Cloey's bedroom and wasted no time in coming up with a word to describe her daughter, 'Whore!'

Her eyes were dry of tears. Not since 13 May 1981 had her tear ducts been so busy; that torturous day when the Pope had been gunned down in his popemobile. The village had mourned then, just as they appeared to be in mourning now. Criminal Jordan was back, an infestation of the worst kind: the human kind. Although human sometimes seemed too big a word for scum like him.

Yesterday, several villagers had watched, appalled, as Jordan had caressed Cloey on her very own doorstep. Mrs Topps had said, 'He felt her up good 'n proper, outside the gate. I nearly pulled a leak on my plasma pouch.'

As word spread like panic through the village, the full gory details emerged. Jordan had come to Cloey's, then pulled down his shorts and wiggled his tattoo-coated bottom. Two out of the five witnesses swore blind that if it wasn't for the aspirin they took, they would have suffered fatal heart attacks.

When Aileen had arrived for Mass that morning, a dark foreboding had greeted her at the church entrance. Fifty per cent of the congregation were in black attire. Father Luke had rubbed his midriff and gestured Aileen to the gate. 'Your attendance is needed elsewhere I fear, Aileen. Young Jordan has brought shame on us with his public display of naked, animal lust with your daughter. You must go and see to her, make her understand the error of her ways. Make haste!' With a quick splash of holy water, Aileen had fled to save Bruckley from the Devil.

Now she made haste, searching through the room for evidence of Satan. Boxer shorts came under that category. Along with men's aftershave, vibrators and packets of condoms. She dithered over a box of tissues wondering to what use Satan could put them. A disturbing thought occurred to her. She crossed herself and the box landed in Satan's growing pile.

As she deftly unzipped the olive-green case, she noticed Claudette hovering at the door.

'Find yourself a new lodger. Cloey is coming to live with me.' Aileen began to fill the case with Cloey's clothes. 'Before you tire me with your girlie banter, remember that for all I care, you can go to hell. It's time my daughter returned to the straight and narrow.' She continued packing.

Claudette walked to her room, mumbling under her breath, 'Stigmatic freak.'

She dialled Cloey's mobile. She had something of great importance to ask. No answer. She texted her:

> *Cloey,*
> *I've run out of Endless Lash mascara.*
> *Be a darling and pop in to Boots.*
> *Rimmel. Brown/black. Hugs and kisses.*
> *Miss World.*

Aileen stood staring at the bottom of the stairs. She kicked the case forward and watched it tumble and bounce to the ground below. Then, very calmly she descended to the last step and sat herself down facing the front door.

She waited . . .

There's no hiding the look of relief when Indians leave a temple, as limbs that have been forced to sit still for over four hours learn to move again. A mass of cracking bones and jellied behinds burst through the open temple doors wobbling like geriatrics and smiling goofy smiles like escapees from a mental home. *One Hundred Punjabis Flew Over the Cuckoo's Nest.*

Just as the car park to the *gurdwara* fills slowly, it empties slowly also. Clans of Sikhs discuss other clans of Sikhs. Who did what with you know who. As in any community, it is always better to be the one doing the gossiping than the one being gossiped about. Unbeknownst to Samir, his name had been batted around over the years like a ping-pong ball. They hadn't known much about him when he arrived in Milton Keynes; all they knew was that he had a healthy wallet, a posh car and good looks. If they couldn't find out about his past, then they would invent one for him. His family were obviously all dead, the Bandit Queen had killed them. Without a family to support him – and this wasn't his fault – he turned out to be gay. That is why for the last seven years he had come to the *gurdwara* without a wife. Until today.

Today, the younger women crowded round Kareena, the new exhibit of the temple. They couldn't help feeling a little jealous. She was stunning: slim, tall, dripping with gold, well spoken. Not only did she have all the womanly goods, but her chosen man was full-on-hunkable-take-me-to-bed-now material. You can't choose your man in an Indian marriage but by golly *chapatties* you can certainly choose your fantasy. The women fired questions quickly, before the men called them to depart.

'How long have you been married?'

'Just over a week,' Kareena answered.

'Where did you come from?'

'Watford.'

'What did you do in Watford?'

'I was a teacher.'

'What did you teach?'

'Kids.'

'No, what subject?'

'Mixed subjects. I was a primary school teacher.'

'We thought Samir was gay.'

Laughing. 'No, he is not gay.'

'Did the Bandit Queen really slaughter his family?'

'Well, it was nice meeting you all. Maybe see you next week.' And we can discuss what medication you are on.

Kareena caught Samir's eyes and he broke away from the congratulatory pats on the back. To be accepted by the Turban King was an honour, enough to keep Samir in smiles for a week. Now they knew he was married, his face was welcome in all their homes, strengthening the ties of the Indian community. He was now one of them.

'Racists!!!!' the voice shouted across the car park. 'Racist bastards!!'

Kareena looked at Samir: was this normal?

He stared back: no it's not.

A man in an orange turban stood by a Mercedes waving a piece of paper. A few children were kneeling on the floor inspecting the tyre. The tickets were free so everyone ran over to see. Who was a racist? Plenty of eyes widened and a scampering of feet shot across the car park making sure that no other cars had been done over.

Samir and Kareena refused to be like the others, running as if they were collecting food rations. They walked over in a dignified fashion. Calm and collected. Now what on earth was going on? thought Samir. Surely it couldn't be as bad as all that—

'Great! Just fucking great!' shouted Samir. 'That's my fucking car.'

Kareena nudged him firmly, trying to smile away her embarrassment at her husband's choice of words.

The Turban King arrived. The Temple Daddy. Combating racism was his forte and a job he did well. He knew how to stand up for his heritage. He was sick to his false back teeth of being called a Paki. Paki this and Paki that. When would the ignoramuses realize you weren't a Paki unless you came from Pakistan?

He barged through the crowd, winding some with his beer gut. 'Ignore references to Pakis, everyone. None of us here are Pakis, understood? We are bloody Indians.' He snatched the note and began to read, his chubby fingers curling round the paper. He looked up through bloodshot eyes. 'Kids. I thought so,' and gave the note to Samir.

Samir read the note and jangled the coins in his

pocket. This was all his own fault, he thought, if he hadn't been such a miser this would never have happened. While they had been sitting inside the temple he had noticed a two-pound coin trapped between the carpet and the white sheet covering it. Carefully and quietly he'd used his car keys to make a slit and work the coin through, totally ignoring the *granthi* and the readings, his eyes wide with greed and his tongue dry with anticipation. He'd nearly punched the air with joy when he had that coin in his grubby mitts. And now, the flat tyre was his payback.

'Have you a spare tyre?' The Turban King said, rubbing his own. He then eyed Samir suspiciously. 'This isn't just to encourage us to buy your security cameras for the temple, is it? A bit of a cowboy set up, if you're asking me.'

Kareena saw Samir's fists clench and she jumped in hastily, 'Uncle ji, why would he wreck his own car, when he could wreck someone else's?'

The Turban King agreed with a nod. 'Good. But we still think you should supply us with a free camera. Racists are everywhere.'

A small child with a topknot spoke up, 'Could have been the Pakis.'

The Turban King frowned. 'Shadhup, Baljinder, don't shame us all by your ignorance.'

Baljinder was hastily wheeled away in his pushchair by his mother.

Samir opened the boot. Normally in a situation like this he would feel as flat as the tyre, but somehow with his wife shining over him with a smile and some kind words, he didn't feel too bad. It occurred to him suddenly that that was the difference between Cloey and Kareena. It was called support. Cloey would have leapt down his throat with a spiteful remark, 'Useless, Sammy. Can't even find a safe parking place. You're going to have to make this up to me now. And that means brushing off the cobwebs on your credit card.'

Cloey would have only offered hindrance. Kareena, on the other hand, was offering help.

'I'm not shagging you in her wedding sari, Cloey, it's off.' Jordan stood naked searching through Kareena's vast but sparsely filled wardrobe for something suitable for Cloey to wear. 'Can't you just be nude?' He checked his watch again. 'For God's sake!'

For half an hour Cloey had been pleading with him to make love to her while she wore Kareena's wedding sari. But the spoilsport had gone all gentleman-like. She admired his bare bum as he burrowed amongst the colourful saris, shaking her head time after time at his choice of garments. Sliding off the bed, she walked over to the chest of drawers still hanging open from her earlier nosing around.

He turned round, holding up a goblin-green *shalwar kameez*. 'What the hell are you doing now?'

'Lighting a joss stick. To help the mood of the room.' Tossing aside a few pairs of lacy knickers, she produced an open packet of patchouli incense sticks and lit one with Jordan's lighter. 'You know how stubborn I can be, Jordan,' she said returning to the messed-up bed. 'I'm not letting you outside the house, until you've been inside of me while I wear this wedding sari. Remember, he used to hit me. Now hurry!'

Jordan had two choices: prison or shag.

He climbed on the bed, then climbed on her, hitching the material up high.

'I'm not staining the sari. Clinton taught all us men a big lesson. I've gone to great lengths to keep my DNA out of this house, so I won't be happy if there's any spillage. Keep your hips still and let me do all the work.'

'You're so crude, I'm not a blow-up doll you know.'

'You are now. Now shut up!'

With his gloved hand he guided himself inside her. Trying to ignore the red and white dots painted above her eyebrows, Jordan endeavoured to enjoy Cloey while keeping a whole bandwagon of guilt at bay. Zara was most likely waiting for her shag at home, with the fridge topped up with celery and the baby room all hoovered. He consoled himself with a thought: only nice people feel guilty.

'If you love me, Jordan, you'll wait until I'm satisfied, before you satisfy yourself.'

'I'm waiting, I'm waiting, now hurry the fuck up,' he said very calmly, disregarding his watch-alarm warning that Mission Snapshot should be over by now.

'Think of me as the Indian virgin bride, prove to me that my parents chose correctly.'

'Well, you'd better hurry up and get jaundice then, because you're the palest Indian I've ever seen,' he said, still sweating, still thrusting, still waiting.

She giggled. 'I love having sex with you, Jordan. It's such a riot.'

And it always had been. The day he gave her her first orgasm, she had been just fourteen and she had screamed so loudly she was sure that if you listened carefully today you could still hear its echo. Afterwards, she had hit him round the head with her denim school bag. 'Who taught you to do that?' Next day at school he'd slipped a vibrator into her bag with a note. 'If I'm moving too quick for you, let me know.' But it was never too quick, and soon they fell into a filthy world not that dissimilar to a drug user's: sneaking off to dingy hideouts to get high on sex, dreaming about their next fix, and even passing sordid notes in class of what one would like to do with the other.

Amid the wisps of incense floating in the sunlight, Jordan helped a sulky Cloey fold up the six metres of glitzy sari. Rushing sex was bad enough, but rushing the after-sex cuddle was awful. A real man would have at least waited until their heartbeats had returned to normal before saying, 'Move it, you stupid cow!'

They tidied away anything they had disturbed, but Jordan knew it would be impossible to leave the room without some traces of their presence left behind. The fact that you now needed fog lights to negotiate the room was, maybe, a bit of a giveaway. He used a pair of Samir's yellow *kacchas* to waft the joss-stick smoke out to the balcony, careful not to put his hands on the bum-crack area. Gloves or no gloves, there was nothing macho about going near another man's undies.

Picking up his briefcase, Jordan stared at Cloey's bulky Elle bag through his Snoopy mask. 'Apart from the photos, is there anything else that you could use as evidence? Like a jagged knife? Or a cheese cutter? Rope? Anything?'

'Sick, Jordan, you're depraved,' she said, following him to the front door. 'I've got the photos, that's all I need.'

This was their first *official* crime together. Cloey felt like giving herself a cuddle. If only clueless Jordan knew why she really wanted to get in this house. If only he knew she had planted something downstairs today that would break open any relationship. Now there was only a manila envelope and some sticky tape separating Samir from his separation, and one practical joke that should add a dash of colour to Samir's whites. Oh joy. Samir and his wife were a dead marriage walking. Even though Jordan didn't realize it, he really was her hero and she slapped a huge smacking kiss on his huge rubber lips, feeling a slight twinge of guilt at having used him.

Still, the house was the most important thing and she couldn't have that without Sammy. She only hoped that love-struck Jordan would appreciate the irony of it all when he realized that he had lost his own relationship with Zara so that she could have her relationship back with Sammy. It was only a matter of time before Bimbo Dimbo Zara found out about the two of them, she could feel it in her bones, or rather, she could feel it in her mobile phones.

They left by the front door, resetting the burglar alarm as they went. The only mistake Jordan could think of with regard to Mission Snapshot was that Cloey had been dropped off in Samir's drive by a taxi driver, who happened to be Indian.

'You stupid imbecile. I . . . I . . . I hate working with amateurs.'

'I'm not that stupid, Jordan, thank you. People

270

know me round this area, they love me, and they also know what car I drive. So stick that up your backside and swivel.' She gave him the bird.

And Jordan gave her a kiss.

Chapter Twenty-five

Loyalty is like a hidden language. An ESP through which people loyal to each other communicate. Like the wife who cheers the loudest for her husband's karaoke when she knows it's crap. Like the wife who tells her girlfriends that her husband is massive – when it could do with another five inches. Or the girlfriend who doesn't tell the wife that she already knows that her husband could do with another five inches as she only shagged him last night. Being loyal sometimes requires being a liar. By this calculation: men are probably most loyal.

Samir glanced over at his loyal wife as they drove slowly out of the temple gates. His dad had told him the test of their relationship would not be in the joy, but in the sorrow. Anyone can be good company when fun and laughter are flying. Throw in a few funerals and hospital appointments and watch the marriage vows creak with the strain. Samir smiled at

Kareena and she smiled back; they had been through their first test. If they could get through changing a tyre together, they could make it through anything.

The car stereo pumped out The Clash's 'London's Burning', and the air-conditioning was blasting. It was a lovely day for a lazy drive. An even better day for a drink. It wasn't really in the Sikh rules, but the best way to recover from the temple ordeal was to get smashed. And the best place to get smashed was the Hogshead in the city centre.

The Hogshead sat among a new complex of pubs and restaurants. If you sniffed due north, there was the aroma of Chinese food wafting towards you, south and you got Italian, west, Indian, and east, Greek. If you decided to spin round and smell the lot, you just threw up. Two huge metal balls and chains sat on the pavement outside. A jest to the men perhaps? wondered Samir: dare you come in to drink in here, or has your wife got you on a ball and chain? It was slightly ironic though, he thought, as they took an outside table beside one of the balls, that in Indian households it's normally the women who are chained. But, to be true to life, the chain would have to have been attached to a kitchen sink or a mother-in-law.

They sat down with their cold drinks in the relaxed atmosphere. It was the kind of place where if you accidentally spilt a drink on someone they would offer to buy you another, as opposed to some of the other pubs Samir had frequented before his marriage where spilling a drink came free with an ambulance to emergency.

Kareena was now part of this place called Milton Keynes. She stared round, taking in the sorts of people who lived here. Every town has a certain aura, a feel. She wondered if she would find it easy to fit in and whether it would ever be home. Home is where the heart is, and very much at this moment, like it or lump it, her heart was still back in Watford.

Idle chat gave way to sterner stuff.

'So, we both lied to each other?' Kareena said, sipping her Budweiser.

'How d'you mean?' he said, slightly concerned.

'On our first meeting, both of us said we hated booze.'

Samir gulped his Bud. 'Yeah, you're right, we lied.' He laughed.

'My point is, what else have we lied about?' She shuffled in her seat. 'We all say things to impress, but now we're married . . . Oh, I don't know.'

He watched her picking at the Bud label, her rhubarb-coloured *kameez* being jostled by a subtle breeze. 'You want us to open up a bit? Clear out any skeletons? I think it's a brilliant idea.' He loosened his tie and undid the top button of his white shirt. 'You go first. You're the lady.' Rolling up his sleeves, he settled back in the aluminium chair.

'It's not exactly skeletons on my part. I'm going to be honest with you . . .'

And she began. The words spilled out of her mouth more easily than she had imagined, no euphemisms, just blunt and to the point. She wanted to know whether Samir would think of her as less Indian if she looked less Indian, if discarding the traditional Indian clothes for things more practical would be insulting to him, whether his vision of an Indian wife would be ruined.

He nodded his understanding. 'Are you asking my permission *not* to wear them? Sounds like you are.'

'Mum said that I've got to always wear them and that I have to ask you—'

He butted in, 'No, you don't need my permission. Fucking hell, I wish these Indian mothers would loosen up a bit. What else did she tell you? That you've got to keep a clean house? Or that you've got to—'

'Sex!' She giggled.

Samir pulled his chair in. This could be very interesting. An Indian mother talking about sex. Not to be missed. Rarer than a pair of golden eagles.

'Sex? I don't even care if you make up the next bit, just make it funny,' he said, watering at the mouth.

She leaned in closer. 'She told me to give it to you whenever you wanted it. Never say no.' Kareena blushed. ' "Keep him happy in bed and he'll buy you loads of gold," she said.'

Samir laughed. 'Didn't see much gold on your mum.' He stopped laughing. 'Whoops. Sorry.'

She remembered her mother's first words regarding sex. A month prior to her wedding, she had closed Kareena's bedroom door, fidgeting with items on the dressing table, moving the make-up around, folding up a pair of knickers and placing them in the drawer, eager to put off whatever she had to say.

Then her courage had taken over, she had spun round, and said, 'On your wedding night, he will pull down his trousers. You mustn't be afraid. No matter how big it is, he will be proud of it. So you must be proud of it too. His eyes will go like a madman's and his *mooli* will rise and double in size right before you.

You must remember: this is what makes him a man. Keep him happy at all times, or his *mooli* may rise for another woman.'

From that moment, her mother refused to stop talking about sex. It was like a whole new world had opened up between her and her daughter. And Kareena was always dubious after that, whenever *mooli* was on the menu.

Kareena continued talking to a studious Samir, 'Apparently I'm not allowed to feel any pleasure myself – as that means I'm not doing my job properly with you. Anyway, I shouldn't even be discussing this with you.' She emptied the rest of the Bud into her mouth. 'Excuse me for being a woman, but a girl deserves the odd orgasm here and there, doesn't she? Indian or not.' Her nervous giggle followed.

'Of course she does,' he said, smugly.

'I look forward to having one then.' Kareena laughed. 'Whoops! Sorry.'

They watched two teenage lads on skateboards roll up to a bin, look inside, and fish out some newspaper. After a few attempts at lighting the bin, the boys gave up. It would probably take another two years in school for them to realize that metal bins don't burn. Their swearing could be heard from a hundred yards away. This was a charming place to be.

'So, what do you want to know about me?' Samir asked, tonelessly.

Kareena positioned her chair out of the sunlight. She spoke, 'Your mother worried me a little bit the other night.'

'I can't apologize enough for her wind.'

'Not that. Something else. She said that you more

or less had to be forced into this marriage.' She raised her eyebrows. 'The impression I got was that you wanted to wait until you were fifty. I find it a little hurtful that you were forced to marry me because of family pressures.'

'Stop right there. Now you listen to me, Kareena. My knees were raw from begging to be married. My family just exaggerates everything. Look what my mother said about your monster-bloated face and how it could be used as a lorry tyre . . . erm, not a big lorry like an HGV or a . . . whatever. Next question.'

She felt as though Samir had simply sprayed air freshener over a bad smell. And sooner or later she would have to bring the topic up again before the stench of his dishonesty choked her.

Her next question was even harder for him to answer. She said casually, 'Oh, I don't know. Why don't you tell me about your past women? It would be interesting to know whether any were special to you.' She giggled nervously again. 'For all I know, you still think about one of them now.' Her eyes seemed to zero in on Samir's shrinking pupils.

And Samir's pupils held his darkest thoughts.

This conversation was similar to one he had had with Cloey many years ago. He'd read somewhere that anyone can make a mistake, but only a fool would make the same mistake twice. Explaining to Cloey about his past women, or rather, past woman, Monica, he had made the critical error of describing her as attractive. It had all gone down hill after that. He would not make the same mistake with Kareena. Women, he was sure, loved being told how beautiful they were. But tell them how beautiful another woman is and get your suitcase, pack your things, and say goodbye, because you are now . . . pond weed!

Samir juggled a few facts in his mind until they made perfect fiction. He had repeatedly told Kareena that his past two lovers had been Indian. Cloey and Monica needed new names and quickly: Calvinder and Mandeep. It would be funny, he thought, if they could hear what he was about to say about them both now.

'Amazingly ugly, the pair of them. Faces like cheap furniture, worn and torn. Personalities so boring that my bum nearly sucked the chair from under me every time they spoke. And their hygiene – it stunk.' He looked up at an engrossed Kareena. Picking up the empty bottles, he walked over to the bin, put them in and returned. 'And *that's* the truth! Quite frankly, I never want to think about either of those smelly women again.' He bent down, kissed her on the cheek, and pulled her up. 'Come on, let's buy my beautiful, exciting wife some English clothes. You smell gorgeous!'

They headed across Midsummer Boulevard towards the shopping centre, hand in hand. You could not have found a happier pair that day in Milton Keynes.

Except for . . .

Cloey and Jordan.

A hundred yards up the road, they sat enjoying a glass of wine and a pint of orange juice in the Sunken Ship celebrating their unlawful entry. Various attempts by the landlords over the years to change the pub's deplorable image had failed dismally. The place was, is, and always would be, a dive. Couples came not only to murder a pint here but to murder each other. It was an unwritten threat that when you said, 'That's it, I'm taking you for a drink down the Sunken Ship,' it was time for a divorce. The landlord had got rich off the wedding rings he had found on the floor after closing hours.

'I've got you a small present, Jordan.' Cloey bent down to her Elle bag and produced a hexagonal silver-covered box. 'Open it.' She gave it a quick rattle. 'It was alive when I wrapped it.'

Half a minute later Jordan had a small rock in his hand. He looked disappointed. 'Thanks.'

She giggled. 'I know you like snow, and I know you like mountains. Wrapping snow is a bit tricky so I got you the mountain instead. Well, part of it anyway. It's from the peak of Everest.' She watched his face begin to light up. 'And it wasn't cheap. It's guaranteed. I had to scrape off Hillary's fingertips; he just didn't want to let go.'

Leaning across the table he kissed her, clearly chuffed to bits. He felt on top of the world, literally, until . . .

'You never did tell me what you liked about Zara. I mean I'm no expert in what a man sees in a woman, but surely it's not all about tits and bums, is it?' Cloey adjusted the itchy wig. 'Surely it's better to talk to someone with a bit of meat in her brain rather than a manky bag of mince? *So*, Jordan, is she good in bed like me? Or is she a bit mincey in that department as well?' She grimaced as she sipped her wine, wondering which vintage this cat's piss belonged to, then continued, 'I once knew a natural blonde who was so dim she dyed her hair blonde. Is Zara that dim? She's had her breasts implanted but what she really needs is a brain . . .'

He let her dig deeper and deeper, each word coated in salt ready to rub into any wound her mouth could open. It wouldn't be long before Zara had been relegated to an amoeba intelligence with a single-celled IQ.

Finally Cloey stopped and Jordan said, 'To put it bluntly, you're thicker than she is. And as regards to sex, only a thick person would ask me to compare. So, thicko, she's better at sex and her tits are real. Drink up.' He gulped his orange juice, semi-pleased with his conversational combat.

After waiting for Cloey's green skin to turn back to pink, he pressed her. 'So, show me these photos then. And I'm not squeamish, I was brought up on close-ups of Thatcher's face, remember.'

Sitting up straight in her chair, she composed herself. 'I don't want you to see me like that.'

'Just pass them over. I want to know what that fucker did to you, I haven't quite finished with that shit yet.' He put out his hand. 'Come on!'

'This is really difficult. Us women who are beaten feel ashamed, we blame ourselves, we can't bear for others to see us covered in bruises. So, don't be cruel, Jordan, let it go.' Cloey tried to remember an episode of *Casualty* she had seen. 'Oh yes, another thing is that we normally don't like to dwell on the macabre experience. I would rather I hide these photos away and never think about them again. Would that be okay with you?'

He paused to light a fag, staring towards a table in the far corner. Four people sat eating bar food like a giant game of Hungry Hippos, throwing the grub in their gobs, ignoring the cutlery, ignoring the red-faced baby crying in the highchair, which was currently being used as a tray for empty pint glasses. Jordan guessed the baby's first words would be, 'Last orders per . . . lease.'

He returned his attention to Cloey. 'You can hide the photos away if you want, but there's no way I'm letting him get away with this. I'll just have to imagine what he did to you before I stick my fist down his throat and pull out his pancreas.' He banged the table with his hand, then stood up. 'In fact, I'm going right now.'

'Noooooo,' she cried, waving him to sit down. 'Don't you dare touch him!' She wanted to reason with Jordan, but there was a wildness to him that she couldn't stop. She had to come clean immediately. 'He didn't hit me, I made it all up. I lied.' She watched his jaw go slack. Not a good sign.

There was an intense silence as Jordan sat back down.

A man with holey jeans glanced back from the pinball machine, smirked at Cloey's wig, then continued playing the flippers. He spoke to his stinky-looking mate who had a fag hanging from the corner of his mouth. 'Twiglet, did I, or did I not, just see a woman wearing a dinosaur's fur ball on her head?'

They both turned their heads towards Cloey.

Twiglet picked his nose and sneakily dipped his finger in his mate's lager. He said, 'You have a keen eye, Raymond, a keen eye indeed, but I'm of the opinion that it is, in fact, a Russian shot-putter's armpit. Now how the hell did it get there?'

They both laughed as Twiglet approached the table, ran his hands down the glossy wig and tugged it, sending it flying across the room, hoping that the man sitting with the wigless woman, who looked like he was about to kill someone, found it as funny as they did. He didn't, and they legged it as fast as they fucking could – Maurice Greene wouldn't have been able to keep up.

Jordan walked over and angrily kicked the wig back across the sodden floor towards Cloey and a bartender thanked him for sweeping up. Brushing it down, she returned it to her head and tried her hardest to look sweet and innocent. The beer dripping on to her shoulders didn't help.

He spoke, 'You used me. Why?'

'Not really. Don't overreact. He did hit me, Sammy did, not with his fists, but when he married his wife. Emotional punches, Jordan, emotional torture.'

'Like fuck. I can even hear the judge now: "Sammy, you have been sent down for fifteen years for beating the shit out of Cloey with emotion." It doesn't wash, does it? Now, you little bitch, you explain to this first-class mug what the fuck we were doing today.'

Something inside told Cloey she was in a lot of trouble. If only she had a pretzel she could have choked on it and then she would have been able to talk her way out of anything. Instead, while Jordan sat back with a look of indifference on his face, she talked her way out of nothing. All she had to fall back on was the cold, hurtful truth that she preferred money to love. Sammy and his house were worth more to her than Jordan and his love, and she'd do anything to get that house back. Anything.

She felt exposed under his steady gaze, as though his eyes were giving her a CAT scan. She relinquished custody of her thoughts. 'You're not a safe bet for me, Jordan. You'd either have an affair or end up in prison again. Sammy will be my husband, I will move into my lovely house, spend his money, order him around, and you, unfortunately, will remain only in my thoughts. Because, as you well know, Jordan, I love you, but you are still a criminal. Aren't you? Horrible, aren't I?'

He didn't bother to answer, just headed to the toilet for some fresh air.

Inside the grubby bog, he screamed mentally. If only the mirrors weren't already broken, he could have broken them; if only the doors were still on their hinges, he could have ripped them off; if the taps had worked, he could have kicked them. Everything that could be broken was already broken, including his heart. Except maybe his willy, but there was no way he was maltreating that!

Through a shard of mirror still hanging on the brick wall, he saw a dazed expression reflected. He hated himself, and he knew why. After all Cloey had just said, all she had lied about, all she had used him for, all, all, all, he still fucking loved her. And he hated himself for it. All of himself.

A skinny man entered and saw Jordan banging his fist against the wall. The skinny man left.

Jordan wished he didn't know what to do. It was so much easier to plead ignorance when you were ignorant. Although in some ways love is just that: ignorant. It doesn't care who it tramples over, it couldn't give a monkey's if you're happily married with four kids; if love wants to visit you again, it will.

Buried deep within the greedy little user sitting

outside in the pub, with a beer-swilling wig and a bucket of false tears, was the Cloey he loved, the *real* Cloey. He wanted her back.

Meanwhile, sitting at the table with a grin on her face, Cloey punched in a text message on her mobile, while Jordan was in the Gents'. It was amazing how much fun you could have bouncing messages off satellites in space.

> *Bimbo Dimbo Zara*
> *Your Jordy fucked me today.*
> *Have a good life.*

With the phone hidden on her lap under the table and her finger hovering over the SEND button, she waited for Jordan to return. A few minutes later, she watched him approach and pull up his chair beside her. It was definitely a shame, she thought, he was bona fide scrumptious-looking, the pair of them would have made *Hello* magazine go weak at the knees with their wedding pics. And that reminded her of what lay unseen in her Elle bag: Sammy's wedding album, which somehow had fallen in. Clumsy.

'You hate me now, don't you, Jordan?' She sniffed, her finger fluttering over the SEND button.

He gave her a kiss on the lips. 'I love you loads. I could never hate you.'

'Really?' Flutter, flutter. 'Do you love me more than Zara?'

'Without a shadow of doubt.' He stroked her wig, and wiped her tears with his hand. 'Come on, finish your drink and I'll get you home, but I'm going to need to take a shower at your place, if that's okay. I don't want Zara to smell you on me.'

'Why? Are you planning on sleeping with her tonight?' Flutter, flutter.

'No. You've satisfied me enough. Remember, Cloey, you and I are blood-tied until our deaths and beyond. Remember that!'

And Cloey's heart went aflutter. She kissed him on the lips as she dropped the mobile back in her bag. If Zara hadn't been blonde, she might even have felt sorry for her.

The landlord, Cage, smiled at Cloey's sobbing as he dried a pint glass, his fingers itching for her wedding ring. It should be flying across the room any second now. He subconsciously willed Jordan to compare her to her mother or slap her round the face; that normally did the trick with women. His moist lips formed a smile. He just loved break-ups.

Chapter Twenty-six

It's a fact: no man has ever died while out shopping with a woman. He's not allowed. When it's paid for, and all packed away at home, then he can die, and not before. Otherwise, he's selfish.

From the car's boot, Samir unselfishly unpacked bag number sixteen containing a delightful pair of Jimmy Choo shoes to go with the contents of bag number eighteen, a zesty, spicy, summer dress. It was at times like these that Kareena wished she had a neighbour, then she could shout up to the face at the window, 'I just couldn't help myself. I only went out for some milk.'

Samir pulled the *Citizen* from the letterbox and joined Kareena inside where she sat proudly among her shopping bags on the bottom step of the stairs. There were items in here that her parents would never have let her wear. Scandalous cuts and slanderous lengths. Clothes so expensive, so sexy, and so perfect that she would most likely be afraid to wear them.

She stood up and gave Samir a kiss. 'Thanks for everything.'

It always amazed Samir how buying clothes for a woman made for a happy home life. He stared at the mass of bags. Kareena should be happy for the next forty years. Each item he had bought her, her smile widened, so much so that at one point he'd had to shout because her lips were covering her ears. But it was nice to have his wallet emptied by someone who appreciated it for a change. And for a nano-second his thoughts turned to Cloey and what she meant to him, or rather, what she didn't.

They sat drinking wine in the kitchen, discussing the day, discussing the flat tyre, discussing past mishaps. Kareena described to Samir the time her father decided that the doctors were wrong and it was time for her brother's plaster of Paris to come off his broken arm, how Mum came in in the nick of time to stop him from using the Black and Decker power saw. Samir laughed.

A bottle of wine soon disappeared and Kareena agreed to go and find the sexiest number she had bought today and come down to be inspected by Samir's judging panel.

Samir flicked through his text messages as he waited for Kareena. Nothing important, nothing that couldn't wait. Even with the tyre business, he couldn't remember a better day than this for a long while. Since . . . since . . . Cloey.

His mind did a wheel spin on her name. Burning rubber on her letters C.L.O.E.Y. hoping to fade the damn thing away. He'd questioned himself before about what love means, and he had a cop-out answer: it didn't matter what love was, you just had to keep hold of it as long as possible. But it did matter really. Cloey mattered. He had loved her and now it seemed he was trying to blank her from his mind. For six years he'd gone to bed thinking about her and had woken up thinking about her. Now he'd sold her out for the ideal Indian marriage. He had fallen all the way with Cloey, just as he could feel himself falling for Kareena now.

He stared at the wine, the mischievous tipple. How many relationships were built on feelings delivered from the mouth of a wine bottle? How many families were wrecked by what went in the bottle bank? Was the bond thickening with Kareena just because of the blood thickening with the booze? His mind fathomed deeper.

Every time Kareena and he had had sex, they had been drunk. Every mindless, laughter-filled chat had been when they were sozzled. Even the frank and open discussions of their Indian backgrounds and Indian worries had been accomplished by the sly, sneaky, red and white truth-juice. He wondered if he was falling for his wife at all. Or was he just falling for his drunk wife while being drunk himself? What kind of marriage did he have if he needed alcohol to touch his wife? Or was this the wine talking?

'Not that booze affects me hey, mate?' he asked the friendly toaster, smiling into the metal grill. 'Anyway, we weren't drunk on our wedding night. So you can shut up.'

The clock on the kitchen wall had either stopped or Samir was now travelling at the speed of light. One way or the other Kareena was in another dimension in the house. The fifth dimension: the woman's wardrobe. If you can't beat 'em, join 'em, he thought with a head so light it was floating with the pixies. He held on to the banister and waited for the stairs to move him up, just like they had in John Lewis. A new bottle of wine was tucked under his arm. He whispered to it, 'Last drinky, or I may give all my secrets away.' He laughed and decided to climb up the stairs instead. It was a lot quicker.

Navigation complete, he found the master bedroom. You've got to be careful with entrances these days, he thought, running at the wooden door. 'Geeeeeronimo.' It gave easily and Samir landed softly on the floor, clutching the bottle like it was his last wish.

Kareena secured the belt on her blue satin robe. A mild chill swept in from the open balcony door. The fierce sunlight could not strip away the blackness in her eyes as she angrily helped Samir to his feet. His irritating laughter ceased immediately at the sight of her cold, accusing stare.

'What?' he said, lying back on the duvet. 'Come and tell me all about it.' He patted the side of the bed.

She pointed to the chest of drawers. 'Have you been through my things?'

He lifted his head up to look. 'No. Why?'

She shook her head impatiently. 'It's obvious, Samir.' Stamping over to the drawers, she threw one open. 'Look. All my personal things ransacked. What were you looking for? My knickers are everywhere. And the joss sticks have all been snapped in half.'

Samir got off the bed and walked over, his mind sobering rapidly. What was all the fuss about? He looked over her shoulder into the messy contents of the drawer. It looked like *The Borrowers* had been busy. Family photos, birth certificate, passport, exam certificates, degree certificate, class photos of the kids she had taught, souvenirs, driving licence, gifts – everything scattered everywhere.

Kareena's mother had always told her not to answer an Indian husband back. But this was not about answers, this was about questions. This was war.

She slammed the drawer shut and turned round to face him. 'What was so important that you had to sneakily snoop through all my *private* things?' She was amazed at how good-looking he still appeared, even though she was so annoyed with him. Somehow that just made her even more annoyed. 'Well!!!'

'I didn't go through your things, I wouldn't do that. Are you *absolutely* sure *you* didn't—'

'Don't you patronize me!' She flung the words at him like a bundle of rags.

A billion Indian women could feel a presence in The Force, a newly-wed Indian woman was battling against the dark side – her husband.

She continued, 'What was it you were looking for? You couldn't take my dad's word for it, could you? You just *had* to see for yourself, didn't you? I saw the way your dad was questioning it. It was like I had committed a murder in his village. How dare I? What were you going to do? Report back to him?'

Samir was now tee-total sober. 'What the fuck are you going on about?'

'Don't act all innocent with me. I know what you were looking for. You were looking for my degree certificate. That's why you bought me all those clothes, to creep back into my good books. Well, you can stick 'em.' She shot over to the bed, picked up the bags and the new clothes, and chucked them in the air. 'Fuck you, Samir!' Calmly, she closed the door and her footsteps stomped down the hall into one of the spare bedrooms.

Kareena had finally used the F word, and Samir needed a good buddy to talk to. Now where was his toaster when he needed it?

Jordan glanced over his shoulder to the rear of the car as he pulled up behind Cloey's Megane outside Lemonly Cottage. The wig was sitting on the back seat with a seat belt around it. He had insisted that she removed it while he drove the car, otherwise lorries on the other side of the road might have swerved into them. Their insurance claim might have read: tried to avoid out of control driver with his baboon.

He waved to a few of the nosy neighbours with his middle finger. It was probably the most exciting thing they'd seen all week. There was precious little they could do about being nosy, just as there was precious little he could do about being rude. He mouthed, 'Just fuck off!' and the nets flew back in disgust.

Cloey turned the key in the lock. As the door opened, she said, 'At least you didn't have to make a skeleton key for this house, Jordan.' They both laughed.

And then both stopped.

Aileen stood up from the bottom step. Eight hours of waiting can cause quite a lot of fluid build-up in the knee area and her creaking joints nearly exploded. She needed lubrication and she needed it quickly. Jordan smiled first. In fact, he was the only one who smiled. Horror was the look of the day in this house.

Aileen pointed to the door. 'I suggest you go, Peasant Boy, this is a family matter!'

Jordan answered by kicking the door closed. He wasn't going anywhere.

Cloey spotted the suitcase. If she looked hard enough, she'd probably spot a travel ticket attached to the handle marked 'To hell'. Her mother was here for a purpose; it had that ingrowing toenail feel about it, a pumped-up, crazy, I'm-going-to-drag-you-by-your-hair-screaming purpose.

Shivering with fear, Cloey faced Jordan and felt the power of his presence: a granite wall, unyielding and protective. He nodded faintly, reassuring her. He'd seen that fear in her eyes before: he'd seen the woman he knew as Cloey become just a scared girl; a cowering infant hiding from the bullying of a domineering mother straight out of the pages of a horror novel. Something had to be wrong when a thirty-one-year-old intelligent woman disintegrates at the feet of her mother. Surely the tie that binds could be untied? Once the fear had been broken, then maybe Cloey could be fixed. Half of Cloey's problems stemmed from this vixen right in front of his eyes.

He stepped forward. 'Look at her, look at your daughter. She deserves so much more than the life you're forcing on her.' He stared fiercely at a quaking Aileen. 'You don't realize how fucked-up your daughter's mind is because of you. I thought religion was supposed to bring people together, not drive a wedge between them. Is it really a sin for her not to

follow the path you lead? Wake up to yourself,
Ailee—'

The slap was directed with both ferocity and speed.
It threw Jordan's whole body slam to the wall behind
him. Aileen stepped forward and made a grab for
Cloey. Jordan snatched Cloey's arm away and pulled
her towards him. Her body was easily concealed by
his large frame and he stood firm, waiting for Aileen's
next move. Did the viper have a sting in her tail?

Aileen's knee came up and hit Jordan in the
bollocks. Wind surged from his lungs and his eyes
crossed and then crossed again. The pain. The Pain.
THE FUCKING PAIN!!! Aileen stood as his body
flopped to the floor and watched him wriggle like a
defenceless worm in agony. She regrouped, smoothed
down her rumpled dress and glared at her cowering
daughter.

'Get up. You're coming home with me. You
obviously can't be trusted to live on your own.'

Through watery eyes, Jordan saw Cloey scared
again. And that was a worse pain than the one he
suffered between his legs. Covering his jewels with his
hand, he rose quickly. It was time to dish out rather
than be dished on.

He turned to Cloey. 'Go in the kitchen.' She gave
her mother a last look and slipped down the hall to
the safety of the kitchen, leaving the wig and the bag
on the floor behind her. Jordan faced Aileen. His eyes
glinted madly. 'You gave birth to Cloey, Aileen, you
didn't just find her on a rubbish tip. If you carry on
treating her this way, she's going to end up hating
you.' He leaned in closer. 'The way you're going, the
only way she'll escape you will be through your death.

Could you honestly rest in peace knowing that? Knowing that your daughter was secretly pleased at your funeral?'

Pulling back, he watched the expression on Aileen's face, checking for a sign of regret, a possible clue that he was talking to a human being and not a machine.

He continued, 'I think that when God put us on this planet, Aileen, he gave us understanding. We all know right from wrong, you don't need the fucking Bible to tell you that. And what you're doing to Cloey is wrong and you know it. You'll go to hell, you will. And from what I hear, it's filled with people like me. No escape.'

Aileen swallowed hard. For the first time, she noticed that Jordan was wearing a gold cross. Its brightness seemed to burn in her eyes. God was supposed to be in everything: look under a rock and you shall find me; feel the wind and I shall be there. But never had she thought God would be inside a tanned, rugged, convict whose green, green eyes seemed to spiral inside her. She'd thought God had standards.

She stared at the door as if it would open itself, then with a determined stride yanked it open herself and slammed it shut behind her, leaving Jordan to collapse in a heap on the floor, cupping his crotch.

His balls were burning with eternal fire.

Chapter Twenty-seven

Kareena sat on the made-up bed in the spare room. This would be where she slept when she hated Samir. It totally lived up to its name, with a spare bed, spare wardrobe, spare chest of drawers, spare TV . . . Why oh why couldn't it have a spare man? she thought. Or two.

She glared at the wall. Samir was obviously asleep now. Very obviously. 'And a spare man who doesn't snore like an elephant,' she mumbled.

Outside, the dying sunlight turned the lawn a darker shade of green, each degree of shade adding a deeper sense of solitude to the house. But how could she be lonely when her husband was only a few walls away? She was just feeling sorry for herself, she thought.

She walked up to a hand-painted picture of Guru Nanak hanging on the wall – signed by a certain Cloey Evelyne. It was the sort of portrait a temple would display proudly; Samir had obviously paid an arm and a leg for it. The painting was entitled: *Roots or Weeds?* and Kareena hadn't got the foggiest what it meant, but something about the image cushioned the nasty thoughts bouncing round her head about her nosy husband, something encapsulated within the carefully chosen oils with golds that blinded and reds that burned.

Kareena knew she was a Sikh, sometimes she just needed reminding of the fact. She smiled and lay back on the bed. Maybe life wasn't so bad. So what if Samir hadn't quite believed her father when he boasted about her honours degree in English? So what if Samir just wanted to take a sneaky peaky look? She had nothing to hide from him. Just like she knew he had nothing to hide from her when she'd nosed through *his* stuff a few days back. His bank account figures topped any honours degree.

Kareena dozed as memories bobbed like corks on a sea of thoughts. She used to have scary visions of the man her parents would choose for her to marry. A man malnourished on good looks but a glutton of deformity. Her future would be filled with a dread of the bedroom. Each rising sun would warn her that a setting sun would soon follow. And each setting sun would remind Kareena that soon her grotesque, perverted husband would leap upon her in bed. He would mount her like a blow-up doll and push his revolting pleasure inside her. He would make no sense of the moans of resistance coming from her mouth, because he wouldn't understand the words she screamed. And he wouldn't understand them because he would be an animal. He would be the nightmare husband that Indian women dreamt about. He wouldn't be the dream husband that Indian parents had nightmares about. Oh, how wrong she had been!

Oh, how right Samir was. He was not what she had expected of an Indian husband, he was not what an Indian husband should be. Kareena had seen Indian husbands before in all their various forms: starting with Dad, then uncles, then cousins, they all tripped up with their same macho boots over the same macho mats. They all fell arse over tit when it came to respecting their wives. The boys who became men were also the boys who became chauvinists. Boys were not supposed to turn into caring, honourable, husbands like Samir. It just wasn't on.

Both Avani and Kareena had formed an alliance when it came to what they expected their parents to choose for them in the husband department. 'We will not be ordered around,' Avani would say. 'It's only fair that the man and woman are equal in the house and they get to share the workload,' Kareena would add. But they both shrank to two inches high when their father glared at them and shouted, 'I don't tolerate fools lightly. Men are the strength in any family. Without us, the family would fall apart. Now whoever we choose for either of you, will be the man you will answer to. But for now, I am the man in your lives and you answer to me. *Now*, go and make the dinner and learn how to take orders.'

Samir would seem weak in her father's eyes. But to Kareena he was stronger than life itself – even if he was a nosy so and so. His demands, if you could call them that, had been simple from day one: any problems they would discuss; any arguments they would try and resolve like two intelligent adults (no throwing cheesecake, then); household chores like cleaning, cooking, ironing were to be shared; if she wanted to go back to teaching, then she could. Kareena had trouble accepting these facts when Samir had first explained his idea of married life. Even now, as she lay there worrying about something as petty as him investigating her university degree, she knew that a luckier Indian woman did not exist. Samir was perfection personified and her parents had unwittingly chosen her the right man. A better choice than she could ever have chosen herself. She had never fallen in love before; she had never been allowed to. But now the nerves in her stomach were singing. She was at the cliff edge, about to jump over. She just hoped she didn't need a parachute. She prayed he would love her in return.

Samir was still snoring like a bison and she felt an overwhelming urge to leave the hate room and cuddle up to him in the love room. It seemed as though they'd been separated for weeks and yet . . . she had only been married one. Maybe this was a foretelling: life together with Samir would be better than life apart. Two Indian people chosen for one another by ancient rules could live happily together in modern times. Sometimes those old codgers of the past did know a thing or two after all.

Guru Nanak was heavier than Kareena thought, as she removed his painting from the wall and carried it down to the kitchen. This picture was too good to be hidden in the spare room. It was time he had a polish. And it would look far better than that blob of green that Samir had hanging by the phone called, *Milton Keynes From Space*. The eyes of Guru Nanak seemed to leap out at her from his youthful face behind the glass. His picture was ingrained in her childhood memory. She could not remember not knowing the face of Guru Nanak. He felt like family. From every relative's wall he watched, in every temple he waited, on every Sikh mind he pressed. He was, and is, what Sikhism stands for – Guru Nanak, *Babaji*, who had founded Sikhism, five hundred years ago. Even though the Sikh religion is the most modern of religions, its values are as ancient as the oldest rock: be a nice person.

The dust wiped away easily with a wetwipe, tightening up every brush stroke and solidifying every colour. The kitchen light bounced from the glass, like a flashbulb, momentarily blinding her eyes. As the image sharpened once more, another picture appeared in the kitchen. The picture of confusion that was now Kareena's face. She let go of the framed painting as if it had bitten her hand, dropping it on the marble floor, making the angry noise glass makes when it shatters. If this had been Gordon Ramsay's kitchen she would have been fired on the spot. As it was, she just sank to her knees and stared, shocked, at the painting of the Guru.

The high-pitched whirring of the fridge was a hazy background noise, as Kareena mentally grappled with a team of ideas that were playing against all she had known, all she had been brought up to know. Someone was either having a sick joke or someone was very sick. There was nothing funny about this at all.

Guru Nanak peered from out of the broken frame with a tiny gold crucifix round his neck. A mocking gesture sneakily painted by the artist, hidden by clever patterning on his clothing. Would a picture of Jesus wearing a turban cause as much anger to Christians? she wondered. Probably.

Kareena respected all faiths, but it didn't take too much noddle to realize that this was the action of someone who was cocking a snook at the Sikh religion, someone who had deliberately set out to cause maximum offence.

Whoever this Cloey was, whatever her beliefs, Kareena wanted to go and see her. And once Kareena had finished with her, she would be one painting that would not be a pretty sight. Maybe it might even win the Turner Prize.

Jordan parked his car as quietly as he could in his garage. It was 11.35 p.m. The end of a long day . . . or so he thought.

The lights were out in all the windows, a sure sign that Zara was asleep. He decided to have a final fag before heading for the sack himself. Nothing quite like that last evening fag when all the world is peaceful, he thought, switching his mobile back on, just in case he'd missed that life or death message. The amount of times he'd stood on this driveway with a blue flashing light for company, he'd lost count. And the amount of times the police had turned up nothing, they'd lost count. But Zara was sick of it. They shouldn't have to keep receipts taped to the back of every electrical item in the house. It was humiliating.

The neighbours had more or less disowned Zara and him on account of the early morning raids that were so regularly bestowed upon their snobby up-market neighbourhood. To have Jordan as a neighbour was to lose status. And status, as far as this area went, was everything. That's why Jordan gave them all the middle finger every time they ignored him. It was very statisfying.

> Text Message 1   2.40 p.m.
> *Jordy, where are you?*
> *Zara*

> Text Message 2   6.00 p.m.
> *Jordy, I'm worried. I'm not sure*
> *whether or not I should phone the hospital.*
> *Zara*

> Text Message 3   8.39 p.m.
> *Jordy, phoned hospitals and mates.*
> *No sign of you. Where R U?*
> *Zara*

> Text Message 4   10.05 p.m.
> *JORDAN, I hope you're in a ditch.*
> *Don't bother coming home.*
> *Flowers won't fix this.*
> *Z*

Jordan stared at the phone again, then back at the flowers. He threw the red, yellow and pink roses in the neighbour's bushes. That's where they'd come from anyway. He turned the key as delicately as possible; it was like breaking into his own house. There had to be an explanation for his behaviour, he just hadn't thought of what it was yet. He only knew one thing: he was in the wrong. Big time.

301

Knowing that you're in the wrong irked some people. Ask anyone who sits across from Jeremy Paxman. And Jordan was irked unconditionally at the moment. This whole day had been an exercise in selfishness, one long mixture of lies and deceit. Zara had been told by Jordan this morning that he would be teaching snowboarding at the SnoZone. A few hours of lessons for a large amount of money. She had been told that while he was on the cold, cold, cold slopes he would be thinking of her in the warm, warm, warm bed.

Zara had eased herself into Sunday like she did most Sundays: a lazy look at the glossy magazines, a lazy watch of the old black and white movies on the TV. That's what Sundays were for: being lazy. But being lazy was so much more fun when you were with your hunky man. And today, Jordan had disappeared off the face of the earth. That scallywag snowboarding would not be allowed to come between her and her sexual Sundays again. Jordan was extra good at sex on Sundays for some reason, and today she had missed out. She had told him once before that if snowboarding was his secret mistress then he could piss off and marry her. That's what he was doing anyway, skiing up and down her big white foamy wedding dress. The snow whore. Men!

Zara's voice leapt from downstairs as the lamp clicked on. 'Where have you been?'

'Oh, you're up.' He wandered in and sat down opposite her. It was too gloomy to make out if she was holding a knife and her face was half in shadow. 'I'm totally fucked. What a day!' He rested his head back and closed his eyes.

'Who is she, Jordan?'

'*Sabrina the Teenage Witch*.' His eyes remained closed as the giant cushion hit his head. 'Not this again, Zara. This is why men don't live as long as women; you kill us with your suspicion.' He smiled at his clever remark. 'I was arrested if you must know.'

'Arrested?' Her teary eyes came out of the shadow. 'Why?'

He huffed. 'Usual. Picking on me. Tailed my car, pulled me over, confiscated my phone, put me in the cell, gave me my phone call, but your phone was engaged . . .'

She jumped up and sat on his lap. 'Poor baby.'

He let her stroke his forehead and kept his eyes closed. 'Oh, Zara, why can't they just leave it? I did the crime, I served my time, leave me alone! Banging on and on they were, just wouldn't leave it, walking past the door, poking a rubber glove through the bars, threatening to give me a strip search. I said only if Sabrina does it.' And she nudged him gently in the ribs.

The beautiful silence was wrecked by Jordan's mobile bleeping. Grabbing it, his heart sank as he saw Cloey's number, and saying Ryan's name he switched it off immediately. As soon as his was off, Zara's mobile rang twice and then rung off itself.

Peering at the display, Zara checked her phone. 'Odd. I never get withheld numbers on this.'

'Turn it off, it's probably a pissed Ryan again, playing silly buggers.'

They both returned to the silence, but inside Jordan's head it rocked. In a few minutes, he was going to tell Zara all about Cloey. He could feel her breathing deeply as she rested her head on his shoulder and felt a lump climb into his throat. Even what he was doing now felt like stealing from her, enjoying her warmth, her smell, herself. These moments didn't belong to him any more. For as soon as she found out that she was snuggled up to a cheat, that he had lied, that he had slept with another woman, she would never want to see him again. Of that he was sure.

He held her close, as they sat on the sofa, and stole one last cuddle from her. Now was *never* better than never in circumstances like this.

'Zara, I love you, and I've let you down,' he whispered, but it was almost a croak.

She pulled away and hoisted up the strap of her skimpy black slip, her heart knocking at her chest like a police raid. 'How so?'

'You're not going to like what I'm going to tell you.'

She closed her eyes, and felt her cheeks burn, cooled quickly by a trickle of tears. She swallowed. 'I know . . . I know I'm not going to like it. It's a woman, isn't it? I know it is.'

He nodded. 'The one who came to the door the other night. Her name's Cloey not Catherine and I've known her since I was a kid. She's a big piece of my life that I never told you about—'

She interrupted. 'Did you sleep with her today?'

'Look, I—'

'You slept with her today then. I could be pregnant right now and you've slept with another woman.' She buried her face in a cushion. 'Do you love her?'

The room fell silent. And it was deafening.

*

Samir's and Kareena's wedding album lay in tatters on Cloey's back garden lawn. Cloey's and Claudette's sanity lay in tatters among the four bottles of wine they'd consumed.

'Separate these phonies,' Cloey said, holding the photo of Samir and Kareena up to the night sky. 'Separate the fake from the fake.' A chilly breeze chopped at her black wig.

Claudette watched, giggling with her bottle of Hobgoblin. She just loved garden bonfire parties, even if she and Cloey were the only two attending. 'Do it, Cloey. Shrivel them up, close the chapter on their love—'

Cloey spun around. 'They don't love each other,' she snapped, hurling another stump of wood into the growing roar of the bonfire, freeing smoke and splinters of glowing ash from the burning mound of heat. 'Love is not random, Claudette, you can't rely on a good throw of the dice to fix you up with the man of your dreams. Love is like a rare animal, you have to hunt it down. And when you find it, you don't go giving it away to the nearest *poacher* like that wife of his. I hate her! She's got my bloody house!'

The fire guzzled the oxygen, sending flames skyward and adding a certain warmth to an otherwise cold-hearted scene. Claudette loved it when Cloey hated someone – as long as it wasn't her. Cloey had the ability to hate people in ways that no one else could. Her mother was a perfect example of that, but after today things would be different, that was for sure.

Today had been the best pantomime Claudette had seen since Beckham received a red card at the 1998

World Cup. Classic. But not as classic as watching Jordan being kicked in the balls by Aileen. Aileen should have been sent off for that – what a dirty move! Claudette had watched and heard the whole scene from the safety of the landing. It had been a perfect blend of violence, action and romance, and afterwards she had felt like running down and giving that big hero Jordan a big hero's hug. But she didn't have her face on. And selfish Cloey had forgotten all about her mascara. Some friend she had turned out to be.

But she certainly knew how to make a fire shout.

Claudette yelled at her, 'Go on, Cloey, more petrol. More!' And the fire was like Apollo rockets shooting out at all angles; as hot as a steelworks, as unfriendly as the look in Cloey's eyes.

Smothering a handful of wedding photographs with Pataka's Tikka Masala Paste, she stared at a giggling Claudette with a 'don't look at me all funny, there's nothing wrong with me' look. Samir and Kareena were now marinating in chilli, turmeric and preservatives and they would make a lovely starter.

Cloey held the snaps at arm's length, masala paste oozing down her arms. 'Free my moneyman from the Devil. Slice their worlds apart. Never let their paths cross again.' She tossed the photographs into the flames as the fire coughed and spluttered. 'Bring him and my house back to me and never let them stray again.'

The chemicals in the photos twisted into blues and greens.

'Bring them to me,' Cloey shouted, 'or I will not be responsible for my actions.' She pulled out five pictures which showed Samir at his best, kissed all five, and then dumped the remainder of the wedding album on the maddened furnace, clutching the five photos like the keys to heaven itself.

Cloey sat watching the deepening orange glow, a growing smile stretching across her charcoal-smudged face. There was something right in doing wrong sometimes. Her mother had fallen by the wayside today, swept aside by a man who was obviously devoted to her. How easy it had been to steal back Jordan's fractured heart. So simple to fool a fool.

And yet, if things went horribly wrong with Sammy, she could quite happily spend the rest of her life with a criminal like Jordan, now she knew he had money (and lots of it). But with every good man comes baggage, and sooner or later, but much rather sooner, Zara's influence on him had to be stifled.

Cloey threw Zara's bubblegum-coloured pashmina on to the vicious flames. 'Burn, you bimbo, burn, you dimbo, give me back Jordan's unconditional love. See to it that he loves me for ever, let it not matter if I don't give him physical love in return. See to it! Hellfire. We are blood-tied until death.'

She laughed at her playful words. Being wicked had many advantages. You never weighed yourself down and you always left your options open. And you always came out the winner. Life was never just about taking part.

Chapter Twenty-eight

Zara had been preparing herself for Jordan's affair since the day she had met him. It could have come at any time, but she knew it would come. It was like that asteroid those scientists raved on about which would one day wreck the earth. Well, Jordan didn't need an asteroid to wreck Zara's earth, just his infidelity.

'Get out!' Zara launched his precious snowboard down the spiral staircase and it flew over the side, landing on the wooden floor below with commendable aggro. It was the board's best trick to date.

Jordan appeared from the kitchen area. The tray in his hands looked suspiciously like a 'Sorry I did wrong' breakfast. The food on the tray looked suspiciously burnt. He ignored the board's mistreatment and tried to feign a smile, it was at times like this that a man wished he didn't own anything precious. Last night had ranked worse than his first night in the slammer. At least he knew then that the prison sentence would end. With Zara, it looked like he would be serving life for what he had done wrong. She would not be giving him time off for good behaviour. Especially now she knew it all, the whole Jordan and Cloey love tapestry.

She walked up to him, took the tray and threw it across the room. 'I don't eat breakfast with adulterers, Jordan. You'll probably find that most women would need something better than a couple of burnt sausages to make amends.' She glared at the crispy, dried bangers lying on the floor. 'You can stick 'em up your arse. Because, to be quite honest with you, Jordan, that's where they look like they came from.' She glowered through eyes swollen from crying. 'I will never forgive you for this, I wouldn't know how to. You're as cold as the ice you ski on. Now please get out. I don't want to see you again. Ever!' She held her hand out for his keys.

Jordan unhooked the house keys and passed them to her. There could be no speech, no justification, no excuses. This was one of those times in your life where you just had to put your hands in the air, and say, 'I deserve what I get. I fucked up.' He left.

Outside Bernie's house on the front porch was a note: No Milk Today. Bernie thought it was hilarious. Above the letterbox was an even funnier sign, No Bills Today.

Jordan knocked on the door. It was 10.00 a.m. He stared back down the short footpath to the gate. The blue sky looked as though it had eaten something bad and was turning a nasty grey. Specks of rain appeared silently on the path and Jordan peered up to the darkening heavens: Bruckley didn't need a little bit of rain, it needed a fucking good hose down.

Bernie swung the door open. 'Hello, Son.' His eyes shifted past Jordan's baggy shorts and down to the holdall by his Nikes filled with his valuables – his collection of snowboards. 'Uh-oh. Get yourself inside, the kettle's already blowing. Wipe those shitty trainers, mind.' He helped Jordan in with a gentle push.

On the table in the tidy living room were a thousand newspaper cuttings. Various titles, various stories, all with one thing in common: biddies. Pictures of old-aged pensioners being led away in handcuffs by the police. Fodder for Bernie's campaign to get the council to vote against planning permission for an old people's home on the outskirts of Bruckley. His main reason was that his ninety-two-year-old mother might move there. His other reason was that it reminded him he was nearly an oldster himself. If he could prove to the council that wrinklies were the scourge of the world, they might vote against the home. Unfortunately for him the average age of a councillor in Milton Keynes is one hundred years old. His argument could fall on deaf ears – literally.

'I've really screwed up this time, Dad,' Jordan said, lounging back on the sofa. 'She's kicked me out.'

Handing Jordan a steaming cuppa, Bernie sank back into the waiting bum mould of his favourite armchair. 'But it's your friggin' house, Son. She can't kick you out of your own friggin' house. That's unpopular that is, very unpopular with me. She won't be welcome round here if that's how she's behaving I mean—'

'Leave it, Dad. It was my fault,' Jordan said, lighting up.

Jordan explained the ins and outs of what he had done wrong. How reason had failed him and love had taken over, how Cloey had used him and had stabbed him in the back once again. He resorted to cheap anecdotes from the movies to describe what Cloey had done. 'She tore my soul apart', 'She drew first blood', and 'She's the wicked witch of the east'.

Bernie viewed his son's idiocy with alarm: what the hell was he doing getting mixed up with Cloey again? And, more importantly, why had he risked losing Zara? He smacked Jordan round the head. Zara was a good woman, just like his wife had been. You don't go throwing away good things. He smacked him round the head again.

'For fuck's sake, Dad, leave it.'

Bernie always tried hard to see something of himself in Jordan. It would be nice to know that nature had decided to pass down your looks; that you were worthy of being taken another generation further, even if it was just in your smile or the curve of your eyes. Anything. Then again – Bernie recalled what he saw when he looked in the mirror – maybe it was a good thing that Jordan looked nothing like him. But still he searched for signs of himself in his son, and he'd always hoped that monogamy was one of them.

Removing his daily cigar from its tin, Bernie brushed it under his flaring nostrils. 'Only a month ago you were banging on about having little uns, couldn't friggin' wait to be a role model, you said, now look at the mess you're in.' He turned his attention to lighting the cigar.

Jordan watched his dad; he was a funny old mix. A milkman who hated milk, an asthmatic who smoked cigars and a rebel without a cause. He was also a Catholic who hated the fucking church. But he was a brilliant father.

He spoke uneasily, 'I hate saying this, Dad, because I sound like a right fucking poof, but I'm in a love triangle.' He laughed nervously. Bernie didn't respond. 'It's like this, I love Zara big time and I love Cloey big time. Selfish, hey?'

Bernie shunted his cheeks around. 'Sounds pornographic to me, Son. I don't know if I want to hear any more.' He had an afterthought. 'And this is legal, is it? This love triangle stuff?'

Shaking his head, Jordan stubbed out his fag. 'This isn't about sex, this is about time travel. I live with Zara in the present, but when I see Cloey I travel back to my past. Can't help it. I still see parts of the Cloey I fell in love with – the old Cloey. But when I'm with Zara and think back to what Cloey did to me, I just want to kill her.' He paused while Bernie took a deep thoughtful drag on his cigar. 'I love her and hate her at the same time.'

'This is serious stuff, Son, very serious. If I had a shotgun and Zara and Cloey were in this room, which one would you save?'

'Zara.' Jordan surprised himself at the speed of his answer. 'Definitely Zara.'

'If you died tomorrow, which one would shed the most tears?'

'Zara.'

Bernie balanced his cigar on the ashtray. 'Okay, if you were on a desert island—'

'Zara, Zara, Zara,' Jordan interrupted. 'I see your point, Dad, I messed up, so what do I do?'

Bernie grinned for the first time that day. 'Son, you know what to do. Make sure she suffers, she's a friggin' witch. You did time for that cow. And another thing, I didn't want to say this earlier, but, between the walls and me, a brown man was seen coming out of her cottage the other day. Know what I mean? Know what I mean?' He winked.

'I didn't see it in the papers.'

'You're not funny, Jordan, I never raised you up to be funny.'

Samir knew that his employees waited constantly for him to slip up. Anything out of place like a badly fitting shirt, or a dirty pair of shoes, even the tune on his mobile. If Samir didn't act or sound like a boss, then he wouldn't be treated like one. Samir had learnt the hard way. Once, just once, he had forgotten to shave and within one month his workforce could quite easily have been called '*Planet of the Apes* Security'. Once, just once, he had forgotten to come into NightOwl and within one month he had been nearly bankrupt from absenteeism. His employees just loved just onces.

And today they were in for a treat; Samir looked everything a boss shouldn't: red marbled eyes; breath so strong it could peel a banana; and pores so clogged with booze that when Samir licked his wrist to see how smelly his breath was this morning he got pissed all over again. Even the shower needed a shower after he'd used it. His final recollection of last night was of upsetting Kareena, but for what he was not entirely sure. Knowing women though, it was something to do with anything.

He found her downstairs curled up asleep on the sofa, the duvet half on and half off, a CD playing softly on repeat in the background – *A Whiter Shade of Pale*, by Procol Harum. He stared at Kareena's socked feet poking out of the duvet. This was no way to treat your wife, he thought. It was an unsaid rule that no matter who was in the wrong, the man slept on the sofa. He gently nudged her awake and prepared to cover her mouth in case she screamed.

She opened her eyes, blinked at her contrite husband, and listened to an apology that stretched for miles. An all-encompassing sorry that accounted for any wrong-doings that may or may not have occurred during the night. He even apologized if the queen's corgis had rabies, and he apologized if they didn't. Kareena was impressed: Samir sure knew how to grovel.

And Kareena sure knew how to take advantage. 'So you will definitely book some time off work so we can finally take our honeymoon? To the destination I choose?' she said, opening a curtain and staring out at the deluge. 'It's pissing down.'

Samir glanced over. 'Yeah, I'm sorry for the weather as well.' He paused. 'What *exactly* did I do wrong? This is getting out of hand. Was it something to do with looking through your drawers? Because I didn't. I wouldn't.'

She looked back. 'Doesn't matter. Anyway, I tried to wake you last night to apologize but you were out of it. I had something to show you.' She led him to the kitchen to see the something.

Samir's heart jolted and his stunned silence seemed to bounce off all four walls. Guru Nanak's portrait sat on the kitchen table, free from its broken frame. A wonderful painting; but this gift from Cloey could be his downfall. Cloey was prone to leaving hidden messages. Cleaning the house of them had been like hunting for that elusive *wodr* in an anagram: nigh on impossible. Little poems were hidden inside CD cases. Between the pages of books were quotes and love letters. Even stuck to the bottom of a plant pot he had found a photograph of her with a note. 'I love to be wet.' What the hell had she written on the back of Guru Nanak?

With sweat forming, Samir turned the portrait over, the picture was heavier than he'd thought. Or maybe it was the weight of his worry:

*Find me God
and
I'll find you
a liar*

The writing was centred perfectly, a bit like Samir's frown. His nerves relaxed, they hadn't quite kicked their slippers off yet, but they relaxed. He looked across at Kareena. 'Why's it broken?'

'I went to clean it and dropped it accidentally.' She paused. 'Do you know about the cross?' She took hold of the portrait and pointed to the gold crucifix.

An Indian kitchen is normally filled with the smell of garlic, spices, *ghee* and ginger. Right now, it smelt of trouble. Big trouble. Samir grabbed the picture and studied it intently. He remembered very well how proud he had felt when Cloey had presented him with the surprise painting. He'd felt really chuffed that she had troubled herself with finding out about his religion and beliefs. And he was overwhelmed at how she had captured the rich Indian colours so beautifully. 'The detail, he had said while cuddling her, 'is remarkable. It must have taken you ages.' And she had giggled shyly. 'Thanks. I'm a little bit cross that it took me so long. Just a tiny little cross though.'

Samir beat back his rising anger. It was obvious from his reaction that he had never noticed the cross before, because Kareena had to wrestle the kitchen scissors from his hands. Hands that were snipping and snapping with the razor-sharp blades desperate to cut the painting to ribbons. How dare this artist insult their faith? What could she mean by it?

'Her mind is poison,' he said, reluctantly remaining calm.

'Well, did you buy it from a shop? Or did you commission the painting? Or—'

'The fucking bitch,' Samir said, not even listening. 'Sorry, what did you say?'

She repeated the question.

'Cloey was recommended by a friend of a friend of a friend. She came round here and I told her what I wanted. A couple of months later she returned with the painting and I paid for it. Sorry, Kareena, this is too much, this is.' He walked through to the conservatory.

Kareena watched Samir, his sad figure was but a dark shadow in the dim conservatory light as the rain bombarded the glass. This must be hurting him badly, she thought. She hadn't realized the depth of his belief. Maybe this was her own fault, for not asking, just assuming that because he was gentle with his Indian rules, then his religion mustn't mean a great deal to him.

Right now she wished she knew Samir that little bit better. Did he want sympathy? Was his emotion best left to settle on its own? Was he the kind who needed a good shout in the garden? She didn't know; she just had to guess.

Standing next to her husband, staring through the window at the thrashing rain outside, Kareena took Samir's hand and squeezed it firmly. There was a closeness here with him, she could definitely feel it. He was her husband, nobody else's, and it was her duty to be there for him, come what may. And this, by all accounts, by the eloquent silence in his stance, was definitely one of those come what mays.

She spoke, 'Just ignore it: she's a sicko. Look at the wording on the back, it's obvious that she's doolally. Don't take it like this.'

'Like what?' he said, pulling his hand away.

'You're taking this very personally. And I did too, to start with, but you can't. She's just thick. Thick people do thick things. This Cloey may be a good painter but she's one shitty person. Anyone can insult anyone if they try hard enough and it seems like she tried her hardest with that crucifix, going to such lengths to hide it like that. She must get a sick kick out of it, knowing that it's up on our wall.' Kareena found she was winding herself up, spurring her own anger on by words that were meant to heal. Her voice rose in pitch. 'Have you got her address? Phone number? Studio? Whatever?'

He turned round sharply. 'Yeah, right. What about Picasso or Dali, do you want their numbers as well?' Then he shouted, 'Of course I haven't got her fucking number. I'm not the fucking Artists' Guide, am I? Just leave it. We're letting her win if we carry on like this. Leave it!' He glanced angrily down at his watch. 'I've got to go. We'll talk later.' He kissed her on the lips, and before she had time to reply he was gone.

Four hundred yards and five thousand beats of his heart later, Samir pulled up in Nutmeg Close. His mobile memory had been wiped of Cloey's number but his mind had it burned in. He dialled the dull tone notes. A few rings later, she answered.

'Hello, Sammy. I saw you come up on the Caller Display. I knew it was you. How are you?'

'Look, can't talk too long but—'

She interrupted. 'I understand, Sammy. Wifee, wifee.'

'Can I pop round now? I really need to see you badly.'

A pause, a gasp, a tiny excited scream. Then, 'I'll leave the back door open for you. You're always welcome here, Sammy, my darling. I can't wait to see you too. I've missed you so much.'

'Me too. I'll be there in half an hour.'

'Byeeeeeeee . . .'

Replacing the receiver, she hoofed it up the stairs in her bare feet, unplugged the mobile from its charger and found Jordan's number in the index. His purpose was over. The last thing she wanted right now was a love-struck Jordan hanging round like a bad smell. It was time to text.

Peasant, Jordan.
Bye bye. It was fun
but Sammy is back.
Which means my house
is back. You're not needed.
This is not a joke.
Cloey. No kisses.
But I still love you.

She sent the text, smiled and skipped over to her wardrobe, flinging it open.

'Now,' she rubbed her hands together, 'what would my Sammy want to see me in?'

Jordan's phone blipped and Bernie jumped from his snooze. He read the message while his father returned to sleep. Sometimes it would be nice to be older and calmer, he thought, watching Bernie muttering to someone in his dream. It would be lovely to be at peace, where the grey matter said it didn't matter. But today, as Jordan checked the shitty message once more, it mattered. There was no way that Cloey was getting Sammy and the house back. No way. Inside the warmth of his dad's house, Jordan closed his eyes, wondering how Zara was.

While outside it rained.

Chapter Twenty-nine

The middle-aged shop assistant, Angela, had been told when she joined Boots film processing service that the job demanded someone with an oblivious nature. Someone who could quite easily hand back a set of nude photos to a customer while holding back the sniggers. Someone who learnt very quickly to say, 'Yes, that is the most beautiful bonnie baby I have ever seen. Very photogenic.' Then, under her breath, 'It would have been nice if you had cut the umbilical cord before you took the photo of Frankenstein's son.' The job required just that little bit more brains than the make-up dolly birds on the Estée Lauder counter who seemed to thrive on being plain stupid, who kept half of the make-up stocks permanently on their faces, and who failed to realize that when a hunky man asked, 'Will you be open on the Bank Holiday?' that he wasn't referring to her legs.

Angela had a choice, to answer the phone or to serve the next customer, who was staring at her impatiently with a handful of films – he hadn't captured some of Buckinghamshire's finest locomotives on ASA400 only to be held up by a nobody. He shook his head and blew off some steam as he watched Angela pick up the ringing phone. He would be writing to his MP about this.

'Boots photos Milton Keynes,' Angela said.

'Yes, hello, I wonder if you can help me,' Cloey began. 'I want to know if it's possible to remove a person from a wedding photograph and in its place' – she fake-laughed – 'in its place, replace that person with the face of somebody else.'

It was important that Cloey knew in advance how she would look standing next to Sammy and his relatives on their wedding day. Kareena, admittedly, did look beautiful and the sari did suit her, but Cloey knew deep inside she would ultimately look the better bride. Plus, because hers would be the only white face, she would show up the best.

Angela liked dealing with the upper classes as opposed to riff-raff; she had all the time in the world for them. She replied in a voice she had picked up watching *Upstairs Downstairs*. 'Oh yar, yar yar yar, oh yar. One so hates these dilemmas, a trifle agitating to say the least, yar, one uninvited guest can so wreck one's wedding—'

Cloey interrupted. 'She's more than uninvited, she's the fucking bride, stupid. Is it possible to rub her out and replace her with me? Yes or no? Yar or nay?'

Angela returned to her professionalism, which brought with it her real accent. 'Sorry, this is Boots, not a Hollywood touching-up boutique. Try it on a home scanner, I hear you can even remove armpit hair with that, like they did with Julia Roberts. Amazing.' Her school bitchiness overcame her professionalism. 'Failing that, try finding your own groom.' You jumped-up little upstart.

Cloey snapped. 'If I wanted the opinion of a louse, I would have asked for it. Thanks for nothing, low-wage earner.' She slammed the receiver down. 'Amateurs. I hate working with amateurs.' Then stared at the picture of Jesus hanging above the phone. 'Best you stay out of my way.'

In skin-tight black leather trousers and a white halter-neck top – her casual, sexy look – Cloey sat in the kitchen waiting for Samir's arrival, thinking how hard this must all be for poor Sammy. Life must be very tender for him at the moment, fighting for happiness when so many selfish people didn't want him to be happy, trying to smile through the mediocre days with his mediocre wife, furious with himself for being pressurized into an arranged marriage. Outside the rain poured on to a dead fire and a dead marriage: a whole burnt album of forced smiles at a forced wedding.

Cloey's smile however was not forced and it nearly split her mouth in two when Sammy opened the back door. The sloshing noises of his feet were moment-arily ignored as she wrapped her arms round him. Then she held him back at arm's length, admiring his width, admiring his height and admiring everything else in between. He was gorgeous, and he was really here.

She grabbed him again. 'I've missed you so, so, so, much. Can you stay long?'

Samir's emotions were lethargic, as if working in a low gravity. It was only a short while ago that standing on this kitchen floor had felt like being in his second home. It was a place where he and Cloey had spent many hours chatting – and more. It had not all been good times, though. There were reminders on the wall of Cloey's anger. Over the door frame was a three-inch-diameter crater. Apparently Cloey had not liked the green marble mortar and pestle he had bought her for a casual weekday present. She had been going through an independent feminist patch in her life on that day. The following day he had tried again and bought her a gold bracelet. She had wanted it engraved with 'Sammy, my darling' – but he should have had it engraved with 'Sammy the sucker'. Cloey was hard to please and expensive to keep.

He untied the carrier bags covering his shoes. 'Can't stay too long. How have you been?'

How the fuck do you think I've been? 'Oh, getting on. I've really missed you though. But then again, I would, wouldn't I? I love you.' Pausing, she watched him perform his muddy task. 'Well? How do I look? Or are you used to a better view now?' She twirled round in her high heels.

Samir replied without bothering to check. 'You look lovely, as ever, Cloey.' He left the wet dirty bags by the back door and followed her through to the living room, led all the way by Cloey's hand. Nothing had changed by the look of things, but something was definitely different with the smell. He sniffed.

'Indian joss sticks,' she said, turning up the Hindi

music on the stereo. 'It's quite relaxing, this music; it takes you there, you know, to India?'

His laughter erupted and Cloey stared at him baffled, a red and gold *bindi* stuck to her forehead and henna doodled all over her hands. The child in Cloey surfaced as easily as did her temper, and it submerged out of sight again just as quickly. She was predictably unpredictable. And men just loved that in a woman. Didn't they?

Cloey fitted herself in next to Samir on the single chair. She didn't like the way his new aftershave smelt. It was sort of boozy. 'How has she been treating you? You're not someone who is easy to understand, Sammy. It took me years to get to know you properly. How long were we together? Six happy years, wasn't it?'

Samir stood up. He'd come with a speech prepared but now, as he looked over at a woman with hope in her eyes and a claim on his heart, he forgot his lines. He couldn't deny that once she had filled his entire existence and broken the glass bubble that Indian life had surrounded him with. Living his life with Cloey had been like walking down a dark alley, hoping that nothing pounced from the shadows. Keeping their love a secret, he realized now, had been half their love. The thrill, the rebelling, the subterfuge, the danger, it had all polished the excitement, sharpening the edges to each and every day. Now Samir finally forced himself to confront the truth. Had he ever loved Cloey? Had their six years together really been as happy as she said? Had he always known in his heart that he would betray her? Was this the cruellest thing he'd ever done?

Sitting back down on the sofa opposite her, he treated himself to a few left-over orange Jelly Babies – some with their heads missing. Cloey hated the orange ones, she said they reminded her of her tanned mother. He spoke through a squelching mixture of arms, torsos and legs. 'That painting you did for me, of Guru Nanak – why did you paint a cross round his neck?'

His voice was unfamiliar to Cloey, hard and argumentative. Jesus had finally shown himself to Samir. About sodding time, she thought. Three years she'd waited for him to notice. 'I tried to merge our cultures together, Sammy. If I did wrong,' she turned her head to one side, 'then slap me.'

He noticed a love bite on her neck. He stared at it with a strange lack of jealousy, almost emotionless. Was this the perfect excuse his conscience was searching for to let him off the hook? To obliterate his guilt? He almost traded his vague confused expression for a smile. He could feel his speech becoming fluid again, ready to fall out of his mouth. He needed something to dislike about Cloey and now he had found it.

'It's over, Cloey. Be honest, the six years we had together weren't really that brilliant. It's always easier to remember the fan, but what about the shit that hit the fan? You and me—'

Cloey dismissed him with a quick shake of her head. 'You're wrong. Your wife must seem exciting to you at the moment, willing to give you blow jobs on tap, but you just wait a few months, and the only jobs you'll be getting will be round the house.' She laughed. 'Think about it, Sammy, how many women would do what I did in bed? How many women would sacrifice their own pleasure to give you pleasure? Did I ever say *no* to you?'

Samir looked at his watch as if it would help him out. 'It's not about sex or any of that stuff. This has nothing to do with what you and I had, Cloey, I'm only realizing that now. This is about what you and I never had. We were aimless, the pair of us, both of us not wanting our parents to discover the truth. Don't you think that if we really loved each other, then what our parents thought would never really have mattered? Or got in our way?' He stared into her unbelieving face, her unforgiving face, her beautiful face. 'Do you think that if I really loved you I would have gone and married someone else? Honestly, Cloey, do you think I would have? You know I wouldn't. We were just kidding ourselves. We got in a rut and became used to each other like a million other couples. The reason we stayed together was fear of the future, fear of being alone. Too scared to make the break.'

Tears rolled down Cloey's cheeks. The dream was nearly over. Her house was being demolished. She cleared her lumpy throat, 'Do you still love me, Sammy?'

The Hindi music didn't cater for the mood change in the room and carried on as jollily as ever while Samir tried to think of the right words, the right sentences, the right paragraphs, to say one word 'no'.

Finally he spoke, 'I'll continue paying your bills for the next six months to get you on your feet. The car is yours, it was a present anyway. It's for the best.'

Cloey sniffed into a tissue filled with tears. 'So your parents won then. I knew they would separate us.'

Her tone went a couple of octaves lower. 'Don't fool yourself, you can't fall in love with a stranger. Come on, Sammy, what are the chances that your parents have chosen you "the one"? Unlikely.' She ripped off her *bindi* and flicked it at him. 'God chooses who we fall in love with, not our parents!'

Samir cocked an eyebrow. 'You don't even believe in God.' He paused. 'Unless it suits you.'

Kareena's mother always said that an Indian man holds his pride in his anger. An emotional energy converted to the physical. She said that an Indian woman shows her pride in her silence and lets her actions do the talking. But right now, as Kareena stared down at the thick book on her lap, this was not about actions doing the talking, this was about fingers doing the walking.

She opened the *Yellow Pages* and began to search for Cloey Evelyne's name among the 'Artist Commercial & Industrial' section. The boxed advert was easy to find and her pride changed from feminine to masculine as she punched the air with her closed fist. 'Got yer!' It was a classily worded advert which grabbed your attention immediately.

Cloey Evelyne
Your imagination is my limitation.
Caricatures, Greeting Cards, Paintings,
Logos, Letterheads, Wedding Invites.
The Lot.
See it and believe it.
Lemonly Cottage, Bruckley, Bucks.
Tel: Bruckley 3846264

She sat on the bottom step, the *Yellow Pages* resting on her knees, and she dialled Cloey's number.

Samir eyed Cloey. 'Aren't you going to answer it?'

'I always let it ring at least six times before I pick it up. You should know that, Sammy. I'm not *that* available, you know.' She strolled nonchalantly towards the phone, her face red and blotchy.

Eight rings, nine rings, ten rings. Cloey smiled at the Caller Display. 'I think it's your wife, Sammy, for you,' she shouted, half laughing, half excited. 'I'll tell her that you're in the shower, shall I?' She giggled freely, her fingers over her mouth trying to hold back the spluttering saliva.

Samir bounded over in two strides and clamped his hand over the receiver, preventing Cloey from picking up. 'Don't you fucking answer that!'

The answerphone clicked on and Samir held his breath waiting for a message, his mind doing all sorts of messy things with the future. How the hell had his wife found out this number? He had bloody visions of the whole Indian community picking out their favourite axes and waiting in line behind Kareena's family for the left-over limbs which they hadn't hacked off his body yet. He was dead! He looked at Cloey who rubbed Jesus's head, talking to her Saviour, 'Well done. Well done.'

There was no message left on the machine, but here was a clear message left in Samir's head: get out here and get home quick.

'Don't pick it up if she rings again. Please, Cloey, se.'

oey continued polishing Jesus, rubbing a month's

worth of dust from his crown. 'You can't just get rid of me that easily, Sammy. You've got one week to leave your wife. I know what you really want and that's me. If you don't tell her, then I'll tell her.' She paused and hung the picture back up. 'I won't pick up the phone if it's her until then. That's if she calls again, of course; that's if she hasn't already found out.'

It was moments like this that deserved framing, she thought. Surely the bitchy wife hadn't already stumbled across the 'marriage breaker' she had planted in the house? She giggled as she watched Samir sweat.

He looked away from her, realizing the situation was pretty grim, but not having the slightest idea what to do about it. He had an overwhelming urge to run home and sob in his mother's arms. But he was a man, and men didn't cry.

Cloey was still giggling when he turned back to say, 'I know you're hurting, Cloey, but don't make me hate you.' Walking into the kitchen, he faced her again. 'If I lose my wife because of you, then I'll make you pay. I really don't love you any more.' The door opened and he disappeared into the rain.

Cloey imitated Samir's last words in front of the hall mirror, her voice was good enough for a cute animal in a Disney film. 'I know you're hurting, Cloey, but don't make me hate you.' She picked the mirror off the wall and threw it hard against the front door where it smashed to smithereens. Her next voice was good enough for the cute kid in the *Exorcist*, deep and revolting, 'You are waking the Devil in me, Samir. You don't know how much I'm fucking hurting. I want my house back. You want your wife

329

Let's see if you love her when she's in an NHS wheelchair.' She made some motions with her arms, wheeling an invisible wheelchair, then said calmly, 'Seven days. I'll have you both back in seven glorious days!!!' And she wheeled herself upstairs, laughing.

Chapter Thirty

Bruckley village store had one shopping basket and one shopping trolley. The trolley had a six foot seven inch metal pole welded on the back, similar to a fairground bumper car. The height of the shop door was six feet five inches. Any attempt at charging out of Morris's Village Store with the trolley would be a mistake. Mathematics, apparently, would not allow that trolley through that door. There probably was not a stingier shop owner in the world than Morris. His name wasn't even Morris, it was Seymour, he just hadn't wanted to pay for the sign to be changed when he had taken over the lease. He had agreed with his first customers who had remarked on the sign, 'Yes, extraordinary coincidence that Morris and I happen to have the same name. God knows how much it would have cost me to have that sign changed if we hadn't.'

Morris knew one thing though, rain kept custome

away. It was already 1 p.m. and he only had ten fucking pence in the till. A float of ten pence. He turned off the light bulb to save on electricity and sat there in the semi-dark on a stool behind the counter waiting for his next customer, listening to a tape recording of *The Archers*. How he prayed for the tinkle of the door bell, how he stared at the bell as if it were his lifeline.

Jordan pushed the door open, the bell tinkled and the lights came on. The smell of damp vegetables shot up Jordan's nose and he glanced over at the offending pile of rotting potatoes, labelled 'Organic'. Bubonic more like, he thought, and stood facing Morris at the counter. There was no love lost between the pair.

'Do you sell "in date" boxes of chocolates, mate?' Jordan asked, scanning the shelf behind Morris's grey bonce. A box of orange-flavoured Matchsticks sat alone.

One of Morris's thrills in life was watching *Crimewatch*, hoping against hope that someone, somewhere had caught Jordan on camera stealing. 'Do you know this man?' Nick Ross or Fiona Bruce would say, and Morris would remove his glasses and squint at the TV in an effort to convince himself that the man was Jordan. One day he was sure it would be.

Morris kept his eyes on the criminal, feeling behind him for his stepladder. 'What is it with chocolates today? Everyone seems to be buying chocolates. I've only got one box left. Matchsticks.'

'I'll have the Matchsticks, then, and a lighter.' rdan was about to make a certifiable joke about tches and lighters, when he noticed his name ten on top of a sheet of paper half tucked under a magazine. Now what would his name be doing in this shit hole? he wondered, swiping the stapled paper sheets, as Morris momentarily took his eyes off the counter, struggling up another step.

Morris arrived back at the counter and blew the dust off. 'That's £12.99, young man.'

Jordan felt his impatience peaking and he grabbed Morris round the neck. 'Tell me the real fucking price!'

'Five pounds,' he answered feebly.

'Now deduct two quid for your fucking cheek; what are you left with, Morris?'

'Three pounds.'

Jordan released his hold. 'Good man. A nice gesture would be for you to offer me the lighter free.'

Jordan received his nice gesture and left Morris with one of his own. Morris was not accustomed to customers dishing him the middle finger as they left his shop. He would be adding a few more fake names to that petition now. Now where was it? Where had he left it?

Outside the shop Jordan sat in his car with the petition on his lap, while the rain pounded on the metal roof. So many people with so much hate. He was amazed to what level people would go to to keep their little world . . . so little.

Do you want to feel safe again?
Then sign here to get rid of the convict Jordan.
(Bernie's son).

Underneath the heading were four pages of names, addresses and comments. The final page was a copy of

the letter that would be sent to the local MP asking
him to put pressure on the government with regard to
asylum seekers.

Jordan's eyes were drawn to some of the first
entries on the list: Cloey's, Aileen's and Claudette's.

Cloey Evelyne   Lemonly Cottage, Bruckley,
Bucks
*I cry myself to sleep from all the pain Jordan has
caused this village.*

*I cannot write any more, for fear my tears will
wet this page.*

*I am hurting. (He ignored me twice in God's
garden.)*

Aileen Evelyne   You know the address.
Posh house at the end.
*Atonement on Bruckley can never be achieved
while Jordan breathes among us. I helped raise him
when his mother sadly left this earth, and the only
thanks I've had for my selflessness is that he has
hated me for being a finer mother than his own.*

Bring back the electric chair. And up the voltage.

Claudette Miss World   Lemonly Cottage.
*Jordan tried to use religion to make me a sinner.
He said, 'The Bible says take up snakes,' and he
forced my hand in his boxers. I was rattled. And
stung.*

*P.S. His fabulous looks and body make me
hate him. He keeps it all to himself and won't
share it round.*

What a waste.

334

Jordan threw the list on his passenger seat. 'Wackos!' He flicked on a Wyclef Jean CD, '911', and sped off. He had learnt a valuable lesson in prison: revenge is a dish best served cold, and as long as someone is still alive, then it's never too late to fuck their life up.

As far as he knew Cloey was still alive and he headed towards her house.

Kareena opened the Whirlpool washing machine and her eyes popped. This was a very unusual-looking white wash judging by the dazzling red colour in front of her. All Samir's shirts, T-shirts and socks were now the colour of strawberries. It was impossible to see which item was the culprit. It was hardly the end of the world though: some of those shirts were only designer anyway. One offs. Nothing to cry about, she thought, plonking the washing basket down in the hall and picking up the phone to dial her mum.

'Why are you crying, Kareena?' asked her worried mother in Punjabi. 'Is he treating you badly?'

Kareena sniffed hard. It wasn't fair dumping her problems on her mother for something so trivial. She was just behaving like a big girl's blouse. She glanced again at Samir's shirts, now they looked like big girl's blouses. 'Do you remember the time Avani did that wash and Dad's jumpers came out with tissues all over them? Well, it's worse than that.' She sniffed. 'Much worse.'

'Will it turn his hair grey? This problem?'

Kareena explained it wasn't about grey hair, it was about red washing, it was about self-esteem and being totally useless. Her mother had previously relayed the importance of not giving her husband ammunition for future arguments. 'Big mistake,' she had said. 'Whenever your father and I argue, he still throws in my face the time I bought frozen coriander instead of fresh. His words every time are, "Bloody frozen coriander. What am I, hey, a bloody Eskimo? Eskimo Singh?"'

The basket of washing looked like a car accident. Any future laundry Kareena did would probably come with a free bit of advice from Samir, 'Make sure you separate your whites from colours. Remember what happened that Monday forty-five years ago? Red Monday.'

'I'm going to throw it all in the bin. He'll never know,' Kareena said, wiping her eyes and feeling slightly better. 'He should have done his own wash anyway.'

There was a silence, carefully planned to send chills up Kareena's spine and she knew she had said something wrong. Yikes! It was like being back at home with her parents again. Double yikes!!

'Ditch those ideas immediately,' her mother began. 'Your job as his wife is to look after him, not to be slovenly and not to take short-cuts . . .' Not to . . . blah, blah, blah.

Her mother lectured from the head not the heart, as the master not the mother. The rules for an Indian woman have been dictated down the corridors of time; it was not for the young Indian woman of today to start editing them. Her life was partly her own but mainly governed by her husband.

Her mother was saying, 'The last thing we want is for Samir to tell his mother how sloppy you are and for her to ring me up and tell me they have made a bad choice for their son.' She paused, and went on sharply, 'We made you a good choice in Samir, don't let him or us down.' She softened slightly. 'And don't let yourself down.'

It was never black and white with Indian parents. It was always brown. Do your best for the Indian way and it would do its best for you. Her mother was right, Samir was the best choice. This was only a basket of washing after all. 'I won't let it happen again. I won't let you down.'

'Put the washing back in the machine on a ninety-degree wash with plenty of bleach. I won't tell your dad this happened.' She coughed. 'He would be *so* disappointed in you. You haven't forgotten that we are coming round tomorrow, have you?'

'No. I'm counting down the seconds.'

As she replaced the receiver, Samir walked in through the front door, slightly wet from the rain. There was a sense of urgency in his step. Maybe the washing Gestapo had already informed him of her blunder, or even the KGB. It was red washing after all.

'What are you doing home?' Kareena said, failing to conceal her surprise.

Samir had driven home dangerously fast in the punishing rain, one thought recurring the whole way, of Cloey on the phone to his wife confessing all: 'He slept with me while he was married to you.' Samir had gripped the steering wheel, wrestling with the winding country roads, willing time to stand still.

Samir stared at the telephone. He wondered whose voice was travelling away down the line. 'Who were you talking to just now?'

'Mum. She was reminding me they'll be coming down tomorrow. Why?'

He walked in. 'Really?'

'Yes, really.'

'Your mum, just now, on the phone?' He turned his back on her, closing the door. 'And what did you talk about? With your mum? On the phone?' He faced her. 'Well?'

'If you must know, I was talking about that,' and she pointed to the red pile. 'I was worried that I'd wrecked all your clothes. No conspiracy theory.'

Samir glanced at the basket. 'Fuck the washing. Who else were you phoning? I tried to ring you earlier. Who else were you talking to?'

He was surprised at how controlling his voice was becoming, dusted with paranoia and distrust. He'd made a great speech to Kareena only a few days ago about how different he was to your typical Indian man. All those rules and regulations were claustrophobic and degrading as far as he was concerned. Apparently, he was the new breed of Indian man. He was Samir *au naturel*. Love him and cuddle him.

Ignoring him, Kareena picked up the basket and walked into the kitchen wondering why he was acting so strangely. Maybe that episode this morning with the crucifix had disjointed his mind slightly. This Cloey woman and her painting had a lot to answer for.

He snapped open a lager. 'Well? Who were you on the phone to?'

Kareena homed in on Samir's expression, there was definitely something dishonest lurking within his eyes.

'I phoned to register with a new doctor as you

suggested, and I also tried to phone that Cloey artist. I found her number in the *Yellow Pages*, I was going to demand a written apology,' she said, stuffing the clothes back in the washing machine. 'Anyway, what are you doing home? And why are you acting so strange? Questions, questions, questions.'

He sipped the lager. 'I'm disappointed in you Kareena, my wife, very disappointed indeed.' He shook his head. 'Your father told me you were honest. Ha! This is honesty, is it? Going behind your husband's back when I specifically forbade you to and sneakily phoning up artists.' He sneered.

But Kareena sneered harder. 'So you forbid me to care about my husband, do you? I did it for you. I saw how upset you were this morning.'

'Did you get through to Cloey?'

'No.'

'Are you sure?'

She frowned. 'There was no answer!'

He followed her sulky walk into the living room. 'Just as well.' He looked out at the rain, pressing his nose against the condensation-glazed window. 'I feel a bit of a dick, to be honest . . . about this morning. I overreacted just like my father would have. We shouldn't let this white woman Cloey and her sick humour interfere with us. Let's just forget it all happened and promise each other that we won't ever mention her again. I won't phone her if you don't. And I wouldn't bother going to see her, because if you're like me, a devoted Sikh, it's probably crossed your mind. But don't do it, we'll be letting her have the satisfaction that we were bothered about the cross. Because we're not, are we? Bothered? We're beyond that, aren't we? Let it lie.' He joined her on the sofa, his nose glistening, his eyes wide. 'Just let it lie, Kareena. Promise?'

She nodded. 'Promise.'

And as Samir sneakily crossed his fingers for luck, Kareena sneakily uncrossed hers for lying.

The first chance she got, Cloey would receive a visit. There was definitely something ghastly hidden within Samir's mind, and as he leant in close to kiss her, two sharp fangs of fear bit deep into her reasoning.

Samir was hiding something, she could just tell. But what? She didn't know, but she guessed it had something to do with the cross. Was Samir a closet Christian? Or was Cloey more than an artist to him?

Chapter Thirty-one

Jordan was still studying the petition on the passenger seat. It was incredible how brave people could be behind the stroke of a pen. Each name on that list had a face and some of those faces wore masks. Mrs Byers, Mr Tilley, Mrs Gabrielle, the Tooks, even cuddly old Mr and Mrs Albany. Villagers he'd known since his nappy days, all wearing the same disguise, all faking kindness when deep down they loathed him. Jordan added them all to his list of revenge. He would have to act quickly though, the Albanys were approaching the end of the runway, their flight to the heavens about to take off.

He glanced at his Rolex, it was just past 3.35 p.m. Jordan had been sitting in his car thinking. Two hours of harsh reality and morality checks, figuring out how best to win Zara back while simultaneously wrecking Cloey's life. It was his own version of yin and yang, a balance of good versus evil. Zara was a no-go area for the time being, her cooling-down period after a normal row was half a day, after an affair he could be looking at a decade. And to be sure his plans for wrecking Cloey's life would work, he had to be sure what to wreck. It was imperative that a couple had to be together before you could officially split them up. Now the question was: were Cloey and Sammy really back together? There was only one way to find out.

Jordan immobilized his car and walked to Lemonly Cottage, ignoring the heavy rain pricking through his orange Roxy snowboarding T-shirt. He knocked on Cloey's front door and, as usual, the curtain at the top window twitched.

Cloey's voice leapt from the open window. 'What d'you want? Didn't you get my text?'

'My phone's playing up. Never mind, I brought you a *present*,' he said, smiling up.

The woeful sight of Jordan standing in the fierce downpour detonated a memory in her head like a small controlled explosion of the day he came out of prison and she turned him away at the door. She'd tried hard not to concede to the feeling of guilt, but now, as she looked down upon the man she was willing to give up, her heart went out to him – could she really say goodbye to him again?

A comb of the hair, change of clothes, a spruce of the make-up and thirteen steps later, she opened the door in her high heels and red chiffon dress. The dress's flirty ruffles and frills were just up Jordan's street – slag wear.

'You're drowned. Get yourself inside, I'll fetch you a towel.' She spotted the blue H. Samuel bag in his hand and prayed to God that he hadn't bought her cheap silver, how she hated cheap silver. 'When do I get my present?' She closed the door and planted a warm kiss on his cold lips. 'There. Better now?'

He followed her to the cosy kitchen, his trainers squeaking on the stone floor. A Weetabix box stuffed with triangles of broken mirror lay by the back door. She'd obviously had a tantrum of some sort – mirror rage?

'The present is for opening when I've gone,' he said, plonking it on the table.

She spun round glaring, then gave him a smile. 'You tease bag.' She disappeared for a while and returned with a fluffy towel. 'Well, come on, you big lug, let me get you dry.'

Jordan stepped closer, Cloey removed his soaked T-shirt, and the drying began.

Each pat to his wet skin with the silky soft towel felt like a treasonable offence. Surely men were not allowed to be built this beautifully, she thought, as her hands worked their artistic movements across his firm, firm muscles. God, how he used to wreak havoc with her snobby upbringing. He could turn the most upper-class woman into a lower-class whore. Cloey smiled at Jordan who had his eyes closed. It made sense to send him out of the door now. Samir was virtually hers, the house was virtually in her name. But if she were to be honest with herself, she could do with a good shag.

She stared sensually at Jordan, while sliding the towel towards his groin. 'I hope I'm not being too rough on you, Jordan. I wouldn't want you to think that I was trying to seduce you.' She kissed his muscular thigh and ran her finger under the waistband to his shorts.

Jordan looked at the hanging, blackened saucepans, at the fridge magnets, at the spice rack. Anything to stop an erection. He wasn't here for sex. His eyes wandered to the ceiling hoping to spot mildew, or spider webs, even cockroaches. Anything to stop an erection. He wasn't here for sex. Focusing hard on the cookery books, the wine bottles, the oven gloves. Anything to—
But it was too late. Way, way, way too late.

'Jordan! Shame on you.' Her fingers felt beneath the elastic. 'I expect you want me to dry in there as well now?'

He edged away. 'No!'

'Don't be so sarcastic. I know what you're like. Of course you want me to touch you there. Who else knows your body better than me? Who else knows all your disgusting dirty thoughts?' She stood up facing him, dropped her dress to the floor, and kicked it under the table with her red stilettos. 'You may be all dry now, Jordan, but I'm all wet. You know you turn me on, but who else turns *you* on like I can? Nobody does!'

She hated to think she was inferior to any woman when it came to touching a man's body. She couldn't bear to think another woman could excite a man more than she could. Whether it be a casual massage, or a quick snog or a fully blown shag, she had to be number one. Jordan, in just a pair of shorts, needed number-one treatment.

She stuffed her hand back in his boxers. 'Come on, I always turn you on. I won't tell Sammy if you don't, and I won't tell Zara if you don't.' Her hand tightened. 'What they don't know won't harm them. Hey?'

Jordan prised her vice-like grip off his goods finger by finger. 'I'm not here for a shag, Cloey. Access denied.' He pulled the wet T-shirt back on. 'Access denied.'

She jumped up deeply hurt. 'This is all blow-up doll's fault, isn't it? Did you leave bimbo dissatisfied as well? I expect as soon as you slammed the front door she reached for the hidden fluffy pink vibrator,' she said, slipping back into her dress.

Jordan hated arguing when he had an erection, it sort of gave off the wrong signals. It was like telling someone you hated violence while beating them over the head with a baseball bat. He pulled the chair from under the wooden table and sat down.

'I don't want to steal your thunder at the moment, Cloey. It's obvious that you're feeling totally rejected because I don't want you anywhere near me. But, I'm feeling rejected as well. A rejected guest. Now, where's my coffee?'

Cloey flicked her hair and kissed him on the cheek. 'I'm not rejected, far from it, actually. Sammy still wants me.' She filled the chrome kettle, placed it on the Aga, turned round beaming and sat down opposite him. 'Both our gods have agreed we should be together.' She watched Jordan light a fag. 'He was supposed to finish with me today, but he just couldn't do it. He took me, there and then. It was like a scene from one of those old black and white movies.' Her face became dreamy, lost in *Casablanca*. 'So this time next week I will be moving in to Sammy's house . . . my house. *It's official*.' She grinned. 'He's promised me he's getting rid of the wife before then and I told him not to let that intruder keep anything. She was only a leach of a lodger anyway.'

Jordan took a lengthy drag of his fag. 'So, you and him are really back together? I'm pleased for you, *really*. I know you only say it as a joke, but deep down, I'm just a criminal. I think you made the right choice.'

'What choice? There was no choice. It was always the house. Shallow I know, but then again, so what? Loads of women do this sort of thing.' She leaned over and stroked his hand. 'Not a day will go past when I won't think of you, though.' She giggled. 'Unless the house burns down.'

He laughed.

The faint whistling of the kettle increased and Cloey jumped up.

Jordan stood up. 'Actually, I'll leave the coffee. I've got work to do, down at the church. My sins have got bigger.'

She followed him to the front door and, as a last resort, desperately threw herself at him, kissing him on the lips and groping down in his shorts again. 'Thank you for the present, Jordan. I'll open it the minute you go. And always remember, you are the second most important thing in my life next to Sammy's house.'

For ten minutes, Cloey and Claudette both stared disgustedly at Jordan's present of mouldy Matchsticks. The audacity. Eventually Cloey opened the back door and hurled the box venomously into the bonfire ashes. What was he playing at? Where was the gold jewellery she had expected?

After pouring a generous amount of whisky into the tea mugs, Claudette handed Cloey hers, and they both sat down on the sofa feeling conned. Surely killing a man for giving you chocolates, instead of diamonds and gold, would be categorized as self-defence under the Willy Wonker clause.

'Bastard.'

'Bastard.'

'Bastard.'

'What a bastard.' Claudette clinked her mug with Cloey's. 'Let's drink to Jordan's downfall.'

Cloey smirked. 'His downfall has already begun, look.' She pointed to the drawing board set up in the corner. A large piece of black card was edged with masking tape and green glittering words shone from it spitefully: Your Boyfriend Cheated On You.

Giggling, Claudette walked over to it. 'I take it this is for bimbo Zara with a Z? Excellent.' She clapped her hands together and rubbed them as if they were cold. 'You are so . . . Cloey.'

'I'm going to wreck their relationship.' Cloey smiled. 'I hate it when he thinks about another woman. I want it like it was before: him and his pathetic pining just for me.'

They both laughed.

The steady flow of whisky slowly entered their bloodstreams as the evening closed in. Outside the walls of Lemonly Cottage, dogs were being walked and the moon shone down in the many puddles. Now the rain had ceased, the evening seemed insignificantly quiet. Mostly, nothing ever happens in a village. And, most definitely, nothing ever happens in a village at night.

Except tonight, in Bruckley.

A drunken Cloey struggled up her mother's garden

path. Her singing voice could be heard for miles. Apart from a few teething problems with the first verse, Cloey's rendition of 'Relax' by Frankie Goes To Hollywood, was better than Holly's himself, and had sent every non-mechanical set of legs to their front-room windows as she swayed past on the journey up here. Under her arm she carried a broomstick with a white handkerchief attached to the end.

She stood waving it from the middle of the garden staring up at her parents' bedroom window. 'Mum, I've come to make peace,' she shouted, swinging the pole from side to side. 'You can't turn your back on your only daughter, your own flesh and blood.'

A forbidding silence was the only response, save for the squelching of Cloey's green wellies in the water-logged lawn. She stuck the flagpole in the ground and then trudged towards the front door, setting off the infrared spotlight with her infrared dress. The sign over the door could be clearly seen from three yards away, Enter And You Are Under Oath. Cloey had lived most of her life under oath, the rebellious oath of a non-believer: thou shalt trample over thy religion. She was sick of the pretence.

The door opened slowly and Aileen moved aside to let her daughter in, pointing to the muddy wellies which Cloey removed immediately. The magical smell of Aileen's famous cookies embraced Cloey as she stood there trying to focus on her neatly packaged mother dressed in her finest cream silk nightwear.

Aileen didn't take too kindly to being out-dressed by visitors at her front door. It was a prerequisite that any limelight in Aileen's house was hers and hers alone. If you tried to arrive at Aileen's all dressed up, then by the time you left you would have had a good dressing down. Aileen's stinging tongue had turned many women of Bruckley to crash diets. 'I've heard they can do miracles with surgery, Mrs Tutkins, just miracles. Tummy tucks, stapled stomachs, chin lifts, bum lifts, breast lifts. Have you thought about having all these done? I'm sure they do discounts for the most needy.'

Cloey staggered forward to plant a sloppy smackerooney on her mother's Oil Of Olay-glazed cheek.

She flinched away. 'You disgusting creature. How dare you come here drunk, wearing a hooker's dress? It's a good job your father is not here to witness this, it would break his heart.'

Aileen grabbed Cloey's arm, dragging her down the spacious hall and into the kitchen. There was only one remedy for an inebriated soul; one cure to sober the Devil. And curing, in this house, unfortunately meant a lot of shouting. Aileen enjoyed the sound of her own tantrums. She placed a plastic bucket beside her daughter's chair.

'Open wide,' she said, pinching Cloey's nose.

Three raw eggs drowning in cod liver oil slithered down Cloey's throat, had a little confab with the contents of her stomach, then barfed straight out into the waiting bucket along with a pint of whisky. In the background Aileen recited the Lord's Prayer.

Cloey wobbled upright. 'I want to tell you something about me and I don't think you're going to like it.' She stumbled weakly to the study, patting around the door frame for the light switch. 'No interrupting me, you must stay quiet, you must let me confess. This is to both you and to God.'

Aileen agreed and guided Cloey to the desk chair, placing the Bible in her lap. Cloey clamped her eyes shut. 'Forgive me, Lord, for I have sinned. Many times I have lied to you, but of course you know that already, don't you?' She paused, swallowed a dry gulp of air, then continued, 'In this house, I have enjoyed the ultimate sin time and time again.' She steadied herself from sliding off the chair. 'At the age of fourteen I gave away my virginity to Jordan in this very room. And I paid for my sin when you took him away from me, when you sent him to prison for my doings.' There was no drunken edge to Cloey's voice, no hesitation, no anger. Yet her words grabbed Aileen round the throat.

Cloey stood up, facing her mother. 'Sorry, Mum, I can't carry on pretending with you, I can't carry on letting you hear what you want to hear. No more.' She raised her voice slightly, 'I'm thirty-one years old; you take me as I am, or you lose me. You must love me for what I am and not what you want me to be. You know nothing about my life, you're so lost in this world of God.' She glanced down at the Bible. 'You get fat on your prayers but you're starved of real life. I honestly don't believe that God can't see through this charade.' She turned back to see her mother weeping.

Aileen wiped her eyes with the tips of her manicured fingers. 'Did you enjoy it? Did you enjoy having Jordan inside you?' she said in a voice that chilled Cloey's heart. 'Tell me he forced himself on you. Tell me he raped you, please.'

'You just don't get it, do you? I love him, he loves me, he still loves me.' Cloey's impatience burned her eyes. 'I drove that car, not him, I committed the crime, not Jordan, and he went to prison, not me. He loved me so much that he lost three years of his life. Three years – and I betrayed him. I live with that, day in and day out. I look at him and I remember how we used to lie in the darkness in Jordan's bedroom and promise each other that if one died, the other would kill themselves like in *Romeo and Juliet*, then we would get embarrassed and turn the light on and help each other with our homework. We had it all, Mum. Once. I lost him. I can see hatred in his eyes when he looks at me now, and then it disappears as if it never came.' Cloey bit her bottom lip to stop herself from crying. 'I don't know what to do with my life. I need you to be my mum. I need you to tell me what to do.'

It had been a long time since Aileen had classed herself as a mum. With an ear not used to listening, and with mounting horror, she heard a story that was more far-fetched than some in the Bible. Cloey explained that on that fateful night in which Jordan was led away to the cells, it should have been her. It was she who had driven Jordan's car like a maniac for the high, it was she who hadn't stopped for the police siren, and it was she who had cackled with laughter as the helicopters joined in the chase. Jordan had pleaded with her to stop; things were getting way out of hand. But the buzz had been too intense, and before long half of MK's police force had been giving chase in their squad cars. Hiding in the churchyard, as the blue lights scorched the darkness, Jordan had ordered Cloey to leg it while he swapped seats. But Cloey hadn't needed to leg it. As soon as she'd opened the driver's door, Father Luke had appeared from the shadows beckoning her to stand beside him quickly before the police spotted her. And the rest . . . was history.

'I will always be in debt to Jordan, Mum.' She twisted her false wedding ring. 'But for some reason, I can't stop hurting him, and that makes me a hateful, jealous person. Especially because I enjoy it so much.'

Aileen felt she wanted to turn away from her daughter, to shun her own flesh and blood. But even though God had made women strong, he had also made women weak, for when it came to turning her back on her own sinful child, a gift from God Almighty himself, she couldn't do it. She pulled Cloey towards her and held her tightly.

Chapter Thirty-two

Most Indian girls learn to bite their tongues from an early age. They become very articulate when keeping quiet and can keep a whole conversation going with itsy-bitsy motioning gestures of the head, tiny flicks of the eyebrows and faint twinkles in their eyes. Without knowing it, the Indian way has made them experts in flirting and masters of containing their opinion.

Even from her nursery school days, when her mother had warned Kareena not to wreck Christmas for the other kids by exposing the myth of Santa Claus, she could remember having so much to say about so many things, but an imaginary zip on her mouth had kept her opinions sealed inside. It had been frustrating at times. Both she and Avani would argue that Indian boys were treated like Indian princes, while Indian girls were treated like . . . plain old Indian girls. Their parents would repeat the same old answer: when both Kareena and Avani were of marriageable age, when they married the Indian man, they could tell their husband all about their opinions. Until then, though – keep it shut.

There would be no keeping it shut today. On this sweltering Tuesday morning.

Kareena straightened down her *shalwar kameez*, it was extremely important that she looked totally Indian today. Not just passably Indian, but one hundred per cent *Indian* Indian. She'd ransacked all her twenty-four-carat gold and draped it obviously over all exposed areas. Neat hennaed patterns were transferred on to her already fading *mendhi* hands. She had beads, bangles and *bindi*. Her apricot-coloured nail varnish matched her *shalwar kameez* which matched her headscarf. She stared into the mirror, admitting to herself that she had made more of an effort today than for her bloody wedding.

Kareena waited for the taxi on the drive. She had never thought that the day she tried to look her best it would be for a woman. Something about this Cloey didn't sit right. It was like a door in her mind that couldn't quite close. If there was something hidden in Samir's past, then she and her parents had a right to know about it.

She checked her watch. The cab was late, which was a relief, she didn't want anything out of the ordinary happening today. The plan was simple. She would go and sort this Cloey out, teach her not to insult religion, and settle her own paranoia. After that, she'd swoop down to Sainsbury's and buy some bits and bobs for her family's visit this evening, then tuck up with Samir and burn a few candles into the night. Simple as A B C.

The taxi driver pulled up, wound down the window, focused hard on Kareena, then said, 'Do you speak English?'

She opened the door. 'Nah, mate, I'm a bit fick when it cums darn to the ol' English. Know what I mean, mate?' She fastened her seat belt. 'Lemonly Cottage, Bruckley, please.'

After frightening the taxi driver into silence by mentioning that, 'I've got a hangover. If you talk to me, I will puke,' Kareena struggled with her thoughts. Just a passing thought but, as it went past, it kicked her in the face. She had a nasty feeling that this Cloey was going to be a stunner. She hoped she wasn't, and she didn't know why it should matter.

She glanced at the graffitied sign outside her window:

Bruckley
Buckinghamshire's Colostomy Bag
5 Miles

'Charming,' said the taxi driver, shaking his head. 'So, what takes you to Bruckley?'

'I think I'm going to puke.'

The car lurched forward.

There's nothing more complicated than simplicity, thought Jordan. The simple word 'sorry' never seemed to work on its own. You had to back it up with a thousand reasons why you were sorry. And right now, as he stood outside his front door, a thousand reasons didn't seem enough. You can't have an affair and expect 'sorry' to bail you out.

Jordan rang the doorbell and waited, dressed in his

dad's spare clothes. Zara had never asked Jordan to prove his love, she believed that love could not be proved, it was like life's impossible equation, along with the Rubik's cube. Cloey on the other hand had needed proof in every form. On her eighteenth birthday, she had asked Jordan for a strange present which would prove to her how much he cared, how much he really loved her. She had begged him to cut himself across his chest, to scar himself. She said if he cut deeply enough, she would be able to see if his heart had her name on it. Jordan had reluctantly numbed his chest with ice, numbed his brain with booze, and set about gashing his chest with a knife, while Cloey watched from her bed, lying on her stomach as though she were watching a good movie, naked and horny, kicking her feet in the air as the blood oozed down his abs. Cloey had known from that moment on that Jordan was prepared to do anything for her. Sex that night had been out of this world and very very sticky.

Zara answered the door, with an almost expectant air about her, as if she'd known he was coming. Her tight, black Escada trouser suit seemed formal, uptight, professional and dangerous. It said, 'You need to make an appointment just to look at me.' Jordan realized that a welcome hug was out of the question when she slapped him round the chops; her toxic glare would have scared a ghost.

'Did you sleep at that cow's last night?' she asked, standing aside to let him by.

'You know I didn't sleep with you last night,' he replied.

She slapped him again. 'Follow me, Adulterer.' Her

pink high-heeled glittery sandals led the way, clomping rhythmically up the spiral staircase. 'Stop watching my bum, you have no rights to it now, Jordan.'

Zara and her friends used to call Jordy an arsonist – he set women's knickers on fire. Last night, however, while Zara's friends comforted her angry tears, Jordy had been referred to as an arsehole. An arsehole who deserved a good kicking.

She opened the door to the nursery. The nursery that patiently awaited the arrival of Jordy Yum Yum Junior. There should have been a note on the door: 'Do Not Enter If You Are Epileptic'. Bright summer colours – yellows, lilacs, pinks and blues – assaulted your eyes and turned your brain into a kaleidoscope. Cuddly toys with flashing pupils stared unremittingly. Hand-painted teddy bears, rabbits and ducks cutiefied the walls and the wooden floorboards. Jordan's proudest addition to the nursery, which Zara had promised to remove once conception had been successful, was a piece of card stuck to the cot, 'If you think I'm cute you should look at my dad'.

Zara pointed at the plastic orange stack 'n' store boxes beside the rocking chair. 'I've packed some of your stuff.' She looked out of the window. 'You've wrecked everything, you know that? Was our sex not good enough for you?'

He sat on the rocking chair, rocking. He tried to see things from Zara's perspective. He knew in his heart that if Zara had done the dirty on him, there were no words she could come up with that could excuse her. And yet, he would want her to try. He would want her to squeeze every known verb and adjective out of her vocabulary to come up with the required sentences to explain why she had fucked another man and then he would say: 'Zara, that is not good enough!'

'Look, Zara, whatever I say isn't going to take away the fact that I put my dick in another woman and she—'

Zara interrupted. 'Please don't be so graphic.' She paused, focusing on his eyes. 'Actually, forget I said that, please, Jordan, be *more* graphic. Give me *all* the filth.' Her voice began to rise, a galloping thunder of wild hooves, a rage of angry decibels. 'What did she do? Dress up in little kinky ski pants and wear a visor for you? Warmed up your cold cock for you, did she? Keep it all warm inside her, did she? What were you doing? Practising for the flipping Winter Olympics with her? Trying to get that missing gold medal, were we? Well, you've already got a gold medal, Jordan: for being an arse. Congratulations. You and your pathetic snowboarding make me sick. Most men would be happy with one woman, but not Jordan. Most men don't go to prison, but Jordan does. Most men have a steady job and don't have the police waking them up once a month, but Jordan does. Jordan has to do everything differently, doesn't he? Jordan doesn't even use a ski ramp, he uses a ski hump. A dirty, filthy ski hump from Bruckley. You disgust me. Adulterer!' And then she stopped shouting, her breathing slowed and her last few feeble comments came in a whisper. 'Did you do that thing you do with your tongue with her?' Her eyes peered into his, then filled with tears, and she knew her heart was broken. 'You did the twister with her, didn't you?' She burst out crying.

Jordan had created all this, he realized that, and it was not his best work to date. How could he have done this to the woman he loved? He stood up, walked across and wrapped his arms round her. Her clinging hug had that awful goodbye feeling about it, like it was their last, and Jordan closed his eyes to stop his tears. They say it is better to have loved and lost than never to have loved at all. Right now, as Jordan felt the fear of losing Zara, he had one word to say to that: 'Bollocks!'

Zara peered up through her tears. 'It's a good job I believe in parallel universes, Jordan, because in the other ones we are still together, with two little Yum Yums to take care of. Unfortunately, I'm stuck with you in this one, in the universe where Jordan failed me, where he went seeking his sexual nourishment elsewhere. Where he couldn't let go of his past and lingered there with his first love.' She wiped her eyes. 'I think you should leave. I won't tell Mummy that you had an affair. She really liked you. She actually loved you.' A silver snowboarding trophy lay on top of one of the boxes and Zara lifted it out. 'Can I keep this?' He nodded. 'Because among all your gold trophies, Jordan, I think this one will remind me of you the most. The man who came second.' She clasped it close to her chest.

Bagging up his clothes, he dithered round in his wardrobe, wondering if a better man would have been able to talk his way out of this, then realized to his shame, that a better man wouldn't have had to. Among the words that Zara might have used to describe Jordan at this moment, he could add a few of his own – derelict brain, being among them.

He must have looked a complete tosser in his dad's clobber, he thought, throwing the milkman's uniform on to the bed and changing into his shorts and T-shirt. Viewing the bedroom with all its fun memories, he choked on a thought. Why? Why couldn't he have opened up to Zara and closed himself up to Cloey? He straightened the duvet and plumped up the pillows. A fear inside told him not to, but to leave this room without looking under Zara's pillow would haunt him forever more. And slowly, like checking under a stone for lice, he lifted the pillow up. The words *Jordy Jordy Yum Yum* glittered up at him, and a tear popped out.

At the front door Jordan kissed Zara goodbye, hugging her hard. 'I'll grab the rest of my stuff in a few days. You will be okay won't you?' She nodded. 'Ring me if you need to spout your mouth off at me again. I know I deserve it. And don't worry about the mortgage and the bills, I'll pay 'em. There's plenty of money in the bank to keep you going.'

Zara pushed him away. 'I want to ask you something and I want you to be honest.' She looked to the floor as she said, 'Would you go to prison for me?'

He stared at her bowed head. 'Yeah, I would. I can't believe I've messed this up big time. I love you, Zara, and I'm sorry.'

A goodbye on the phone was bad enough; in a letter even worse; but in flesh and blood it was terrible. Zara collapsed on the other side of the door, sobbing. No man should be so powerful he could make a woman feel so weak, but, Jordan was her man, Jordan was her love and Jordan was definitely *the one*.

Outside, a few streets away, sitting in his car smoking a fag, *the one,* was acting very peculiarly, searching a map of Milton Keynes for Stacey Bushes.

The word 'payback' had dropped out of his mouth to start with like a slip of the tongue, but by the time he knew exactly where Samir's NightOwl security firm was based, it was a fully blown chant. Payback was coming and it was heading Cloey's way.

Jordan flicked his fag out of the window and keyed in a number on his mobile.

A bloke's deep voice picked up, panting. 'Wot?' It was Ryan, Jordan's mate. He was in the middle of pleasuring a woman whose name he was not familiar with – as yet – and, judging by the look of disappointment on the woman's face, with whose erogenous zones he was not familiar yet, either.

'If the town clowns ask, I was round yours Sunday morning, nine until one thirty. Am I covered?'

'As ever.'

'Cheers, mate. Catch you later.' And Jordan chucked the phone down and headed off towards NightOwl Security, listening to 'Firestarter' by Prodigy. It was the prefect lullaby to get him in the mood.

Chapter Thirty-three

There is no vehicle that travels as fast as the mind. It can whip you off to places more quickly than the speed of light and take you on journeys that otherwise keep you at bay. Kareena's mind had journeyed many miles by the time they reached their destination, zooming ahead of the taxi, guessing what type of place this Cloey would live in. Avani had once told her: 'Never be fearful of the man, always be fearful of the woman.' No matter how faithful a man is, there is always one woman who thinks she can steal him. As Kareena paid the taxi driver his ten-pound fare, she realized that, indeed, her sister was right, this Cloey had become her fear for no other reason than a woman's sixth sense: suspicion.

Kareena sat on the edge of a worn wooden bench hiding under a huge oak tree, its thick branches shading her from the roasting sun. She stared out, forgetting her troubled mind for the moment. The superbly cut bowling green in front of her echoed with visions of men smoking pipes, wearing clinical white clothes, jovially singing each other's praise with, 'Good shot'. The thatched hut near the back of the green held a newly painted sign, Bruckley Scouts. The whole place perspired with respectability. It demanded that you came furnished with a picnic hamper, a blanket and a good book the next time you were here. And a nose peg.

You can spend most of your life wanting to be right about things, but sometimes you just want to be wrong. Kareena stood and nervously made her way to Lemonly Cottage in her apricot-coloured *shalwar kameez*. As she trod slowly up the path to the quaint-looking cottage, her eyes widened and her heart banged in her chest: all her fears were right. There, broadcasting from the leaded window pane, were the tell-tale signs of misbehaviour.

These Premises Are Protected By
NIGHTOWL SECURITY

Sometimes you want to be right, sometimes you want to be wrong, and sometimes you just don't want to know. The only blessing at this instant was that Kareena was looking her best even though she was feeling her worst. But blessings in Bruckley never lasted too long, and within two thumps of Kareena's heart, the front door of the cottage swung open. There, standing at the entrance, with half a smile, was a beauty of a brunette in a short figure-hugging excuse of half a dress. She didn't look like any artist Kareena had seen, she looked more like a centrefold in a man's dirty magazine; and Kareena would kill Samir if he had been down that particular centrefold. Or up it.

Kareena composed herself with a smile. 'Are you Cloey?' Cloey nodded. 'You don't know who I am, but—'

'Oh, I know who you are all right, Kareena.' Cloey waved her through. 'And I especially know who Samir is. Come in, it's small but homely, nothing like your place.'

Cloey watched, amused at Kareena's unease as she sat on the sofa in the living room. She had never seen an Indian woman cry before and she couldn't wait. By the time this little visit was over, her pretty little Indian face would be swelling with sadness. Oh joy! Cloey plonked herself next to Kareena, she didn't want to miss one facial dip, one slippery tear, or one untidy fall to the ground. How dare she turn up at her cottage unannounced, how fucking dare she!

Cloey began, 'I used to be feeble like you, all insecure, no confidence. You remind me of a little butterfly I killed once. Pulled its wings off and told it to fly away. But it couldn't, so I stamped on it. Shall I light a joss stick?' She flicked on the stereo with Hindi music and lit up a patchouli incense stick, then returned to the sofa. 'Ahh, the smell of India, my homeland.' Cloey tilted her head to the side, trying to downgrade Kareena's beauty by searching for hidden blemishes, surely there must be a zit somewhere. Anything. She'd never seen something so horrible in her life – Kareena was beautiful.

Cloey continued, 'I saw you have sex, you know? That night you were cooking for his family. Samir asked me to watch from your garden, he said it was the only way he would get through fucking you. He came to me the following day, and I did things to him that he would be ashamed to ask of you.' Cloey breathed in the smoke, moving her head like a charmed snake, enjoying the sight of the tears building up in Kareena's eyes. 'I've got his child beating inside me right now, come on, feel.' She grabbed Kareena's reluctant hand and clamped it to her stomach. 'This child is conceived from pure love; six years of love growing in my womb.' Cloey laughed. 'Your parents really did choose you the wrong man, didn't they? And Samir's parents forced him to marry you, but of course you wouldn't know that. You're expendable. You don't really matter. Nice *bindi* by the way.'

Kareena remembered hearing on TV about a woman who had been flogged a thousand strokes of the whip in some far-away land for some far-away crime. She remembered thinking: No way, I couldn't cope with that. But right now, she would have swapped the whipping for the torture she was suffering at the hands of this bitch.

Kareena rose, Cloey's laughter frayed the air, catching on her eardrums and sinking deep inside. She had to get out of this place. She fumbled at the front door, almost suffocating.

Behind her Cloey's voice emerged. 'I think you know I'm telling the truth, but if there is still that one per cent doubt that your husband fucks me, then I suggest you see what's hidden behind that vulgar picture of Milton Keynes hanging above your phone. Hanging in the house that *I* decorated. And I think you'll agree, I did a rather good job. Can't wait to move back in with my Samir and our baby.' She followed her up to the gate. 'Oh, by the way, there was one thing I did lie about, I bet you're dying to know. Your *bindi* is disgusting. Goodbye.'

Cloey shut the door and her smile slowly withered to nothing. It was the most fun she'd had for ages. But fun, like most good things, costs. By the time Kareena had walked twenty yards up Conker Avenue, it occurred to Cloey just how costly that fun might be. Why, oh why, couldn't she keep her mouth shut sometimes? After what she had just done to Kareena, there was no way Sammy would take her back. She had more or less just kissed her house goodbye.

It wasn't all doom and gloom though. After all, Jordan had a lot of money. She picked up the phone and dialled Jordan's mobile, the answerphone flicked on. 'Jordan, I'm feeling really horny, if you don't get over here soon, I'll dial Sammy's number instead. You can't pretend any more, Jordan. We love each other and I'm willing to give up the house for you. Did you hear that? I'm willing to give up the house for you. Don't be long. Ciao.' She slammed the receiver down, sank to the floor and sobbed into her hennaed hands, not knowing if she was crying with happiness or sadness.

Kareena's tears, however, were definitely for sadness. The rule for an Indian woman who finds out her husband is having an affair is to ignore it. But, returning to the bench in a whirlwind of emotions, Kareena decided it was time to break an Indian rule. There was no way she could ignore this. Only a feeble, insecure woman with no confidence would be able to brush this under an Indian rug.

Kareena spotted the taxi, wiped her tears with her *chunni* and hailed it. She sat in the back of the cab with a stern face. It was obvious from her brief encounter with Cloey that Samir went for bitchy women.

Well, if it's a bitch he wanted . . .

Sitting in his car, Jordan flipped the two-pound coin. The trusty chunk of metal served many purposes when it came to tricky decisions. He had chosen Zara's lingerie on the toss of the queen's head. Heads he nicked it, tails he spent cash. Sex in stolen underwear, Zara said, was the ultimate. It was like stealing orgasms. He flipped again, still not believing his string of bad luck. Five heads in a row.

He looked at the NightOwl sign, admiring the Uzis on the owl: tasteful. He'd promised himself if the coin landed tails, then without further ado, he would storm the building. Flipping the coin again, he willed it to land tails: it landed heads.

'Fuck it.' Jordan put on his John Lennon shades, immobilized the car and headed to the entrance of NightOwl. He didn't need Lady Luck on his side today, this was purely man to man.

Inside, Jordan was asked to wait on the sofa, while a dippy woman handed him a cup of coffee, a handful of her biscuits and an eyeful of her breasts. Another woman shook her head once and returned to her calculator.

'Samir shouldn't be too long, he's on the phone. I'm Madeleine by the way.' She giggled and bounced back to her chair, slotting herself behind the desk. 'You've got lovely legs: sporty, tanned, toned, lovely.' She snapped a biscuit in half. 'You should be ashamed of yourself wearing shorts with legs like that, it makes me go all—'

'Stop it, Madeleine! Leave the customers alone,' Samir said interrupting, then turning to Jordan, 'You have got gorgeous legs by the way.' He laughed. 'What are you selling?'

Jordan stood up, thinking, 'Erm, insurance.'

'Not interested. I've got the lot.' He glanced Jordan up and down. 'Bit of advice, though, you won't be selling much insurance while wearing shorts and a T-shirt like that, nice legs or no nice legs.'

Jordan smiled. 'I'll give you a bit of advice, mate.' He leant across and whispered in Samir's ear. 'Fucking two women doesn't pay off.' He pulled away and asked, 'So, are you interested in my insurance?' His eyes glinted. 'Wife insurance?'

Samir had never nodded so hard in all his life as he led this stranger with nice legs through to his office aware that he was acting like a guilty man, aware that he *was* a guilty man. Being accused by someone you didn't know of extracurricular sexual activities was the adulterer's version of a citizen's arrest. It wasn't that serious – but it was serious enough.

Jordan plonked himself down on a chair. 'I'm Jordan, Cloey's ex. Sorry I'm late, I came as quick as I could to save you from—'

Samir interrupted, 'Jordan? Cloey's ex, as in ex-con Jordan? Prison Jordan?' He casually opened his desk drawer and deftly pulled out a truncheon, holding it out of sight, his eyes locked on Jordan's relaxed face. 'Woman basher, Jordan?'

Jordan tapped out a fag and lit up. 'Well, our sex

was pretty rough but I wouldn't go as far—'

Samir clenched the cold metal of the truncheon. 'Four fractured ribs and a broken nose, I'd say that's pretty fucking rough. Not to mention the months of counselling, the restless nights, I'm surprised they let you out.'

Jordan leant forward swiping Samir's NightOwl coffee mug for an ashtray. 'I'm no angel, but I'd never—'

'And why did you have to beat up her mother as well?' Samir asked sternly.

'Enough! I've *never* laid a finger on Cloey or that freaky witch of a mother. You've been sucked in by her bullshit, just like I was when she cried to me that *you* beat the living crap out of her. Unfortunately, I did not have the privilege of her telling me that you also beat the crap out of her mother, as that is one image I would have treasured for life. Now put that fucking truncheon back in your drawer.'

'Cloey wouldn't lie about something like that, I've seen her cry buckets over it.'

Jordan gave Samir one long hard stare. 'You just don't know her, do you?'

Within an hour, Samir knew all there was to know about Cloey's crippled morals; how time had turned the slightly fruity Cloey into a fully blown fruitcake. Samir paced his office listening to how Jordan and Cloey had entered his house, bypassed his security system, and while Jordan had waited in the torture-chamber room, Cloey had swiped the wedding album, and injected red dye into the white-wash capsules so Samir's wife would look incapable and—

Samir appeared dumbfounded. 'Did you slash my

car tyre?'

'Nah, I couldn't touch a man's motor, it's like messing with his woman.'

'And you honestly broke into my house to collect photos of Cloey's beatings, which I did not do?' Samir sunk into his leather chair, shaking his head. 'No, no, this is wrong.' He glared at Jordan. 'I should pick up that phone right now and shop you to the police. I mean, look at this shirt.' Jordan squinted as he tried not to laugh at Samir's pretty pink NightOwl shirt. 'Well, it may be funny to you—'

'Look, I'm here to tell you she's only after your house and your money. The last thing I am is a grass. But she's screwed me over too many times. I'm not here to hurt your feelings, mate, but take a closer look at that torture-chamber room of yours. Read the words. I snowboard, just look at it, you'll know what I mean—'

'So what did she want to break in the house for? It couldn't have been just for the wed—'

'The wedding photos. Yes. Pathetic. I broke into your house for some shitty wedding photos – no disrespect.' Jordan eyed Samir earnestly. 'If you're thinking of leaving your wife over her, don't.'

Samir felt like he'd been experiencing the PG version of Cloey, while everyone else was viewing the X rated. For six years he'd struggled to keep her boat afloat when she was having a hard time dealing with the effects of the abuse that Jordan had supposedly dished out. For six years he'd tried to comfort her. 'Please don't raise your voice to me, Sammy, you scare me. That's what Jordan used to do before he used to beat me.' And for six years he'd spent thousands and thousands of pounds trying to cheer her up. Samir was beginning to hate her. And as with every beginning, it must have an end; he just hoped that it didn't end with him losing his wife.

'I'm not leaving my wife for Cloey, that's final, and I don't want my wife to leave me because of Cloey either.' He stared into Jordan's green eyes. He somehow trusted Jordan, the man who had broken into his house. Something about him seemed paradoxically honest. He laid himself open to him. 'I'll be frank. I screwed up. I slept with Cloey while I was married and I've been losing sleep over it ever since.' He lowered his voice. 'Time's caving in on me, I know it. She's given me a week to tell my wife and leave her or she confesses all. I'm sort of hoping she's bluffing.' Samir raised his eyebrows to his new-found friend.

'Cloey doesn't bluff about wrecking people's lives, mate, she actually gets a kick out of it.' Jordan paused, thinking. 'Let's just say it amuses her.' He walked over to the wall planner and then turned round. 'How do you feel about blackmail? Shutting Cloey up once and for all?'

Samir stroked an invisible beard, trying to get a grip on the last hour. 'You mean, kill her?'

'Don't be so fucking stupid. How can you blackmail someone when they're dead? It's more subtle than murder. Let me explain . . .'

Chapter Thirty-four

Cloey set up the tape recorder beside her bed. She was going to tape herself having sex with Jordan and send it to Zara. It should finish their relationship once and for all. It was time she had Jordan all to herself again. They were meant for each other. Samir had been a good reserve, keeping the ovary tank ticking over, but he never gave her the rush of adrenaline that Jordan provided. It was time that Jordan and she thought about marriage. Seriously.

She knelt on the floor in her black lacy lingerie with her eyes closed and her hands held together, speaking clearly. 'Our Father, who art in heaven, hallowed be thy name, our kingdom come, thy will be done, on earth as it is in heaven. Please bring me Jordan.' Cloey opened one eye, smiled up at the ceiling and stood up. 'As if, Lord, like I need *you* to help me get what *I* want with the man who *I* want.' She laughed. 'He's besotted with me. Amen.'

Cloey sprayed a devilish amount of Baby Doll perfume on to her gleaming skin and glanced out of the bedroom window. Now where was he? Her man, her lover, her soon to be fiancé – she'd left two messages on Jordan's phone already.

A knock at the door sent her scooting down the stairs in her lingerie. At last!

She opened the door to see Samir standing there. Oh hell!

Cloey ran her eyes over his face. No bruises, no blood. After the little pep talk she'd had earlier with his feeble wife, Cloey had expected at least one set of fingernail lacerations across his traitor face. As it was, his face was perfect, but his timing was naff.

'You can't just turn up at my house when you feel like it,' she said, taking a step back. 'But as you're here, you may as well have a look at what you're missing out on.' She twirled round twice, then squared up to him. 'I told you, asylum seeker, this community doesn't take too kindly to lowly ethnics, you're supposed to use the service entrance round the back.'

Samir slammed the door behind him and stood facing the woman he used to think of as an angel. Her perfectly beautiful face wasn't fooling him any more.

'I've come to tell you I've cancelled all my direct debits. You'll have to pay your own bills from now on. I'm not your fucking mug, Cloey.' He stepped towards the Caller Display and began pressing the turquoise CALLS button, checking to see whether his wife had called here again.

Cloey smiled, drawing her own conclusions. Kareena had not told him that she'd been round here yet. Maybe she couldn't, maybe she was dead, maybe she'd killed herself after seeing what was hidden behind the picture of Milton Keynes.

She giggled. 'That spineless wife of yours hasn't phoned again. You're still in the clear, Sammy, for the time being. I would offer you tea, coffee or razor blades but I'm expecting somebody.' She glanced at the Caller Display, checking the time – where the hell was Jordan? She was gagging for him.

'My wife's never going to find out, because you're not going to tell her.' Samir smirked.

'Is that so?' Cloey picked up the phone and began to dial. 'I don't know the Indian word for "an affair" but I expect she'll understand the English version, "Your husband fucked me."'

Samir grabbed her wrist and jammed the receiver down. 'You'll have to get used to that, Cloey, fighting for the phone in prison. Aileen's going to be so proud of you when you go down for burglary.'

She jerked her hand from under his. 'What d'you mean?'

'Oh come on, Cloey, you don't honestly think that the boss of Milton Keynes' top security firm wouldn't have cameras fitted in his own house. What do you take me for? A moron?' He paused, watching the sculpture of her beautiful face change before him, her jaw muscles tightening, her eyes cramped wide. She looked like she was about to be run over. 'I didn't recognize you at first with the black hair, it threw me. But it was not a very clever disguise, Cloey. At least your associate had the sense to keep his face covered with a Snoopy mask.'

Cloey listened in disbelief as Samir went on to explain the story Jordan and he had concocted. A fictitious drama spiked with a few facts. Her face froze when he described the pixel quality of his indoor cameras and how his deep paranoia of being burgled had encouraged his super-duper indoor surveillance.

'You could say that you've had your fifteen minutes of fame,' Samir said, relaxing back on the sofa, enjoying the moment.

'You are such a control freak, Sammy. Why the cameras in the house? So that you can catch your wife bonking another man while you're at work? You are *so* sick!' She wanted to cry, nothing had turned out as she'd planned. 'And these cameras, they can see everywhere, can they?'

'All entry points in the house. Why?'

'No reason. Just curious.'

Samir shook his head faintly. 'So we have an understanding? You keep away from me and my wife, and that tape will stay locked up in my safe.' He stood up. 'I used to be so sure I loved you, Cloey.'

Her flushed face shifted up to look at him. 'But?'

'But nothing. Take care.' And he left.

Cloey did her best to control her rage. Nobody treated her like that. It was customary for her at a time like this to throw something of Claudette's, but, instead she picked up the phone and dialled. It was answered almost immediately. 'Hello, Kareena? It's Cloey. I thought you'd best know that your cheating husband has just left my warm bed. Next time wash his shirts better so that they don't come out pansy pink. He hopes our child is a boy. Goodbye!'

Now she could throw something of Claudette's and her house-mate's Prada handbag was lobbed up the stairs. 'Hag bag!'

Feeling better, she dialled her master of masculinity

– Jordan. His answerphone switched on. 'Hello, gorgeous. Best come over right now, sex is off, this is more important – if that's possible. Sammy has just been here threatening to drop us both in it. He had hidden cameras, the sneak. I think you may be going to prison again, Jordan. Hurry now. Ciao.'

Jordan sat smoking on a wonky headstone in the cemetery, his tanned bare back facing the afternoon sun, the drumming bass of his radio-cassette player vomiting out Limp Bizkit. He fancied an easy day today. Maybe he'd paint one plank, just to keep the church's very own charlatan, Father Luke, happy, and then head on down to the ski-slope to cool off. His mobile rang and he imagined a hundred skeletons all reaching for their mobiles from their graves. It was Cloey, again, and he ignored her, again. He checked his watch, 4.00 p.m. If the plan was being executed correctly, Samir should be out of Cloey's life by now. It was enough to give him a resurgence of energy to paint another plank. Well, almost.

He viewed the church, the hub of the village community, thinking of the generations who had sung and worshipped here. Jordan puffed out smoke, its greyness diluting to nothing in the sun's glare. How many people came back to visit their great-grandparents? Let alone their great-, great-, great-grandparents. As far as Jordan could see, your memory on this earth lasts only as long as those who remembered you. After that, you're a washed-up soul with no place to go. Jordan smiled. Unless, that is, you make your mark on this world. Unless you give it no choice but to remember you.

He tried to motivate himself to stir the paint can, but that meant motivating himself to look for a stick or a bone, and that meant getting off his arse. He even smoked the fag lethargically, just breathing nicotine into one lung, it was too damn hot to do anything. The noise of an ice-cream van tolled in the distance. What he wouldn't do now for profiteroles and ice cream. Those sweet chocolate-coated balls of vanilla ice cream being spoon-fed into his welcoming mouth by the best spoon-feeder of them all: Zara. God he missed her. He cast an eye upwards, God it was hot. Help!

He lay beside the headstone on the dry, raggedy grass, hands behind his head sunbathing, keen to even out the paler patches of skin under his arms. Maybe he could find the motivation in his dreams to stir the paint. He snoozed until a gloomy damp crawled across his chest, and he peered upwards.

A paralysing voice dropped down from the silhouette, 'Wake up, Peasant Boy. Rise!'

Jordan tried to focus on the figure but all he could see was a banana. Or was it a pineapple? He struggled to his feet and stood staring at Aileen who was wearing a bright, custard-coloured dress. She smelt like she'd just come out of the washing machine.

'If it's not the beautiful Aileen. The mother I never had.' He searched for his top.

'Your mother lies decomposing over there.' Aileen pointed her thumb over her shoulder. 'And you,' her finger slammed into his chest, 'you turn God's dormitory of the dead into a disco. Have you no shame?' She bent down and switched the racket off.

'Turn that fucking music back on, my mum likes

listening to Eminem.' He moved in closer, grabbing his T-shirt off the aluminium stepladder. 'Just because they're dead, doesn't mean they can't live a bit.' The music blared back out as he jammed his finger down. 'What were you baptized in, Aileen, Devil's puke?' He threw his T-shirt on, shaking his head through the top. ' "God's dormitory", how *do* you come up with them?'

For a moment, it seemed that he had finally pushed Aileen over the edge as, with the grace of a fencer, she produced from her brown leather handbag the sabre of her choice: a gleaming silver letter opener, engraved with the words, Blessings on the Messenger.

She drew a sharp breath and thrust herself forward, bringing the point of the metal within an inch of Jordan's gulping testicles. There was an efficiency to her movements that would have warped the stiffest courage. 'You stole my daughter's virginity out of wedlock and you shall pay a heavy price, Peasant Boy. In front of the Lord, you dirtied my Cloey with your disgusting seed. She was only fourteen. She was an innocent girl!'

'And I was only an innocent boy of fourteen. And maybe someone like me could never be good enough for your daughter. Too common. But remember this, Aileen, when you drive up to the pearly gates, God won't give a shit if you arrive in a limo or a Sinclair Five, all he's going to care about is if you're good, or if you're bad. So fuck off out of my face and get your hands away from my nuts. You do nothing for me.'

God had served Aileen well for many years and now she would serve him in return. To rid yourself of hate, you first had to rid yourself of the object of that hatred. And Jordan topped her list.

'Say your last prayer, Peasant Boy.' She closed her eyes. 'Get ready to join your mother.'

A voice came from up yonder. 'Aileen!' It was Father Luke and his bowling-ball head scampering across the gravestones towards them, his large crucifix swinging from side to side across his tubby belly. 'Don't do it, Aileen.' His sweaty hands hooked her under her armpits and, using his full weight, he pulled her back. 'Thou shalt not kill, Aileen, thou shalt not kill.' He eased her wiry body away from the flash point, snatched the letter opener from her grip and set her down on the grass. The music still rocked in the background.

Jordan's high was over and he watched as Father Luke tried in vain to comfort a sobbing Aileen. He picked up his Tupperware container, opened the lid and walked over.

'Fancy a sandwich?' he asked. 'I've got cheese and pickle or ham and French mustard. They're a bit manky now the sun's been at 'em, but they'll fill a hole – excuse the pun, Aileen.'

Father Luke locked his pinprick vision on Jordan. 'I suggest you go. You're determined to hurt people, aren't you?' Father Luke's hand soothed Aileen's back and he whispered, 'There, there, come on, come on, Aileen.' It almost sounded like a start to a Dexy's Midnight Runners song.

Jordan knelt down on the rough grass, his eyes glinting. 'Call yourself a decent guy, Lukie Baby? I came here to talk to my mum so many times when I was a kid and you told me that she wouldn't be able to hear me because I broke the rules, because I was a sinner. Remember that?' He stood up. 'You told me that God doesn't normally favour the poor, that he has little time for the black sheep of his flock. You told me that if I carried on my bad ways, then God, your buddy, would wipe me off the face of this earth. Remember that?' Jordan turned his attention to the snivelling Aileen. 'I loved Cloey more than anything in this world, I would have done anything for your daughter. Anything, Aileen. Remember that.'

Chapter Thirty-five

If you look for the word divorce in the Indian dictionary, you won't find it. Instead are the words, 'Go and bloody well look up another word. Suggested word to look up: shame.' And it is shameful. One life, one partner, one death, no divorce – it's as simple as that. Most Indian grannies spit on the sidewalk when the name of Liz Taylor is mentioned and if you utter just the first few syllables of Zsa Zsa Gabor, you may find a joint of halal meat plummeting towards your head. It's amazing what an Indian biddy will keep under her trusty white sari along with her bank book and her 15,000-decibel personal rape alarm.

But it's not a spitting matter. It's a splitting matter. And sometimes people just don't hit it off, and sometimes bastard men hit it off with other women. Kareena knew she must have an in-built *ignore* switch, but just at this precise moment, as she was packing her suitcase, she couldn't find it. Her mum had advised her, 'If he shouts at you, ignore it. If he doesn't help round the house, ignore it. If he leaves a black rim round the bath, ignore it. Just ignore everything.' Kareena flung in a handful of underwear, ignoring the lingerie that Samir had bought her. Bastard!

Her parents surely couldn't expect her to ignore Samir impregnating another woman. Or maybe they could. She would soon find out. They were due in less than an hour for a family dinner, and Samir had been due more than an hour ago for his overdue slap. Bastard!

Zipping up her overcrowded case, Kareena stuffed it into the wardrobe, almost laughing at the ridiculousness of her life. Oh, what a delightful feeling, she thought, as she threw a NightOwl badge across the room, knowing that not only were you a man's wife, but you were also his bit on the side and he was really in love with someone else. She gazed at her reflection in the full-length mirror, with wide eyes, wondering if the eyes that peered back were worthy of being called eyes at all. Why hadn't she managed to see this coming? Samir had seemed too good to be true with his slack Indian rules and daring challenges to the traditions of the Indian way. Now she knew why: butter up the wife at home and prance on over to spread the legs of his mistress. She wondered why he had bothered marrying her at all when he obviously loved someone else.

Watching Streakers scratching himself on the lawn outside, she smiled at the cuddly cat's lack of worry about life and relationships. He never wondered about the meaning of life, he knew it already: food. But Kareena did wonder about the meaning of life, her life. She sat on the bed secretly knowing the answer as to why Samir had married her when he was in love with someone else, the only reason that ever matters in Indian households: parents. From the moment you are born they inject into your skull the idea that the arranged marriage is the only way it is the Indian way. Like it or fuck off. And as you become older, nearer marriageable age, those syringes get bigger and those injections become more painful. The truth, you find, is that you never had a choice.

The sound of her parents' BMW arriving dislodged her melancholy thoughts. Kareena bounded down the stairs, stairs that she now hated, through the hall, a hall that she now hated, in a house, a house that she now hated. And why did she hate it? Because that horrid Cloey had chosen every damn thing from top to bottom, that's why.

She opened the door, dressed to the nines in Indian get-up and threw her arms round her mother's shoulders. It was like winning the pools seeing her family again. And it was important that her effusive welcome extended to the whole family, including her brother, Arun.

Kareena gave him a cuddle. 'You okay?'

He shrugged. 'Maybe, maybe not.'

Kareena's father interrupted, scolding him. 'Stupid boy, why don't you just forgive her. Well?'

Arun feebly forgave Kareena. It was ridiculous bearing a grudge over A-level grades after all. But how could he hold his head high knowing that he had scored less than his sister? Oh, the humiliation when the results arrived a few weeks back. Oh, the torment. He had felt like writing a suicide note, but he wasn't keen on the dying bit.

Avani folded her arms, studying her sister. 'Has he hit you yet, Kareena?'

Her father intervened, his short temper getting the better of him. 'Stupid girl, there are questions you don't ask.' He pulled a white hanky from his suit trousers and dabbed his balding head.

Avani hobbled through the hall in her favourite sling-backs, confused. 'Well, if there are questions you don't ask, then how can they be questions?' she said, arriving in the living room and glancing around. 'Kareena,' her voice grew louder, 'he still hasn't got any photos of you up. Selfish is what he is, pedigree selfish.'

In time, all Kareena's family were sitting with tea, biscuits and Bombay mix. There were fifteen conversations going on at once, which was strange, seeing as only one person was talking, always talking – Dad. He was about to begin his sixteenth conversation when Samir's arrival had everybody on their feet, except Kareena. She had been kind of hoping that her father would have managed to keep quiet for just one minute before her cheating husband arrived so she could explain to them that she wanted a divorce. Kind of hoping never got her anywhere. You had to hope with a passion to get her father to shut up.

After an explosion of, '*Sat sri akal*'s', laughter from Avani at Samir's poofy-pink shirt, and Samir's apology for arriving late, the family gathered round the dining-room table ready to be fed. The evening had officially begun.

Kareena's emotions were like a stone wall. And Samir's wall, the one he had built on lies and deceit, was about to come tumbling down.

Jordan stood, waiting for Cloey, in the dried-up stream that used to run through Bruckley. If you followed it far enough it led you past the farmer's fields and up to the distant hills which overlooked Milton Keynes. The water was long gone, but Jordan's memories were still fresh.

He lit a fag, wishing he had a lager or two. This place meant many things to him. Dreams, hopes, escape, all the things that little boys are made of, along with slugs, snails and puppy-dogs' tails. Most of all, this place meant Cloey. With its steep muddy bank and surrounding trees, no one had been able to touch them here. It had been their island. They had constructed their plans for the future here, deciding on two kids, a boy and a girl, deciding on a huge mansion in Hampshire, deciding they would love each other for infinity.

Jordan heard a rustling in the thick hedge that topped the stream bank, and stretched his head up to see the dense bushes giving birth to Cloey. First her head emerged, then her shoulders, then the rest of her. A healthy, bonnie girl, dressed in a slutty slip of a mauve-coloured dress with matching Reeboks, stood staring down at him. Taking into consideration she had just jogged half a mile and climbed through a jungle, she looked fucking fuckable.

'For Christ's sake, Jordan, you sure know how to treat a girl to a fun evening,' she said, struggling down the dry bank. 'I wanted you in my bed. You know? A place without leaves and worms?' She fell the last foot and landed in his arms – on purpose. 'Whoops!'

He threw down his fag, and pulled up the bottom of her dress. 'Whoops!' Just as he had expected – no knickers – and took a step back, adding some breathing space between their groins. 'Give me the ring Sammy bought you.'

Cloey twisted the fake wedding band off her finger and plopped it in Jordan's palm. 'Easy. I told you it would be. I've got no problem getting rid of anything of Sammy's. I'm yours now, Jordan, I love you. I'll throw away all the presents he gave me, except the car.'

He felt the weight of the ring, then threw it for six over the bank. They both watched its trajectory long after it had flown, as if somehow the ring would boomerang back, and then stood looking at each other. Jordan grabbed Cloey's hand, pulling her towards him, wrapping his arms round her welcoming body. Nothing was said, nothing needed to be said that wasn't totally related to sex.

Jordan unhooked the small straps of her slip, holding it briefly before letting it fall to the crusty mud. He brushed the hair from her face and kissed her, toying with the idea of moaning some obscenities in her ear, first in English, then in French and if she was really lucky in ficking Irish. Language can heighten any sexual adventure, but nothing compared with the language of Cloey's artistic fingers as she expertly massaged him through his shorts.

A scattering of bird wings above loosened his concentration, undoing some of his wild thoughts. Jordan peered up. It was all right for the birds and bees to do it, but when it came to humans, not a second's peace. Now, fuck off!! he thought, as he led Cloey up the crumbly bank, gently pushing her down, then removing his clothes. He had always loved extreme sports, and that included extreme sex. He pushed himself inside her, pleased that he had made the right decision this time: when having sex outdoors, *always* make sure the woman is on the bottom. He began to thrust hard. Extremely hard. Work work, busy busy, bang bang. It was a tough life being a sinner.

And as he made love to Cloey, as they wallowed in their own moans and groans, the silt of the last hour settled to the bottom of his mind. Cloey's frantic tears earlier on the phone had needed some serious calming, a dextrous use of sympathy mixed with a hardened assertiveness. She had explained about the video tape Samir was holding of her and Jordan breaking into Sammy's house and how she had already confessed all to Samir's wife earlier. She worried about going to prison and referred over and over to a place she'd heard of called Tempo. Jordan explained it was called Tenko, the Japanese horror camp, and she had cried some more.

If there was such a thing as the truth coming from Cloey's lips then this was it. He understood how hard it was for her to dig up those old words that had remained buried for years, he knew how difficult it was for Cloey to say sorry. Sorry for sleeping around while he was in prison and keeping him hanging on. Sorry for using him while trying to win Sammy back. Sorry for ever letting him go. Sorry for giving him up for money. And sorry for never being sorry before. It was a sorry affair.

Cloey gazed over at Jordan, lying exhausted beside her. 'Promise me, you'll never become complacent with your lovemaking, Jordan. That was fantastic. I want it like that all the time,' she said, brushing away the moss and dirt from her bottom.

He stood, yanked his shorts up and looked down at her. 'I don't care how screwed up you are, you've got one fucking beautiful body.'

Jumping to her feet, she moved in closer, tracing her fingernail across the scar on his chest. 'I'm glad you and blow-up doll are finished. She was never your type. *I am!*' She paused. 'Am I more beautiful than Zara?'

'More.'

'And do I turn you on more than Zara?' Her hand slid down into his Raggedy snowboarding shorts.

'More.'

'And do you love me more than Zara?'

He paused, as if working out the averages. 'Much more.'

Cloey bent down, and dropped his shorts then peered up. 'And when are you going to marry me?' Her eyes wide and questioning.

'Erm . . .'

She squeezed his erection, stood up and glared at him. 'Well? *Are* you going to marry me? Don't you think we're both sick of pretending, Jordan? We're made for each other.'

He looked into her hazel eyes, sure of what he was seeing. 'Of course I'll marry you. I've been waiting for you to . . . I've been waiting for years.'

She sunk back down to her knees, the happiest she'd been since before Jordan went to prison.

Jordan felt his body charge like an electric storm, tingling with anticipation of events soon to unfold. Sometimes it was far better being a peasant than a prince. Peasants, like blondes, always had more fun.

Chapter Thirty-six

As Kareena watched her family tuck into their hot chicken jalfrezi, she waited for the right moment to turn up the heat. It came soon enough.

She interrupted the quiet munching, 'Samir, why don't you tell my parents about the woman you're sleeping with.' She sipped some water, her heart on standby for a heart attack. 'The white woman in Bruckley who you secretly go and see while I stay here and cook your dinner.'

You could have heard a timid mouse fart, it was that quiet. A silence hung at the entrance to everyone's mouth. Gob-smacked. And then it became so noisy you wouldn't have been able to hear a bloated elephant fart. A deafening roar of accusations, denials, cross-questionings, and crosser questionings. Only one person refused to participate in the oral frenzy – Avani.

Very slowly she scraped her chair back across the

wooden floor and, taking three steps forward, she hissed angrily in Samir's face, 'Is it true? Are you filling someone else's hole?'

Her father's voice became a siren, ordering everyone to their bunkers. 'Sit down, shut up and let me sort this out.' Family issues were dealt with by him and him alone. He faced Samir. 'Is there a grain of truth in anything she has just said?'

'She's lying.' Samir pushed his half-eaten food away. 'Every day I get this from her. It's almost like she wants an excuse to get out of this marriage.' He checked their watching faces quickly, then looked over at his crying wife. 'Why do you keep accusing me? Why? I want to know. I need to know.' He turned sideways to Kareena's mother. 'I am at my wit's end. I was going to phone you and explain about this problem she seems to have and ask you to talk to her. I've really had enough.' His lying eyes pleaded, trying to elicit sympathy from his mother-in-law's face. 'I'm losing weight with worry, you know.'

Inside Samir's head, brain cells were dying rapidly. Gangs and gangs of cells all trying to help their master out of a spot of bother, realizing the full scope of the problem, then performing acrobatic kamikaze leaps against his skull wall. Cell dead, brain dead, Samir was dead – if he couldn't talk his way out of this.

Only a few hours ago, this untidy problem seemed to have been all stitched up. A tidy mend of a loose thread: Cloey had been bribed. The score had been settled. The problem was supposed to have faded away. Surely there was someone in this world who got away with having an affair? Why couldn't it be me? he thought, as he listened to Kareena's screams.

'He's lying! Don't believe him. I saw his woman today. She told me everything.' She wiped her wet eyes with a napkin, then turned to Samir. 'She told me everything, Samir. Don't you *dare* deny it!'

Her mother escorted her weeping daughter out of the dining room, with Samir's words flying behind her, 'Please try and talk some sense into her.' Kareena's mother knew about talking sense, and it usually meant leaving men out of the discussion. In Pandharpur, the village where she grew up, the women used to have a saying, 'God gave man one present: his intelligence, unfortunately he never told man how to open his present – *jhalla*.' And the women would laugh as they slapped the wet washing on the smooth, round rocks.

Kareena sat next to her mother in the conservatory, the dim evening sun still managing to soak the room with its orange tinge. She could feel the weight of her mother's stare and feebly shrugged as another tear plopped on her *kameez*. Her mother knew that to reach through her daughter's tears and find the source of her spring sometimes necessitated patience and understanding. But affairs and sleeping around were items she had neither patience nor understanding for. She just prayed her daughter had been duped by her own imagination.

'You'd better be right,' she began, squeezing Kareena's hand, giving her encouragement. 'These are serious allegations. No one will prosper out of this if you are wrong. And if you are wrong, then he has every right to treat you badly, you would have deserved it.' She paused. 'Now tell me what the real problem is.'

Kareena withdrew her hand. 'She's pregnant with his child.'

'Barrrstarrrrd,' the word slipped out.

Kareena wasn't sure whether her mother was referring to the kid or to Samir and she set about explaining her suspicions and conclusions: how Cloey had confirmed her worst fears and why her suitcase was now packed upstairs. Instantly her mother dismissed many of the so-called pieces of evidence: how the house seemed put together by a woman, Samir's up and down behaviour and even his lax Indian rules. She waved away these snippets of information as though they were choking smoke. They were not pieces of the jigsaw puzzle. Cloey, however, was.

'How sure are you that this woman is not telling you a pack of lies? You haven't even discussed this with Samir, Kareena. You said yourself that she must be doolally to have painted a crucifix on our Guru Nanak. I'm under no misapprehension here, I can see that you believe what you're telling me, I am your mother of all things and I know when you're telling the truth.' She tucked a cushion behind her back, stiffening her posture, and with a sterner expression she continued, 'If you are one hundred per cent sure that Samir is seeing this woman, then I, and your father, will take you home right now. No going back to Samir. But if this woman is dilly dally doolally like you say she is, then how do you know she isn't making all this up? How do you know that, without having talked it over with Samir?' She paused. 'Are you *absolutely* sure?'

'Yes and no,' Kareena replied slightly embarrassed. 'I don't know.'

Her mother shook her head, tinkling her twenty-two-carat gold earrings. 'I think it was unfair of you to have brought this up without speaking to Samir first. You talk it over with him and you let us know in the morning. If you still want to come home after discussing it with Samir, then your dad will drive up and collect you. But you must be *totally* sure.'

Sure? Kareena thought. I was sure until you opened your big mouth.

Kareena and Samir stood uneasily at the front door as her sombre family departed. Avani walked backwards to the car, her eyes continuously on Samir. She hissed, 'I don't trust you, Samir, watch yourself,' then blew Kareena a kiss, and stepped into the BMW, keeping her suspicious eyes on him until the car left the drive. She might only fill samosas for a living but she could spot dodgy ingredients anywhere. Her brother-in-law was food poisoning as far as she was concerned. She just hoped her sister had the bottle to barf him up.

Samir closed the door, bolting it. 'I can't believe you did that. I can't believe you put me in a position like that.'

Ignoring him, she headed into the dining room and viewed the messy table with sadness. She always liked to think of the empty plates and empty bowls as the ghosts of a good time, the spirits of laughter. Today, with half the food destined for the waste disposal, her memory was only of five shocked faces all staring tunnel-mouthed at her announcement. It was not quite the traditional Indian way of spicing up the evening.

Kareena expertly shunted all the leftover food into a

serving bowl with half a naan, careful not to splash any on her *kameez*: turmeric was hazardous waste as far as expensive clothes were concerned. She was grateful for Samir's avoidance of clean-up duty, thankful for the time to think. Her mother had scattered a handful of doubtful seeds amongst a field of mistrust, urging caution when judging her husband. Suspicion could be a very sharp tool and should be wielded wisely. Men were built on ego, it was your duty to massage it, not to search for flaws in their character.

'I want you to see this,' Samir said, hovering at the doorway to the dining room.

She turned her head away from a plate stained with curry towards a man with a face stained with worry. In his hand, he gripped a chunky photo album with a black corrugated cover. Lifting up the corner of the tablecloth, he set the album down on the polished mahogany table and flipped back the cover, revealing various black and white photographs all meticulously stuck to their pages with good old-fashioned Indian *ghee*. Samir wanted Kareena to see the various branches of his family tree, all the way down to the last twig.

He spoke in a voice heavy with anger, 'You have hurt my feelings, Kareena, I can't believe you think that I have been with a white woman. It's really low of you to think that of me.' He pointed to a picture of his grandparents. Two old-timers looking petrified by the flashbulb. 'Do you honestly think that I am a freeloader? Do you think that I could let our ancestors toil and grind the ground to dust, to pave the way for our future, so that our parents could come to England

and live a better life and then for me to wreck it all with my selfishness?' He slammed the album shut and kicked a chair with his foot. 'I'm a fucking Sikh, it's in my blood, it's in your blood. It's not our way to mix bloods. How dare you even contemplate the idea I've been with this *Cloey*.' He almost spat in fake indignation. 'How fucking dare you!' He glared at her. 'You sneak off, after promising me you wouldn't, you go to this mad woman's flat, you listen to her lies, and then you come back here and doubt me. That ain't my bloody idea of marriage. It may be yours but it certainly isn't mine.' He kicked the chair again. 'I had to explain myself to your father. Can you even begin to imagine how I felt? Can you? *Can you?*'

Kareena slumped into a chair, feeling slightly tipsy with humiliation. One more comment from Samir and she'd have a huge hangover of guilt by morning. She *so* wanted to be wrong about all this, and faintly, like an insignificant worm coming out of the ground with a miner's helmet, she could see some light at the end of the tunnel. Just a little.

She wondered whether, if this same situation arose ten years from now when she knew Samir better, she would be able to recognize when he was lying. Each doubt was like cholesterol, clogging her thinking, blocking any peace of mind; there were still some niggling questions that needed answering.

Samir poured out two glasses of white wine, picked up the kicked-over chair and sat down facing her.

She took a gulp of her drink. 'Cloey phoned me this afternoon, telling me you had just left her bed and you were wearing a pink shirt. How would she know about your shirt?'

Samir stared at his pink sleeves. 'Look at it! The whole of Milton Keynes probably knows about it.' He glanced up, searching through his dishonest mind, hunting for a lie like an alley cat hunts for fish bones. He found one, cleaned it up, then regurgitated it. 'I expect after you left this nutcase's *flat* she headed on down to NightOwl security to look through my window to see what I was wearing. Hey?' He threw back some wine. 'And then she phones you and you believe her. So you think all her other lies are true? Hey?'

Samir coloured in his story, adding humour where needed, twisting the whole episode into a mini-drama in Kareena's mind. Using the photos as props was a wicked idea, he thought. He'd known his grandparents would come in handy one day. And that classic line he'd just thrown in about Cloey's flat – unreal. Now just to tie up a few loose ends and this marriage could return to . . .

'She said she's pregnant with your child, Samir. How do you explain that one?'

'Pregnant? Child? Mine? Baby? Her and me?' Samir reached for help from the gurus. Surely after all his praying at the temple they could grant him a little favour. 'Not possible, we haven't had sex.' He stood up, grabbing her arm. 'Come on, put your coat on, we'll go and see her. Let's get this all out in the open. Let's all embarrass ourselves. Now where does she live? *Her flat*, Kareena, where is it?'

'Flat? It's a cottage.'

He stared at her as if she were a fool and shouted, 'Well, I wouldn't know that, would I? I haven't seen it, have I? She told me she was an unemployed artist who worked and lived on the eighth floor of a block of council flats.' He bellowed the next bit, 'She said the height gave her inspiration!'

Kareena frowned. 'But she's got a NightOwl sticker on her window.'

Samir slapped his hand to his sweaty forehead. 'Well, she would have, wouldn't she? I gave her security advice on how to deal with the rapists and druggies who hang around the entrance to her block of flats – *that's my job*. I was only trying to be nice. I won't bother next time. I thought she was a lesbo, if you must know.'

The warm night stretched until dawn as Samir slowly wriggled off his hook. Kareena knew their future happiness together depended upon trust, there could be no stability without it, and it needed sorting out tonight. And as she fell for Samir's charade, as he convinced her with his fake display of hurt, she concluded two things: Samir was either the biggest liar on earth, or, she had been listening to her heart and not her brain. And, as every Indian girl knows, she must never listen to her heart.

Samir and Kareena, now empty of talk, both looked at their bed with tired, greedy eyes. At that moment they both loved that bed so much, they'd probably have named their first kid after it: 'Bedjinder Singh.'

Kareena rested her knackered head on the pillow, holding on to relief, as sleep finally took her.

Samir rested his bullied head on the pillow, holding on to his sanity, as sleep refused to take him. How could it? He had a pregnant Cloey to think about.

Chapter Thirty-seven

Claudette was drunk and depressed at 10.00 a.m. Last night a lanky thirteen-year-old lad from MK had asked her to sleep with him. He'd said, 'I heard you were a slag and would sleep with anyone.' Had her life come to this? And, as if things weren't bad enough, her lifelong friend was getting married. Jordan had finally popped the question and Claudette was jealous as hell.

Tucked up in a towelling robe, jammed into the corner of the sofa, she swigged from a hefty mug of Amaretto and coffee. People say they can't remember the sixties – because they were too high. Would she say something similar? 'Can't remember the nineties, I was too busy getting fingered and fucked.' Shouldn't she receive an OBE for services to mankind? Order of the British Empire for shagging. Or even a knighthood. After all, she did spend most of her nights putting little hoods on men's cocks.

'Babe alert,' Cloey said, traipsing in and throwing open the curtains. The sun burst through like a dog who had been waiting outside in the rain. 'Another scorcher on the second day of my engagement.' She giggled. '*Scorchio*.'

Claudette toasted her, 'Scorchio.'

Cloey swung round, her bum resting on the window sill. 'I want you to be nice to Jordan. Don't make me choose between you and him. Don't test me, Claudette, you will come out the loser.'

Claudette rolled her eyes. 'I can't believe you're engaged to prisoner 4253 when you have no idea of the state of his bank balance. It's so unlike you.'

'It's called love, Claudette. Look it up sometime.'

She eyed Cloey, assessing her friend's choice of come to bed threads. What appeared to be a backless red dress was being worn the wrong way round, leaving her breasts half exposed. Experience had shown Claudette that men lacked imagination. They didn't need any with this dress. It was explosive.

'So, will you choose between Jordan and your stigmatic mother? Or is this another case of 'leave my mother out of it?' Claudette slurred.

'Actually, like I said to you, she's either with me, or she's against me. My mother and I have a new understanding, I think it's called keeping her fucking nose out of my life. I think that's what it's called.' She smiled. 'She will be told about the engagement as soon as Jordan has slipped the ring on my finger. Did I tell you where he is going to officially propose? No?' Cloey walked across and sat next to Claudette. 'It was all my idea. Ask yourself, Claudette, what does Jordan love the most? Excluding me of course.'

'His mother's grave?'

'Wrong. Try again.'

'The prison cells? Budweiser? Zara? His mates? Wanking? Wanking over his mates in a cell while being served Budweiser by Zara?' Claudette was urged to keep guessing, until finally she said, 'I know, it's completely obvious now: snowboarding?'

Cloey jumped up. 'Yes, you've got it, he's going to propose to me on top of the ski-slope in Milton Keynes. All my idea of course. I said to him he's got to get down on one knee on top of the ski-slope, ask me to marry him, and then we slowly snowboard down the slope together like two snowflakes melting into one.' She hugged herself, rocking from side to side. 'It's so romantic. His two true loves under one roof.'

Claudette grimaced. 'Well, make sure you wear something warmer than that, you look like a right slut!'

Cloey shook her shoulders like a swan ruffling its feathers. 'I'm ignoring that comment as you're clearly drunk. Make sure you apologize to me when you're sober. Anyway, a woman can never be too sure when her lover will pop in, so, I say, be prepared.' She paused. 'Shouldn't you be phoning in sick before you get totally hammered? I mean if I were your boss, I—'

She was interrupted by the first ring of the phone. By the second ring she was answering it. 'What do you want, Samir?'

'You bitch! Couldn't leave it, could you?'

Oh joy, she thought. 'She came to my door. What was I meant to do? Remember, Sammy, you were in the wrong, you sneakily married her and it was *you* who let *me* down. I don't really think you've got any moral high ground with me, do you?'

Samir took the blow and carried on with the fight. 'My wife tells me you're pregnant. Are you?'

Rubbing her stomach in circles, she answered, 'She's lying. Do you honestly think that I would carry a brown baby in my womb? I can't think of anything more disgusting, can you, Asylum Seeker?'

Samir felt chills on the back of his neck. Could he really have loved this woman?

'I really didn't know you, Cloey, did I?' He swallowed hard.

'I'm not a gold digger by nature, but you were such easy prey, Sammy, I would have been a fool to pass you up with all your money and your eagerness to pay my bills.' She paused, trying to send a smirk down the phone. 'But in answer to your question, no, you never knew me. That distinction only goes to one man, his name is Jordan, he's the only person who really knows me. And he's the only man who I ever loved. Ever!'

Samir said, 'How sweet,' and hung up.

But there was no sweeter feeling than this. Samir felt as though his life had been resurrected. To have found out that Cloey was not pregnant with his child, was like a rebirth. He had been given another chance.

Last night his marriage was sinking, a one-way voyage to the bottom of the ocean. *Twenty Thousand Sikhs Under the Sea*. And his only way out was lies. An amalgamation of whoppers thrust down his wife's throat, hoping that none of them rebounded on him.

Most Indian marriages start at the same place, two strangers thrown together, sent off on a wing and a prayer to work it out for themselves. Some couples become real couples quicker than others, love gets a grip and takes hold of them at the outset. Some take years, decades even, to reach that same happy state. And others never find love at all, and live to old age and die with romantic feelings that were never allowed to exist.

But Samir knew he was one of the lucky ones. With Kareena, against all the odds, he knew his love for her was taking hold. He thanked the gurus for giving him this second chance. He thanked his parents for finding him Kareena.

There was a knock on Samir's office door and Mickey swaggered in. 'You called, Chief?'

Samir pointed to the chair opposite him. 'Sit down!'

Mickey's head moved round the room like a bird in a cage, then flopped to the chair in front. 'How come you're in jeans and a T-shirt, Chief? It's not very boss-like, time management is your problem, spot it a mile away. What you—'

'Shut the fuck up.' Samir ground out the words, 'What I would like to do, Mickey, is get another full-time person in to do your job. Okay?'

Mickey beamed. 'Chief, you're promoting me? About time. With all due respect I'm your best security guard. In fact, you could almost call me a security god. Let me shake your hand.'

'You're sacked, Mickey. Here's your P45.' Samir threw the screwed-up form at Mickey's head.

'Sacked?'

'Fired!'

Mickey opened up the crumpled form, chuckling, this had to be a joke. He flattened it out, staring at the date of leaving. He checked his digital watch for today's date and it matched. 'Why, Chief?'

Samir explained the reason why security guards were called security guards. Ever since Mickey had taken over the graveyard shift of the Communiqué Communications site, two computers had gone missing, one fax machine, stationery, bog rolls, Dictaphones, food . . .

'Basically, Mickey, you nick everything. You're a crook. Since I spoke to the director yesterday, it has also come to light that you have been through people's personal drawers.'

'So? Everyone does it, you're just too blind to see it, Chief.'

'It's other things, too. You may not think so, Mickey, but some people are dead proud of their children and that's why they bring cute little photos of them and place them on their desk.'

'So?'

'It's not for you to scribble little notelets explaining how "fucking ugly" their kid is. Is it?' Samir had nearly had to chew on his tongue to hold back his laughter when he was told of the list of remarks that Mickey had left on his clients' framed children's photographs: 'Freak!', 'Dingleberry kid', 'Crossbred child', 'Next time use a condom'.

Mickey demanded a fuller explanation as to why he was being sacked for such a minor offence.

'I found out through another source that my house alarm was set off last Sunday. Marvin asked you what to do, as you were the duty controller on that day and you told him to ignore it. You said, quote, "If Samir's wife can't be bothered to come through the front door, then we can't be bothered to fill in the report book. Let one of his precious Mohammeds do it. Stuff him." So, on that note, stuff you, Mickey.'

Mickey stood. 'It's a mistake for you to sack me, Chief. You'll regret it. This is racism of its worst kind.'

Samir shook his head wearily. 'Just get out.'

At the entrance Mickey turned, ripped up his P45 and tossed it to the carpet. 'You'll regret this. I know Keyser Soze.' He left the office door open.

Kareena's mother had received the phone call like someone expecting the results on a dodgy smear test, 'Well, can I breathe again? Are we in the clear? Have you nipped it in the bud? Do we have to find you another husband?' After Kareena had explained that for the time being Samir would do, her mother had cried joyfully down the phone in Punjabi, her Indian pride now restored. 'So we won't hear about this matter again? You are one hundred per cent happy with Samir?'

Kareena had said, 'I won't mention it again, and yes, I am happy.'

But as Kareena replaced the handset in the hall, her smile faded quicker than a goose bump in a sauna. Questions still remained. How had this Cloey known who Kareena was before she'd even introduced herself? How come Cloey had known that Kareena's parents had chosen Samir for her? These were questions she should have asked last night. And now, lingering in her muddled mind like the stench of rancid meat, was the carcass of an uneasy thought. What, oh, what lay hidden behind the picture in the hall? Behind the satellite photo of Milton Keynes from space.

Kareena looked at the large framed print. A green blob. The picture said nothing, did nothing, just hung there looking all innocent, but underneath it could be hiding treachery of the worst sort. She wondered if she trusted Samir enough to ignore what was concealed behind the photo. Or maybe, hopefully, trustworthily there was nothing there at all, just the backing.

She checked the kitchen clock. Only 11.30 a.m. Time can slip by so quickly when you're having fun. But leave a woman at home, in a five-bedroom house, without a well-hung vibrator, and you've got Bored Housewife Syndrome and the clock don't get any slower than that. Kareena checked the time again. Only 11.30 a.m. and 49 seconds.

She picked up the local rag, flipping through the pages to the employment section, trying to resist temptation, trying to forget the photo. The top of the job page read:

If you **can** read this sign without the help of a friend, then you have no excuse for **not** finding a job in Milton Keynes. We take on even the thickest! The Inland Revenue.

Go for the interview. Go on, go on, go on, go on, go on, go on, go on, go on, go on . . .

A loud knock at the front door set the dog alarm barking and without thinking Kareena told the dogs to pack it in and behave. There was another alarm she had to attend to, her Indian modesty alarm. Was she dressed appropriately to answer the door? Were her nipples showing through her tight vest top?

She opened the door wrapped in her winter coat: it was the only thing to hand in the hallway closet. 'Hello.' She tried to remember the visitor's name. 'Samir's not here, he's at work.'

'It's you I've come to see. Your bastard shit of a husband has sacked me. Wanker!' Mickey's eyes darted this way and that, unable to meet Kareena's gaze.

Kareena looked sympathetic. 'I'm sorry, but it's between you and him. I'm sure he had good reason. Sorry.'

Mickey scratched the back of his earlobe, closing one eye and baring his teeth. 'I'm not a rat, grassing ain't my thing, but I've been unfairly dismissed. This is how I see it. It's swings and slides. Swings and slides.'

'You mean swings and roundabouts.'

Mickey laughed. 'Out of towner. You say swings and slides in Milton Keynes. Roundabouts are a sore topic, if you catch my drift. Anyways, he fucks me, and I fuck him. Sorry to do this, you seem like a nice lass, but you best know.' He paused while he checked his trouser pockets and pulled out a piece of paper, holding it for Kareena to take. 'He's 'aving an affair, with some chick called Cloey.' He watched her hands become shaky. 'It's for the best. Nobody gets one over on the Mickey. Nobody takes the mick out of the Mickey.' He jumped into his Astra and sped away, his music, Atomic Kitten, trailing behind him.

Kareena looked at the empty driveway, her fingers clutching the folded A4 sheet and her heart dancing wildly. She had heard her father say that love is just a state of mind. Right now, her mind was just a state.

Inside, with her back to the door, Kareena opened the paper, fixing a cold stare on the writing, promising herself that whatever words were written on the page, she would remain calm.

Samir's bold handwriting, unmistakable and confident, covered the paper with its scrawl. She read the first three words: 'My darling, Cloey', and then she glanced to the middle: 'My wife will only become my wife, she will never be my lover, my friend, my reason to get up in the morning . . .'

What had her parents married her to?

Chapter Thirty-eight

The switchboard picked up the phone. 'Thames Valley Police, how can I help?'

Cloey sneered at the voice. She imagined the woman at the end to be butch, a right hefter, a woman in a wrestler's body. She said, 'Yes, hi, I would like to report some sort of chemical spill in Milton Keynes.'

The gruff voice sounded surprised. 'Chemical?'

'Yes,' Cloey continued. 'I was just this minute in the vicinity of Waterfalls when I saw these three dopey-looking cheap blondes entering a house. I think you may find you have a peroxide spill on your hands.'

A pause. 'Peroxide? Hang on, I will put you on to our . . . Hang on a minute, this is a wind up, isn't it? Do you know that this is wasting extremely valuable police time—'

Cloey interrupted, 'Just get rid of the bitchy blondes in Milton Keynes, will you. Arrest them for being so fucking bamboo, bimbo skinny. Do your bloody job.'

She slammed down the receiver, walked out of the phone booth and back to her Megane parked fifty yards up the road. God, she hated resorting to childish phone gags to get her kicks, when fun of a nastier kind was just minutes away. But now that Jordan was hers once again, her grudge against Thames Valley Police had been rekindled. Their few wasted minutes on hoax calls was chicken feed to the three years they had stolen from her Jordan's life. She'd never forgive them. They took him away, and they shall pay. Town clowns.

Back in her car, Cloey resumed her spying. This was getting ridiculous – an hour she'd been waiting. If Zara's two dim make-up trolleys didn't leave the house soon, the champagne would be warm. How could one celebrate with warm champagne? Twenty minutes later, the door opened and, like a tightly buttoned blouse, four silicon tits burst out of the house, masking their eyes in designer shades. Air-kissing Zara goodbye 'moi moi', they screeched off in a red convertible BMW, their blonde bonnets dragging in the air, Destiny's Child, 'Survivor', cooking it.

At last!

Cloey walked up the drive, two glasses in one hand, a semi-chilled bottle of bubbly in the other. To drink to the downfall of someone was good, but to drink to a blow-up doll falling down was so much better. She tightened the grip on her corked surprise for the has been, imagining the bubbles getting all excited for that fizzy explosion as the cork rocketed up and Zara's face plummeted down. Cloey's smile reflected from the varnish of the front door, it was time to bully the bunny girl.

She rang the doorbell, waited, then rang it again.

Zara answered, cagily. 'What do you want?' One yellow Marigold coated in bubbles held the door ajar. 'If you're looking for Jordan, he's not here.'

'On the contrary, Zara, I'm here for you.' Cloey raised her eyebrows, chinking the bottle against a glass. 'Well, let me in then. I'm not in the habit of washing my sexy laundry in public.'

The open-plan space had taken a step backwards since Cloey was last here. It had already lost the collective aura of a happy couple. Sometimes too much of a woman's touch is just too much. Glossy women's magazines were scattered all over the wooden floor, branded carrier bags still filled with branded clothes, an unopened box of Milk Tray (sacrilege), a fluffy pink photo album, and a box of tissues. The room reeked of dejection and self-pity.

Cloey sunk into the white sofa, placing the bottle and glasses by her stilettos. 'Jordan proposed to me last night – hence the champagne.' She smirked. 'Well, aren't you going to congratulate me? Or have you already forgotten your manners?'

Zara peeled off the Marigolds, letting them drop to the floor. With a tongue-tied brain her mouth struggled. 'No . . . it can't be true.' She sat on the edge of the armchair as a tear slithered down her cheek. 'We were going to have a baby together.'

Cloey momentarily lost her balance. Baby? Quickly, she recovered her composure. 'Yes, he told me all about it, he said he was afraid to have a child with you as you would most likely beat it. He said your temper could not be, how did he put it now? Ah yes, stemmed.' She returned to the main topic of conversation – herself. 'You've got one month and that's because I like you, in a pathetic kind of way.'

Zara plucked out a tissue and dabbed her eyes. 'One month for what?'

'You stupid woman.' Cloey stood up, extending her arms. 'For this. Jordan's too nice to ask you, but I'm not. We want the house – including all the furnishings. It's a lovely house. It deserves a loving couple.'

Cloey's eyes scanned the open area methodically, a prickly excitement settling inside. All this, each corner and echo, would be hers. Then her smile came to an abrupt halt. The wall in the dining room area was plain, with no deviation in its whiteness, except for one thing. And as far as Cloey could remember this one thing hadn't been there before. She walked briskly over to the hanging picture: Jordan and Zara, tanned and smiling, overlooking a snow filled valley in the French Alps. It was captioned, 'There's no love like snow love. Jordan and Zara Always.'

She turned and said, 'Was this after or before he fucked you on the mountain?' Cloey returned to inspect the photograph. 'Jordan always said you were a frigid fuck. He said you were unfamiliar with what a man wanted, what a man needed. He said—'

'Get out you spiteful cow.' Zara's voice rose to a scream. 'Get out!'

Cloey lifted the picture off the wall and dropped it to the floor, cracking the glass and breaking the frame. 'Whoops!' She stamped over and glared into Zara's red face. 'Now, you listen to me, you *little whore*. Me and Jordan go back a long way, you can't get love stronger than ours, it's reinforced by time. It's reinforced by our past, our youth, our teenage years.' She grabbed Zara's blonde hair and yanked it roughly. 'I was there when his mother died, you bimbo, I was there to ease his pain.' She yanked again, sending a tuft to the floor, ignoring Zara's scream. 'He'll do anything for me,' she shouted. 'Anything! Now, we're going to drink that champagne and we're going to celebrate my engagement and we are going to be civilized about this.' She marched over to the kitchen, dragging Zara by the arm. 'And please stop that babbling and open the bottle.'

After chinking glasses and sipping the champers, Cloey air-kissed Zara 'moi moi' on the cheek and made for the front door. Just before departing, she said, 'You dare squeal to Jordan and I'll bury you.' She slammed the door.

Zara knew Santa Claus didn't exist, and she knew fairies didn't either. She just wasn't that sure about monsters any more. How in a million years Jordan could fall for that and want to marry *that creature* was beyond thinking.

Zara felt like she'd stubbed her brain on something sharp. Nothing made too much sense about what had just occurred. Snivelling, she picked up the phone and with a trembling manicured finger punched in Jordan's number. His voice was the only voice she wanted to hear right now. As soon as he answered, she burst into noisy tears. She loved him too much and wasn't afraid to beg him to come back to her. She was only afraid of one thing . . . afraid he didn't love her any more.

*

Samir returned to his idling car with a bottle in a brown bag. He checked the time, 6.00 p.m. He swigged. Even with all the guilt and regret, he couldn't wait to get his hands on his wife tonight and finally shut the book on Cloey. She had been a few chapters of his life that he wished had gone straight to the slush pile. The rejection slip should have been pinned to her head with an axe.

He switched on the ionizer, and in his mind thanked Guru Nanak for supplying the safety net for yesterday's fall. It had been a close shave. And Sikhs are not supposed to have close shaves – they're supposed to keep their hair long. But the experience proved a myth correct: men can't concentrate on more than one thing at once, and that includes women. And, God, he couldn't wait to get his hands on his legitimate woman and finally be the good husband she deserved.

He swigged again, spitting out the Listerine in a drain beside the car parked outside Boots. There was no way he would be getting his leg over with Kareena tonight stinking of salami, spring onions and mango pickle.

With a minty mouth, and gums so numb you could pierce them with cocktail sticks, Samir leisurely drove home to the sounds of Elton John. Sir. He decided he would not discuss this Cloey business again with Kareena as that would show guilt. And guilt is the last thing a guilty man wants to show.

Wiggling the front door key, Samir pushed open the door. 'Honey, I'm home.' He laughed at his own joke, taking in the smells of cooking. Perfect. A hard day at work, dinner on the table, and a beautiful wife some-where in the house. Abandoning his briefcase on the hallway carpet, he found Kareena sitting on the sofa watching CNN. The huge screen showed President George W. Bush, the First Lady, Laura, and their two dogs, Barney and Spot stepping off a helicopter. Bless. The world was in safe hands.

Kareena accepted Samir's kiss. 'Good day?' she asked smiling.

'Tops. Apart from sacking that dope, Mickey. I sort of felt sorry for him really, but, well, it's a business not a charity.' Joining her on the sofa, he picked up *The Times* and checked out the headlines. 'How's your day been? Food smells lovely by the way.'

'Your problem is you're too nice. I'm sure you sacked him for a good reason, you're not the sort to make waves.' She switched the TV off.

Samir turned a page. 'Mmm, something smells lovely.' Another page. 'Mmm.'

Kareena examined Samir's profile. He was very symmetrical. His lying face looked just like his lying arse. She spoke, 'When was the last time you slept with Cloey?'

Samir threw the paper across the room and it rained pages. 'Are you just trying to hurt me, Kareena? We sorted this out last night. Over and over and over, I told you, and you promised me, you *promised* me that you believed me. What do you want me to do? Invent a fucking time machine and take you back with me? I'm telling the bloody truth. A true Sikh does not lie.' He was seething. 'Will you just *believe* me? Sometimes I wish I had slept with her, then at least I would deserve this torment you're inflicting on me. I'm your husband, Kareena. Please please, *please* treat me like one.'

Kareena jumped up off the sofa, walked out to the

hall, and returned with the photo: *Milton Keynes from space*. 'Cloey told me, if I wanted proof of you and her together, then I should look behind this. Do you want to say anything before I rip it open?'

Samir smacked his forehead hard. This was no time to think retrospectively, but right now, he wished with all his heart he'd never met Cloey. 'I've nothing to say, except that my wife obviously takes the words of a mad woman over mine. No trust in our marriage. That's what's missing between us. No trust.' His words had that spider-trying-to-crawl-up-a-waxy-surface feel about it. Desperate, and hopeless. 'I *forbid* you to open it.'

She eyed him coldly. 'I expect you didn't *forbid* her to open her legs though, did you?' She began to peel off the beige masking tape, its glue less sticky than when she had first removed it three hours before. This time, though, there would be no tears: there weren't any left.

Samir sweated as his tortured mind sent an urgent SOS to the gurus, 'Save our Samir'. He even sent one to the Pope just in case, 'Save our sinner'. And then he sent one to his mum, 'Save our son'. He watched as the backing was pulled away and then shivered as he noticed Kareena's wedding ring was missing. The next few seconds blinked by slowly, as the tipped-up contents spilt to the carpet. Samir heard the sucking of air, soon realizing that it was himself heading towards hyperventilation.

He uttered one more lame, 'I'm a Sikh,' then turned his head in shame from the Polaroid pictures of him and Cloey together – nude. He was fucked. And he knew he deserved it.

How Cloey had talked him into painting a scar

across his chest, he'd never know, but it was scant humiliation compared to the photos of his knob up in the air being buttered by Cloey with one of the villager's homemade jam. Very scant.

Kareena picked up a few of the love letters from the floor. Reading these had been even harder than seeing Cloey with a mouthful of jam. She dropped them on his lap along with the note Mickey had given her, then withdrew to the opposite armchair, kicking off her trainers, and tucking her bare feet under her.

'It's bad enough you've done all this,' she began, watching him staring into space, 'but using our religion as a ticket to weasel yourself out is the pits. "My Sikhism is my blood. I would never trade it for a quick shag with a white woman." That's what you said, wasn't it? "If God had wanted us all to mix, then he would have made us all brown." Isn't that what you said? The list of your lies is endless.' She opened her eyes wide, refusing to spill another tear, her voice trembling. 'You said in one of your letters to her that you had made a mistake marrying me. You said you could never love me . . .' She looked at Samir, her throat a swollen lump. 'She's got your baby inside her.' And then she sobbed into her arms.

Everything catches up with you in the end. The smoker loses fitness, the soap-watcher loses sanity, the sweet-eater loses teeth, the boxer loses brain cells, and the adulterer loses his wife. Samir sunk to his knees, scooping up the Polaroids, letters, cards and a pair of black lace undies – everything that Cloey had hidden when she'd broken into the house.

Solemnly he walked to the kitchen and dumped it all in the chrome bin. His distorted face reflecting back from the lid was as misshapen as his life was right now. Returning with some flowery kitchen roll he put it on Kareena's lap, almost afraid to open his mouth, worried he might start lying again. As of late, he could have woven a threaded story that would outdo the Bayeux Tapestry. But there are limits even to the best of liars' imaginations. And sometimes those limits are called looking like a right prick. God, he hated himself.

The truth may never really fix a lie, but it can try. Samir told Kareena everything: from meeting Cloey to hating Cloey. The whole shebang. It wasn't exactly the scoop of the year that a man had betrayed his wife's trust. But it read like the front page to Kareena, 'The Sorriest Sikh'.

She watched Samir beg and crawl for forgiveness. Some of the words he used to describe himself were uncouth, disgusting and meant for late-night viewing. He said he would accept any punishment except death and blamed no one but himself, also understanding that if she had bouts of depression he would be held responsible. He asked for a chance to explain deeper . . .

And deeper . . .

And deeper . . .

Right into the abyss.

And over the next few days, Kareena gave him that chance. She knew the consequences if she didn't. If she returned to her parents as a daughter and not a wife, they would marry her off again pronto. The standard of man who they looked for this time would drop. *Plummet* might be a better word. Indian girls were like cars, perfect when brand new, but their value depreciated after they'd had one owner. Second-hand

Indian girls are hard to shift. You never knew if the prior owner had been thrashing her too hard. A re-stitched hymen is not quite the same as a recon-ditioned engine. Kareena knew she would probably end up having to marry a divorced man. And it would beg the question: why was he divorced?

Samir's regret was blatant, it followed him like a gloomy rain cloud. He explained himself constantly, pouring out apologies, saying he understood it might take time. Kareena pointed out that time couldn't heal everything, she would never be able to forget, but she would definitely try to forgive.

And forgiveness begins with a kiss.

'What's that for?' Samir asked, packing the last of the suitcases in the car boot.

'For being strong enough to go against the Indian way. For at least questioning your parents and finding out about love for yourself. I could never do that. I haven't got the guts to go against the Indian way.'

'It's not all it's cracked up to be, believe me,' he said, giving her a kiss back.

Samir walked up to the front door to make sure it was secure then took a step back to view the new burglar alarm. DareDevil Security 24–7. The house was now in safe hands.

As they left for their belated honeymoon in Mauritius, Kareena smiled at the recently planted sign outside the gates.

For Sale.

Chapter Thirty-nine

It looked like Thor, the Thunder God, had swapped his hammer for an ice-cream scoop and lifted up half a mountain of snow, dumping it down in central Milton Keynes. The enclosed man-made ski-slope, Xscape, was a powerhouse of slippery, frost-bitten fun. It was the outdoor life – indoors.

With their noses pressed up flat to the safety glass, Cloey and Claudette watched the gutsy skiers and snowboarders weaving down the 170-metre slope. Cloey wondered if the skiers would all look so cock-sure and cocky if she was facing the glass aiming a loaded shotgun at them. God, she hated people who were good at things she was crap at.

Claudette elbowed Cloey through her hired ski jacket. 'It's just impossible, Cloey. How are you supposed to tell the hunks from the monks when they've covered their gorgeous faces in goggles?' She pointed up the slope with a glove that would have fitted a goalie, 'I had my eye on that one until she took her hat off.'

Cloey laughed nervously. Nervous because she hadn't skied since a school trip to Austria, nervous because Jordan was late, and petrified because after the engagement she would have to face her mother with her new fiancé. Her mother's latest theory on Jordan was that he had been baptized with the water from hell's well – the unholy hole.

Cloey watched yet another skier rocket to the bottom, while her mind contemplated a cringeable thought: understanding Jordan like she did, she knew after today he would be going out of his way to call Aileen Mum. Cloey cringed, then sighed. She supposed it was better than him calling her mother Witch.

'Sometimes I wish I was still a virgin,' Cloey said, fanning her flushed face with a coffee-shop menu. 'Just once, I would love to look at myself in the mirror and not see a slag grinning back. Imagine it, Claudette.'

Claudette huffed. 'Are you implying that when I look in the mirror I also see a slag?'

'No, not at all, you see Miss World looking back. You're *absolutely* gorgeous – in your own mind.' Cloey unzipped her skiing jacket an inch. 'It's just the rest of us who see Miss Slag.'

The slap of wood on concrete startled them both, and they turned to see Jordan standing astride his snowboard, wearing a black woolly hat. He stood under the No Smoking sign with a fag in his mouth, his Worn 'n' Torn snowboarding jersey bore the words, 'Swallow my Frozen Yoghurt, Bitch'.

Removing his fag, he leant forward and kissed

Cloey's warm lips. 'Sorry I'm late, Cloey. Couldn't give a toss about you, Claudette.'

Cloey wrapped her arms round him, enjoying the emptying of her nerves, toying with a thousand dirty thoughts of making love tonight as an engaged couple. She knew Jordan would do anything for her, but right now, as his strong arms hugged her tightly, she knew she would do anything for him in return. Anything. She smiled at Claudette, whispering, 'Be nice to him, Claudette, or I will drop you like a can of used hair spray.' Then she pecked Jordan on the lips before pulling away. 'I can't wait to see the ring, Jordan, where is it?'

He patted his snow pants' back pocket, 'Safe.' Then he sniffed the air, nodding agreeably. 'Nothing like it, the smell of snow. Pure as my conscience. Cold as my—'

'Heart?' Claudette interrupted, then apologized. 'Sorry, Jordan, slip of my tongue. By the way,' her eyes slipped to his boots, '*choice* board, very choice.'

Jordan's snowboard, Deliverance, had been painted by a criminal for a criminal, and as such, the mural was criminal in content. A pair of metallic-green handcuffs decorated the surface. Inscribed on the left cuff was 'Pigs Can't Ski', on the right cuff, 'I Eat Pigs', and on the back, 'Squeal Piggy, Squeal'. It was a present from an ex-con and Jordan rode it with pride.

Ignoring Claudette, he picked up his board and all three headed for the snow peak. Cloey had given Claudette precise instructions: ski carefully to the bottom – without breaking your leg – and then wait at the bottom of the slope. Take the cap off the camcorder, and don't dare miss a single frame of this most important event of my life.

The perspective had changed: instead of looking up at ants, they were now looking down at a tantalizing landscape of white dust, ploughed by the skis and harvested by the fearless heart. To snowboarders, fear was a four-letter swear word and snow was their four-letter ride. It paid to be good on the slope, but you had to pay to be good on the slope. And nothing beat the experience of the open mountains of France.

Jordan threw himself down the slope, his board an extension of himself, himself an extension of his mind. And his mind? Sometimes he wondered where it went.

Cloey felt the gritty taste of jealousy. Surely Jordan had not forgotten what he was here for? How could frozen water take precedence over *her*? Could a snow-woman give head? She doubted it very much.

'Get down after him, Claudette, send him back up. Chop chop.' She gave Claudette a gentle shove, watching her zig-zag to the bottom on her skis. Fairly impressive for a slag, she thought, hoping her bottom would look more elegant than Claudette's. Hired ski-wear were not the most complimentary of clothes. And Cloey did not have the most complimentary of thoughts either: hippo-arsed Claudette.

Cloey stared impatiently down at the tiny figure of Jordan. Even from this vantage she could tell he was engrossed. But engrossed in what? She removed her tinted goggles and edged closer to the lip of the artificial mountain. Squinting and squirming, she could make out that his attention was focussed on a small cluster of women down at the bottom. Her envy circled like a vulture. What sort of place was this? A pick-up point for lost dogs?

Time melted by and finally Jordan returned with a

huge smile like a crescent across his face. He slid up beside Cloey, signalling at the bottom with his glove. 'Wave, Cloey, Claudette wants to see if you're in shot.'

She waved, smiling. 'And who were those women you were talking to?'

'Just ex-pupils of mine, telling me about their skiing holiday. I get it all the time, I had to be polite.' He sounded apologetic.

Cloey glared. 'I'm a very jealous kind of woman, Jordan, you should know that. You've got to respect my wishes if you love me. I can't have you teaching women. Understood?'

Jordan twirled on his board. 'Bollocks to that. You either fucking trust me or you don't.'

Cloey wanted to put her hands on her hips, but she was afraid she might slip over. 'Trust? Just like butter-brain Zara trusted you? I would like to call you a peasant boy right now, but I can't any more, as I'm going to marry you. I refrain. So don't cheese me off. Don't swim in the deep end with me, Jordan, you'll bloody well drown. This is supposed to be a special day. Now, where's the ring?'

His hand delved into his bottoms, fishing out a blue box. He snapped open the lid, sending shivering sparkles of light in all directions. The sapphires and the diamonds in all their glory amidst the angel-white snow. This was the ring that had been meant for Cloey eight years ago, stored away in Jordan's locker for all that time.

Jordan's hand held the box out steadily. 'I spent three long years in that shit-hole slammer thinking about you day and night. The screws all gabbing on and on about how our wives, girlfriends, boyfriends were all sleeping around. While the cat's away . . . and all that. But I laughed at them, I howled when they tried to wind me up, because I knew that you and me had something those pig-bastard screws would never have. Not once, not even in a dream, did I ever think you would sell out our love. I would have died for you.' His previously steady hand was now trembling and his eyes glinted madly. 'I fucking trusted you, Cloey. Don't you dare talk to me about trust. Got it?' There was a pause, his breath foggy and hot. 'You trust me now, or the ring hits the snow.'

The constant noise of the ski lift grinding people to the summit and the screams of falling kids made little mark on the ringing echo of Jordan's voice. If this were a real mountain, there would have been an avalanche by now. As it was, the only tumbling rocks were the tears from Cloey's eyes.

'Why can't you accept that I made a mistake?' she sniffed. 'This is why I hate you sometimes, I know you'll never love me like you did before. I know I lost the real Jordan, my Jordan. My sweetheart. I know I'll never get you back like before. But I accept whatever there is left. And that is something, if you asked me a month ago, I would never have been able to do.'

A loud message came over the intercom.

'Will the two people standing at the top of the slope please show consideration for the other paying customers . . . You may be an ace snowboarder, Jordan, but it's not your slope. Show respect, Deliverance.'

Jordan bent down on one knee, steadied himself, then

425

looked up. 'Cloey, put your goggles back on, I can't bear to see your tearful eyes.' She grinned and pulled them down. 'I've waited years for this. I don't think, even now, you realize how much I loved you.' He put out his hand and she quickly removed a glove and placed her hand in his. Jordan stroked it against his cheek, feeling the sweaty warmth. 'You were my princess, my hopes and dreams. No man on this earth could have ever loved you like I did.' He paused, thinking. 'This is going to be so romantic, Cloey.' He smiled at her, while removing his woolly hat and tossing it behind him. 'I am never going to forget how beautiful you look right . . . now . . . right . . . now . . . NOW!!!!'

Suddenly, like a sledgehammer from the blue, two hands came thundering into Cloey's back with immense force. As if falling out of an aeroplane, Cloey disappeared from view, shooting down the slope like an out of control rubber ball. She made no attempt whatsoever to look graceful as she tumbled down the snow, bouncing this way, then that. Two leisurely skiers heard her screams and just about moved out of her way in time, her momentum building rapidly. One ski spun outwards as her hat flew off, her high-pitched wails giving the distinct impression that she was not enjoying her engagement.

Jordan hurtled down after her, eager to witness all of her rather inventive descent. Two kids standing near the bottom, never a pair to miss out on a mishap, began to throw well-aimed snowballs at Cloey's swiftly moving bonce. Finally, her body came to a juddering halt near someone's skis, the journey at last complete.

Jordan grabbed Cloey under the shoulders and

dragged her to her feet. 'Tell me you're okay, Cloey.' He saw Claudette still filming them and beckoned her over.

Cloey brushed away the snow, her breathing heavy, her eyes searching upwards for the culprit. 'I was pushed! I want you to get the person who did this.'

Claudette arrived, not quite managing to stop in time, knocking into both of them. 'Got it all, every bit, Cloey. Let's have a look at your ring then. I can't believe you did a stunt like that, it was amazing.'

Jordan shook his head and grabbed the camcorder, smiling at the skier who had just arrived. 'She fell quicker than I thought she would.' He laughed. 'One minute she was there and the next . . . bong, she was gone.'

Zara laughed along with Jordan. 'It was like pushing a box of stale Cornflakes.'

Cloey looked at Jordan. 'But . . .' Then, grinning madly she looked at Zara. 'He shagged me last night, he said he wanted my baby.'

Zara smiled. 'Jordy was with me last night, you sad little animal. And the night before that. Do you honestly— Oh, never mind.' She belted Cloey hard round the face. 'That's for making me drink champagne.' She belted her again, sending her sprawling. 'And that's for yanking my hair and messing with my man.'

Claudette helped Cloey to her feet. They held on to each other like two drunks. Cloey glowered at Jordan. 'You were never going to marry me, were you?'

'Nope. I was just having a bit of fun, playing with your head. And you should think yourself lucky you chose a ski-slope as the scene for our engagement and not a parachute jump or I might just have cut your fucking strings.' He grabbed Zara's arm. 'Let's go.'

Cloey lunged forward, blocking his path. 'Those three years you were in prison, when I promised you I would lay flowers on your mother's grave once a month on your behalf? Well, guess what, Peasant Boy? Not once did I do it. Not once.' She grinned sweetly.

Claudette laughed.

Jordan looked at Zara with a Z. She was special with an S. She was all that mattered with an M.

He eyed Cloey. 'Try and be nice to someone. I know deep down there is a nice person in there, I've seen it. Hurting people the whole time, as you do, you'll only end up hurting yourself eventually.' He stared at Claudette. 'And as for you, Princess Vomit Face, there's a gurning competition on in Cornwall. You'll win it, just like that.' And Jordan and Zara left, arm in arm, across the slippery snow.

Outside in the seething sun Jordan donned his John Lennon shades admiring Zara's behind as it wiggled over to the queue by the ice-cream stall. It was a hot day, but that had nothing to do with why most men's tongues were shining their shoes. Zara had a knock-out body and a minimalist wardrobe: you could have made four Zara outfits from just the one Bond girl's bikini top. Jordan was used to men ogling, but if they touched her . . .

He wiped his forehead, sniffed under his arms and nodded with respect for Right Guard. He peered at the shuffling queue ahead, a short man of ample circumference seemed to be holding everyone up. His

Weight Watcher plan allowed 2000 calories a day.
That meant twenty 99s and one wafer. Jordan dialled
Zara on her mobile, uttered a few filthy words,
watched her face go red, and then asked her to order
a 69er. She hung up.

A few minutes later, Zara trotted over with two ice
creams dripping like bird shit behind her. They passed
by the various diners attached to the Xscape complex.
People on diets generally avoided the area at all costs,
the wafting aroma alone added inches to waistlines.
Allegedly, the 'Smell All You Like' buffet down at
Rickies' Rodeo Ranch was to blame for most of MK's
obesity.

Just outside KFC, Jordan opened the boot of his
car, and loaded up the snowboard. Zara watched his
every move. If he treated his women like he treated his
board, then she'd do all right. The boot slammed shut
and she was almost sure she heard Jordan whisper,
'Goodnight' to it.

Leaning against the car, he lit up a fag then grabbed
her waist. 'When can I move back in?'

Zara removed his shades and planted a soft kiss on
his cheek. 'You will have to prove yourself first. You
hurt me very badly, Jordy.'

He handed her the fag, a confident expression on
his face. 'Prove myself, yeah? Cover my space.' He
turned round and pulled his surfing shorts part-way
down – exposing his tight bottom. 'Check it out.'

Zara made a yeaking noise upon spotting the new
tattoo. Prouder moments than this did not exist in
Zara's world. Still slightly raw, the finely detailed
artwork showed a snowboard with the words, 'Zara
Yum Yum' inside, and outside in perfectly neat

Gothic writing, 'I'm not snow-blind'.

She yeaked again. 'Jordy Jordy Yum Yum. I *so* love you.' Pulling his bottoms back up, she plopped his fag back in his mouth and hugged him with an epic smile. 'I want you to marry me.'

He spoke into her hair, 'I'm supposed to ask you, but the answer's yes. I won't let you down again.'

Zara pushed him away gently, looking up into his eyes. 'I want the full works. A church, a white dress, everything. And in return, I'll grant you the dream honeymoon.' She ran her fingers through his damp hair. 'A honeymoon for four weeks in . . . the French Alps.'

Jordan yeaked. Sex, snow, snowboarding, skiing, su-fucking-perb. 'What did I do to deserve you?'

Her neat eyebrows raised neatly. 'The catch is Jordy, you can smell the snow, feel the snow, shag me in the snow if you like, even eat the snow, but you're not allowed to surf or ski on the snow for the whole month. That's your punishment for sleeping with Cloey. I think you got off lightly, don't you?'

Jordan's face became glum, as if he'd gone fishing and reeled in a wellington boot. He'd been punished before, sent to the corner of the room, hit with the headmaster's cane, detentions, lines, sulks, even prison. But this? It sucked. Then he found the sense to see sense. He was lucky to be here even talking to Zara, let alone arranging a wedding. He moved in for the kill and lifted her off her feet. 'I love you under any conditions.'

After landing, Zara whispered in his ear, 'Remember, Jordy, every woman has a little bit of a Cloey in them. Be very afraid.' She kissed him. 'Come on, let's go ring buying. I've already got my eye on one.'

'Oh goody.'

She gripped his hand. 'But first, I need to get to a grocers quick.'

'Grocers?'

'Jordy, I'm gagging for some celery.'

They looked at each other.

Jordan smiled up from Cloey's bed. She touched his face. 'I love you, Jordan. Say it back.'

But, unfortunately, the old curling Polaroid couldn't talk. He just stared in his school uniform, gripping a sledgehammer with one hand, a fag hanging from his bottom lip. Looking back on better days is never cheap, it always costs you a tear or two.

From the open window she searched the distance, viewing the wild fields and hedges. What an exquisite spot, with the birds singing, butterflies playing, the peaceful breeze stroking. God could make such beauty, but he could also deliver such misery.

Cloey cursed the ceiling. 'Why do you keep taking Jordan away from me? Can't you see he needs me?' She shouted, 'I know you made the sands but do you have to always bury your head in them?'

Holding up the Polaroid of Jordan, she kissed it lovingly. 'You were my first and only love. We made a blood promise that we would love each other until the day we died.' She kissed him again and smiled. 'I will never *ever* let you go, Jordan, you are mine. For ever.'

**POCKET
BOOKS**

Also by Nisha Minhas
Chapatti or Chips?

For twenty-three years, Naina has saved herself for
the man her parents have chosen for her to marry.
They've chosen well: Ashok is handsome, kind and
considerate. Although she's met him only twice,
Naina knows he would make a good husband.

Dave, on the other hand, would not. Although, like
Ashok, he's goodlooking and charming, he's also
unreliable, thoughtless – and an incorrigible
womaniser.

Dave is Trouble with a capital 'T'. And with six
months to go until her wedding day, Naina knows
she shoud keep well away from him.
So why can't she stop herself . . .?

PRICE £6.99
ISBN 0 7434-3045-X

**POCKET
BOOKS**

Irish Girls About Town

When it comes to spinning a good yarn – creating
stories to tug at your heartstrings or make you cry
with laughter – the Irish are the best in the
business.

Join Cathy Kelly for a madcap road trip across the
States. In Maeve Binchy's *Carissima*, an old friend
returns to Ireland from Sicily – with unexpected
consequences. An independent woman answers a
Lonely Hearts' ad – with surprising results. And
discover an unusual method of getting rid of an
unwanted wedding ring.

Whether they're provocative or poignant, raunchy
or romantic, all the stories in this fabulous new
collection are infused with a peculiarly irresistible
brand of Irish charm. So put your feet up, take the
phone off the hook, open a box of chocolates –
and treat yourself.

PRICE £6.99
ISBN 1-903650-26-7

**POCKET
BOOKS**

Scottish Girls About Town

Scandalous, scathing – and scorchingly good: a
scintillating collection of stories from some of
Scotland's best-loved women writers.

A high-powered businesswoman metes a
devastating revenge on her cheating husband. A
bored housewife contacts an old schoolfriend –
with unexpected results. Two flabby flatmates
race each other in a hilarious weight-loss contest.
And a night at the Edinburgh Fringe goes
disastrously wrong for Jenny Colgan's hapless
heroine.

All this and much, much more in a fabulous
collection of brand-new stories which proves –
if proof were needed – that Scottish girls are not
to be messed with.

**PRICE £6.99
ISBN 0-7434-5036-1**

**POCKET
BOOKS**

Swansong

Victoria Routledge

Rosetta Mulligan, seventies rock-chick, fashion
icon and friend to the stars, has never fully
embraced her role as mother to her four sons.
They, in turn, have never fully accepted her as
'Mum' and certainly have their doubts as to who
to call 'Dad'.

Twenty years on, the angelic Mulligan babies have
turned from flower power children into four very
different adults, and Rosetta now feels the time is
right to parcel up her past and move on – but not
until she has written her revelations of life on the
road. The trouble is, there could be an awful lot
that is news to her boys . . .

'A sparkling story of complex relationships and
intense love . . . Imagine Marianne Faithfull's
secret diary' *Company*

PRICE £6.99
ISBN 0-7434-1519-1

**POCKET
BOOKS**

These books and other **Simon & Schuster/Pocket** titles are available from your book shop or can be ordered direct from the publisher.

☐ 0 7434 3045 X **Chapatti or Chips?** £6.99

☐ 1 903650 26 7 **Irish Girls About Town** £6.99

☐ 0 7434 5036 1 **Scottish Girls About Town** £6.99

☐ 0 7434 1519 1 **Swansong** £6.99

Please send cheque or postal order for the value of the book, and add packing within the UK inc. BFPO 75p per book; OVERSEAS inc. EIRE £1 per book.

OR: Please debit this amount from my:

VISA/ACCESS/MASTERCARD ....

CARD NO...

EXPIRY DATE..

AMOUNT £ ....

NAME...

ADDRESS...

....

SIGNATURE..

Send orders to: SIMON & SCHUSTER CASH SALES
PO Box 29, Douglas, Isle of Man, IM99 1BQ
Tel: 01624 675137, Fax 01624 670923
www.bookpost.co.uk   email: bookshop@enterprise.net
Please allow 14 days for delivery.
Prices and availability subject to change without notice.